ANNIE STANLEY, ALL AT SEA

Annie Stanley,
All at Sea

Sue Teddern

MANTLE

First published 2021 by Mantle
an imprint of Pan Macmillan
The Smithson, 6 Briset Street, London EC1M 5NR
EU representative: Macmillan Publishers Ireland Limited,
Mallard Lodge, Lansdowne Village, Dublin 4
Associated companies throughout the world
www.panmacmillan.com

ISBN 978-1-5290-2503-3

1 3 5 7 9 8 6 4 2

A CIP catalogue record for this book is available from the British Library.

Typeset in Sabon LT Std by Palimpsest Book Production Ltd, Falkirk, Stirlingshire
Printed and bound by CPI Group (UK) Ltd, Croydon, CR0 4YY

Visit **www.panmacmillan.com** to read more about all our books
and to buy them. You will also find features, author interviews and
news of any author events, and you can sign up for e-newsletters
so that you're always first to hear about our new releases.

For my parents, Gaggi and Teddy

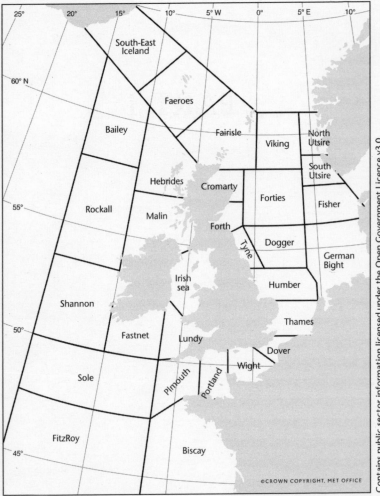

25°   20°   15°   10°   5° W   0°   5° E   10°

60° N

South-East Iceland

Faeroes

Fairisle

Viking

North Utsire

Bailey

Hebrides

Cromarty

Forties

South Utsire

55°

Rockall

Malin

Forth

Fisher

Tyne

Dogger

German Bight

Shannon

Irish sea

Humber

50°

Fastnet

Lundy

Thames

Dover

Sole

Plmouth

Portland

Wight

45°

FitzRoy

Biscay

©CROWN COPYRIGHT, MET OFFICE

PART I

Chapter One

'Becoming Cyclonic Later'

I wake with a start. Someone's snoring and it's me. Even as six-packed superheroes are triumphing over evil at an ear-piercing volume on the multiplex screen in front of me, I've managed to nod off, with my fist submerged in my popcorn bucket.

I pull myself upright and wipe a string of stray dribble from my chin. The twelve or so other people dotted around the auditorium, mostly singles like me, are unlikely to notice the dozing woman in her usual seat at the far end of Row G. I expect one or two of them are 'resting their eyes' too.

Silver-screen matinees are the best and you don't even have to be over 60. If you get there ten minutes early, there's a free cup of tea and a budget Bourbon. If you get there on time, there's a plate full of crumbs and an apologetic shrug from the staff member on biscuit duty. Sometimes I pop into Greggs before the midday screening for a sandwich or a slab of bread pudding, Dad's favourite. Last Friday, I slid out of bed and into my comfiest jogger–cardy combo for a late morning Japanese animation, with an ice-cream tub of cold spag bol to sustain me.

There's something slightly illicit about going to a daytime

screening. But if I see a film at night, I might bump into friends (or worse, ex-colleagues) in the foyer and be forced to make small talk. Early afternoon films offer anonymity. Having said that, on the way home from one last week, I pulled up at the traffic lights alongside Nia Ronson-Tanner's mum's Berlingo, doing the school run with a carful of kids. I could guess what Nia was saying: 'Hey, it's Miss Stanley. OMG, state of it!'

I manage to stay awake for the rest of the film and blink into the daylight as I emerge from the Odeon. My car is in the usual car park and I've yet to get a ticket if I'm late returning to it. I've got this cinema thing down to a fine art. Plus it's good to leave the flat every few days and get some fresh air. Vegging out on the sofa, shouting at *Pointless* contestants, has lost its charm and I'm bored with choosing the right villa for retired couples from Lincoln, seeking 'their place in the sun'.

It's a dull Tuesday afternoon. I could pop home, find the stray trainer that's missing from my sports bag and do a forty-five-minute circuit at the gym. Or go wild and randomly take whichever class is about to start. Except Zumba. Zumba is for show-offs in expensive kit who roll their eyes at unco-ordinated heffalumps like me. I don't have the frigging funk and I never will. Can they recite the alphabet backwards in Finnish or teach a roomful of rambunctious 13-year-olds the chemistry of coastal erosion? I very much doubt it.

If I can't find my trainer, I could still grab my swimming things and do a few laps of the leisure centre pool. Then pick up a pizza, polish off that opened Merlot and hunker down in front of the latest 'acclaimed film' Netflix has specially selected for me.

There again, I could do the gym and/or pool tomorrow. Maybe get up early – half nine at the latest – and use the morning to wash and bag up my kit so I've got no excuse. Great. I have a plan. Starting tomorrow. Once I find that trainer. Or buy new ones that don't squash my little toes.

Or not. Fuck it, I hate the gym anyway.

Traffic is light and I'm home in fifteen minutes. Maybe I should jog to the cinema next time. I park in my usual slot, click my car locked and walk to the front door, patting the pockets of my Puffa jacket for the key. I suddenly remember a budget pizza buried in the bottom drawer of the freezer that I can pimp with tinned pineapple. Result.

I don't expect to find Kate, sitting on the step, punching a text into her phone. She gives me her signature glare. 'At bloody last. Where have you been?'

'The gym, okay. Are we meant to be seeing Dad tonight?'

She stands, brushing down the pencil skirt of her Zara suit. 'I've been trying to reach you all afternoon but your phone's off. Dad's in hospital.'

'The physio for his knee? That's not for ages, is it?'

Kate takes a deep breath. I think she's tired of lecturing me on why a) I should keep my phone turned on, b) I'm so flaky and c) *she's* always the first port of call in a crisis.

'Annie, just listen, will you? He's been rushed in by ambulance. He collapsed. Bev rang me and I said I'd ring you. She was beside herself.'

Dad. Collapsed. Ambulance. I swallow hard, forcing Kate's words to engage. I spot some popcorn on my cuff and eat it.

'We'll go in my car,' Kate commands, over her shoulder, as she strides back down the path, waving like a tour guide for me to follow. 'He was in such good form on Sunday. All jolly and silly. Going on and on about some cheap headphones he'd bought at Lidl. Like he needs new headphones. But they were "such a bargain". You didn't see him, but he was.'

I'm still scrabbling for my seatbelt as Kate screeches her Mazda into the afternoon traffic. 'He kept asking why you weren't there. Bev too.'

'I *told* them. I was busy.'

I stare out of the window, looking but not seeing. Is that a new hair salon in the parade of shops by the bus stop? Or has it always been there and I've never noticed it before? I concentrate hard, trying to remember.

'Busy. Yeah, right. *So* busy.' Kate overtakes a bus with her usual brazen confidence. 'And then you have your phone turned off all afternoon because you're so "busy" at the gym.'

'I was. Ask my Zumba instructor if you don't believe me.'

'And I have to search St Albans to find you.'

I don't reply. What's the point?

'I just wish you could share the load, do your bit. You're the big sister around here. But you do fuck all. You only make an effort when I nag you. It isn't fair. It *so* isn't, Annie.'

I suddenly remember: that new hair salon used to be an off-licence. With the flirty manager. Ric, was it? No, Vic. He asked me out once. As if! And now it's gone. When did *that* happen?

I let Kate drone on, say her piece, get it off her chest. Path of least resistance. And okay, maybe there have been times when I've taken a back seat, excused myself from my responsibilities. Kate's just better at that kind of thing, so why compete and fall short?

'Come on, come on.' Kate thumps her steering wheel at some slow emergency traffic lights. I give her a reassuring 'we'll be there soon' smile, but she's staring straight ahead. The lights change and a yellow-bibbed lad with a 'Go' paddle waves us on. I recognize him as a former pupil. Mason McIsaac. Shame. I thought he'd gone to uni.

Kate accelerates, to make up for lost time, her knuckles whitening on the steering wheel as a sign for the hospital appears at the roundabout.

'It sounds serious, Annie. Let's assume it is so that we can be pleasantly surprised. And we need to do this together. *Don't we?*'

'Stop going on. I'm here, aren't I? Just stop going on!'

The ICU visitors' room has a TV in the corner, turned on but muted. A programme about antiques, is it? Or upcycling? I have to stop myself scrolling through the daytime schedule in my head. It doesn't matter, you idiot.

Bev is sitting in a corner armchair, away from a noisy family who are celebrating with each other that their mother is on the mend. 'Typical Mum, putting us through the wringer because she likes the attention.'

Bev looks up as Kate and I approach. Her eyes are ringed with damp mascara and she's forgotten to apply her ever-present coral lipstick. I clock the relief in her eyes as we sit each side of her.

'Oh, thank God you're here. Pippa's on her way but she had to ask Mark's mum to pick up Elliott and Evie. She shouldn't be long. I won't text her if she's driving. I don't want to distract her. She should be here soon. Thank God you're here . . .'

Bev runs out of words and searches her pockets unsuccessfully for a Kleenex. I pull a trail of toilet roll from my Puffa pocket and pass it on. Least I can do.

Unfeasibly grateful, she gives me a spontaneous sideways hug which I have to twist round to accept. I hug back. This angular, unfleshy woman with whom I rarely, if ever, make human contact, needs comfort from me and I don't like it.

Kate gives a weird little hiccup of supressed emotion and sandwich-hugs Bev from the other side. Eventually and awkwardly, we free ourselves, sit back in our chairs and remember our surroundings.

'What happened?' Kate asks, taking Bev's hand.

Bev shakes her head, trying both to recall *and* delete the memory. 'We went to the garden centre. You know how keen your dad is to get those raised beds planted for the summer. We bought some things for lunch in the farm shop: cheese, bread, that spicy chutney he slathers on everything. I laid the kitchen table and Peter carried all the things through to the garden. You know, round the side of the bungalow. From the car. I called out "Ready!" but he didn't whistle back. He whistles back when it's mealtimes.'

Bev pauses to blow her nose. 'He'd collapsed on the path, you see. I didn't realize. If he'd collapsed in the garden, I'd have seen him when I was slicing the bread.'

She stops, indicating with a wave of the hand that she's too distraught to go on.

'Did you dial 999 straight away?' Kate asks.

Bev nods, filling up.

'Did you try CPR?'

'I didn't want to do it wrong so I got a pillow and made him comfortable. I sat on the path and held his hand. The woman on the phone was very reassuring. They think it's a heart attack. They were there so fast. I can't fault how well they responded. Or you two. Your dad will be so pleased to know you're here to look after me.'

I try to scrunch away the negative thought but it lingers. This woman, whose hand now pats my arm, has got it so wrong. We aren't here for *her*, we're here for *him*. Isn't that bloody obvious?

I walk to the window and take in the view, six storeys up: a car park; a single-decker bus disgorging visitors; three paramedics grabbing a quick coffee break. One of them leans in and says something and they all laugh. In a job like that, you have to laugh to keep sane. Teaching geography's a breeze in comparison. I'm a lightweight.

The door swings open and Pippa bustles in, bearing a palmful of hand sanitizer from the dispenser outside.

'I squirted too much. May I?'

She takes my hand and wipes a dollop onto it. I catch Kate's eye and we exchange a look. That is *so* Pippa, so typical of how she behaves. Like her mother before her, she has invaded our family without being asked.

Pippa hastily rubs in the last of the sanitizer so that she's hands-free to hug her mother. If Bev's held it together until now, the presence of her only child gives her free rein to break into wracking sobs which startle one of the noisy family's children so much that he has to be taken to the chocolate machine for a consoling KitKat.

As Pippa rocks her mother, she looks to Kate and me. 'Well? What's happening? How is he?'

'I'll find a nurse,' Kate replies, clacking away down the corridor in her work stilettos. I want to go too, but Kate would have asked, if she'd needed me. Which is the whole problem in a nutshell. She accuses me of not being involved but chooses to exclude me. And I let her.

'They think it's a heart attack,' I tell Pippa.

The words sink in. A heart attack. People die of heart attacks: my neighbour, three days after last Christmas; Toby's mum when he was 16; Stephen Gately. No, he died of a pulmonary oedema. Is that the same as a heart attack? I have no idea . . .

Should we have seen the signs? If I'd gone to Dad and

Bev's for Sunday lunch, would I have noticed that he was breathless or wheezy or sweaty? If I'd got my lazy fat arse in gear and driven the twenty minutes to their house, could I have stopped this?

Pippa is saying something. I allow the words to drift past me. She tries again. 'I'm getting Mum a cup of tea. Do you want anything?'

I could murder a Mars bar. I saw them in the machine as we left the lift. And now that little boy is making a smeary meal of his KitKat.

'Not for me, thanks.'

'Keep an eye on Mum, will you?'

Or your mum can keep an eye on me because that's my dad in there, in intensive care. And he could die and I've already lost my mum so I'm the one who needs taking care of, thank you very much, Pippa.

'Maybe a Mars bar if they've got one?'

The noisy family have left and Bev and I have the visitors' room to ourselves. Why are Kate and Pippa taking so long? When will we be allowed to see Dad? Why did I ask for a Mars bar when I know the very first bite will make me heave?

Bev pats my hand. It's a gesture. Of sorts. Is she acknowledging that we're both running the same anxious thoughts through our heads? Or is she gently reminding me to be the 'dutiful daughter' in Pippa's absence?

I give it my best shot. 'How are you doing, Bev? Finding Dad like that, it must have been horrible for you.'

'Oh, Annie. It was. Of course, I've been here before. Not here, I mean. Not the ICU.' She lets out a heavy sigh. 'When I lost Keith, I couldn't possibly imagine I'd be going through all this again.'

'Nobody's "lost", okay. Dad's collapsed but we haven't lost him.'

'Absolutely. We mustn't jump to conclusions. But you can't help it, can you? Worst-case scenario. What if he doesn't make it?'

I try not to raise my voice, lose my rag. 'Dad's a stubborn old bugger. Always digging his heels in, not giving up. He'll come through.'

Bev takes comfort from my words, even though *I'm* not totally convinced by them. He is stubborn though, and he often loses patience with my 'oh sod it' attitude. Kate's more like him. Diligent, conscientious, responsible; she hated learning the piano but still got her certificate. I gave up the violin after two lessons; Dad was always teasing me that I could have been the next Vanessa-Mae.

'It was different with Keith, of course,' Bev continues. 'Still a shock. Still out of the blue. But it was instant. That lorry ploughed into his car and he felt nothing.'

I know how Keith died. I've heard the story countless times and yes, it was sad and ghastly. But, if I'm really, *really* honest, I can't find it in my heart to care about a man I never met. A man I was only aware of, post mortem, because of his connection to a woman I hardly know and barely tolerate.

'It was different with Jackie too, wasn't it?' Bev says, sifting through our shared losses. 'Peter's often told me how painful it was for you all to watch your mum fade away like that.'

'Yes. It was.'

'What's worse, I wonder? Losing someone in an instant, like I lost Keith. Or knowing they're in dreadful pain, month after month, and they're going to die.'

'Bev, we're *all* going to die,' I snap. 'Didn't you get the memo?'

11

Bev chuckles, enjoying my little joke. I can't even get angry with this silly woman without her seeing it as a bonding moment.

'I knew your dad was a good man on our very first date. It wasn't really a date. He came to the garden centre with me to help me choose a new lawnmower, then we had lunch in the cafe.' Bev's chin quivers as the irony hits her. Will the garden centre symbolically bookend their relationship?

'We sat there on the terrace for a good couple of hours and he told me about Jackie, how she'd fought off the first bout of cancer and they thought that was it. How he knew before she did that something was wrong. He was so loving and caring as he talked about her. A proper *gentle* man. And I thought to myself: Crikey, Bev, this one's quite the catch.'

I bite my tongue. Dad *didn't* know before Mum that the cancer had returned; she'd been so careful to hide the signs because she feared she wouldn't survive it a second time. So did he rewrite the story of her illness, or did Bev? I'll have a word with him when he's back on his feet.

He will be back on his feet. I *won't* lose two parents in five years. No bloody way!

And then Kate and Pippa return. Pippa holds two paper cups of tea and the top of a Mars bar pokes out of her pocket. Kate is pale. She squeezes her eyes tight shut, then blinks them open again. She tries to find the words but they don't come. She sits down with a thump, lucky to find a chair behind her.

He is gone.

Chapter Two

'Rough or Very Rough'

Nearly noon and I'm curled up on the sofa, still in my washed-to-death Boyzone T-shirt and equally ancient leggings. I've dragged the duvet off my bed and tucked it around me as I channel-zap through daytime options, finally settling on something with dogs. At the next commercial break, I shall make some tea and polish off the last two Tunnock's teacakes. They never used to make me feel queasy but, with determination, I'm pretty sure I can eat through that.

I am an orphan.

I went to sleep – eventually – with those four words in my head and they were still there, like an insistent cluster headache, when I woke up, befuddled and exhausted, at five to six this morning.

I am an orphan.

My dreams have been chaotic and strange: no foretaste of grief to come, no Kodachrome moments of a young Mum and Dad beside us at the seaside or round the dining table. That would make sense. Last night I dreamt I was living in a dystopian city which held a big parade to celebrate the vanquishing of an alien force. But the aliens hadn't left. They were still there and I was the only one who knew.

13

The front door clicks open and Kate enters, weighed down with Tesco bags and post from the communal hall. I wait for the almost imperceptible look of disapproval; I'd promised to be dressed when she returned. I might even have said I'd tidy up . . .

Kate stomps past the sofa and dumps the shopping in the kitchen. 'Sod it, I forgot kitchen towel. I'll pop out later.'

Cupboard doors thump open and closed. Cutlery is put away. A tap is turned on and plates immersed in sudsy water. Kate is also now an orphan, but her response is busy-ness and order. I hear her stop what she's doing and take a deep breath to collect herself. Then she returns with two glasses of orange juice and perches on a vacant corner of sofa.

'How long's the dishwasher been out of action?'

'Couple of weeks, a month maybe. It's no biggie.'

'It isn't if you remember to wash up, Annie. You know? Hot water, little scratchy sponge to loosen the porridge and dried-on ketchup?'

She kicks off her shoes and gets under the other end of the duvet, forcing me to shift my legs. We stare at the TV.

We are both orphans.

'Well, at least we know what we have to do, second time around,' Kate says eventually.

'Do we? Last time we had Dad. Plus Mum told us what she wanted. Which songs, which poems. Tell everyone to wear something red. Hey, d'you remember the Cousin From Tenby?'

Kate only just manages not to spit orange juice across the duvet. A mash-up of grief and light relief catches us unawares and we laugh hysterically for a full minute.

'Oh God, the Cousin From Tenby!' Kate tries to recover herself. 'Did we ever find out who she was?'

'Dad claimed he knew her but he was on autopilot all day.'

'And we didn't defrost those sausage rolls properly and they were rock hard in the middle. But the Cousin From Tenby still ate about ten of them.'

'Those bloody sausage rolls. Why did we buy so many?'

'We must have known she was coming,' Kate says and the hysteria returns.

'Well, unless she's in Dad's address book, we don't need to invite her again.'

'She was pushing 90 six years ago. She's probably dead.'

Dead. She hears the word leave her mouth and it's enough. Just before the tears come, typical Kate, she carefully puts her glass on a side table and finds a clean hanky.

'I keep thinking, "I can't believe it",' she sobs, in jerky gulps. 'And then I think I can't believe I'm thinking I can't believe it because it's such a bloody cliché. This time yesterday, he was alive. It isn't even twenty-four hours, Annie.'

I scoot along the sofa to put my arm round her. I may not have a functioning dishwasher and my flat is a tip. But I give good hug. At least I know how to do that.

'Do you remember, after Mum died, how everyone asked how Dad was?' I say. 'And we'd reply that he was bearing up. "How's your dad, how's your dad?" No one ever asked how *we* were, Kate. It's like we were, I don't know, bystanders. Not daughters who'd just lost their mum.'

Kate blows her nose and pushes stray fringe from her eyes. 'Maybe at Dad's funeral they'll finally ask how *we* are.'

'They bloody won't! Not when there's "poor Bev" to take care of. She's been in our lives, what is it, four years, but she'll be the star turn at Dad's funeral, not us.'

15

'I don't want to be the star turn.' Kate shrugs. 'Whatever that is.'

'Neither do I. But Bev? Seriously? I better be tranquillized or pissed to get through it without laying in to her.'

Kate frowns. 'You can't, Annie. You'd feel awful afterwards. Everyone would.'

I pad into the kitchen, returning with the two remaining teacakes. 'She'll have her fingerprints all over everything. It will be *her* day and we'll get sidelined. You know we will.'

'I don't care.'

'I do. And so do you.'

Kate nods. Magnanimity's overrated. 'But she'll have to respect our wishes for the funeral. *We're* his next of kin.'

'Exactly. It was her choice not to marry Dad. Which means we can do it our way.'

'I don't want to make waves, Annie. She and Dad were really happy and we didn't expect that. We should be grown up about this and let her take charge of the day.'

There is so much to do: registering the death, contacting the solicitor, undertakers, DVLA, electoral roll, passport office . . .

Kate takes charge, I take instruction. In one packed day, we manage to tick seven and a half things off a list she's drawn up with asterisks (urgent/less urgent) and two shades of highlighter pen (pink/Kate, green/Annie). Meanwhile Bev takes it upon herself to break the news to her own friends and family. It means she's occupied and these are the people she and Dad socialized with as a couple: the local Ramblers, Terri and Bill from their walking holiday in Austria, the proprietor of their favourite curry house.

Kate nips home to get her hair straighteners and a couple of changes of clothing; even though she doesn't live far away, we soon realize we need to be together and she only makes a minor fuss about the thinness of my sofa-bed mattress. I'd forgotten how loudly she snores, through two walls and a closed door. I'm amazed that she can disengage her brain and nod off so swiftly. At the end of day two, we're both in bed by ten. By quarter past, Kate's honking like an adenoidal sea lion.

And then the stream of unwanted, mostly trivial, thoughts invade my head, often returning for a second or third visit. All the things I need to do; all the things I should have done and didn't or have done that I shouldn't. Nothing important. That will come later.

I lie board straight and wide awake, staring at the ceiling and tracking the occasional flash of car headlights that crosses the ceiling. Do I have black polish for my best shoes? . . . Who did the registrar remind me of? . . . Why does Kate wear contacts even though she hates them? . . . Cromarty.

When Mum's cancer returned, she insisted on getting a new cat. Flo had died a couple of years earlier of chronic flatulence and immense old age. A kitten would be a distraction from the terminal elephant in the room. Flo's replacement, a long-haired piebald tabby, was almost certain to acquire a cutesy little boy's name, if Mum had anything to with it: Benjy, Barney, Bobby. But Dad insisted that it was his turn to choose and she acquiesced. She must have known the cat would outlive her.

Dad's victory was hollow. All his suggestions were bad puns that no one laughed at: Clawed, Hairy Potter, Purr Favor. Defeated, he scanned his trusty Shipping Forecast tea towel for inspiration: Malin? Bailey? Fitzroy? He settled on Cromarty, where he and Mum had gone on their honeymoon.

I adored Cromarty (more than I had Flo, although I never

told Mum) and used to call him Monorail because of the way he straddled the back of the sofa to look out of the front window. He was unusually sociable for a male cat and was a huge comfort to Dad after Mum died.

Bev wasn't a cat person but, when she and Dad got together, Cromarty, now fully grown, was an integral part of the package. When they sold their separate homes and bought the bungalow, fitting a cat flap was Dad's first job. On the rare occasions I visited, freaked to see furniture or saucepans I'd grown up with in this ugly, alien little house, Cromarty would seek me out. When I could locate no warm feelings for Bev, I could still give love to this daft, klutzy animal painfully kneading my lap.

Cromarty hadn't been old enough to appreciate the loss of Mum; he'd barely adjusted to replacing his own mother with these larger, fur-less parents. But Dad had spoilt him rotten and the cat will definitely notice his sudden absence.

Will Bev remember to feed and cuddle him? Will she know that the only way he'll swallow worming tablets is encased in expensive Waitrose salmon pate? If Bev doesn't care for or about Cromarty, might I have to adopt him? Great in theory but it's patently obvious that I'm barely responsible for myself. And I've got no outside space. And, well, I just can't.

After two hours of failing to fall asleep, I give in and get up to make a cup of tea. Normally, when insomnia hits me, I spend an hour or two in front of Netflix, waking with a jolt at the dawn chorus and stumbling back to bed. But Kate is honking for England on the sofa bed, so that's not an option.

I rest my elbows on the worktop, waiting for the kettle to boil. I flick the radio on, hoping to catch the last gasp of the midnight news.

As I dunk my tea bag and clock two new packets of

Hobnobs (hurrah for Kate) in the cupboard, the Shipping Forecast kicks in. North Utsire, South Utsire, Dogger, Fisher, German Bight. And finally it hits me like a cold slap of sea water in the face.

Dad is dead.

I hadn't found it in me to cry before. There were even times when I thought I wouldn't need to, the way I'd cried for Mum. What did that mean? Didn't I care enough? Was I now such a detached, callous cow that I'd become hardened to loss?

This sudden wail of grief takes me by surprise . . . Portland, Plymouth, Lundy, Fastnet. It comes up from my belly and bursts from my lungs. It hurts . . . Shannon, Bailey, Rockall. As I try to control the jagged lurch of sobs, it dawns on me that every night after the midnight news, every morning at 05.20, this sing-songy, all too familiar, irritating mantra will remind me that Dad is gone.

I hear a thump and 'fuck' from next door as Kate gets out of bed; she must have walked into the coffee table. I barely register her coming into the kitchen. She hugs me, crying in sympathy.

I don't need to explain myself. Faeroes, Fair Isle, South-East Iceland says it all.

'Shall I turn it off?' Kate asks gently.

'No! He hasn't got to Sandettie Light Vessel Automatic yet.'

Kate parks me on the kitchen stool and makes the tea. The announcer runs through inshore waters . . . Cape Wrath, Rattray Head, Lyme Regis, Carlingford Lough, Ardnamurchan Point, and wishes his audience a peaceful night's sleep.

As soon as the first chord of 'God Save the Queen' strikes up, Kate turns off the radio. That's the rule. Dad's unconditional love of the Shipping Forecast was a constant, as was his disdain for the Royals.

'Sandettie Light Vessel Automatic.' Kate laughs. 'I still don't know what that is.'

'I don't suppose we need to.'

We settle on my bed sipping tea, a pyjama party minus the party.

'Bloody Shipping Forecast,' she mutters. 'Soundtrack to our lives.'

'What was he like? Living his whole life in landlocked St Albans but he had to know if a storm was brewing off Selsey Bill.'

'Once a sea cadet, always a sea cadet.' She does her own approximation of a salute. 'And always home from work by five to six, so he could catch it on Long Wave.'

'Mum reckoned he listened to it to wind us up, because we hated it so much when we were kids. And then it just kind of stuck. Part of what glued us together as a family.'

Kate nods. 'Do you remember when we had friends for tea on a Saturday and we had to tell them to keep quiet while it was on? I know it scared off Michael Atkins. My first-ever boyfriend. God, I was so embarrassed.'

'Shame it didn't scare Bev off.'

Kate doesn't respond. We long ago agreed to be tolerant of her but Kate is better at this than me.

Bev came into Dad's life when he'd just about learned to get through each day without Mum. He'd got back into reading again, sometimes a book a day. He'd taken on an allotment and joined the Ramblers.

Bev was a Rambler too; that's how their friendship began. What upset Kate and me was when it rapidly became more than a friendship. We didn't have to like her (we didn't) to be distressed at how quickly she displaced Mum. That was Bev's only crime. That and her fondness for little carved stone ornaments and parsley garnishes and turquoise as a default colour choice for everything. And Lionel Richie.

'We need to cut her some slack,' Kate says carefully, knowing this suggestion has sparked arguments in the past. 'She's lost him too.'

'I know. How could I not know that, Kate?'

'And, let's be honest, it suited us that she was in Dad's life. She looked after him so we didn't have to. She went to the theatre with him. She cut his toenails. Bev being there meant we could stop worrying.'

'I worried. Sometimes.'

'Did you? Really? It wasn't always obvious, Annie.'

'I did. But I just had so much other stuff to deal with: work . . . missing Mum . . . Rob.'

'He knows, right? You've told Rob about Dad.'

I stare at the last cold mouthful of tea in my mug.

Shit! Rob!

Kate shakes her head in disbelief. 'Oh Annie, that's – that's really – Dad loved Rob. Promise me you'll tell him first thing tomorrow.'

'Could you?'

'Are you serious? You are, aren't you? Jesus!'

'I'll take that as a no then.'

Kate unfolds her long legs and gets off the bed. 'First thing tomorrow. Promise me.'

I nod. I will. At some point tomorrow. Definitely.

'Right. I've got a 9 a.m. meeting. I need to sleep. Night-night, An-An.'

'Sleep tight, Katkin.'

* * *

21

Around half six, I get a sense of someone moving around in the kitchen and bathroom, slamming the front door and clacking down the lino-ed stairs. Kate will have found the coffee, bread and cereal because she lugged them home from Tesco. She's already discovered the clogged shower head, the incapacitated dishwasher and the temperamental latch on the communal front door.

Two hours later, an insistent ringing rouses me with a jolt. Doorbell. Probably the latest girlfriend of Tony in Flat 2 who's always locking herself out. Or some poor harassed parcel delivery person needing to drop-&-go. Because I'm home so much these days, I sometimes think I could set up in business receiving neighbours' shipments from Amazon and eBay. A tenner a parcel doesn't seem unreasonable . . .

The doorbell rings again. I get out of bed and tweak the blind. Waiting on the front step is Rob, with Josh slouched behind him fiddling with his phone. I scuff into some nearby sweatpants and pad downstairs to let them in.

Rob looks ashen. He gives me a massive hug, then steps back so that Josh can hug me too. I *had* been intending to phone him. I really had. Bloody Kate must have got there first, convinced I wouldn't follow through. Okay, it isn't exclusively my news, but Rob's *my* ex so I should have been trusted to tell him.

I wave them into the living room. Kate has closed the sofa bed, re-scattered the cushions and thrown the throw. If it wasn't for some neatly rolled bedding behind the armchair, it would be as if she was never here.

'I'm so sorry, Annie,' Rob says, sitting on the sofa and cocking his head for Josh to put his phone away and sit too. 'It's awful news. Just awful. Peter was a brilliant bloke.'

I nod. It is. He was.

'She shouldn't have told you. I said I would.'

'She was still in shock. Very emotional, losing her drift. She kept insisting that he'd want me to have his tools. But I really can't get my head round that right now.'

'His tools?'

'So thoughtful of her. They made a great couple.'

Finally. It makes sense. 'Bev told you?'

'She rang the morning after he died. She said she'd got to "F" in her address book and suddenly realized she'd rather talk to me. I won't lie, I nearly lost it. Didn't I, Josh?'

Josh confirms with a grunt. His phone judders in his pocket. Maturely he ignores it.

'But *I* was going to tell you.'

'Hey, it doesn't matter now. Maybe she wanted to take the pressure off you.'

'Why does everyone around here think I'm useless? That I'm incapable of doing stuff, handling stuff, behaving like a grown-up?'

'I wish you *had* called me, lovely. I'd have been round like a shot.'

'Kate's been here. She's running the show. And then Bev will take over and I can get back to my jet-set life.'

'Jet-set. Right.' Rob stands. 'I'd love a cuppa. You too?'

'And some toast? I haven't eaten since yesterday morning.'

Rob tuts and goes into the kitchen. 'Got any unhealthy, sugar-laden drinks for Josh?'

'Not for me thanks.' Josh rolls his eyes. 'Anyway, I'm meeting Rhys at half eleven. I just wanted to say, you know, I'm really sorry about your dad and everything.'

I can't deny I still miss Rob. You don't just un-love someone. But Josh generates a different kind of love: the nearest I'll ever come to being a mum. He has his dad's tight curly reddish-blond hair and skinny frame. He definitely has his black-treacle eyes. He's taking a while to outgrow the acne but he acts as if it isn't there.

'See you then, Miss Stanley. Bye Dad.'

He gives me a wraparound hug, kisses the top of my head and leaves.

'He wanted to come,' Rob says from the kitchen doorway after we hear the front door slam. 'He was asking me all the way here what was the right thing to say. Bless him, he was only 2 when *my* dad died. And his mum's old man will still be out on the golf course long after the rest of us are worm food.'

'How did Bev sound?'

'When did you last speak to her?'

'At the hospital. Kate has, though.'

'We could pop round if you like. Maybe take her out for lunch.'

'No! I can't. Not yet.' Suddenly I feel suffocated, cornered.

'Fair enough, lovely. I could take *you* out for lunch though.'

'I just want to sleep.'

'I get that. I do, Annie. But I want to help. What's that bollocks they say on the telly? I want to "be there for you".'

He says it in a really bad American accent and I can't help laughing. It's even worse than his all-purpose yokel accent. He's always made me laugh. When Dad first met him, after disapproving for months that I was dating the father of a pupil, he was instantly disarmed.

I go to the loo to have a little cry and brush my teeth. When I return, the coffee table is laid with mugs of tea and a plate stacked with toast, cut on the bias, one triangle slathered in lemon curd and the other in marmalade. He

24

knows me so well. The 'St Clements Special' was our favourite lazy Sunday breakfast, if we didn't go out for brunch.

Rob gives his tea a stir and takes a sip. 'Bev said it was sudden. How he died.'

'He never regained consciousness. The paramedic promised us he wasn't in pain.'

'It's just too quick, too soon. He had so much life in him . . . Top bloke.' He pauses, momentarily overcome with sadness. 'I wish I'd met your mum.'

'You'd have won *her* over too.'

'I haven't cracked it with Kate though. You sister remains one hundred per cent underwhelmed.'

'Hey, don't be so hard on yourself.' I grin. 'Eighty per cent, more like.'

He grins back. Water under the bridge now.

'So,' he says eventually. 'What can I do? How can I help? I've got a day off between jobs and I want to be useful.'

Not a good idea. 'Kate's on the case. And she reckons we should let Bev make all the decisions for the funeral, even though we're next of kin.'

'Cremation or burial?'

'Cremation. That's what Mum had.'

An awkward pause. This is the man I thought was my soul mate for life and now we're doing awkward pauses.

Eventually he breaks the silence. 'Peter wasn't too impressed with my tool box. Remember? When I helped him lay that decking. He's got – I mean, he *had* – a hammer that belonged to his dad. Just imagine all the nails it bashed in, all the stuff it made. I'd be honoured to have his tools, Annie. That's if you and Kate don't want them.'

'And then you can pass them on to Josh so he can make things with them too.'

'He can't even make his bed.'

Rob watches me dispatch the last triangle of toast, then run my finger round the plate to wipe up any missed marmalade. Job done.

'I need to deliver a cabinet to a woman in Luton, then I'm all yours,' he offers, probably kicking himself for his choice of words. He isn't mine any more. But I'm not quite ready for him to be anyone else's.

I look at him looking at me. I think he still loves me. Maybe the grief of losing Dad has cleared my mind and we could try again. Is that a good enough reason? I can't even begin to think about it just yet.

He waits for a response: how can he 'be here for me'?

'There is one thing, Rob.'

His face lights up.

'How are you with dishwashers?'

Chapter Three

November 2014

Just one more hour – fifty-four minutes to be precise – and Annie could pack up and depart. Some of her workmates were planning to decamp to the Plough, get a few rounds in and compile nominations for this year's unofficial Parent/ Teacher Awards: rudest parent, pushiest parent, least fragrant parent, hottest parent, coolest parent; plus a special award for the daftest question.

Annie intended to nominate Nia Ronson-Tanner's father for both 'rude' *and* 'pushy'. Plus he had thrust his IT business card into her hand, when his wife wasn't looking, and told her that he'd be happy to 'update her system' any time, wink-wink. He certainly wasn't 'hot' or 'cool' and she hadn't got close enough to assess his aroma.

Cameron, the head, had stationed her in a classroom some distance from the central hub. Annie suspected that several parents had been unable to find her, despite all the laminated signs, but she wasn't going in search of them now.

Those she had seen, apart from Nia's dad, were in the main friendly and polite. They understood their kids and had reasonable expectations of them, bearing in mind the muddled, unfair and unpredictable world beyond Rangewood

27

High School. In fact, Annie's most repeated advice was for their sons or daughters to aim higher: Seema Patel should definitely study engineering, and Mason McIsaac was easily university material. It felt good to be the voice of optimism and positivity. It reminded Annie why teaching beat the corporate world hands down, even if the salary was hardly commensurate.

She checked her phone to make sure it was still the Plough and not the Queen's Arms, which was closer but mankier. There was a text from Kate reminding her that it was Bev's birthday on Saturday and did Annie want to go halves on the turquoise necklace she'd already bought in Accessorize? And not to forget a card. Annie replied twice: 'Yes' and 'I haven't'. She could nip in to the newsagent's tomorrow and pop something in the post, more to please Dad than Bev.

Annie began noodling around on Facebook, checking on her ex, Toby; they were no longer on good terms but he had yet to unfriend her or tighten up his privacy settings. She didn't miss him, not one bit, but she resented the presence in every photo of his fiancée, an American City lawyer called Madison. Toby was welcome to her, in all her size 6, Stella McCartney-clad glory.

'Ahem.'

Annie jumped, so caught up in Toby and Madison's weekend in Barcelona that she'd not heard anyone approaching.

'Sorry. Did I startle you?' the man asked, apologetically.

'Just a bit.'

'Am I too late? I'm Joshua Tyler's dad. Rob Tyler. Hi.'

Annie gestured for him to sit. He took the chair beside her but kept looking to the door, then his watch.

'Honestly, you've got ages yet, Mr Tyler.'

He turned to face her properly, to give his full attention. Curly red-blond hair, long legs which didn't sit comfortably on the utilitarian school chair and the deepest brown eyes. Annie mentally ticked 'hot' but she wasn't going to tell her colleagues just how hot.

'Sorry. I thought my wife would be here. She said she would be.'

Wife. Of course there was a wife. They're either gay or spoken for – wasn't that the rule?

'We can give her a couple of minutes,' Annie suggested, 'if you think she's close.'

'No. Let's start without her. I had a feeling she wouldn't make it. I don't mind her taking it out on me but she shouldn't punish the lad.'

'How is she doing that?'

'We separated last month,' he said, looking down at his shoes. 'Not permanent, just a trial to give ourselves breathing space. And, well, it's all been a bit . . . fraught. Right now, we're not very good at being in the same room, even if it's a classroom with a teacher present to keep the peace. Anyway, it's not your concern. So. Josh Tyler. How's he doing?'

Annie knew and liked Josh. If she could only adhere to her brief and disengage from those molasses eyes, she could do this. She rebooted herself into teacher mode and gave a thorough assessment: Josh is diligent, bright; good manners (mostly); needs to take assignments more seriously because he can't get by on charm if he keeps missing deadlines; definitely university material, if that's what he wants.

Mr Tyler looked pleased. 'That's great, Miss Stanley. That's really good news. He's an only child, you see. So all the tension at home lands on him, however hard Maggie and I try to keep him out of it.'

29

'Perhaps, when the trial separation's over, things will be easier.'

'God, I hope so.' He tried an optimistic smile. 'We just need some time apart. We'll come through this stronger, all three of us. I know we will.'

Annie reciprocated the smile. God, those eyes. They'd really done a number on her. She collected herself. She'd dispensed her words of wisdom but there was no harm in a bit of informal conversation, was there? Otherwise he might just leave. Or, worse still, Mrs Tyler might skid into the room, apologizing for her lateness.

'You're a carpenter, right? I remember Josh mentioning it in class when we were discussing global warming. He was very concerned about deforestation.'

'We didn't worry about that kind of thing when I was a lad. Dinosaurs still roamed the earth, of course, so we were too busy wrestling them.'

Annie felt a frisson of attraction. Bloody hell, Mr Tyler was hot *and* funny. She wondered how he smelled. Wright's Coal Tar Soap with a hint of wood shavings? Stop it, stop it, calm down, you ridiculous woman.

And then she said it, before she could stop herself. 'Do you do small commissions? What I mean is, do you make things for ordinary people? Or is it just big stuff? Shop fitting-type stuff? Or small stuff too . . .?'

'Ordinary people? Not sure what you mean.'

Annie felt her face redden but she'd started, so . . . 'I'm looking for someone to make a cupboard for my kitchen. The units I've got are discontinued Ikea but I need more storage space. So I thought I might get a carpenter to make something in a dark wood to match the worktops. Um, can you recommend anyone?'

'Ah, I'm with you now.' He laughed. 'So you're just an "ordinary person", are you?'

'Absolutely.'

He felt around in his pockets, eventually pulling out a crumpled card. 'There's a link to my website, such as it is. You can see the kind of jobs I do. I'm just finishing a study of bookshelves, floor to ceiling, for a mate of a mate. If you like what you see, I could squeeze you in after that.'

Stop it, stop it, Miss Stanley. You're making a show of yourself now. Pull yourself together.

'Great,' Annie replied. 'I'll check out your website. Good to meet you, Mr Tyler.'

Chapter Four

'New Low Expected'

One Tuesday morning, in that strange period post-shock and pre-funeral, I wake up early. I even *get up* early, rather than turn over and go back to sleep. Before 8 a.m., I have tipped the contents of the laundry basket into the washing machine and set it to 60°C, made and eaten porridge with banana and washed up two days' worth of plates and cutlery. I am also showered and dressed. What has happened to me?

Years ago, I used to be good at early mornings. Maybe not at uni, unless I had a 9 a.m. lecture, but I could do it if I had to. It was how I'd been brought up; Dad thought he was late if he was on time and Mum was just very organized. So, when I worked in the City, it wasn't hard to be suited, booted and on the Tube to Canada Water by 7.30.

I kept it up when I became a teacher. Finally I was doing something worthwhile, after all those years of pretending to find satisfaction in the corporate world, and that was definitely worth getting up in the dark for.

Mum's cancer returned just as I was starting my PGCE teacher-training course. I offered to postpone it, but she wouldn't let me. She said that me becoming a teacher, after my seven-year fling with mammon, was more therapeutic than any chemo. 'You were born to do this, love. I never saw you as a City person.'

So . . . I qualified as a teacher and moved back to St Albans two months before Mum died. My silly City salary meant I had enough put by for a tiny flat and a tiny mortgage. I didn't become a teacher for the money, that's for sure, but I was sufficiently cash-cushioned to take the leap and it was important to be close if Mum needed me.

And yet, however much I knew it was the right move, it was always tainted. She didn't live to see that I *was* a good teacher: motivating sullen kids, keeping up – at first, at least – with all the prep and marking.

Once she'd gone, it became harder to get out of bed. Slowly, incrementally, I began to lose my nerve and my way. When I met Rob, I was still a good teacher but even his support couldn't put off the creeping burnout. Working for an international merchant bank had its moments but teaching is on another level of stress because the 'product' is people. Young people. There simply aren't enough hours in the day to do everything.

I experienced breathlessness and palpitations. Twice, I was convinced I was having a heart attack; the second time in the middle of a lesson. My GP put me through all manner of cardiology tests and my heart got the all-clear; there was nothing physically wrong with me. I was, however, diagnosed with stress due to excessive workload and bereavement, and signed off work on full pay for the first hundred days, with half pay to follow.

I coped without Mum. We all did. Dad coped by hooking up with Bev. Kate coped by shagging unavailable men and being a control freak. I coped – for a while – by being loved unconditionally by a wonderful man. But I didn't deserve it and, pretty soon, I extricated myself from the two things that gave me a purpose. I resigned as a teacher and I ended it with Rob because he could do way better than me.

Kate called it a breakdown. Maybe it was; I don't honestly know. I simply decided I didn't deserve to be a teacher and/or Rob's girlfriend any more. So I stopped. Dad quizzed me a few times on my plans but I couldn't tell him what they were because I didn't have any. Keeping things simple was the only way I could get out of bed in the morning – although, more often than not, I didn't.

Perhaps if Dad hadn't met Bev, he might have been more proactive in pushing me. But suddenly his life was full again and he was too busy selling the family home and moving into the bungalow with Bev . . . or hiking in the Tyrol with Bev . . . or holidaying with Pippa's brood in Dorset. With frigging Bev!

I will go back to teaching. Or I won't. Cameron has said numerous times that there's a job for me at Rangewood, if I want it. Do I? Fuck knows!

But today, I am up and dressed and I will use the day wisely. There's nothing left to organize for the funeral. Bev and Kate have liaised about the music and the words; I'm down to read a Walt Whitman poem. Pippa and Kate have downloaded a pdf template for the order of service booklet and will collect it from the printers tomorrow. They've also booked a pub function room not far from the crematorium. Bev and Pippa have chosen the finger food and pastries Dad would have liked and will put £200 behind the bar.

I have done bugger all.

On a whim, I drive to The Galleria in Hatfield, half minded to find something to wear to the funeral. I still have an expensive black Hobbs work suit from my past life, but it doesn't seem appropriate. Plus I was a stone lighter back in the day and I manage to bust the zip trying it on. Lucky I didn't get it dry cleaned.

Mum wanted everyone to wear red at her funeral but Dad died so suddenly that we have no instructions. Bev believes black is respectful and Kate relays this information to anyone who asks.

I park underground and wander aimlessly around the shopping mall. I am not one of life's shoppers and none of the window displays feature outfits that tempt me inside the stores. Why isn't there a formal version of trackie bottoms and sweatshirt?

I try on a couple of things in M&S: a black dress with a wild turquoise flower print. Bev would love it. And a longish pleated skirt in a shiny fabric that reminds me of the curtain at the hospital when we were ushered in to see Dad's body.

I buy the dress. It can go to Oxfam next week.

That evening, Kate and I are summoned to Bev's; she says she has some things for us. I can't concoct an excuse quickly enough to refuse and Kate is keen to pick me up. In the car, she sets the usual ground rules.

'Just because I'm driving, doesn't mean you can get pissed, Annie.'

'Yeah-yeah.'

'Seriously. We'll get through this by being considerate and accommodating. We'll bite our tongues. Agreed?'

'Kate, I'm not a kid. I've behaved up till now, haven't I?'

She doesn't reply. Clearly not. I don't pursue it because then we'll argue and it'll turn into an even more uncomfortable evening.

This way, we're both still talking to each other when we

ring the bungalow doorbell. Pippa opens it and directs us to the garden room, Dad and Bev's pride and joy. En route, I try not to take in our old family Welsh dresser, now boasting a set of turquoise serving platters and a row of little carved stone ornaments. Mum used to display her much-prized collection of Poole Pottery milk jugs on it. That's what it was for.

Last time I visited, I got unfeasibly distressed that Bev had changed the knobs on the drawers . . . from the slightly scratched wooden ones I'd grown up with to white porcelain faux-Victorian ones, each one hand-painted with flowers. She and Dad had bought them in a craft market in York. She threw the old knobs out, not that I'd have known what to do with them if I'd asked for them. But even so.

Pippa brings in glasses of iced tea and bowls of nuts and olives. She puts the nibbles beside me and I tell myself to ignore them. I know her game. I *will not* scoff the lot like last time.

'So,' Bev says after we've cheek-kissed and settled ourselves. 'We're nearly there.'

'Nearly where?' asks Kate before I can.

'Saying our farewells, celebrating Peter,' she replies. 'There's such a big build-up to the funeral and then, after that, we just have to get on with our lives. That's how it was when I lost Keith.'

Pippa chips in. 'You took it one day at a time, Mum. And that's what you'll do now. You've got no choice.'

'Dad was just the same after Mum died, wasn't he, Annie?' Kate is determined to draw me into the conversation.

'He said each day had its own personality,' I recall. 'Mostly sad, sometimes surreal. Or tied up in miles of red tape, like that day he tried to cancel all her magazine subscriptions. We did laugh a lot though, the three of us, didn't we? I can't even remember what about now.'

Kate smiles. 'The music box that wouldn't shut up.'

At this point, Cromarty hurtles in from the garden and scoots under Bev's chair, as if he's playing hide-and-seek with an invisible pal.

The cavalry has arrived. Cromarty is one of the Stanley clan. I lean forward and wiggle my fingers under the chair rung to tempt him out. He loves chasing my fingers. But he won't budge.

'Come on, Cromarty,' I plead in the squeaky voice we use to communicate with each other. He squeaks back but will not shift.

I know what it is. He is bereft without Dad. Obviously we all are, but at least *we* know that Dad is gone and that he won't be coming back. Cromarty will be anxiously expecting his back-rubs and treats, bless him. Now he must learn to tolerate Bev who, as she has constantly reminded us, is not a cat person. Just thinking about Cromarty's loss and confusion nearly sets me off. When will our beloved moggy realize that Dad is gone?

Bev wiggles her fingers under her chair and he appears with a friendly chirrup, barely acknowledging Kate and me. He leaps onto Bev's lap, turns around three times and settles into a croissant, head tucked under back paws. Within seconds he is purring loudly, utterly content, with the occasional twitch of his tail.

It shouldn't matter but it does. Cromarty is totally at home here, in this neat, characterless little house with its turquoise accent colours and reminders of *our* home: the table lamp that used to be in Mum and Dad's bedroom; the Matisse print that hung on our landing; the little bowl containing the nuts that I brought back from a holiday in Portugal. (In fact, I brought back two but the second one got broken one lively Christmas.)

I didn't mind seeing these things, *our* things, in the bungalow while Dad was still around to use them. But, like Cromarty, they now belong to Bev, and what will happen to them when *she* dies?

Bev scoops up the cat. 'Off you get, Marty. I need to fetch something.' She pours his sleeping form on to my lap where he stays for all of five seconds, then dashes back into the garden.

'Since when's he called Marty?' I ask, ignoring Kate's 'don't make waves' frown.

'I think he prefers it,' Bev replies. '"Cromarty" is such a mouthful, isn't it?'

'But it's his name.' I know I sound ridiculous. I shove a fistful of peanuts in my mouth to stop myself from making this into a 'thing'. Bev is oblivious.

We chat in a desultory way, Kate, Pippa and I, while Bev is gone. Pippa is seven years younger than me, four years younger than Kate. But she wins whatever competition there is between us because she is married with two adorable children, currently being cared for by her amazing mother-in-law, while Kate and I are spinsters.

'Elliott and Evie are too young for the funeral,' Pippa tells us. 'Better they don't come than they get upset. They adored Peter. We all did.'

We adored him more.

Kate and I catch each other's eyes and transmit the same thought. He was ours. You just borrowed him for a bit. He was *ours*, not yours.

Bev returns with a large cardboard box and a well-stuffed bin bag. She puts the box on the coffee table with a grunt. It must be heavy.

'Your nana's best tea set,' she explains.

38

Kate unscrunches some old newspaper from around a teacup, nestling among others at the top of the box. It's white with a 1940s wheatsheaf design and a fiddly handle. Mum never liked this tea set and rarely used it. But she didn't have the heart to chuck it out. Dad must have moved the box from our family home to the bungalow without ever unpacking it, so he probably felt the same.

'There's four place settings and a teapot,' says Bev, clearly wanting them gone. 'Or it can all go to the charity shop, along with these old tablecloths and napkins and whatnot.'

The contents of the bin bag smell musty. I pull out an old checked tablecloth, permanently stained with spilled Ribena, then some napkins I won for Mum in a Brownies' raffle that never came out of the dresser drawer. Nothing here is of use to me. And Kate only likes new things, ideally from Next Interiors.

And then I spot it: Dad's Shipping Forecast tea towel. It's creased and faded and the bottom hem is fraying. But this tatty rectangle of Irish linen, denoting Dogger, Fisher and German Bight, says everything about our lives and our dad.

When he first bought it, from a little ships' chandlery in Whitstable, he wouldn't let us use it. He treated it like the Turin Shroud. He even bought a plastic clip-frame for it, saying it should take pride of place on the kitchen wall. A semi-serious suggestion that Mum refused point-blank. He knew she would. So it joined the other tea towels in the dresser drawer and clearly got a lot of use.

'Oh, that,' says Bev, waving it away dismissively. 'You have it, Annie. Use it as a cleaning rag.'

I take the tea towel, carefully refold it and put it in my bag. I want to cry but I won't, not in front of Bev and Pippa.

Chapter Five

'Occasionally Very Rough Later'

On the morning of the funeral, I nearly have words with Bev. She thinks Kate and I should travel to the crematorium with her, in the car behind the hearse, but I can't think of anything worse. Kate 'isn't fussed' but I am. I know I'm being childish and petulant and I try to snap out of it but I just can't. In the end, Bev is accompanied by Pippa and Mark, while Kate and I hitch a lift with Rob and Josh, fortunately *not* in his white work van full of tools and timber.

Like father like son, both Rob and Josh look uncomfortable in smart clothes. Rob wears his darkest jeans and a brown tweedy jacket I made him buy when we were together. We'd booked a weekend break at a flash hotel and I feared he might be turned away from their three-star restaurant if he rocked up in his usual casual gear. He even has a tie in his pocket that he won't put on until the last minute. Josh wears one of those tight-legged, short-jacketed suits that work on boyband members and shop-window mannequins but look lumpy as soon as you put your phone in your pocket. I'm touched they made the effort.

Kate and Rob aren't exactly frosty with each other but they've never really found common ground. He made her some alcove bookshelves, soon after he and I hooked up. She moaned that he took too long and it wasn't the shade of wood stain she'd chosen. He moaned that she was too fussy and he'd bloody written down midnight blue, not cobalt, when she commissioned him. I kept well out of it.

I used to have this visual image of me as the middle joint of a chicken wishbone, with Rob and Kate pulling either end. Whoever tugged hardest and got the biggest bit of bone would win my soul. When Rob and I split up, Kate won by default. She could have been a bit more magnanimous in victory, and nicer to Rob, but the pattern had been set.

Never one to hold back, when she has her first sight of my black funeral dress, with its lairy turquoise flowers, she stifles a giggle: 'Well, at least Bev's going to approve.'

She has already been picked up by Rob and sits beside him in the passenger seat. She's wearing trousers and jacket in a sort of aubergine colour that pretends to be black. Kate always looks smart, crisp and businesslike; she's rubbish, however, at looking relaxed, creased and casual and certainly wouldn't take lessons from me.

I know my dress is awful but I don't care. I just need to get through the day. Then we can cut Bev adrift and do our mourning our way, without her fingerprints all over everything. I will behave, I will be gracious and respectful. I can do this.

'Have you learned your poem?' Kate asks as we pull into the crematorium car park.

'No! Why would I?'

'So that you don't have to hold a rustly bit of paper and everyone will see your hands shaking.'

I ignore her. The poem is printed in the order of service

booklet so no rustly bit of paper is required and, that way, some kind soul can take over if I can't get through it without falling to bits.

I grudgingly give Kate credit. The Walt Whitman poem I'm to read, 'Song of Myself', is actually very beautiful. When she first showed it to me, I said she should be the one to read it. She declined, quite forcefully because a) I'm the eldest so it should come from me and b) she has a horror of public speaking that I've always found strange in someone so straight talking and shoot-from-the-hip.

We get out of Rob's car and switch into daughter mode as people hug us and say soothing things. Yes, he was a wonderful man. Yes, we will miss him. Yes, he died in his garden. Yes, he was at peace. No, if you don't mind, could you sit next to his friends from Royston so that we can squeeze our old neighbours, Maureen and Ray Gorringe, in beside Dad's colleague Derek from the insurance office.

Maureen gives me one of those frowny-smiley nods, to convey her sadness, across the packed pews. It was good of them to come; I must tell her to thank Kim, their daughter and my first best friend, for her condolence card. Kim often joked that she'd happily swap her dad for mine because he made her laugh and didn't mind chauffeuring us back from parties the other side of St Albans.

The service begins with 'In My Life' by The Beatles and I'm amazed I don't cry, even though I know I will every time I hear it from now on. The celebrant talks about Dad's career, his happy first marriage to Jackie, and his two wonderful girls. I have a terrible urge to stand up and give everyone a cheery wave at the mention of my name. I emit a silent giggle. Kate glares and I pull myself together. Hysteria is a dangerous thing.

Then we get on to Bev and how happy she made Peter in their twilight years. Does the celebrant know Dad was only 65 when he died? That's not twilight, that's barely bloody teatime.

I am called to the front to read my poem. I suddenly have no fear, no nerves, even with all those caring, expectant faces focused on me. I see Rob, scrunched in between Auntie Jan and a pillar. Josh stands at the side; he must have given his seat up for Uncle Frank. I take a deep breath and remind myself to take it slowly:

> I bequeath myself to the dirt to grow from
> the grass I love,
> If you want me again look for me under
> your boot-soles.

I stop for a moment and see a little cluster of Dad's Ramblers pals nodding in unison at the boot-sole reference. Bev too. That's how they knew him, in his Berghaus boots, sturdy fleece and cargo shorts, with a rain-protected OS map on a cord round his neck.

Yes, he loved tramping the hills and rewarding himself with a pint and a ploughman's afterwards. But Kate and I have a more engrained image of this funny, friendly, stubborn man and before I know it, I put the poem down and my own, initially stumbling, words echo round the room.

'Dad wasn't just a Rambler, although he loved his walks. Obviously. He lived in St Albans, with no sea for miles around. But he had this thing about coasts and lighthouses. He liked to imagine little fishing boats bobbing about at night and ferries going to Dieppe and Rosslare and Shetland. He loved the Shipping Forecast. He bloody loved it. He saw it as a kind of security blanket, wrapped round the British Isles, keeping us all safe.'

I stop for a moment to mop my eyes and blow my nose, then I go on. 'Ardnamurchan Point, Lough Foyle to Carlingford Lough, Sandettie Light Vessel Automatic, Channel Light Vessel Automatic, Machrihanish flipping Automatic. Those names were as much poetry to Dad as anything by Walt Whitman or John Lennon.

'When I was 17, Dad drove me up to Norwich so we could check out the University of East Anglia. Mum didn't come; it was when she first got ill. Anyway, I was map-reading and I saw this place on the coast of Norfolk called Happisburgh and it made me laugh. Happy's Berg. Quick as a flash, Dad turned off our route and drove us there to see the famous lighthouse. And, as I'm sure some of you will know, it's pronounced "Haisbro", not "Happy's Berg".

'So we get there and we look at the lighthouse and it's a very nice lighthouse, as lighthouses go. And we eat our cheese-and-Branston sandwiches, and it's really windy and it starts to rain. And we're happy in Happy's Berg, Dad and I. And I make myself remember it, there and then, as a special moment. And, well, it was, it *is*, a day that will always make me happy. Sorry. Thank you.'

I stumble back to my seat. I can see I've made at least four people cry. Kate puts her arm around me and the coffin trundles off behind some curtains, like the ones at the Odeon, and the celebrant says a bunch of words I don't even hear.

I grit my teeth for the final piece of music, as listed in the order of service: 'Wind beneath my Wings', specially chosen by Bev. I will try not to hate it. I've said my bit and deviated from my instructions. I will let Bette Midler wash over me, hoping I need never hear it again.

But it isn't Bette, it's 'Sailing By', the soporific signature tune to our family's lives. The congregation looks surprised. One or two chuckle. Rob and Auntie Jan applaud.

Kate squeezes my hand. She did this: for Dad, for Mum. But mostly for us.

Chapter Six

'Moderate, Occasionally Poor'

Everyone tells me that the bereavement process can really only begin after the funeral. So much is invested in the day: who will attend, who will say the wrong thing, who will eat too many goat's cheese straws and Portuguese custard tarts? (Answer: me.)

Dad was the reason for all the planning and organizing and gathering, and at least it distracted us from our grief. But now it's over and we need to make a stab at dealing with his absence and trying to get on with our lives.

Which is fine for Kate, who has just been promoted at work and is super-busy. And it's fine for Bev, who is spending a few days with Pippa, Mark and the kids. It's even fine for Cromarty, who gets fed, stroked and spoilt rotten by Two-Doors-Down Dawn whenever Dad and Bev go away. *Went* away.

My 'normal' life, however, is fucked. It was fucked before Dad died but back then, what seems like a million years ago, I could at least pretend I was merely taking a sabbatical from teaching, a time to recoup and re-energize. Going to the pictures, not going to the gym, getting up late with a long nap in the afternoon . . . these were medicinal mechanisms designed to get me well again. And I was sure I'd get well because I knew Dad would worry if I didn't.

But now, who honestly cares? I don't.

Three days after the funeral, I'm trying to haul myself out of bed. The sun is streaming through a gap in the blinds and the milk in my fridge has fermented. At least I don't need to get dressed to get milk. That's the great thing about living 24/7 in the same T-shirt and leggings; people think you're off for a run and you must be so flipping keen to get out there and clock up the 20k that you've forgotten to brush your teeth or put a comb through your hair.

I return with essentials: a litre of milk, a loaf of white sliced and some creme eggs. As I walk up the path, I see Rob parking his van. Oh great, he's checking up on me. At the funeral, he told me he would, and I said he didn't have to and he said he did and I closed the conversation by biting so enthusiastically into another Portuguese custard tart that the filling fell on my lap. Damn, now I'll have to wash that dress before I take it to Oxfam. Unlike the dishwasher, my washing machine *does* still function.

That's why Rob's here. He couldn't fix the dishwasher and Kate told him I'm still living in a tip and I can't even wash up and she fears it's the thin wedge of a slippery slope.

'Don't pull that face,' he says, following me in. 'Your sister's worried about you.' He clocks the creme eggs. He never liked them: too sweet and gloopy. I should have taken that as a sign that our relationship was doomed.

'And I'm worried about *her*,' I reply. 'She's gone straight back to work and she's stressed enough as it is.'

Rob only has to look around the flat to see that I have indeed let things go a wee bit since Dad died. Rob is one of life's unfeasibly tidy folk. When I moved in with him, it was his place and space so I made an effort. I really did. I even thought I'd stopped being messy forever.

He looks at his watch and nods to himself. 'Right. It's five to ten. I need to be back on a job in Tring by noon. Get showered and dressed. We're off to Currys to get you a new dishwasher.'

I'm tempted to tell him to sod off. I don't need anyone frogmarching me anywhere. I'm doing fine. I have six plates, six knives, six forks, so that's nearly a week I can go without washing up, if I stack carefully.

But actually I do feel a bit stir crazy. The walls are thick, so I can cry for hours, not that it helps. The people in the other flats barely say 'Hi' to me, which means that at least I haven't had any do-gooders pitching up with nourishing casseroles and platitudes about Dad being with Jesus. Even so, I do need to break my non-routine routine. Currys it is.

Rob's van is spotless. No Lucozade bottles or semi-munched KFC detritus kicking around the floor. No trodden-in sawdust or wood shavings. He even has his familiar, and now faded, passenger's cushion in the seat beside him. I bought it at a school fayre because the fabric has a Minions design; they make him cry with laughter.

'How long has the dishwasher been out of action?' he asks.

'It hasn't been right since I moved out of yours. My klutzy tenant must have broken it but I didn't realize straight away.'

'And then it was too late to make a fuss and keep back some of the deposit. That's so typical of you, Annie.'

'Isn't it. Once a flake, always a flake.'

'I didn't mean that.'

'Good.'

We barely converse after that. I haven't come on this mercy mission just to be reminded of my failings. I can do that perfectly well from the comfort of my own sofa *and* watch *The Repair Shop* at the same time.

Rob turns into Apsley Mills Retail Park. If this isn't hell on earth, you can certainly see it from here. But actually, this day out feels good. We used to love a shopping trip: buying a birthday present for Josh; treating ourselves to a new high-tog duvet or a belated non-Christmas treat. It felt so intimate and couply. I miss that.

A dishwasher is a dishwasher is a dishwasher. My only caveat is that I like my white goods white. I see one. It will do. But Rob takes it upon himself to quiz the 12-year-old shop assistant (whose badge tells us he's called 'Ash') about cycles and eco-washes and how many place settings this machine will take. As if I'm ever going to have thirteen people round for dinner. I honestly don't care which one I buy but I'm liking that Rob does. He's impressed with the Serie 2 SPS24CW00G Slimline and, yes, it's white, so why not?

We queue up to pay. Rob tells 'Katrina' on the till that we don't need to book a delivery. He can transport it in his van right now and even take the old one away. Typical Rob, he's got it all worked out.

I know it's just a 'thing'; a new thing replacing an old thing. But I like what this little outing represents. It's a reminder that Rob wants to help me. That he still cares about me. We have a history and it can't be deleted, just because we couldn't make it work. *I* couldn't make it work.

'I can't believe they make black dishwashers,' he says as we pull out of the car park. 'That should be against the law.'

'Even grey is wrong,' I reply, enjoying the banter. 'I mean, what are they? Grey white goods? Grey grey goods? Didn't anyone think this through?'

'Fi has grey white goods but she calls them "matt silver".

Sounds more like a Seventies rock star to me.' He chuckles to himself. This quip is new to me but obviously not to him.

I stare straight ahead. A roundabout. This way A41, that way A4251.

I can't help it, I have to ask. 'Who's Fi?'

Rob has rung the job in Tring to tell them he's running late because he needs to pick up some extra brackets. Rob isn't one to skive or take the piss. He's got a great word-of-mouth reputation for hitting deadlines, being reliable and doing a proper job. But he must be so keen to explain the Fi thing to me that he doesn't want to rush it.

He parks in a layby, with a catering truck nearby selling bacon butties and mugs of paint-stripper tea.

'Do you fancy a fried-egg sandwich?' he asks as we settle on a picnic bench.

'Yes. Maybe. I don't know.' I shrug. 'It was a simple question, Rob: who's Fi? You're making it into a big deal. Is it?'

The smell of frying rashers wafts over. We sit for a minute inhaling it. Then he takes a run and launches into his little speech. Has he been rehearsing it since our 'white goods' bantz?

'We met online. Last month. *She* found *me*, actually. I'd registered, done the daft questionnaire, posted a photo. That one in Ventnor where you can't see my bald patch. But I don't know, I just couldn't summon up the *cojones* to contact any of the women. I was still a bit bruised.'

I remember that photo in Ventnor. Rob is squinting into the sunlight. He has just eaten a hot dog. He looks bloody lovely. I took that photo.

'Anyway, I kept getting emails from women wanting to meet me for a coffee, a glass of wine, whatever, and I wasn't interested because I wasn't sure. You know. Is this what I really want? Am I ready? And if not, why not?

'Fi was funny and persistent. Not in a stalky kind of way. Keen but cool, I suppose you'd call it. So I met her and I *still* wasn't sure. So I met her again. We went out for a Turkish meal. And then, a week later, we went to the pictures plus a walk in Verulamium Park the next afternoon. And I thought to myself, This is nice. I like her. Just go with it, Rob. Live in the moment, not in the past. And I don't want to put a curse on it and, yes, it's early days, but it's going really well.'

He concludes with, 'You'd like her, Annie.'

He actually says that.

I wished Rob and Fi well. It would have been spectacularly churlish not to, especially after he persuaded Josh to meet us at the flat so that they could get the new dishwasher up one flight of stairs, remove the manky old one, load it into the van and take it to the dump. He even plumbed it in. Fi's fallen on her feet all right.

When my first serious boyfriend, Duncan, and I broke up a year after uni, he didn't deal with it very well, especially when I started seeing one of his friends a few weeks later. I didn't do it to get at him, and the new relationship lasted less than a month. It was a cleansing thing for me. But it was a kick in the teeth for Duncan.

We were still living in our shared house in Moulsecoomb, on the non-trendy fringes of Brighton, with two other ex-students, all of us trying to decide what to do with our lives. And then Duncan decided. He upped sticks and fled back to Edinburgh, leaving me to pay the rent on our double room, which I could only manage for a month before, fortunately, I got The Job in London.

So I learned back then – what is it, crikey, fifteen years ago – that it's better not to be bitter when your ex meets someone new. Duncan and I had a mutual parting of the ways, of course, but with Rob, I was the one who ended it and I know it hurt him. Behaving like a spoilt brat who doesn't want anyone else to play with the toy you've chucked out of your pram is not a good look.

Rob met me when he was newly separated from Maggie and there was still the possibility of them getting back together again. So my initial role was 'transitional girlfriend'. Then it developed into something more. Dad thought I was breaking up a marriage but I really wasn't. Like the aggrieved child who has nothing to do with the smashed vase, 'it was already broken when I got there'.

It's a well-known fact, however, that transitional/interim girl/boyfriends have a short shelf life. Fi could well be Rob's life partner. Good for him. Happy for them. I just hope she connects with Josh too. He's a bloody brilliant young man and I miss him.

I can't deny, the new dishwasher prods me into trying a bit harder to keep on top of things. I will eat more vegetables, I will do Zumba. I will say hi to my neighbours. Even Tony in Flat 2. Instead of watching daytime dross, I will read. Or listen to podcasts while I make soup. I make soup. From scratch. I even eat some of the soup I don't tip down the sink because grief has stolen my appetite.

Kate rings every couple of days to see how I am. She's ridiculously busy 24/7 so it makes sense that, over the past year or two, she's become the one who initiates the call. She'd only get angry if I were to disturb her in some high-powered meeting or en route to catch a train.

I'm just pushing some stubborn lumps of spicy cauliflower soup down the plug hole when she calls. She's on a train, ten minutes from Euston, so we can't talk for long.

'How are you doing?' Kate always asks how I'm doing. She prefers a 'fine, thanks' reply and sometimes she even gets one.

'Fine, thanks. I've just made soup.'

'Cream of tomato? Like Mum used to give us when we had a cold?'

'No, real soup from scratch.'

She can't hide her shock. 'Hey, that's great. That's really great, An-An.'

'It's frigging soup, okay! I haven't married Hugh Fearnley-Whittingstall.'

Her voice cuts out, then returns just as I'm about to give up and hang up. 'And? How does it taste?'

'Yummy.' The line crackles again. We're going to have to keep this brief.

'You haven't forgotten Sunday, have you?' she asks in her sternest headmistress voice.

'Um, remind me.'

'Dad's birthday.'

I may be the scatty, unreliable older sister but how could I forget that. 'Do me a favour. Of course not.'

'Lunch. With Bev. To celebrate his memory. Not sure what she's got planned. I know how empty your diary is so don't you dare pretend you're busy.'

I hadn't forgotten that Dad's birthday is on the 10th or that Bev had invited us over for Sunday lunch. I'd just forgotten that the two things were connected.

'Honestly, Kate. I'll be there. I said I would, didn't I?'

I hear one of Kate's signature sighs. The one that signifies weariness at always being the nudger, not the nudgee. 'I'll

53

pick you up at half twelve. Wear something clean and bring flowers. Bye.'

I take out my resentment on the final, stubborn lump of cauliflower that gets mashed down the plughole with the business end of a ladle.

Bloody Bev. You had Dad for four years. You made each other happy. I couldn't say that at the start but I can now. Do I have to like you? Can't we just move on from all that fake affection and connection?

Sunday lunch symbolizes warmth and family and being loved and nurtured. Bev may make the world's best roasties – way better than Mum's – but I don't want her to misinterpret my presence. I will be there under sufferance and then, fingers crossed, I need never see her again. And I honestly won't miss her.

Bev's roast potatoes are a triumph. The pork crackles with crispy skin and the vegetables – four kinds – are cooked to perfection. She also makes great puddings but she won't tell us whether it's crumble or sticky toffee. Dad put on over a stone when they moved in together. Was she a feeder? Did Bev kill him with kindness? I shove another spud in my mouth to obliterate the thought.

On the drive over, I made it clear to Kate that this would, in all likelihood, be my final encounter with Bev. It would be the height of hypocrisy to continue a faux relationship with a woman I'd barely chat to at the checkout in Tesco. I know Kate feels the same, but she's been too busy with work to process awkward, uncomfortable thoughts like this. But, hey, I'm the oldest so I'll do it for both of us.

'We can't,' she said. 'That would be so cruel.'

'You keep up the pretence, then. I won't do it.'

We never finished the conversation as we arrived at the house and Kate parallel-parked her Mazda outside. But we will finish it. And I'm not shifting one inch of ground on this. I owe it to Mum.

It turns out to be trifle for pudding, made with chocolate custard, chocolate Swiss roll and tinned pears. It's bloody lovely and I have two helpings. Bev looks inordinately pleased, as if liking her pudding is proof that we'll be pals for life. Don't get your hopes up, love, I think to myself as I push my scraped-clean bowl away.

'It was so good of Rob and Josh to come to the funeral,' Bev says as we settle in the living room for coffee and home-made petits fours.

'Absolutely,' I reply.

'He said I'm to contact him if ever I need anything done around the house. He's very handy, isn't he?'

'He did a great job on my bookshelves,' Kate chips in supportively, even though we both know she's never been happy with them.

'Rob is such a lovely man,' Bev coos. 'And young Josh is turning into quite the dreamboat.'

I smile my agreement and eat my fourth petit four. Must be where the name comes from.

Bev sighs melodramatically. Kate and I leave it hanging there, hoping it won't be the start of something that might set me off.

But it is. 'Peter was so upset when you ended it with Rob. He thought you'd finally sorted your life out with a lovely chap like him.'

'Dad didn't approve when we first got together,' I say, through gritted teeth.

'He was worried about you having a fling with the father

of a pupil. The ethics of it. He didn't want you to get into trouble.'

'Rob was separated,' says Kate. 'Annie didn't do anything unethical.'

Bev nods. But it's too late, she's said it now: Dad was on Rob's side when we split up, not mine. This is a woman who doesn't think before she speaks, who can never self-edit. Something pops into her head and out of her mouth. I don't know how Dad put up with it, even for just a handful of years.

'Your dad only wanted his girls to be happy.' Bev turns to Kate. 'You with your career and your promotion and everything. And Annie . . . well, he desperately hoped you'd get back to teaching and settle down with Rob. Happy ever after. That's all he ever wanted.'

She dabs her nose with some Kleenex. 'And he'd so love to have been Grampa Peter. He adored Pippa's little ones, of course. And they loved him to bits. Always giving them piggybacks and singing "Jake the Peg", complete with silly walk, and finishing their broccoli. Even so, it's not the same as having grandchildren of your very own.'

There we are then. We were a disappointment to Dad. We failed him. Kate tends to have relationships with married men who don't have plans to procreate. And I've well and truly missed the boat. Rob and I never discussed kids because he'd been there, done that with Josh. Kids were not on the cards when we were together and I can't see it happening for me now. Besides, I couldn't be responsible for a small human. I'm a danger to a guinea pig.

I make a conscious decision to zone out of the rest of the conversation until it's time to leave. Kate can fill the silences. Not that there are any with Bev. Now she's talking about how lovely they've been in the walking group and that she can't seem to stop buying mushrooms, even though she's never liked them and Peter's not here to eat them.

Talk of walking reminds Bev of another item on the agenda. Dad's ashes. 'They're in the dresser at the moment. I can't bear to look at them. But I do have plans.'

'Plans?' asks Kate for both of us.

'I'm going to scatter him in the Tyrol. Where we went on holiday last year. I think that would have made him happy.'

I can't help myself. 'The Tyrol? That's Austria, right? How do you know he would have approved? Did he say so?'

Kate shoots me a look: leave it.

Bev is taken aback. 'How could he say so? He was fit as a fiddle back then. Don't you think I should scatter him there, then?'

Of course I bloody don't, you stupid woman. He went there once. With you. The Tyrol has nothing to do with us, our dad, our lives.

I fume quietly. Saying it out loud won't help. The bloody Tyrol, though. The words embed themselves in my brain on a loop. The bloody Tyrol, the bloody Tyrol. The wrongness of it is so obvious.

Before we leave, I go to the loo. Before I go to the loo, I go to the dresser, take the urn of Dad's ashes and cram it into my Fjällräven backpack which I left in the hall. The zip won't close so I cover the urn with my scarf.

Dad isn't being scattered in the Tyrol.

End of.

PART II

Chapter Seven

Cromarty

I put Dad on my bedroom mantelpiece, next to a framed photo of Mum, taken the year before she died. I place them together like this in a misguided attempt to make myself feel better, as if my moment of madness was *their* idea, not mine.

What on earth possessed me? Perhaps I should pop round to Bev's tomorrow with a bunch of daffs and sneak the urn back into the dresser while she's making us coffee.

I can't sleep. I daren't tell Kate what I've done although I know she wasn't happy with Bev's Tyrol plans either. Okay, maybe she didn't say so *as such* but for all our differences, we agree on the important stuff: politics, climate change, Nutella on bagels. Scattering Dad's ashes in the Tyrol is plain wrong and I'm one hundred per cent sure Kate thinks so too. Well, I'm fairly sure she does.

My sleep is patchy and broken. At half three, I make myself a cup of tea and watch some old Boyzone videos on my phone. At half four, I let the World Service lull me into semi-consciousness.

I wake with a heart-thumping start at those oh-so-familiar words: 'Good morning, and now the Shipping Forecast, issued by the Met Office on behalf of the Maritime and Coastguard Agency at 05.05 on Monday the 15th of July.'

North Utsire, South Utsire . . . Portland, Plymouth, Biscay, Trafalgar . . . Even after the apocalypse, an announcer will be reading these place names into the one surviving microphone. I find myself moving the urn closer to the radio so that Dad can hear the forecast too. I have seriously lost it.

He called it poetry. 'The poetry of our isles.' Once he made Mum take a photo of him at a Bierfest, chomping on a knackwurst, just so that he could use the caption: German Bight. He used to say 'Rockall' instead of 'fuck all'. My middle name was nearly Malin. Our cat, Cromarty, is living proof of his obsession. So much family folklore, so many memories and daft moments.

That's when I decide. Sod the Tyrol. Mum and Dad visited Cromarty on their honeymoon and they had plans to return on their fortieth wedding anniversary, which would have been . . . this year. Cromarty. That's where he will be scattered. It's so obvious, so appropriate, so perfect.

Best not tell Kate just yet, though.

Two days later, I'm on the 09.00 train from St Albans to Luton Airport and I'm checked in half an hour after that. I had yet another sleepless night, fearful I'd doze through the alarm, so I'm out cold for most of the flight. By 12.30, I'm waiting for my overnight backpack to come through on the conveyor belt at Inverness. Dad gave it to me when Bev bought him a new one, with all sorts of fancy straps and pockets. This one is a bit faded and tattered but it packs like the TARDIS and it smells of retsina – I broke a bottle in it when Rob and I went to Corfu.

The urn raised a slight eyebrow when my hand luggage

was checked by the security man at Luton. I couldn't pretend it was anything other than what it was. I suppose they might have suspected that I'd filled an urn with pure-grade cocaine which I was county-lining to the Highlands. Fortunately, I had the funeral order of service with me and the Shipping Forecast tea towel, which has lived in my bag ever since I saved it from the charity shop black sack. I explained the purpose of my trip to the nice man and I couldn't stop my eyes filling and my chin quivering.

For a split second, he welled up too. His mum died last year. She wanted to be scattered in the Grand Canyon and all the red tape was a nightmare. No paperwork required for an internal flight, though. Crikey, I hadn't even thought of that. He waved me through and gave me the understanding smile of someone still grieving. I had a little weep in the Ladies'.

I marvel at my travel nous. This journey is a piece of cake. A bus transfers me to downtown Inverness, a woman at the bus station in a hi-vis vest points me to 'Stance 4' and I'm soon settled on the 26A to Cromarty. The fifty-something man with the steel-grey crew cut sitting in front of me has also travelled all the way from Luton and we do one of those understated, slightly awkward, nods of recognition.

'Don't tell me, you're stalking me,' he says, swiftly followed by a hearty chuckle to ensure I don't take him seriously.

'How did you know?' I chuckle back.

'You're going from Luton to Cromarty too? Small world, eh.'

'Minuscule.'

As the bus crosses the Moray Firth and we pass signs for Glack of Kessock, Bogallan and Drumderfit, we get into conversation. In fact, when a bunch of noisy schoolkids get on at Fortrose and insist on sitting together, he takes the seat beside me.

'I normally leave the car at the airport but Hazel needed it today,' he explains. 'And it's a nice wee journey when the sun's out.'

'It's pretty,' I say inanely.

'Not where I work, it isn't. Port of Nigg.'

My face tells him I have no idea what that is.

'Dry dock, cranes, marine logistics. Big employer round here. I'm Don, by the way.'

'Annie. Hi.'

He asks where I'm staying and I tell him I don't know yet. Fortunately Hazel's sister, Liz, has a B&B and before we've reached the outskirts of Cromarty, my accommodation is sorted and I've requested the 'full Scottish breakfast'. Apparently Liz makes her own white pudding and it's very popular with her regular guests so she'll be sure to put some by for me.

Don and I get off the bus at Victoria Hall. He recommends the community market that's held there. 'It's a shame you've missed Potato Day. You could have cleaned up on seed tatties, only 15p per tuber.'

He directs me to Liz's B&B and waves me farewell. We've practically crossed the UK together. A Range Rover pulls up beside us and the driver hoots the horn; Hazel has come to pick him up, then they're popping over to see his mum, who's housebound after a knee op.

My B&B room is cosy, with fish-themed ornaments and a view of the lighthouse. I check on Dad. I secured the lid with parcel tape before leaving my flat so he's still all there. Then I kick off my trainers, tip forward onto the bed, and fall asleep in an instant.

* * *

I'm awoken four hours later by a polite knock on the door. I've slept like a sack and my arm's numb where I've been lying on it. I stumble to the door and Liz is there, in a fish-themed apron, bearing a cheese scone on fish-themed plate.

'I'm trying out a new recipe,' she explains. 'Are chopped chives and sunflower seeds one step too far?'

I haven't eaten since a hummus sandwich at Luton and I threw most of it away. I am ravenous.

'There's two pats of butter. Say if you need any more.' Liz turns to go, then spins on her heels and pulls a phone out of her pocket. 'Ooh, nearly forgot. Call for you.'

I'm instantly covered in a sweaty film of guilt. Bev must have found out that I've done a runner with Dad's ashes and she's called the police. But how does she know where I am? Even I don't know where I am. Not precisely anyway. Liz leaves me to it.

'Hello?' I say tentatively. I'll come clean. What else can I do?

'Hello, Annie. This is Don. From the bus.'

Annie to armpits: Please can you calm down now?

'Oh. Right. Don. Sorry, I was asleep. My brain hasn't engaged yet.'

'Shall I call back? I didn't mean to disturb you.'

I sit on the bed and get my bearings. A print of a leaping salmon next to the wardrobe. A shell-edged mirror above the bedside table. Three fake starfish in flying-duck formation.

'Not at all,' I tell him. 'I'm glad you did.'

'Oh, that's a relief.' Don does one of his hearty chuckles. 'I told Hazel about us being on the same flight, the same bus, and she said we should take you out for supper, if you don't have any other plans.'

While he's been talking, I've demolished half the scone. It's barely touched the sides. 'That would be lovely. Thank you.'

I pop the phone back in its cradle in the hall and catch myself smiling in the shell-framed mirror. This is going really well. With this distraction tonight, I can forget that Dad and I are parting company tomorrow. Don might even have some suggestions on a good place to scatter him. And I could murder something stodgy and comforting like pie and chips. Result.

I have half an hour to tidy myself up and change into a clean T-shirt. I turn my phone on to check the weather for tomorrow and it practically jumps off the bed, acknowledging all the texts and missed calls in a series of angry beeps. Then it rings again.

'Annie, where the fuck are you?'

'Hi Kate. I'm the fuck here. Where the fuck are you?'

She makes a noise like a macerating toilet. I've always been super-good at winding her up. 'Seriously, where are you? I'm worried sick. I even went round to your flat but the curtains were closed. You're not there, are you, Annie? Please tell me you're okay.'

'I'm fine, Katkin. I truly am. I feel like I've finally got my mojo back.'

'So where are you?'

'Cromarty.'

There's a pause while she tries to join up the dots. 'What about Cromarty? Has he died? Oh God, poor Bev, she doesn't need to bury the cat on top of everything else.'

'I'm *in* Cromarty. With Dad. I took him from the Welsh dresser. He's sitting on top of my bedside table and I can see Cromarty lighthouse from my window, Kate. I'm looking at it right now.'

'This is you "with your mojo back", is it? For fuck's sake, Annie!'

'I'm going to scatter his ashes here. I should have told

you. Hey, if you catch a plane from Luton first thing tomorrow, we can do it together.'

'You stole Dad's ashes? I can't believe you'd do such a – actually I totally can. Bev will be so upset. Oh, Annie. What were you thinking?'

'Bev is not next of kin. *We* are. Dad is ours, not hers. And we both know he shouldn't end up in the bloody Tyrol. Please come, Kate. I should have told you. I see that now. Please let's do it together.'

She hangs up on me. I'm guessing that means she's angry and not that she's gone straight online to book an early flight to Inverness. Yeah. She's angry.

Then I notice that one of the unread texts, among eight of Kate's, is from Bev and please can I ring her back. She must have clocked the missing urn. I'm really not ready to talk to her yet and, besides, I need to be downstairs in three minutes to meet Don and Hazel.

I've already behaved so badly. I reckon I can risk saving Bev for later . . .

We eat at a pub in Rosemarkie, a ten-minute drive away. Don and I plump for steak-and-ale pie, Hazel gets into a long discussion with the waitress about the salmon and what kind of sauce it comes with because she's gluten intolerant. She'll have it *sans* sauce but with extra veg and will help herself to most of Don's chips. I like her already.

'We always eat here when Don's been for a meeting in London, don't we, Don?'

He nods enthusiastically as steam comes out of his mouth, which is full of scalding gravy.

'Is this your first time on the Black Isle?' Hazel asks.

'We're on an island? I had no idea.'

Don is back in the conversation. 'It's a peninsula. We like to exaggerate.'

'So is it your first time?' Hazel persists.

I nod. 'My parents came here on their honeymoon. They were planning to come back for their fortieth wedding anniversary but, well, they died. Mum in 2013, Dad three weeks ago.'

Don glares at Hazel. Trust you to stick your nose in.

Hazel gives my hand a little squeeze. 'Join the club. I'm an orphan too. Oh, hey, you're little orphan Annie. That's sad.'

'Dad used to call me "Annie Lummox" because I was a very clumsy child.'

Don and Hazel love that. Dad has made my new best friends laugh. I so want to tell him. I suddenly feel bereft and Hazel picks up on it. She strokes my arm with one hand and takes the occasional chip off Don's plate with the other. I explain why I'm here.

They have several suggestions for places to scatter Dad: from the Cromarty–Nigg ferry would be good. Or along the coastal path up by South Sutor.

'It's a fine walk,' Don says. 'I reckon your dad would like that.'

I've managed to push Bev's message to the back of my mind for an hour or so but it doesn't go away. She won't understand why I took the urn. And suddenly I'm not sure either.

'I stole Dad,' I tell Don and Hazel as they scan the desserts menu. 'I took him without his partner's permission.'

They look suitably shocked and don't know how to respond.

'They weren't married, Dad and Bev, so it's not like she's next of kin or anything. The thing is, he shouldn't be scattered in Austria. He should be here in Cromarty. So he is. Here.

With me. Well, he's not here-here, in my bag. He's back at the B&B. On the windowsill so he can see the lighthouse.'

The waitress asks if we've decided on puddings. Hazel bats her away with a friendly smile; we're not quite ready yet.

'You mean Bev doesn't know you took him?' Don asks.

'She didn't, but now I think she does. She left a message to call her back.'

'And have you?' says Hazel, gently. 'Will you? You will, won't you, Annie?'

I nod, suddenly feeling so guilty and fucked up and ridiculous. But part of me still understands my flawed logic. Don and Hazel didn't know Dad. Or Bev. They don't appreciate what these past few years have been like, watching Mum fade away . . . seeing Dad start a new life with a woman I can't warm to.

They drive me back to the B&B. Hazel tells me firmly that I should call Bev tonight and makes me take her mobile number in case I want to de-brief with her tomorrow. I think, secretly, she wants to know what happens next: her very own soap opera and she's a secondary character in it.

I make myself a cup of claggy hot chocolate from a sachet by the kettle. I put on my jim-jams, get into bed and dial Bev's number. She's a proper nightbird – Dad never was – so 10.30 p.m. isn't too late. I won't sleep unless I talk to her.

Bev answers on the second ring. 'Annie? Is that you?'

'Hi Bev. Sorry to call so late. Shall I ring back tomorrow?'

I hear the TV being muted.

'Not at all, love. I was just catching up on last week's *Casualty*.'

I don't know where to start. 'Anyway, how are you?' is all I can muster.

There's a brief pause while *she* tries to work out where

to start too. Then she launches straight in. 'Kate rang. She told me where you are and what you've done.'

'Wasn't that why you texted me?'

'Not at all. I wanted to see how you are. I wouldn't have known the urn was missing if she hadn't told me. I could have gone months without realizing. Maybe not until I'd booked my trip to the Tyrol.'

I have no appropriate response. I feel awful, even though I still stand by what I did.

'I've been thinking about this,' she continues. 'Ever since Kate rang. I think I understand.'

'Do you?' I hear myself say, instantly regretting my petulant tone.

'Of course I do. I never wanted to compete with you and Kate for your father's love. He had enough for all of us.'

I feel a big blobby tear wobble down my cheek. I daren't utter a word in case it turns into an anguished wail.

'You loved him all your life, Annie. And he loved you from before you were even born. I've only loved him for four years. But I did – I do – love him and he loved me.'

'I know that, Bev.'

'Now, if you want to scatter his ashes in – where is it again?'

'Cromarty. Like the cat.'

'Cromarty, that's it. If you want to scatter him there, it's up to you. And Kate, obviously. You do what you think best.'

I'm shocked. I was expecting her to demand Dad's return asap. Which she then kind of does.

'But, Annie, you should know that you've got the wrong ashes.'

I catch my reflection in the shell-edged mirror. My jaw genuinely drops.

70

'Peter is still in the dresser in a temporary urn. A bit like a Pringles box, only bigger, and it's got a woodland scene printed on it. You've taken my first husband, Keith. In the Chinese-looking urn. I never found the right moment to scatter him. Not sure why.'

I look over at 'Keith', enjoying the view of Cromarty lighthouse by night. I've transported the ashes of a total stranger across the UK. My moment of madness is even more bonkers than I could possibly have imagined.

'Oh God, I'm so sorry.'

'First thing tomorrow, I'll courier your father to Cromarty Post Office. And perhaps you could send Keith back to me.'

'Or I could just come home with him first thing tomorrow.'

'No, no, if you want your father scattered in Cromarty, so be it. I wouldn't dream of stopping you. It's really up to you.' Her voice trembles. 'And now it's rather late and we both need our beauty sleep. Night-night, love.'

Three texts from Kate when I wake up the next morning.

Text #1: Did U ring Bev?

Text #2: Promise me U did.

Text #3: Oh An-An, this is bad even by yr standards.

Liz's full Scottish breakfast is indeed amazing, especially the white pudding, which I'd approached with trepidation. Afterwards, I pack my few things into the rucksack, leave it in Liz's kitchen with her permission, and take Keith to the post office. Several miles of bubble wrap later, he rests securely in a firm cardboard box and begins his couriered journey back to Hertfordshire.

I am at a loss for what to do. Cromarty is very pretty, and very windy, but I've covered it in half an hour or so. I could visit Hugh Miller's Cottage. He seems to have been a big thing around these parts a couple of centuries ago. I could check out the coastal walk Don recommended and find a suitable spot to scatter Dad, when he gets here.

Instead I ring Hazel, and half an hour later we're 'ladies who coffee' in a funky little cafe on the high street. I tell her about Keith. She concentrates hard on stirring her latte for longer than necessary, then emits a loud yelp of laughter. An elderly couple across the room turn to see what's happened.

Hazel tries unsuccessfully to pull herself together. 'I know, I know. It isn't funny, Annie. I shouldn't be laughing but – oh my God, wait till I tell Don.'

As I see it, I've got two options. I can either storm off in a huff, hurt by her insensitivity. Or I can laugh too. It *is* funny. I have cocked up on a major scale. Pretty soon we're gripped by uncontrollable, rib-hurting hysteria. The waitress brings us a carafe of water and two glasses. Eventually we recover. I can't speak for Hazel, but I feel surprisingly refreshed afterwards.

'Bev sounds like a good woman,' Hazel says, flapping a napkin at her face. 'She must have made your dad very happy.'

'She did, I suppose.'

'Would it be so wrong to have him scattered in Austria?'

'I could live with it,' I mutter begrudgingly. 'But Cromarty meant something to him for much, much longer.'

'Because he came here once? With your mum.'

'On their honeymoon. *And* he named our cat Cromarty, from the Shipping Forecast.'

Hazel likes that. 'You could hardly call a cat Dogger.'

I feel the need to show her proof of his obsession. I pull the Shipping Forecast tea towel out of my bag and unfurl it on the table.

'He'd only dry up dishes with this tea towel, no other. It drove Mum spare.'

Hazel surveys sea area Cromarty and finds the Black Isle peninsula. Seeing it on a faded, frayed, much-loved rectangle of Irish linen, it still feels slightly surreal.

I am here. I am here *now*.

'And there's St Albans,' I say, pointing vaguely at an area to the north of London. 'Hundreds of miles from Sole and Fastnet and all the rest of it.'

'Maybe you should take your dad on the full tour,' Hazel suggests. 'From, let's see . . . Norway to Portugal and from Ireland to Iceland. Why stop at Cromarty?'

'Yeah, right,' I snort. 'And how long would that take?'

'Weeks? Months? I've honestly no idea. Anyway, you've probably got lots to get back to in St Albans. I wasn't being serious, Annie.'

We finish our coffee and Hazel hugs me goodbye. She has to take Don's mum to the doctor's. I can't imagine Dad will arrive until tomorrow morning so I ask Liz if I can stay an extra night at the B&B.

'No problem,' she tells me. 'You just can't resist my white pudding.' Then she giggles, realizing how end-of-the-pier that sounds.

I noodle around the shops again: a pottery, a Scandi design shop. I check out the cheese shop and think about my university boyfriend, Duncan, who moved back to Edinburgh after we broke up. Last I heard, via a friend of a friend on Facebook, he'd opened an artisanal cheese shop. When we were together, he lived on Kraft cheese slices melted onto crumpets slathered with Branston. So something – or someone? – must have broadened his taste-bud horizons.

I'm heading back to Liz's for an afternoon nap when

suddenly the heavens open. Not just a short sharp shower but stair rods of rain that go straight through to my bra. I spot the open door of a church hall and hurtle in. Shelter from the storm and all that. After I've shaken myself down like a damp spaniel, I turn and see ten pairs of mostly bespectacled eyes focused on me. It looks like some kind of meeting.

I offer an instant apology. 'Ooh, sorry, I didn't mean to interrupt. I'll leave you to it.'

A nippy, silver-haired woman wearing a stunning Fair Isle waistcoat beckons me over. 'Nonsense. Sit by the radiator and dry off or you'll catch your death.'

She introduces herself – Joyce – and explains that they meet every Thursday afternoon for a knit 'n' natter session.

'Wendy there wanted to call it "stitch 'n' bitch" but we never bitch, do we, ladies?'

Wendy pulls an invisible Pinocchio nose and they all hoot with laughter. Lesley makes me a cup of tea from the urn and Eileen snaps open the lid of an old plastic biscuit box loaded with home-made, chocolate-dipped oat shorties.

'Can you knit?' Lesley asks. She is sewing buttons onto a rainbow-striped children's cardy. There's a tam-o'-shanter and scarf to match.

'Me? God no. My mum tried to teach me but everything I made came out full of dropped stitches and knots where the wool got tangled.'

The woman next to me, who is either Doreen or Dorothy, pulls a circular needle and a ball of raspberry-pink wool from her hessian shopper and hands them to me. She is knitting squares for a blanket – sixty-seven so far. 'Rule number one: you can't have your hands still at the knit 'n' natter club.'

When she sees I've forgotten how to cast on, she takes

the needle and in about twenty seconds I'm good to go. 'Thirty stitches times four inches. You *can* do garter stitch?'

Garter stitch, garter stitch . . . That's the one where you pick up the stitch at the back for every row, rather than forward-back in turn. I give a brave smile and get started, remembering from the recesses of my brain that the first row is always the hardest.

'Where are you from?' Joyce asks.

'St Albans. Hertfordshire. Just north of London.'

'I went to London last year,' Wendy chips in. 'I thought it would be too busy, too noisy, but I loved it. I should have moved there in my twenties.'

'Are you in Cromarty spending time with family?' Joyce still needs the full picture.

'Kind of,' I reply. Well, I will be when Dad's ashes arrive.

Before I'm interrogated further, a large woman with a hennaed bun mentions someone they all know in Inverness whose daughter's been done for fraud. And off they go, clacking and clucking, stitching and bitching for Scotland. They pull no punches, none of them.

I stay and knit for an hour. They mostly ignore me, moving from the daughter in Inverness to someone who used to be in the group but left without saying why. When I'm dried off and ready to make a move, Eileen wraps two oat shorties in cling film for me to have later.

Doreen/Dorothy won't take back my lumpy pink strip of knitting, or the wool and needle.

'You need to finish that yourself,' she says. 'You'll have your own tension.'

Very perceptive of her. I should be less stressed when Dad's ashes arrive, though.

Chapter Eight

January 1995

Anne was ready to give up. Why had she thought she was remotely capable of this? She planned to shove the wool, pattern and needles back into the Woolworth's carrier bag, hide it under her bed and try to forget she'd ever attempted it. Or maybe Mum could use the wool to make a matinee jacket for next-door's baby. But it was red, and who dressed babies in anything but pink, blue, lemon or white? Mum could have the wool for free, even though it had cost her a fair chunk of last week's pocket money.

Katie was in the garden, helping Dad build a brick barbecue in optimistic anticipation of a decent summer. At 10, Katie was no expert at mixing cement or using a trowel but she could fetch water and relay orders for a mug of tea and a slab of banana bread, still hot from the oven.

Every so often, Anne would see Katie staring back at her through the lounge window, her face so close to the glass that she created a mist and her cheeks left smudges. Anne ignored her and had another go at casting on the 140 stitches needed to get started. This would be her third attempt and she wasn't filled with optimism.

'Anne! Homework!' Mum shouted from the kitchen.

Anne didn't respond. If it was a choice between knitting this flipping hat or writing an essay on Atticus Finch . . . well, she wasn't wild about either.

Mum came in to investigate the silence. She was wearing her baking apron. Banana bread made, she was now trying out a Delia Smith recipe for carrot cake. She loved baking. Anne reckoned there should be a contest, maybe even on the telly, to find Britain's best cake-maker. Mum would win hands down.

'Are you planning to do your homework some time before the millennium?' Mum asked, wiping her hands on the tea towel flung over her shoulder. She was also very good at sarcasm.

Anne threw down her knitting. 'I can't do it. I hate it.'

Mum sat on the sofa. She looked to Anne for permission to pick up the needles, with their scrunched row of tightly packed stitches. Anne shrugged a 'whatever'.

'You need to cast on more loosely, love. Do you want me to start you off?'

Anne shrugged a second 'whatever' although secretly she'd been hoping all afternoon that Mum would take over.

'It's a lovely colour. Does he like red then?'

Anne nodded, still not quite ready to snap out of her mood. Kim had told her that Stephen's favourite colour was red and Kim knew everything about Boyzone.

'It's for Rowan, is it? The ginger one.'

Anne was forced to respond. 'It's Ronan, not Rowan. He's blond, not ginger. And anyway, I prefer Stephen now. It's for his eighteenth birthday on 17 March.'

'The little dark one? He's quite cute, isn't he? Show me a picture.'

Mum's adept fingers cast on the required stitches as Anne

77

sought out the latest *Smash Hits* on the coffee table, under all the sections of Dad's *Sunday Times*.

'That's Stephen, that's Ronan. Then Mikey, Keith, Shane.'

Mum stopped casting on and peered at the photo. 'And you like *him* best? Not Keith? Seriously?'

Anne rolled her eyes and looked heavenward. 'No-err! Not Keith.'

'Well, if *I* found him in my bed, I'd give him twenty-four hours to get out.'

Mum giggled and got back to her knitting. Anne pretended to be horrified. She'd never tell Kim or Janet what her mum had said about Keith because they'd pretend to be sick and then she'd have to, too. But actually she liked it when she and Mum had shared moments like this.

'It was Marc Bolan in my day,' Mum said with a sigh as she knitted the first row super-fast. 'One day I liked David Cassidy, the next day I was potty about Marc. Such lovely hair.'

Anne had heard about Marc Bolan before. Mum occasionally played her old LPs on the music centre, to annoy Dad. One Saturday, she sang 'Ride a White Swan' at the top of her voice to drown out the late afternoon Shipping Forecast. Honestly, her parents were over 40 but sometimes they behaved like a pair of daft kids. So embarrassing . . .

Mum finished the row with a flourish. 'There you go. The first row's always the hardest. Over to you, An-An.'

Anne picked up the needles and set to work. Mum returned to the kitchen to check on her carrot cake. A waft of cinnamon sweetness entered as she exited. Outside, Dad was laying a third row of bricks while Katie raced round the garden on her scooter.

'Garter stitch is when each row is back-back, not

forward-back,' Anne told herself as she doggedly picked up Mum's relaxed stitches and knitted them tight onto the needle again.

She'd attempt at least four rows before giving up in sweaty-handed frustration and make Mum finish the hat for her. Stephen need never know.

Chapter Nine

Forth

After another full Scottish breakfast with white pudding, I swing by Cromarty Post Office to see if Dad has arrived. He has. Bev coddled him in as much bubble wrap as I did Keith, plus a heavy-duty padded envelope. She has also enclosed a little card with a turquoise flower design, sending me lots of love. I have a pang of guilt but I have to see this through. My return flight to Luton leaves at 11.40 so if I'm to find a suitably spiritual scattering spot off the Cromarty coast, I need to get a wiggle on.

The 'eco-friendly scattering tube' does indeed look like an oversized Pringles container, just as Bev described it. Dad was more your Kettle Chips kinda guy and he would have preferred a seascape print on the outside, rather than a bluebell-filled woodland glade. It doesn't matter now.

I have a coffee and look up the South Sutor coastal path on my phone. I should be able to get there, scatter Dad and say my farewells, then catch the bus to Inverness and just make it onto the plane with minutes to spare.

I hear my brain running through the schedule and I actually scare myself. I can't do this. It's too rushed, too wrong.

'Take your time, Annie Lummox,' Dad used to say. 'Do it well or don't bother.'

I recalibrate. Okay, I'll scatter Dad in my own time and catch a later plane. Maybe even stay an extra night if Liz has room at the B&B. Who's eagerly awaiting my return? No bugger, that's who.

Or . . . or . . .

Hazel said I should take Dad on a tour of the Shipping Forecast. I know she wasn't being serious. But what if I do it? I spread out my tea towel map to see, quite literally, where the land lies. Viking, Forties and Dogger are just big swathes of sea, with no land mass or coast whatsoever. How could I possibly get to them? Other sea areas skim the coasts of Norway, Spain, Portugal and Iceland . . . Would Dad expect to 'see' them too?

If I take him to all thirty-one sea areas, I could be gone till Christmas. And I've only got clean pants and socks for one more day. But the idea is starting to take root. Okay, maybe I can't cover all thirty-one of them. That would take forever and cost a fortune. Maybe I can just visit the ones hugging the British coastline. That would whittle it down to a more manageable fourteen. How long would that take? A fortnight? A month?

I wish Dad was here to tell me if this is remotely do-able or downright daft. He might even say 'do it well or don't bother, An-An' and he'd have a point. What if I just set off and see what happens? Perhaps I'll find the perfect place to scatter him in Tyne or Thames, Portland or Plymouth.

All I know is that I'm not ready to let him go.

* * *

The bus back to Inverness soon fills up, picking up Twirlies with tartan wheelie shoppers, a lad in overalls with leaking ear buds, two sullen schoolgirls in blazers brazenly bunking off. We pass the pub in Rosemarkie where I went with Don and Hazel what seems like several weeks ago. Dad is squeezed into my backpack, taking up the space vacated by Keith – as he did in life, I suppose . . .

At Inverness station, I have time to buy a sausage bap, a carton of Ribena and a two-pack of pants before catching the train to Edinburgh, three and a half hours away in Forth, the next sea area of Scotland. I've been to Edinburgh a couple of times before and it seems like the obvious destination while I think this through. There's more to making this trip than having sufficient knickers.

For a 'resting' geography teacher, I'm all wrong on our route. I somehow assumed the train would follow the coastline, thus giving me a good gander as one sea area blends into the next around Aberdeen, according to my tea towel. But no, we head inland, stopping at lots of places I've heard of – Aviemore, Pitlochry, Perth, Kirkcaldy – and many I haven't. Kingussie for one.

'Monarch of the Glen,' says the elderly, anoraked man next to me who got on at Carrbridge and is slowly working his way through a bag of Maltesers. I think he's sucking the chocolate off first.

'I beg your pardon?'

'They filmed *Monarch of the Glen* in Kingussie and all around. I was in the background in one scene, though you'd miss me if you blinked. Lucky I was with my wife and not one of my fancy women, eh.' You can tell he's made this joke before.

He offers me a Malteser – 'take two, go on, treat yourself'

– then gets back to his *Daily Mail*. He gets off at Inver-
keithing. As the train pulls away, he waves and I wave back.
He reminds me of my grandad. Dad's dad. Same slow,
pained walk, same fruity sense of humour, same way with
a Malteser.

I arrive at Haymarket station in Edinburgh, a modern
terminus, all chrome and steel. Because I'm tired and because
I did 'cosy' in Cromarty at Liz's B&B, I opt for an impersonal
chain hotel not far from the station, popular with business
travellers on a budget.

I watch a bit of telly, pop out to pick up pasta salad, an
iced coffee and some jelly beans from M&S which I polish
off in bed while I watch more telly. Home from home or
what? I even knit a few rows of my pink square. It's actually
quite addictive and pretty soon it's finished and doesn't look
too shabby. I take a photo but don't know who to send it
to . . .

Dad, in his Pringles tube, sits on the window sill but, sadly,
can see no ships, just a view of the car park and some over-
stuffed skips. Excitement enough for one day. I fall asleep
wondering what the hell I'm doing.

I will ring Kate first thing tomorrow and get her up to
speed. If I can explain it convincingly to her, I might even
begin to understand it myself.

My hotel offers a pale imitation of a continental breakfast
so I opt for a mug of tea and a bacon sandwich at a nearby
cafe. As good a place as any to call Kate.

There's a long silence after I tell her I'm thinking of taking
Dad on a tour of the Shipping Forecast. Then a sigh, then
a silence, then, 'Oh, for fuck's sake!'

'Bev gave me her blessing,' I remind her. 'She was happy

for me to scatter Dad in Cromarty. But I couldn't do it. I wasn't ready.'

'So let Bev take him to Austria. You're 37, An-An. Try being a grown-up for a change.'

'I've been trying for years. I'm just not very good at it.'

'What do you want me to say? Do you want *my* blessing too?'

'It might help.'

'Will it help *you*, doing this? Will you get your mojo back?'

'I haven't had a mojo in years.'

'Don't make me the grown-up here, Annie. It's not *my* job to tell you what to do.'

'You think I should come home, don't you?'

Kate stays schtum. She's always been good at that, even when we were kids, forcing me to say more than I meant to, so that I was the one who got the telling off, the early night and no hot Ribena.

But this time I get it just right. 'Okay then,' I ask her. 'What do you think Dad would want me to do?'

She makes that 'aargh' sound. I have my answer.

The last time I came to Edinburgh was August Bank Holiday at least ten years ago. Toby and I stayed in a ridiculously expensive boutique hotel – we were both on silly City salaries – and did the whole festival thing: theatre, fringe, art, stand-up, weird walking tours at midnight and an improv gig where I was pulled up on stage and had to pretend to be an Alaskan signpost. Toby posted a photo on Facebook for my mates to see. I looked like a rabbit in the headlights, all pink eyed and petrified. It got eighty-seven likes.

I suddenly realize it's Saturday, which must be why Princes Street is busy with weekend shoppers, on top of the crocodiles of Italian schoolkids and selfie-sticked Japanese tourists. I'm a tourist too so, on a whim, I buy a ticket for a hop-on-hop-off bus tour of the city. It's somewhat breezy on the top deck but it's a good way to get my bearings and I'd never visit Holyrood otherwise . . . even if I don't actually 'hop off' at that stop, when everyone else does.

I think about Duncan, my first proper, serious boyfriend. His folks lived away from Edinburgh's city centre, near somewhere with 'Links' in the name. We spent one Christmas with them. I got a bit 'pished' (as Duncan always called it) and had a heated discussion with his dad about Scottish Nationalism. I don't remember which side I was on; he was just one of those people you feel duty-bound to disagree with.

I look up 'Edinburgh . . . Links' on Google Maps and there it is: Bruntsfield Links, a big open space just north of Morningside. But the tour bus doesn't go anywhere near and, even if it did, what would I be looking out for from my top-deck front seat? A blue plaque to commemorate the hardcore blow job I gave Duncan down a dark close at 2 a.m. on Boxing Day because he didn't like shagging within earshot of his parents?

As our bus stops to pick up a noisy American family, all wearing tam-o'-shanters with nylon ginger hair attached, I log in to Facebook, seek out an old uni friend and send her a breezy message: 'Hey there, hope you're well. I'm in Edinburgh and would love to look up Duncan but my stupid phone wiped all my contacts and he isn't on FB. Do you have a number?'

If she has, will I ring him? Seriously? Good idea or a totally stupid one? We lost touch long ago, and sleeping with his mate Simon didn't help. I'm just deciding not to 'go there' when my phone beeps. My uni friend has lost touch with

Duncan too but seems to think he does food markets. Any help?

Google tells me there are three in Edinburgh, two on Saturday, one on Sunday. We've just driven past the Grassmarket, two stops back, so I hop off and retrace my steps. Even if he isn't here, this is a great market with fudge and felting, jewellery and Japanese noodles, candles and cupcakes. And I can always check out the other two markets. What's to stop me?

I'm distracted from my mission by a knitting-wool stall and fall in love with a ball of hairy thick-and-thin yarn in variegated shades of dark red, sage green and mustard. I buy it and hope it will like the circular needle Doreen-Dorothy gave me at the knit 'n' natter session. Was that really only the day before yesterday?

But there's no sign of Duncan or his cheese stall. Maybe he's at the other food market in Leith. Disappointed, I decide to hop back on my bus and complete the circuit, stopping off at Calton Hill, where I remember amazing views.

And then I spot him, loading a fistful of fish into a soft roll, smearing it with sauce and passing it proudly to a waiting punter. Aha, so he's not a cheesemonger, he's a fishmonger. Actually I smell the smoky aroma first. It's like bonfires and wood-burners and Nana Hedges forcing fluorescent orange kippers on us for Sunday tea.

Duncan is every inch the artisan hipster: short back and sides, massive beard, little woolly hat. He looks like Tintin's mate, Captain Haddock. I should suggest that to him for his business name. 'Hawthorn Smokies' is fine but not quite as quirky.

I amble past, pretending not to know that he's just feet from me. The Boxing Day blow job suddenly flashes through my mind and I shudder with a combination of embarrassment and horniness. He doesn't see me; he's giving the punter change and exchanging bantz. So I pick up a tub of his special horseradish relish and earnestly study its ingredients list.

'Annie? Is it . . . fuck me, it only bloody is.'

Result.

I turn, totally surprised. 'Duncan? I don't believe it. Crikey, Duncan, look at you.'

He comes out from behind the stall and gives me the biggest bear hug. He always gave good hug. I need to act surprised for a bit longer so I shake my head and blink at the sight of him.

Steady on, Annie. You're not up for an Oscar.

He's pleased to see me, he really is. I'm glad I washed my hair this morning in the foaming gel the hotel provided. I'm a bit thicker round the middle than I was fifteen years ago but my T-shirt is loose and I bet he's got a tum on him too.

'What the heck are you doing here?' he asks.

'Oh, you know. In transit. Afternoon to kill. I just bought some wool.'

I hold up the brown paper bag to prove it. I haven't been stalking you, Duncan, honest. As we chat, a customer approaches the stall and gives Duncan a wave of greeting.

'Hey Jim,' he shouts. 'Won't be a mo.' Then to me, 'Well, if you've got an evening to kill too, you must come to ours for supper.'

Ours, eh. So he's a 'we', not a 'me'. Stands to reason, he's aged extremely well.

I do a 'wouldn't-want-to-be-any-trouble' shrug but he insists. I'm to meet him back at the stall at 5.30 and we'll head for his, if I don't mind sharing a van with any unsold produce. He makes me a massive smoked mackerel sandwich and won't let me pay.

I do another circuit of the city on the hop-on-hop-off bus, as planned, but my mind is racing and I barely take in any of Edinburgh's sites. Duncan's drop-dead gorgeousness, plus the obvious success of his fishy business, has caught me unawares.

When we parted back in Brighton all those years ago, his only plan was to take up a job as a journalist in Scotland, working for a trade paper. Hipsters had yet to be invented but I'd never have had him down for one anyway. Back then he wore contacts and blinked a lot. Heavy hornrims suit him. I suppress the blow job image yet again.

When I return to the Grassmarket, Duncan is all packed up and ready to go. The smell of smoky fish has seeped into the upholstery of his van; I inhale it as we drive off.

'Oh God, is it really bad?' he asks. 'I hardly notice it any more.'

'It's noticeable but it isn't bad. Far from it. And that sandwich was amazing.'

He doesn't take his eyes off the road but I can see a happy grin. He's as keen to impress me, after all this time, as I am him.

'Where are we going?' I ask, as we head east.

'Portobello. We moved there when Calum was born.'

'Duncan, you're going to have to fill me in on who "we" is.'

He chuckles. 'I do that a lot. I've forgotten how to be me in the singular any more. Okay, I live in Portobello with my wife, Yasmin – she's an artist – and my two children. Calum is 10, Finlay is 7. My brother, Tom – remember Tom? – he and I set up Hawthorn Smokies in 2014. It was a bit of a punt but we're finally making a name for ourselves.'

'Wow, I'm impressed. I always thought you'd end up editor of the *Scotsman*.'

'And I thought you'd be something amazing, whenever you decided what that might be. Do you have kids?'

'I had an unofficial stepson for a while. Josh. But no. No kids.' I can hear the regret in my voice so I swiftly change the subject. 'Dad-hood suits you.'

'It really does, Annie. Don't know why it took me so long to get around to it.'

Duncan parks the van outside a redbrick house, with a smoky mauve front door and a neglected patch of lawn. An abandoned child's bike and a stack of orange fish crates take up half the path. I help Duncan unload, as does his son, Fin, though he's very shy around me.

I'm directed to the kitchen and the smell of smoked fish is replaced by something meaty and stewy, with a hint of burnt Le Creuset. Duncan's wife wipes her hand on a tea towel to shake mine. She is big breasted and ample hipped, with long black hair caught up in a messy ponytail, kohl-rimmed eyes and a big smile.

'Annie, hi. I'm Yasmin. Please tell me you're not vegetarian. Duncan didn't think to ask.'

'I eat anything, everything.'

'No change there then.' Duncan grins, unscrewing a bottle of red.

Calum is sleeping over at a friend's so it's just us four for supper. We eat in the kitchen, a disorganized dumping ground, with piles of paperwork balancing on over-stuffed bookshelves and some half-constructed Lego castle on the sideboard. I am so envious. For all the chaos, it feels like a proper home with a beating heart. Duncan has made a life for himself. This life.

What have I made? What have I lost?

'How do you know Daddy?' Fin asks, finally finding his voice.

'We were friends at university. Good friends. But then we lost touch.'

Duncan gives me a knowing look. 'That's one way of putting it.'

I push a potato around my plate to wipe up the last bit of gravy. 'I wanted to get in touch so many times. But you don't have a presence on social media and whenever I Googled Duncan Hawes, all I could find were newspaper articles from years ago.'

'That's my fault,' Yasmin chips in. 'I said we should stitch our surnames together when we got married. Hawes plus Thornley equals Hawthorn.'

'I'm Finlay Ranjit Hawthorn and Cal is Calum Ashok Hawthorn.'

Fin wants to read to Duncan once he's in bed so Yasmin and I move into the slightly less chaotic front room. She shifts some cardboard boxes from the only armchair so that I can sit, then settles on the sofa.

'Greetings cards,' she says, nodding at the boxes. 'I sell them around the city. I didn't have the concentration for painting proper after the kids were born so I took a temporary detour. Duncan's going to build me a studio at the end of the garden, when I'm ready to get back to it, but Smokies is going gangbusters so I'm not holding my breath.'

I see a card at the top of the box. It features a stylized watercolour of a fishing boat tied up at a quay with a seagull right up close in the foreground, as if it's taking a selfie. It's very cute.

'Help yourself. Please, Annie, take a handful. They're last year's design so I really need to shift them.'

I take one to send to Bev, one to Kate . . . one to Rob? He doesn't know about me stealing Dad's ashes, unless Kate's dobbed me in. She probably has. She likes being in charge of the news headlines.

'What do *you* do?' Yasmin asks, tucking her feet under her and squishing down a couple of cushions to get comfy. 'I asked Duncan but he had no idea.'

'I worked in the City for a bit, after Duncan and I, um, parted company. But it wasn't for me so I did a PGCE to become a teacher. Geography. In St Albans where I grew up. That's about it, really.'

'Wow, that's some gear shift. Do you love it? I bet you do.'

It's been a while since I had to explain my downward/sideways career trajectory to anyone. 'I'm taking a sabbatical,' I reply, all perky and positive. 'Health reasons. Stress. Chest pains that turned out to be nothing at all. Plus Mum died. And now Dad has too. Just recently. I'll go back to it in a bit. Teaching, I mean. Or maybe I won't. Who knows?'

Yasmin leans forward to pat me on the arm, but I'm not quite close enough. And I really don't want her to, in case I cry.

'Oh, Annie. That's tough. That's way too much to deal with. Are you dealing with it on your own?'

She wants to know if I have a partner. I would too, if I was her. 'Mostly, yes. Along with my sister and – some other people. I'm doing okay. Really.'

Duncan comes in, bearing a bottle of whisky and three glasses. Before closing the door, he bellows up the stairs. 'Lights off now, Finlay Ranjit. I mean it. We did "one more page" five minutes ago.'

He settles down next to Yasmin and pours us each a 'wee

dram'. I don't normally drink whisky but it feels like warm honey as it goes down.

'What have I missed?' Duncan asks.

Now I feel awkward. It was so much easier opening up just to Yasmin because I don't know her. Duncan took up a big chunk of my life all those years ago and everything I say now will be tinged with our shared history.

But, hey, why not? 'My dad died and Bev, his lady friend, wanted to scatter his ashes in the Tyrol so I stole his urn. I'm thinking about taking him on a tour of the Shipping Forecast.'

Yasmin's eyes widen. Duncan frowns. 'Sorry to hear that, Annie. I liked your dad. Not sure he liked me though. He was convinced *I* was the one distracting *you* from your essays.'

He holds up his glass for a toast so Yasmin and I follow suit.

'To Paul.'

They clink and drink. I do too.

'He did like you actually, Duncan. He thought you deserved a medal for taking me on. And it's Peter, not Paul.'

We do it again. 'To Peter.'

'Sorry, Annie. My bad. Hey, what was his nickname for you? You used to get so hacked off whenever I used it.'

'Annie Lummox. Because I was a lummox. I still am.'

Yasmin has been quietly processing my confession. 'I'm just trying to work out how long it would take to visit all the sea areas. I don't even know how many there are. Won't it be expensive, getting to each one? Will you give the ashes back when you've finished?'

Good questions, all of them. 'It wouldn't take too long if I only covered the British coastline. Mum left me and Kate a bit of money when she died. Quite a bit actually. It was from an old aunt of hers; Mum was determined we should have a nest egg. I treated myself to a Persian rug and a weekend in New York but I've never known what to do with the rest. This feels right.'

'And Bev doesn't mind?' Yasmin wants to know.

'She says she doesn't.'

Yasmin nods knowingly at the way I worded my answer. 'That's good,' she finally responds.

'You don't think I should?'

Duncan attempts to speak for both of them. 'It's not for us to say, hen.'

But Yasmin's having none of that. 'I don't know you, Annie. Even though I know *of* you, obviously. So you're perfectly entitled to ignore what I think. And what I think is, if you reckon it will help you process your grief, bloody do it.'

I'm genuinely surprised. I wasn't expecting that.

'Does that help?'

'It does, Yasmin. Thank you. I still have to work out how to do it, though. I only packed a small rucksack. I need clothes, an itinerary . . . a plan.'

Yasmin jumps up and heads for the door. 'I've got a spare wheelie suitcase Duncan's mum gave Fin. Have that. Everything else, you can sort out as you go along. What size are you?'

'A 12, sometimes a 14.'

'Perfect.' I hear her thump up the stairs.

So Yasmin has a plan, even if I don't.

I offer to order a cab but Duncan insists on driving me and my new Star Wars wheelie suitcase back to my hotel. 'Save your money for sea area Malin,' he tells me as we buckle up and drive off.

93

Duncan is quiet and just stares at the road ahead. It's not until we're passing Holyrood Park that I break the silence.

'Yasmin's great,' I say. 'And Fin. He's the dead spit of you. Does Calum look like his mum?'

Duncan takes a deep breath before answering. Then it all comes out in one angry rush. 'This trip, stealing your dad's ashes, not having a plan but doing it anyway . . . That's typical Annie Stanley. I thought you might have changed, fifteen years on, but you're just the same.'

'I've gone up a cup size,' I reply, trying to lighten the tone.

'Your dad was right. You really are Annie Lummox. Take something bad and make it even worse. Do you remember when we were staying with my folks that Christmas?'

Oh, dear God, please don't mention the al fresco blow job.

'And you broke a little Chinese vase in the guest room. But you didn't come clean, you just swept all the bits into a drawer. And my mother didn't find it for weeks. She hated the bloody vase – that's why it was in the guest room – but what she hated more was that you didn't bother to tell her.'

I have no recollection of doing that but I can't let on to Duncan.

'Take something bad and make it even worse. That's you all over.'

Does he think saying it twice will give it added veracity?

'I know I can be a bit klutzy sometimes,' I say quietly.

He does a hollow laugh. I'd forgotten how good he was at those. 'It's klutzy when you break a vase. It's more than klutzy when you mess with people's lives and plans and emotions.'

'Bev's given her blessing. I swear she has.'

I nearly tell him that she even facilitated the ashes swap

after I accidentally went off with Keith. But I sense that won't help my defence.

Duncan pulls up with a judder and parks by the Meadows so he can totally concentrate on my character assassination.

'I don't mean Bev although, God knows, she must be pretty upset, whatever kind of blessing she felt obliged to give you. I mean us, Annie.'

Us? I took something bad and I made it even worse? Oh no, I'm not having that. Okay, I might have had a bit of a thing with his mate, but that was *after* he and I broke up.

'We both knew it was time to grow up and move on, Duncan. You wanted to be a journalist, I wanted to be – actually, I didn't have a clue what I wanted to be. We couldn't live the student life when we weren't students any more. You got the job in Scotland and we broke up.'

Duncan looks as if he's going to self-combust. 'It's Mum's vase all over again. Jesus! We didn't break up, Annie, you dumped me. That's why I took that cruddy job and had to move in with my folks for six months. And then you fucked my best pal, just to make sure I got the message.'

'It was just sex. It didn't mean anything.'

'Not to you, maybe. Or to Simon. But I was gutted. You broke my heart and then you stamped on it in your Doc Martens, for good measure.'

'I'm really sorry, Duncan. I didn't mean to hurt you.'

He starts the car again. He's said his piece. He can draw a line and move on. Lucky old him. When he drops me outside my hotel, he looks calm again.

He kisses my cheek. 'Maybe this is your moment to take a bad thing and not make it even worse. Reckon you can manage that, Annie Lummox?'

Chapter Ten

Tyne

I sleep fitfully, trying to recall Duncan's mother's sodding Chinese vase and why I didn't tell her I'd broken it. I sift through his comments about me always making things worse, which I can't help feeling is rather unfair. Yes, I'm a bit scattergun in how I deal with things and okay, I've been known to plough on with a stupid idea, convinced that it's got legs, when all around have walked away. But I'm more than that, aren't I? I'm not always a lummox.

I really didn't think it through with Dad's ashes, though. I took the urn from the Welsh dresser in a brief mad moment. Then, when I realized what I'd done, I justified it, rather than quietly returning it, before it was missed. I get that now. I do.

But why won't anyone believe me when I tell them that Bev is one hundred per cent fine with this? I wouldn't be here now if she wasn't.

Also . . . I didn't dump Duncan. I'm sure I didn't. It was an amicable split, then we went our separate ways. And while I was adjusting to singledom, I had a fling with Simon, who just so happened to be a mate of Duncan's. In retrospect, I could perhaps have chosen my fuck buddy more wisely but, guess what, I didn't. Guilty as charged. I hurt someone

96

I truly cared about. And, clearly, he's never let it go. *So* pleased he was able to get it off his chest like that and dump it all back on me. How cleansing for him.

I wake up at five and listen to the Shipping Forecast. It's soothing and hypnotic, like a Buddhist chant. It doesn't make me cry, as it has often done over recent weeks. It's like a prolonged hug from Dad. 'I'm gone but we still have this, don't we, An-An?'

Fair Isle, Faeroes, South-East Iceland.

I click open my Star Wars suitcase, thinking Dad and his urn will be happier stowed safely in there. Yasmin has packed me two Sea Salt T-shirts and a pair of boyfriend jeans, all with the labels still attached. There's also a card, one of her own designs, featuring the selfie-snapping seagull in front of Edinburgh Castle. She has very artistic handwriting.

Dear Annie

I hope these fit. Give them to your favourite charity shop if they don't. I bought them last year as incentive to lose weight. But I like bread too much.

I hope you find what you're looking for on your journey. Duncan often talks fondly of you and I'm sure he wishes you the very best too.

If you're on Facebook, please do let me know how (and where) you are.

Love Yasmin xxx

So *she* definitely thinks I'm making this trip with Dad's ashes, which is really sweet and trusting of her, while Duncan assumes I'll klutz it up. I tell myself I should only do it if I can make things better, not 'even worse'. That phrase of his will be stuck in my head forever.

The sea area after Forth is Tyne which, according to Google, stretches from Berwick-upon-Tweed to Flamborough Head. I unfurl my trusty tea towel and spread it out on the hotel bed to see where *I* am and *it* is. I've never been to the North-East of England and have no idea where to head for.

I take a safety pin from the complimentary sewing kit, close my eyes and stab it into the tea towel. On my first attempt, I spear a stylized fish in sea area Dogger. After two more goes, I strike land and yes, it's in Tyne but it's not by the sea. The nearest place I've heard of is, however, Scarborough.

I know someone in Scarborough: Kim Davenport-formerly-Gorringe, daughter of Maureen and Ray, our old neighbours. She was my first-ever best friend and pops up sporadically on my Facebook feed whenever our algorithms align. She's still potty about Boyzone, judging by her posts, which generally fall into three categories:

1) All matters Ronan Keating-related, occasionally even a selfie of him and Kim, with her looking all shiny-faced and starstruck.
2) Grave warnings about the latest online scam, followed by a sheepish follow-up confirming it's a hoax and . . .
3) Nights out with her gal pals; all clinking cocktails, pouty lips and bunny ears.

After my encounter with Duncan, I wonder how sensible it is to keep dredging up people from my past. Kim should be fine, though, because we were besties and we go back to a much more innocent time. She sent me such sweet notes of condolence, via her parents, when Mum and Dad died. Her words were brief, unflowery and came from the heart. I'd like to see her and thank her.

I go straight online, book myself a room in a nice hotel and a one-way train ticket from Edinburgh. I am going to Scarborough.

I know I should call Kate but I honestly can't deal with her weary tone when I tell her my plans, such as they are. So I text her. 'I'm fine, please don't worry. Leaving Forth and heading for Tyne. Am feeling moderate to good. Love you. xxx An-An.'

I have a pasty, popcorn and coffee, plus a window seat on the seaward side of my train carriage so I can take in the glorious scenery as we trundle down the rugged east coast towards Newcastle. Yasmin's jeans fit perfectly, if I don't mind super-big turn-ups, and one of the T-shirts, white with blue horizontal stripes, feels suitably nautical for the purposes of my trip.

I know I won't feel so positive about this journey when I'm struggling through a Force 8 gale off Orkney or waiting at some isolated station for a cancelled train to the arse end of England. But right here, right now, I am not Annie Lummox. I left her in my Edinburgh hotel room, along with the last few jelly beans and a tube of toothpaste. They have toothpaste in Scarborough. I will survive.

At Durham, a woman gets into my carriage and takes the seat opposite me. She is Bev's age, or thereabouts, and wears a jaunty tan beret, a jazzy silk scarf and short-sighted specs. She pulls some knitting from her bag and clacks away. She is so proficient, she can even risk gazing out at the passing countryside, without fear of dropping a stitch or losing her thread. She seems to be knitting a square but not back and forth in simple repeating rows, as I was *re*-taught to do in Cromarty. I can't help watching. Her dexterity is compelling.

'KFB,' she says suddenly.

I must look confused. She puts down her needles and repeats. 'KFB. Knit front and back. I'm making diagonal corner-to-corner squares for a cot throw.'

'I thought you could only knit horizontally.'

'I wish. Kira, my daughter, bought all the wool for the cot blanket herself, to match the nursery wallpaper. But she's got no idea about knitting so some of it's two-ply, some of it's four-ply. I've got one ball of DK and another chunky.'

She tuts knowingly at me, as if I can see what the problem is. I shrug because I can't.

'Corner-to-corner squares suit different ply yarns,' she explains, finishing a row and holding it up for me to see. 'So you can mix and match wools and still come out with squares that are all the same size.'

I think of the luscious thick-and-thin wool I bought yesterday at the Grassmarket. Maybe I could knit that corner-to-corner to ensure it will be the same size as the Cromarty square. I watch Kira's mum carefully. When I still can't figure out what she's doing, she knits in slow motion until I get it. She even lets me do a row.

My wool is at the bottom of the suitcase, acting as padding for Dad's urn, along with my circular needle. Maybe I'll give it a go tonight in Scarborough . . .

The hotel is on the Esplanade, one of those creaky old establishments that hit its heyday in the Fifties, before the Costa Brava was invented. Now it's part of a national chain so some marketing bod has imposed a corporate colour scheme in fifty shades of navy, from reception to brasserie to bedroom, plus lots of splodgy modern art on unframed canvases, churned out by chimps by the yard.

I have a sea view. And a huge double bed which is wasted

on me because I still only sleep on the left side, from Duncan, through Toby, to Rob . . . plus one or two others in between. I have an extensive range of beverage options, including the ever-present sachet of claggy cocoa, and some classy-looking toiletries that will all go into my wash bag tomorrow. At my last hotel, the watery, grey shampoo and handwash bottles were nailed to the bathroom tiles, as if I'd be unable to resist nicking them otherwise.

Dad is settled on a little side table by the window so that he can view sea area Tyne in all its glory. I wonder if I should take him outside to enjoy the bracing sea air. It didn't occur to me in Cromarty or Forth. My bad. I have an image of me sitting on a bench on the West Pier, chatting animatedly to an oversized Pringles tube, and decide against it. All this Shipping Forecast malarkey is mad enough already.

I find and 'friend' Yasmin on Facebook to thank her for the clothes and to let her know I've arrived safely. I also message Kim Davenport-formerly-Gorringe to say I'm in Scarborough and shall we meet up? I'm relieved I don't have her phone number. Reconnecting via a message has to be less awkward than an out-of-the-blue call. If she isn't up for seeing me, she needn't reply until I'm en route to sea area Humber. I can live with that.

Facebook was just becoming a 'thing' when I signed up in 2007. I was working in the City and it was imperative to have as many Facebook friends as possible, to prove how clubbable and connected you were. On quiet nights, I would sit at my desk, trawling madly through other people's time-lines in order to click anyone who looked vaguely familiar. Quantity over quality. I'd lost touch with Kim but I must have friended her back then. Or maybe she found me?

When I became a teacher, I reined in my presence on social media. I really didn't need any vengeful pupils sharing photos of me in a straining bikini or inappropriate clinch. And then, when I stopped being a teacher, I had nothing to say, nothing to boast about to online 'friends', apart from the occasional hundred per cent *Pointless* score, and who honestly gives a toss about that?

I know Facebook is inane and occasionally all-consuming but it's easier to stay than flounce off and it does keep me in contact with people like Kim. Kate doesn't do social media of any kind and Rob thinks social media is 'futile and self-absorbed' so I know they won't be checking in on me. Josh might, even though he thinks – quite correctly – that Facebook is for crumblies.

There's a glossy magazine beside my bed, listing all the hotels in the chain – from Abingdon to Aberystwyth – plus things to do in Scarborough: the Stephen Joseph Theatre, the Casino, Anne Brontë's grave, an art gallery and a museum. Maybe tomorrow.

Right now, all I want is a cup of Earl Grey, a Brontë shortbread and, in an hour or two, a fish supper, in tribute to all the trawlers bobbing on the waves out there in Tyne, Forties, Fisher and beyond.

I dig out my circular needle and the wool I bought in Edinburgh and have a go at knitting a corner-to-corner blanket square, as taught to me by Kira's mum a few hours ago. It's thrilling to watch the variegated colours and thicknesses of yarn form an ever-growing triangle and then, when I decrease, a neat, complete blanket square. A silent hour goes by and it's finished, without help from anyone else.

I did it. Me! I did! I couldn't be more proud.

My silenced phone bounces on the bedside table. I pray

it isn't a terse text from Kate. Or maybe Bev's had second thoughts about Dad's ashes and her blessing is herewith revoked. Neither. It's a Facebook notification to say I've been messaged back by Kim.

'Hi Anne, how brilliant to hear you're in Scarborough. Been thinking of you loads since my dad told me about your dad. Such a fab man. So sad. Would love to meet up & remember all our wild 'n' crazy times. Plus all our Boyzone adventures. Ronan rules!!! Then 'n' now. Hugs 'n' stuff Kimmi G xxx ☺.'

Kim lived in the next street to us; the Gorringe garden backed on to ours and we often chatted through the trellis. Kate and I called her parents Auntie Maureen and Uncle Ray; they were like family, but nicer. Kim and I became best friends on day one of secondary school and for a good few years we were inseparable.

We didn't have a massive amount in common, but a fanatical obsession with Boyzone made up for that. Kim would buy *Smash Hits* and I'd buy *Number One* so that we could swap, once we'd pored over every page. She loved Ronan, I loved Steo, so sharing out the pin-ups was always amicable. There was also a Mikey fan in our gang but we froze her out because we went to her house once for tea and got a bollocking for being too loud.

Mum and Dad were friends with Auntie Maureen and Uncle Ray. Not close, but close enough to feed cats, water plants, borrow lawnmowers and host sleepovers. Every 28 December, we went to theirs or they came to ours for turkey sandwiches, cheese footballs and the remains of the Christmas cake. Uncle Ray once gave me a tiny tumbler of Baileys, which I thought was the most sublime drink ever invented. Literally. Like ever.

Our friendship fizzled out when I went off to uni. Kim was dogged but not academic while I was clever but lazy. Kim got an office job and married an electrician called Nick. I went to Sussex, hennaed my hair and shacked up with Duncan. We did meet once for coffee in St Albans but the conversation drained as quickly as the cappuccinos. Plus she was still potty about Boyzone while I'd moved on to Gomez and Elbow.

I got an invitation to her wedding but said I had exams and couldn't make it. Mum bumped into her once in Asda and said she was pregnant with her second child. I didn't even know there'd been a first.

Mum and Dad stayed friends with Maureen and Ray, even after Kim and I drifted apart. They still did the post-Christmas cold turkey and warm Baileys thing until Mum died and Dad hooked up with Bev. And they came to both funerals, which made me feel bad for nearly not recognizing them and barely talking to them.

Kim and I message back and forth in a giggly faux 14-year-old style and arrange to meet. She suggests a fish restaurant on York Place tomorrow night for a 'big-time catch-up'. I hadn't planned on two nights in Scarborough, but Dad and I are in no hurry to be anywhere. Why not?

I'm too knackered to go out so I order a club sandwich and a glass of Sancerre from room service. I'm in bed by 8 p.m. and sleep like three logs.

After breakfast, I set out to see Scarborough. It's bucketing with rain and buffeting with wind so I'm pretty much self-propelled over the Spa Bridge and into town. I buy a cheap kagoule but it can only keep out so much rain. Even so, I'm determined to get a sense of the place and to fill my day.

I take refuge from the weather in a series of Scarborough landmarks. First, the indoor market, where I buy a blue 'souvenir of Scarborough' egg cup from a vintage knick-knack stall, then on to an amazing Fifties throwback coffee bar near the pier where you half expect the Fonz to serve you your peach melba. I buy fudge in a sweet shop on the windy seafront and spend a couple of hours in Scarborough Art Gallery, where I see yet more windswept coastline, but this time in oils and watercolours.

Throughout the day, I get texts from Kim: to tell me that she has short blonde hair now and is wearing a red jacket. Then to say she's a twat and she isn't wearing her red jacket today, she's wearing her brown check jacket. And black trousers. And a beige blouse. And finally to let me know that she doesn't wear glasses any more. I've had a good squint at her timeline on Facebook so I know exactly what she looks like, as I'm sure she does me. She looks pretty good actually.

I'm a bit early so I find a table, order a glass of wine and write my selfie-seagull cards to Kate and Bev. Yet more reassurance that I'm fine and Dad's fine and Scarborough looks nice and I'm meeting an old friend and everything's fine so please don't worry. If Bev's having second thoughts, she needs to know I haven't done anything irrational or ominous. I'm a 37-year-old woman on an adventure and I know what I'm doing. Kind of.

On the dot of 7.30, Kim appears, as promised, in her brown check jacket. She spots me and rushes over. We nearly hug, then think better of it, then hug anyway. She used to wear horrible glasses with thick lenses. She looks like she's always been blonde. It suits her.

'This is one of my oldest friends,' she tells the waitress

excitedly. 'I haven't seen her in a gazillion years. Pretty much joined at the hip, weren't we?'

The waitress and I nod politely at each other, then she leaves us to it. I still have half a glass of wine but Kim insists on buying a bottle of Prosecco to celebrate our reunion. She sits down and beams at me.

'Anne Stanley, as I live and breathe. Flipping heck, who'd have thought it.' We chink glasses and toast our old selves: Anni S and Kimmi G, those wild 'n' crazy Boyzone superfans who cried hysterically at 'Love Me for a Reason', laughed hysterically at 'When the Going Gets Tough' and discussed for hours on end which of the lads we'd have if we couldn't have our best boyz, Ronan and Stephen. Like Mum, I favoured Keith, but for Kimmi it was Ronan or no one.

'Look at us,' I say. 'The Boyzone Over-Thirties Appreciation Society.'

Kim snorts with laughter. 'Pushing 40, more like.' She refills our glasses. 'Right then, missus. To what does Scarborough owe the pleasure?'

I could tell her about Dad's ashes, the Shipping Forecast and my mad flight to Cromarty. I could catch her up on what I've done with my life since we last saw each other. I could but I won't. Kim always saw me as the go-getter, the trendsetter. Why prick her bubble?

'I've been catching up with an old friend in Edinburgh and fancied a stop-off on the way home.' Not a total lie, right? 'I've never been to Scarborough so I thought, why not? Plus I wanted to thank you in person for your condolences. We got so many cards and letters. Not just from family but from all over; people really loved him . . . them. Yours meant a lot, Kim. Thank you.'

We both go a bit wobbly-chinned and our eyes fill. Kim

fiddles with the pepper mill while she regains her composure. 'Your folks were so cool and so nice to me. My dad could be a right sod with his moods, but your dad never was. I know I was a strange kid but he always made me feel welcome. And your turkey sandwiches were way nicer than ours.'

'Redcurrant jelly, brie *and* mayo. That was the secret. Yours too. Your parents, I mean. Not your sandwiches.' We giggle. Auntie Maureen's sandwiches were challenging; heavy on the stuffing, light on the turkey.

'It was so great to see their faces in the congregation at Dad's funeral. At Mum's too. I didn't get to thank them for coming. I wish I had. It was all a bit overwhelming. Please send them my love.'

'Brie *and* mayo. That's about four million calories. It's probably illegal now.'

'So. Catch me up, Kim. Facebook's all very well but it just skims the surface.'

She does a dramatic eye-roll. 'Long version or short version?' It's obvious she's dying to tell me her life story, year by year.

'I'm all ears. But could we order some food first? I'm starving.'

Over two fish pies, each the size of my head, she fills me in. And actually, it's fascinating. It would be brilliant to find out where *all* my ex-friends, flatmates and fuck buddies ended up and how they got there, in every eventful detail.

'Me and Nick lasted eight years,' Kim explains, wiping a blob of white sauce off her chin. 'We were ready to go our separate ways after Jenna was born but we stuck it out until our tenth anniversary. That was, let me see . . . ten years ago. That's right because Jenna's eighteen in August. Love her to bits. My boy, Jackson, he's sixteen. He wants to join the Royal Navy. Smart lad, that one. Clever as anything. Must have got it from his dad.'

She whips out her phone and scrolls through files of photos until she finds the one she's after . . . Kim in a mauve silk wrap-over dress and feathery fascinator, with a beaming teen each side. I can't recall a thing about Nick but he must be large boned and lantern jawed, judging by Jenna and Jackson.

'That's my wedding. Second time lucky or I'll be wanting my money back. Credit note, at the very least.'

She shows me another photo from the same batch, of her and a tanned, shaven-headed, smiley man in a morning suit with a mauve rose buttonhole to match her dress. 'That's husband number two. Stuart. Fit, isn't he?'

She gazes at the photo for an extra second, blinking at her good fortune. Then she remembers herself. 'Well, go on then, Anne. I've shown you mine, you show me yours. What was your chap's name? Malcolm? Andrew? Duncan, was it? I bet you and him are living in a farmhouse, weaving muesli and you've got seven kids.'

'No Duncan, no kids. Actually, I'm a free agent right now. That's how I like it.'

'Treat 'em mean, keep 'em keen. You go, girl!' She does a 'whoo-hoo' fist in the air and clinks my glass.

We can't decide on desserts so we share some ice cream. Kim used to be a bit of a pudding herself back in the day but she's slim and streamlined now. She's also happy and fulfilled, despite divorce, and her kids are so obviously her reason for being. I hadn't intended to be envious of her, but I am.

'Well, go on, mystery woman,' she says after we've polished off our pud. 'You still haven't told me anything about yourself. Hey, you don't work for MI5, do you?'

'Dammit, my cover's rumbled. Now I must kill you.'

Bless her, for a split second she looks anxious. Then she grins and punches my upper arm. 'Oh, *you*.'

So I rattle through my employment history: my soul-sapping job in the City and how I hated it and blah-blah-blah and how I decided to become a teacher and moved back to St Albans. I tell her a bit about Rob but stick to bullet points, not the whole sorry mess. Something about her genuine, sincere interest makes me over-protective of my thin skin.

Kim is loving this trawl down memory lane. 'Your mum's carrot cake with the cream-cheese frosting. I had four whole slices once. Hey, didn't she knit a bobble hat for Steo?'

'Because my attempt looked more like a string bag. I can knit properly now.'

I go to pour out more Prosecco but it's finished. How did that happen? The alcohol has lubricated our friendship and we're wild 'n' crazy Kimmi G and Anni S again, lusting after Ronan and Steo in each other's bedrooms, learning every lyric, aping every dance move and crotch grab.

I suggest brandies in the bar of my hotel so we link arms and totter along the main drag, pretending to be more pissed than we actually are. Scarborough is a bit tacky and faded, especially by night, but aren't those the best kind of British seaside towns? I don't do fate or karma but I can't help thinking that my safety-pin-in-a-tea-towel decision to stop here has turned out well. Maybe it's a portent for the rest of the trip.

At the hotel, I treat us to double Courvoisiers. We could perch on bar stools, beside the two suited business types who look as if they've been here since they finished work hours ago. Or we can sink into plush blue velvet armchairs, upholstered to match the corporate colour scheme. Music from a hits channel on the flat-screen telly above our heads is just loud enough to distract but Kim and I are too busy nattering to notice. Take That blends into Natalie Imbruglia, Shalimar segues into The Cranberries . . .

Kim takes me through her CV; she drifted for a while: dental assistant, teaching assistant, shop assistant. But she's recently found her calling in sales at a holiday apartment development. That's how she met Stuart.

And then suddenly we hear the opening bars of a song so familiar, it's practically in our DNA. We catch each other's eyes. It is! It bloody is! 'Picture of You' by our own special boyz. It came out in July 1997 and was 'penned' by Ronan himself, as Kim was always keen to point out.

Mum and Dad bought me the album for my sixteenth birthday: *Where We Belong*. Kim and I could practically act out the 'Picture of You' video, frame by frame, with her as Ronan and me as Stephen. Lucky we didn't have the technology back then to record ourselves on our phones, for bum-clenching posterity.

It could be the Prosecco or the double brandy. It could be that I can do what I like in Scarborough, where only one person knows me and she's thinking what I'm thinking. It could be the cumulative hysteria of a week on this wild 'n' crazy trip.

I jump up and start dancing as I would have done nearly a quarter of a century ago. Kim gives it a second – she *does* live here, after all – then joins me.

The barman grins, does a thumbs-up, and carries on polishing glasses. It's obvious we're not two out-of-control drunks, just a pair of giddy women having fun. The business types at the bar watch us, intrigued, then they come over and start dancing too. The younger, better-looking one, with his slick suit and artfully loosened tie, is a typical dad dancer who doesn't know it. The other one, paunchy and balding, can seriously bust a move. He tears off his jacket, Travolta-style, to expose a straining waistcoat, and hits the dance floor like he's been dying to do this all his life.

Boyzone fades out and the four of us grind to a sheepish halt. Best sit down now and pretend it didn't happen. That's the British way. And then, and then . . . on comes 'U Can't Touch This' and off we go again. We are seriously Da Bomb. Paunchy Bloke is amazing, even removing his belt, so that his trousers can bag at the crotch like MC Hammer's. The barman does a few hip swivels and finger-clicks as he passes by to collect our used glasses. He's loving this too.

As I rock and swirl, I realize that I am in the moment. The one that will be gone in a nano-second, like a snowflake on the tongue. As a rule, I don't do 'being in the moment' because I'm usually worrying about just now or last Friday or next Wednesday. Or lately, if I *do* pick up on the right-here-right-nowness, it's invariably to castigate myself for zoning out on the sofa in front of *Escape to the Country* while I chomp through a pack of Hobnobs. Somehow I've forgotten how to inhabit those rare moments when I actually feel good about myself.

When did that stop? Why did it stop? And can this moment – *this one right now* – go on for a bit longer because it feels fantastic?

The two men give us each a hug and depart. We make to leave but the barman brings us brandies on the house; he's not closing for another hour. Kim and I slump back in our armchairs and grin, unfeasibly pleased with how this evening has panned out.

She shakes her head and does one of her snorty giggles.

'What?' I ask.

She giggles again. 'Do you remember when we skived off school so we could go to London and wait for the boys outside Radio 1? They were on the *Jo Whiley Show* to promote *Where We Belong*?'

'Oh my God, yes. I had to give Kate £1 not to blab to Mum.'

'And we stood out there for hours and hours and it was raining.'

'And we'd changed out of our uniforms in the loo at John Lewis. And we got soaked because we didn't want to wear our blazers.'

We sigh in unison. Happy days.

'Worth it though, eh,' Kim says.

'Deffo.'

'I've seen them loads since then. I went to three shows on their Farewell Tour and did a meet-and-greet and got selfies and signed photos with all of them. But seeing them that very first time outside Radio 1, being that close to them, getting a smile from Shane when they went in, even though I really wanted one from Ronan . . . well, that was one of the best days of my life.'

'Better than marrying Stuart?'

Kim's guilty grin says it all.

I suddenly remember another shared passion. 'Who were those two lads we fancied from Batchwood? I can see their faces, clear as anything. I can even remember that I liked the dark-haired one. But their names? Not a clue.'

Kim hasn't forgotten. 'Malcolm Robbins and Chris Walling. I preferred Malcolm but you said I had to have Chris.'

'Did I? Really? They were both DDG.' Our secret code for Drop-Dead Gorgeous.

'Chris had acne. That's what swung it for Malcolm. Hey, there was that night we went out with them. Proper out, not just hanging around by Burger King. Do you remember, Anne?'

Vaguely. Distantly. 'Go on, remind me.'

'They were going to a party somewhere miles away . . . Potters Bar, was it? And they said: did we want to come too? And we were so gobsmacked, we said yes.'

'We did?'

'And Chris had a car and all these cans of Strongbow on the back seat. And we didn't want to look like wusses, even though I don't like cider, so we drank two each.'

It's starting to come back to me. 'Oh God, and you threw up.'

'That's just it, Anne. I didn't. I told Chris I was going to throw up, to stop them. Because I twigged that there *was* no party in Potters Bar and I got scared. And I didn't want to snog Chris in some deserted layby. Or be made to do anything else. Seriously, Anne? You don't remember that?'

I do now. I thought Kim was pathetic. I was on a promise with Malcolm Robbins – who I'd fancied for years – and that was all that mattered. Why did she have to spoil it?

'I pretended I was about to throw up,' Kim continues. 'And Chris panicked because it was his dad's car. So they dumped us at a bus stop in the back of beyond at 2 a.m. and I found a phone box and rang for a minicab and we made it home. And my folks were fast asleep when I got in and they never found out.'

Malcolm and Chris totally ignored us after that. Or they'd do puke noises whenever they saw us, until they lost interest. I blamed Kim. I was fucking furious with her for ruining my chances with Malcolm Robbins, even though I see now that she was the responsible adult that night and I was the wild child.

Kim was lucky. Dad was waiting for me when I got home, shivering because I'd gone out with no jacket, and stinking of cider. He was low-volume and calm, which was way worse than a tongue-lashing. And I couldn't go to bed until I'd answered his questions: Where had I been? Who with? Was I drunk? Who dropped me outside just now? Why didn't I ring, if I needed a lift?

I remember lying in bed afterwards, feeling pretty pleased with how I'd saved my skin. I'd had no choice. It was all Kim's fault, I told him. Going to the party with those two lads was like totally her idea. I didn't want to, I really, really didn't, Dad. But she wouldn't listen. It was only my quick thinking that got us home, safe and sound.

Dad was all for stomping round the next day to tell Auntie Maureen and Uncle Ray that Kim had led me astray and put us in danger, but I persuaded him not to. He and Mum agreed that, from then on, I should give Kim a wide berth, knuckle down to my A levels and get the grades I needed for university. So I ghosted her, although we didn't have a name for it back then. I caused our friendship to die and it wasn't because our paths were about to diverge.

'So shall we?' Kim is saying.

I haven't been listening. 'Shall we what?'

'Get together next time I'm in St Albans visiting my folks? It's been so great catching up with you, Anne. Sorry, but I just can't call you "Annie", however hard I try.'

'That would be great.'

'I can't wait to tell Mum and Dad that we've met up. They'd love to see you too. Any time. They've been in that semi nearly forty years now so you know where to find them.'

I nod, a bit too enthusiastically.

'Anyway,' she says, hauling herself out of her armchair, 'I best get home or Stuart will worry.'

We hug. She turns and waves twice before spinning out of the hotel's revolving door.

Back in my room, I make my claggy cocoa for something to do. I feel ashamed. I took a bad thing and made it worse, even though I was pretty damned smug at the time. I didn't need Kim's friendship for much longer so I happily chucked her under the bus. Is that how it all began, my inability to be a good friend, a good partner, a nice person?

'It wasn't Kim's fault that night,' I tell Dad's urn. 'It was me. I made you think less of her, probably for the rest of your life, and she never knew.'

My sleep is fitful. I keep remembering the thoughtless, heartless girl I once was. Where did she come from and why is she still here?

I must do better. I need to do better. This isn't who I'm meant to be.

Chapter Eleven

March 2001

Mum said: Just go! She sounded irritated and impatient, as if she couldn't wait to see the back of them. Honestly, Annie and Dad were making a silly fuss about nothing. And anyway, she'd rather visit the next university on Annie's wish list, Sussex. Who'd say no to a day out in Brighton? She even started singing: 'Oh I do love to be beside the seaside'.

'If you're sure, love.' Dad's forehead was creased in a concerned frown. 'Or what if we visit Sussex University first? UEA isn't top of your list, is it, Annie Lummox?'

Now it was Annie's turn to frown. Yes, the University of East Anglia *was* top of her list. She liked what she'd seen in the prospectus, her favourite teacher, Mrs Bates, was an alumna and it was a two-hour drive from St Albans – far enough away to be independent, close enough if she had a sudden craving for cake and hugs. Plus Janet the Prannet's older brother, Colin, was in his second year of a law degree there. She'd snogged him at Janet's sixteenth birthday party and it felt like unfinished business.

'Oh, don't make such a thing of it, Peter,' Mum sighed. 'It's just a stupid doctor's appointment. I don't need you

116

there to hold my hand. She'll probably send me home with a flea in my ear and a prescription for antibiotics.'

She returned to the kitchen to finish making their packed lunch: cheese-and-pickle sandwiches, some cartons of Ribena, two fat doorsteps of sticky bread pudding, plus the essential bag of humbugs. If they still wanted crisps, on top of all that, they could buy them at a service station.

The Ford Sierra gleamed in the driveway. Dad had cleaned it thoroughly inside and out yesterday morning. He'd checked oil levels and filled the tank. He'd even burnt all his favourite tracks onto a blank CD. 'You can't have a road trip without road music, An-An.'

Annie was fairly certain what the road music would be: Graham Parker & the Rumour, Brinsley Schwarz and Dad's absolute favourite band, Dr Feelgood. He knew he could get away with it if Mum wasn't coming with them. She'd insist on non-stop Radio 4 or a 'nice family conversation'. They'd only just weaned her off I-Spy.

'I'll call you from the campus,' Dad insisted as he gave Mum a big hug that rocked them both sideways from foot to foot, until she pulled away. 'And tell Dr Golding about *all* your aches and pains, love. That's what she's there for.'

Mum looked heavenward. 'Oh, just bugger off, will you, pardon my French.'

She stood on exaggerated tiptoes and kissed the top of Annie's head, then bustled them out to the car. She still wanted to clean the kitchen before heading off to the health centre for her 9.10 appointment. Then she was meeting her best friend Judy for their monthly coffee and catch-up in Abbots Langley.

Dad had studied the route the night before and needed no navigational assistance from Annie, but the *AA British*

Road Atlas was in the side pocket, just in case. She kicked off her uncomfortable shoes and wiggled her toes. Mum had insisted she look smart but this was just the open day, not some all-important, make-or-break interview.

The A1 became the A505, through Baldock, where Dad had once reversed into a bollard, and Royston, where she'd lost a purse full of pocket money. Then the A11 and their favourite sign: Six Mile Bottom.

'I'll have a six-mile bottom if I eat all that bread pudding,' Annie giggled.

'And I'll have a ten-mile tum. Or, let's see, a forty-acre arse.'

'A hundred-metre middle, a fifty-foot front.'

'You win. Sheesh, who made you such a clever clogs?'

'Must have been Mum. She's the smart one out of you two.'

Dad feigned affront. 'Right. No bread pudding for *you*, madam.'

They stopped for a wee and a coffee at Newmarket, then cracked on. Dad couldn't wait any longer. On went the first CD, starting with 'Reasons to Be Cheerful, Part 3'. Dad knew every word, every single stanza of nonsense and trivia. He'd even looked up Bonar Colleano, who turned out to be an American film star.

Dad was as encyclopedic and obsessive about Seventies pub rock as he was about the Shipping Forecast. If only Dr Feelgood had recorded 'Sailing By' to a thumping, jack-hammer beat, Dad would have been sorted for life.

Annie knew what Dad would say next. She did a silent countdown from fifty but got no further than thirty-two before he trotted out his well-worn comment.

'Proper, sweaty, eardrum-splitting music this, Anne. Not

like your pimply 12-year-old Irish lads with their wishy-washy covers of other people's songs.'

'I told you. I'm Annie now. Anne was a schoolgirl but Annie's going to uni. Got that?'

'Loud and clear, Miss Lummox. Anyway, best live band ever, best gig ever. Southend Kursaal, 1975. I barged my way to the front row so I wouldn't miss a thing. I was wearing this new white T-shirt and I got covered in beer. The Feelgoods had it all back then. I was gutted when Lee Brilleaux died of cancer, when was it, '94? Only two years older than me. Put him up against your Boyzone boy and he'd have had him for breakfast. With extra bacon and a sausage.'

Annie gazed out of the window, watching the Thetford Forest flash past. Dad had no major issues with Boyzone. He just liked to wind her up. But these days it didn't work. She'd lost interest in the boyz, although she would always retain a deep affection for Steo. He'd come out a year earlier and she was pleased for him. What a relief, rather than living a lie. She'd never had any fantasies that they'd marry anyway. Not like her friend Kim, who still hoped she was in with a chance with Ronan.

The traffic had been light and Dad's road music suited fast-lane driving. They were in a car park on Norwich's eastern ring road by ten and were early, really early.

'All part of the plan,' Dad said. 'I thought we could do a bit of sightseeing first. Norwich Castle, maybe, or the Sainsbury Centre for Visual Arts, which is on campus.'

Annie groaned. If in doubt, Dad always suggested something cultural and wholesome. He never said: 'Hey, let's find a funfair,' or 'Who's up for crazy golf?'

He picked up on her underwhelmed response. He could

hardly miss it. He leant over to grab the *AA British Road Atlas* from the side pocket and put it on her lap.

'Go on then, Annie-not-Anne. You come up with something we can do in less than two hours.'

Annie located East Anglia on page 29 and scanned it for suitable destinations while Dad thrummed his fingers on the steering wheel. 'In your own time, smart arse.'

She traced her finger along the A47 until she hit Great Yarmouth.

'Seriously?' Dad groaned. 'You'd prefer that to a nice bit of culture?'

She ran her finger north, up the coastline, finding fantastic place names along the way . . . California? Scratby? Eccles on Sea? Happisburgh?

'It's Haisbro actually, not Happy's Berg.' Dad suddenly perked up. 'Happisburgh lighthouse. It's on my Shipping Forecast tea towel. Where sea area Humber meets sea area Thames, I do believe. Now you're talking, An – I mean, Annie. You navigate, I'll obey your every word.'

He screeched out of the car park and they hurtled towards Happisburgh, with yet more thumping Feelgood as their soundtrack. Annie wished she'd brought her Boyzone CDs, just to piss him off.

It was a lighthouse. Fairly old but just a lighthouse. Red-and-white striped like a Man U woolly hat. There was a sign saying it was open on occasional Sundays in the summer, but today was a Tuesday in March. So all they could do was walk round it a couple of times, then perch on a bench and eat their picnic.

Dad gazed out to the horizon, happy as a happy berg. He loved it when his tea towel destinations came alive. He inhaled the seaweedy smell and waved his sandwich at the view. 'Not bad, eh, An-An. Not flipping bad.'

'Yup. Pretty good. Although I think Mum went a bit light on the Branston.'

'Ha-ha-ruddy-ha! What I don't get is that you want to study geography and yet our glorious British coastline leaves you cold.'

'Only because you bang on about it all the time, Dad. North Utsire this, Rockall Hebrides that.'

He chuckled. 'Guilty as charged. Okay then, what *will* you do with a geography degree? Become a travel agent, an air hostess . . . a weather girl?'

Annie shrugged. She didn't know. She hoped university would make all that clear.

'Derek's youngest's got a whizzy job with a City bank,' he continued. 'Even though she did English at uni, not economics. You tell me, what was the point in all that studying? Why did she do that?'

'For the money?'

'Probably. You'll be working your whole life, An-An. Just think about that. What you do has to be about more than just "the money" or you'll go mad. How about teaching? I reckon you'd be brilliant at that.'

'Do you?'

'We both think so, your mum and me. No pressure, though. It's your decision.' He delved into the Tesco carrier bag. 'Bread pudding o'clock, d'you reckon? That Mrs Stanley of ours makes an ace bread pudding. How about we share one bit now and keep the rest for the drive home?'

He began to unwrap the cling film, then stopped and gazed out at the horizon again. 'I hope she's okay. You know what she's like when she's under the weather. Won't

121

make a fuss, won't say what hurts or how much. I hope she's okay.'

It started to rain. They grabbed their things and made a dash for the car. It was time to drive back to Norwich anyway, if they didn't want to be late for the open day.

Chapter Twelve

Humber

Before going to sleep, I watch *Newsnight* and start to knit another square. The wool came from a charity shop near Scarborough station. It's school-jumper maroon and it feels synthetic so no sheep caught a chill in the spinning of this yarn. It very much looks like I'm knitting squares for a blanket of my own, one for each sea area: Cromarty, Forth and now Tyne. Like taking Dad on this tour of the Shipping Forecast, I'll do it until I stop.

The other thing I do before bed is book a hire car, one that can be dropped off at my destination, wherever that may be, for the next leg of my journey. Dad taught me to drive over one summer before I went to uni. He also instilled in me the joy of the open road. I need a break from train platforms, bad coffee and small talk with strangers who want to know where I'm going and why. The only down side is that I can't knit while I drive.

Next morning, I load up on the full breakfast at my hotel: from tinned grapefruit and poached eggs to two rounds of toast and a chocolate muffin. Starter, dinner and pudding all in one meal. Last night's barman is now this morning's waiter. He gives me a knowing wink as he brings over coffee and directs me to the hot buffet. They have one of those annoying conveyor belt toasters where the bread tumbles down the slide either pale white or pure charcoal.

I pack Dad carefully into my Star Wars wheelie suitcase, knowing he may have to lie on his side in the car boot. I wrap him in Yasmin's T-shirts, after introducing them to each other. I have seriously lost it.

The car is a Kia, which I'm used to. The car-hire bloke – 'Wesley' – mansplains the dashboard, as if I've just popped in from the 1950s, and makes me check the bodywork for scratches. 'Not that we don't trust you, my love, but you never know what you might bump into.'

Soon I'm on the A64, heading south. White clouds scud across the ceiling of the sky and there's a refreshing breeze if I open both windows. In the rear-view mirror, I catch sight of myself smiling. This is good. I am mistress of my own destiny, God of my very own moving metal box. I can talk to myself, sing to myself, swear to myself.

I am on my way. I don't have a specific destination in Humber, which stretches, I think, from Flamborough Head to Great Yarmouth. But I hope I'll know when I get there.

I haven't forgotten last night with Kim and have plenty of time to rerun it as I tootle down the A165, direction Bridlington. She thinks I'm still the dog's bollocks because I once was. She'll be telling her workmates – and Stuart and Jenna and Jackson – what a laugh she had with her wild 'n' crazy bestest bestie ever. She might even think we'll pick up where we left off, despite the two hundred or so miles between us.

I feel my cheeks burn. I don't deserve her friendship. I chucked her overboard, just to avoid a ticking-off and a week without pocket money. Dad didn't want me associating with someone who he regarded as 'no better than she ought

to be'. He took my lie on trust. He never doubted my version
of what happened and I let him believe it.

My lie soured our family's friendship with the Gorringes.
Nothing was said, but something had changed. The post-
Christmas get-togethers continued. Plants were still watered,
cats fed, lilos lent. But now we were just neighbours, nothing
more. Auntie Maureen and Uncle Ray were sidelined by
proxy and *they'd* done nothing wrong either. They came to
both funerals, for fuck's sake.

And all for a snog with Malcolm Robbins. Which I didn't
even get.

'Look, Dad! Bridlington,' I hear myself say as I'm funnelled
round the predictable ring road of Lidls, car showrooms and
self-storage solutions. Bridlington is, of course, one of the
coastal stations of the Shipping Forecast, after Boulmer and
before Sandettie Light Vessel Automatic.

I wonder why Dad was never on *Mastermind*. If he'd
chosen the Shipping Forecast as his specialist subject for round
one, he could have nailed it with Dr Feelgood for round two.
I visualize him in an open-neck shirt and his best sports jacket
in the *Mastermind* chair, looking dead pleased with himself
for sailing through it with no passes, and my eyes fill.

I drive through Lissett and Beeford and Brandesburton
and they don't make much of a mark. Then a sign appears
on the road. I mean, literally, a sign that reminds me why
I'm doing this.

Beverley. I am passing the outskirts of Beverley.

Before I have time to think, I depart from my route and
follow signs for the town centre. I park in Ladygate, buy
some boring beige wool and find a newsagent's selling post-
cards. I choose one of Beverley Minster in bright sunshine,

just like today, and buy a book of stamps, while I'm at it. I'm not ready for food yet, after my massive breakfast, but I could murder an Americano so I settle in a Costa and write the postcard.

Greetings from Beverley, Beverley.

I put my pen down. What do I say? 'Hi there. I haven't scattered Dad yet because I don't know where to do it and I'm not ready to let go of him. But doing this has to be better than sitting on my arse, doing sweet fuck all. Please bear with me while I put your grief on hold. I'm sorry I don't like you as much as I should but now that Dad's dead, it doesn't matter any more, does it. Kind regards, Annie.'

Instead I make up some guff about the nice weather and the nice town and has she ever been here and I better get back on the road. I try to write 'love' but my hand just won't cooperate. There is no love. I sign with a flourish and post the card before I can tear it up.

Back in the car, I check my route on my phone. It would be a lot easier if I actually had a destination so I tap in King's Lynn, for want of anywhere better. And I'm off.

It's a long drive. A really, really long drive. Why didn't I spot that when I set off? Crossing the Humber Bridge feels symbolic, significant. But it isn't. It just gets me to the next bit: the long, flat, uninspiring landscape of Lincolnshire, with place names that sound like Dickens characters – Utterby and Sutterby – or throat clearings – Haugh and Louth – or Fifties film stars – Mavis Enderby and Gayton le Marsh.

The car radio manages to keep me distracted from the distance I still have to cover. I dip into local phone-ins about the controversial new bypass and interviews with stars of the latest production at the Embassy Theatre, Skegness. I re-tune to Radio 4 for an interesting documentary about suffragettes. Hurrah for Sylvia Pankhurst.

But ultimately it's Capital Gold that sustains me; I sing along to everything. I give good Garfunkel on 'The Boxer'; I show Emeli Sandé how it's done on 'Read All About It'; I even get to singalong to Dr Feelgood's 'Back in the Night'. If I had one of Dad's home-made CDs, I'd happily play his favourite band all the way to East Anglia.

Rob used to hate me singing in the car. Even when I wasn't giving it total welly, I'd absentmindedly la-la-la, then chuck in a random lyric or two, hum a bit more, maybe noodle in some harmony. In my head, it sounded awesome.

When you love someone, you're meant to love everything about them. Even their singing. Not Rob. And he'd get ridiculously wound up if I got a lyric wrong. What did it matter that I sang: 'Ebony and I agree . . .' or 'Don't sleep in the subway doorway'? His intolerance of my singing wasn't the reason I broke up with him. But it probably didn't help.

Beyond Boston, I stop at some services to stretch my legs and buy a road atlas so that I can get a better sense of distances. Back in the car, I allow myself five minutes' shut-eye but it turns into nearly an hour. It would have been longer if it hadn't been for some pesky kids banging on the window as they pass, screeching with lolz when they see me jolt to life.

Two hours and change later, I have reached my destination. Not King's Lynn, not Great Yarmouth or Southwold, where Toby and I once went to a ludicrously fancy wedding and had a massive row on the drive home.

I am in Happisburgh.

As soon as I saw it on the map, my destination was obvious. I park, take Dad's urn out of the suitcase and pop it in my backpack, just in case I have a sudden urge to scatter him here. Then I head for the lighthouse; so old, so sturdy and wind-battered, still standing up to the elements.

When I came here with Dad, on our detour from the UEA open day, I had yet to study geography, let alone cover the subject of coastal erosion with a classroom full of kids. If you want to see it in reality, go to Happisburgh. I don't recall where the land ended on my last visit, but it must have retreated incrementally since then, crumbling away, inch by inch, day by day. When (or if) I go back to teaching, I really should bring my students here, to see for themselves what the wrath of the sea can do.

It's weird and a bit loopy, I know it is, to sit on the grass with Dad beside me. I have no cheese-and-Branston sandwiches. No bread pudding made by Mum. No frantic dash to Norwich afterwards to check out the university . . . which I decided not to study at anyway.

Just Dad and me and the North Sea, here, now, sitting on my spread-out jean jacket. And a big gaping hole in my life where he should still be. Like the Happisburgh coastline, he's inching away from me, day by day. Will my memory of his face – his over-exuberant eyebrows and that slight chin dimple – will that memory crumble away too? Coming to Happy's Berg maybe wasn't such a great idea. Please may I rename it Sad Berg?

The clouds darken to grey and a shiver runs through me. I haul myself up from the damp grass and shake out my jacket. If I wasn't sure before, I am now. I have no choice. If I scatter Dad here, I end our time together and I'm not ready to do that.

I know I can't take him to *every* sea area because some of them are just that: areas of sea, like Sole, Bailey and Forties.

And some are attached to other countries and will make the trip much more complicated and costly, like Fitzroy, Biscay and German Bight. So, together, we'll cover every sea area of our coastline. I feel a pang of guilt that I can't do all thirty-one but I couldn't bear to fail; fourteen feels at least do-able.

'Mum's bread pudding was brilliant, wasn't it, Dad?' I say out loud as I pack him away. That whole day was brilliant. Just me and him going on an adventure. I could have done without the non-stop Dr Feelgood though.

I can almost hear his reply: 'That's proper music, Miss Lummox. Listen and learn, listen and learn.'

What's to stay for in Happisburgh, pretty though it is? I've done what I needed to do. An hour later, I'm checked into a room above a pub in Bungay, on the Norfolk/Suffolk borders. While my few grubby clothes get soaked and spun in the nearby launderette, I wolf down fish and chips on a bench under an ornate shelter called the Butter Cross and ignore a small gang of disaffected youth who want me gone so that they can sit here, as they probably do most nights.

They cycle and circle round each other in some kind of ancient mating ritual. The girls ignore the boys, the boys ignore the girls. Kim and I did just the same outside Burger King. We ignored Malcolm Robbins and Chris Walling. (We should have kept ignoring them.) The world keeps turning . . .

My Sadburgh sadness won't shift. Watching the shyest girl in the group smile at the cockiest boy, seeing them slouch off together down the deserted high street, feigning lack of interest, I wonder if they know what they're letting themselves in for. Be nice, I want to tell them. Don't sing in the car, just to wind him up. Don't play games. Don't cause pain.

Don't take something bad and make it even worse.

I resist an urge to ring Rob. He'll be with Fi, doing all the couply stuff you do together when you've only just hooked up and the novelty has yet to wear off: midweek meals out, Netflix and chill on the sofa, shagging every which way instead of *Newsnight*. They won't have started farting in front of each other yet or having stand-up rows in Ikea or finishing the milk without asking. They won't have lost that first glow of 'Phew, I'm not single any more'. Yep, they'll definitely be shagging now. We were, at every opportunity, when we first got together.

I can't phone Rob. So I phone Kate. She picks up on the first ring and sounds disappointed that it's me.

'Annie. You're still alive then.'

'Kate. You're still grumpy then.'

She sighs, as if she really doesn't need this right now. 'I'm tired, that's all. Plus I thought you were someone else. I'm waiting on a call from – a colleague. So how the heck are you, stranger?'

O-kay. This conversation isn't going to lift my spirits or shrug off my sadness. I wonder why I bothered.

'I'm fine. I'm in Bungay. That's sea area Humber. Off to sea area Thames tomorrow. Quite possibly Canvey Island because of Dr Feelgood. Because they came from Canvey Island.'

'You what?'

'Dad reckoned they were the best band ever. You must remember that?'

'The Gospel according to Dad. He also loved salami but that doesn't mean you have to trek off to—wherever salami comes from.'

'Italy.'

'I can't believe you're seriously still doing this.'

'We agreed that Dad would have wanted me to. We did, Kate.'

'I was humouring you.'

'Why are you being such a cow?'

'Because you're being such a child, stomping off like that. You'll still be throwing your toys out of the pram when you're on a Zimmer frame.'

I hang up. I don't need this. I leave the shelter of the Butter Cross and return to the launderette to retrieve my clothes from the tumble dryer. The remaining disaffected youth reclaim their bench and make just-within-earshot snarky comments about me as I retreat. But I *do* have a lard arse, so I can't argue.

My room at the pub is even cosier than the B&B in Cromarty, probably because it's not heaving with nautical knick-knacks. The bed is hard, just how I like it, the towels are soft and there's a kettle and the usual cocoa sachet to go with some pre-sleep knitting. This maroon 'wool' may be synthetic but it slides from needle to needle like a dream. Or maybe I'm finally learning to slacken off on my tension. A lesson for life . . .

I've just turned off the bedside light, a good hour before the Shipping Forecast, when my phone rings. It's Kate.

'I'm sorry, An-An. You're right. I *was* a cow.'

'You really were.'

There's a long pause at the other end. 'This isn't a great time for me right now,' she finally admits. 'And not just because of Dad.'

I can only imagine she's being given the runaround by her latest married man. I stopped asking ages ago. Her business, not mine. But maybe this time, she wants me to.

'Is it, um, Rory?'

Her laugh is hollow. 'Rory's ancient history. Remind me to tell you about Rory some time. Sheesh, what a charmer he turned out to be.'

Another pause. I wait.

'I've just come back from a work thing in Coventry. Overnight. Work's a bit fraught at the mo. Nothing I can't deal with but, well, it's all a bit fraught.'

'Tell me, Katkin. Maybe I can help.'

'You! Hardly!' She actually bursts out laughing.

I am shocked and hurt into silence. Where did that come from?

'I'm sorry,' she says, sounding calmer. 'I didn't ring to have a go. Bit of a shit apology, isn't it?'

'I've heard nicer.'

'It's just, I'm still not convinced you should be doing this. This trip around Britain. Are you sure it's helping? Because if it isn't, you need to come home first thing tomorrow.'

'I'm not sure,' I reply. Because, honestly, I'm not. 'But I'm not ready to come home.'

'If that's how you feel.'

'You know what would help, Kate? What would really, really help.'

'Go on,' she prompts cautiously.

'Come to Canvey Island. Do the next bit *with* me. Please, Katkin. It would help us both.'

'Of course I can't come with you,' she snaps. 'Have you even listened to what I've been saying? About work being difficult right now. I can't take time away. I just can't.'

'Not even one measly day?'

'No! This is your project, not mine. I'm sorry if I'm still being a cow. That wasn't my intention. But no, I absolutely can't join you. Now, let's both get some sleep, okay.'

I lie in bed rerunning our conversation. Was I wrong to invite her to join me? Why is she so bitter and brittle? We're both grieving, but can't we process it better together?

Chapter Thirteen

Thames

It's an easy drive to Essex. My phone estimates it will take two hours and it does. I declined my breakfast in Bungay, just wanting to be on the road, so the sausage sandwich and mug of coffee at a pitstop near Needham Market are just the ticket. There are short stretches of pretty village and windy road on the first leg of the journey but, once I'm on the A14, skirting past Ipswich, Colchester, Chelmsford, it's just mindless dual carriageway. I can do mindless, with the help of Radio 2.

Canvey Island really is an island. I had no idea. But once you've driven over the thin stretch of water that separates it from the 'mainland', you could be in any densely built suburb. I don't know what I'm looking for or where best to take in the essence of Essex so I drive until I reach the far coast, which doesn't take too long. I park by a low-key fairground, optimistically called Fantasy Island. Despite the bracing, salty wind, it's far from deserted: dog walkers, cyclists, a noisy bunch of Orthodox Jewish children chasing each other.

A rock-solid wall keeps back the sea. Once you're the other side of it, Canvey Island disappears behind a faded,

Sue Teddern

peeling mural in episodic form which tells the tale of the floods of 1953. It's actually quite moving.

I sit on one of the benches and watch two massive container ships approach and pass each other on the Thames estuary, like two trucks on a B road. Dad would have loved this. I wonder if he ever came here . . .

I wish I had a dog; everyone else walking the length of the sea wall seems to have one. A creaky Jack Russell with grey whiskers and a pot belly waddles over to sniff my shoe. Some dogs smile and this one is positively beaming.

'Sorry love, she's a right tart, my Olga.' A wiry man in his seventies, in a flat cap and fake fur-trimmed parka sits down next to me with a pained sigh. 'Cor dear, I don't know whose arthritis is more of a bugger. Hers or mine.'

He cuts Olga some slack on the lead so that she can sniff bench legs and get in the path of a pair of power walkers and their Nordic poles.

'Why's she called Olga?' I ask. Obvious question really.

He chuckles. 'Don't tell my late wife. Not that you could anyway because she died five years ago. Olga was a girlfriend from when I was in the Merchant Navy, long before I got married. Linda, that's my late wife, she thinks we named her after Olga Korbut. You know? That nippy little Russian gymnast from the '72 Olympics. Now look at her. About as nippy as a sack of spuds, bless her.'

Olga emits a weary grunt and takes the weight off under the bench, occasionally sniffing my shoe in case she's missed anything.

'We do this every afternoon, rain or shine,' the man says. 'Dogs keep you fit. You ever had a dog?'

'A cat.'

'Never saw the point. Neither use nor ornament.'

134

I'm not having that. 'Cromarty's part of the family. As was Flo before him.'

'If you say so.' He isn't convinced.

We gaze out at the container ships that have – at long last – passed each other. It's impossible to sense their size or speed from here. They look like moving shopping malls.

'Why's your cat called Cromarty?' the man asks.

'My dad was potty about the Shipping Forecast.'

'Was *he* a sailor and all?'

'Not even remotely. He lived in St Albans. As landlocked as you can get. He just liked the names, the rhythm . . . Sole, Fastnet, Shannon, Rockall.'

'He might not have been such a fan in a Force 8 off Biscay. Rough as old Harry.'

I nod to the mural behind us, with a panel listing the lives lost from the North Sea floods: Netherlands, England, Belgium . . . 'You can't have been born when that happened.'

'I bloody was. I was 4. We lost our telly.'

'Your telly?'

He looks so pleased to explain. 'We was still living in Leyton. My dad bought one of the first tellies. Size of a small shed. Anyway, it went on the blink and his cousin Ken, who lived on the island, he said he could fix it. So Dad drove it down and left it with him. All our family survived the floods, thank God, but the telly got swept away. Could have been a lot worse. It was for some. Fifty-eight drowned on Canvey alone. Terrible business. This sea wall is like a shrine to them.'

He sighs, as if he still can't quite fathom the enormity of it. 'Linda and I moved here from Becontree when I retired. And then she died. But I thought, Sod it, I'm going nowhere. It suits me, this place. And, well, here I am. Me and Olga.'

I nearly take his hand. I so want to. Instead I divert it to patting Olga's warm little head which has caught the sun. She snorts her appreciation, then re-settles behind her owner's feet, safe from the occasional cyclist.

'So you weren't here in the early nineties? You were still in Becontree?'

'Not living here, no, love, but visiting. Why d'you ask?'

'My dad loved the Shipping Forecast *and* Dr Feelgood. I just wondered if you'd known any of them, Lee Brilleaux, Wilko Johnson and the rest. Canvey's such a small place.'

It's as if I've suddenly plugged him into the mains. He sits forward on the bench and his eyes shine with enthusiasm.

'I wish! Only the best bloody band ever, bar none. I'm starting to like your dad. I'm guessing he's not with us any more, right?'

I nod. 'He died last month.'

'Sorry to upset you, love. Me and my size 10s.'

I shake my head, to clear the tears. 'You didn't. Anything but. I reckoned he'd have liked you too.'

Olga wakes with a start. A poodle, plus owner, is passing by and territorial rights need to be established. She barks with a fury you wouldn't expect from such a mature dog. The moment is broken.

The man pulls himself to his feet, groaning again. 'Bloody arthritis. God's way of telling you that lad in the Merchant Navy is just a folk memory.'

'Course not. He's right here.'

'In your dreams, love. In your dreams. Anyway, nice chatting with you. Come on, Olga.' He gives a wave and they head off, Olga looking up at him every so often for reassurance.

I stay for a while. Adrian at the Airbnb in Leigh-on-Sea asked if I could check in after five so I'm in no hurry. And then my phone rings. It's Kate. Is she calling to apologize – again – or to have another go at me? Shall I even answer? I give it a couple of rings but I can't not.

'Annie, are you in Canvey yet?'

'Yes. Why?'

'My train's just pulling in to South Benfleet station. That's the nearest I could get. So . . . are you going to pick me up or just leave me here?'

The Airbnb turns out to be a well-appointed loft conversion with views across the estuary. We have a big double bed, a dinky little en suite, a microwave and a kettle. Adrian and Jonny, our hosts, assume we're a couple. I'm not fussed what they think, but Kate's super-keen to set them, quite literally, straight.

'We're sisters. We're not, you know, together. Well, we are but not like that. We're sisters.'

Adrian beams. 'We're the last ones to judge, hun. Now, there's home-made sourdough rolls and raspberry conserve in the garden room at 8 a.m., if you fancy it. I'll leave you to settle yourselves in.'

Kate kicks off her shoes and lies on the bed. I climb out of my trainers, chuck a stack of Orla Kiely cushions to one side and join her. It feels like being on a therapist's couch for two. Maybe we can talk to each other without eye-rolls and sarcasm if we're both staring at the ceiling.

'You said things were too fraught at work for you to come,' I ask tentatively.

'They are. I pulled a sickie. Apparently I've got a terrible migraine, I've been sick three times and I can't even open my blinds.'

This is a first for Kate. If she lost both legs in a freak

skiing accident, she'd still wheel herself into work on a supermarket trolley. She's slim, bordering on skinny, because she skips lunch to finish an urgent report or plough through emails. She works at a small start-up software company and I reckon the couple who started it up – Ros and Ross – take advantage of her loyalty. But she doesn't mind.

'It means a lot that you came, Katkin. Oh crikey, you don't want us to scatter Dad's ashes tomorrow, do you? Off Southend Pier? I'm not ready to say goodbye to him yet.'

'Course not. I'm a completist. You know I don't like things unfinished, like when I had to read every Harry Potter. So I totally get that you want Dad to visit all the Shipping Forecast. I really do, An-An.'

I explain that, in actual fact, I can't possibly take him to *every* sea area because it's just too ambitious and unwieldy. But if Dad and I can work our way round the Scottish, English and Welsh coastline, ignoring Ireland, that will reduce the stops from thirty-one to fourteen. So that's what I'm doing and I think he'd approve. Kate agrees, right?

She doesn't reply. Is she taking issue with my assessment of the situation? Does she think I'd be letting Dad down if we don't make it to either Utsire? No. She's fast asleep. She'll be annoyed that she's nodded off in her Toast linen jacket, but what's a crease or two? Merely an acknowledgement that she doesn't have to achieve perfection 24/7. Me, I've never had that problem.

She wakes with a start an hour later, has a shower and changes into tight cropped chinos and a white T-shirt. She really is effortlessly stylish and extraordinarily gorgeous. Mum and Dad were just practising parenthood on me, ironing out the glitches for Daughter Number Two, who is everything I'm not.

We walk into downtown Southend. It excels at a tackiness that Scarborough can only aspire to. The naff souvenir shops, banging arcades and lairy theme pubs are cocky and brazen. They don't give a stuff what any bugger thinks. You don't come to Southend-on-Sea for subtlety and nuance. 'If you don't feckin' like us, jog on.'

Kate has a sudden urge for curry. She normally takes little interest in what she eats so I'm more than happy to indulge her. If we over-order – which we do – we can always warm up the doggy-bagged leftovers for breakfast in our micro-wave. Welcome to *my* world.

We glug down our Kingfisher beers, I karate-chop a pile of poppadoms into manageable pieces and we're off. This is so great, eating out in a proper restaurant with my baby sister. I can't help wondering why it's such a novelty. What stopped us going for a balti in St Albans? Why must we be far away to be close?

'This is so great,' I say out loud as I smear mango chutney on to a shard of poppadom.

'The pickle's a bit vicious.'

'I meant us. This. Being all sisterly in Southend. I'm really glad you came.'

'Yeah, well. I didn't have much choice.'

'I asked nicely, Kate. I didn't bloody force you here.'

She stops eating and does one of her humourless laughs. I am about to be bollocked.

'An-An, this may come as a shock, but the world doesn't revolve around you. I needed to be somewhere else and Canvey Island, Southend, wherever we are, was as good a place as any. More a case of self-preservation than visiting sea area – which one is it again?'

'Thames.'

'Thames. That's it. Shall I order more beers? God, I must have been thirsty.'

Kate does one of those international hand signals to the waiter and two more beers appear. I am chastened, silenced. Self-preservation? From what? Does she want me to ask or will I be told off for being too nosy?

She pours her beer and finds her voice. 'I said things were a bit shit at work, didn't I.'

'Fraught. You said fraught.'

'It started at fraught, moved on to shit and now, and now, I am in Olympic-level, A-grade, proper fucked-up-big-time territory.' Her voice wobbles. This sounds serious.

'I told you we had a meeting in Coventry. Presentation to a new client. Ros and Ross wanted me along because apparently I add gravitas. So there was me, Ros, Ross and Charlie, our production manager. And we were put up in a nice hotel. Nice meal out, nice company. All very . . . nice. And then I ruined it. I ruined everything.'

My mind fills with possibilities. Kate's idea of ruining everything could be using the fish knife on steak or spilling her wine. She doesn't cut herself much slack.

'Well, go on. What? How?'

'After the meal, one of the Coventry people suggested a club so me and Charlie and a couple of them said yes. Ros and Ross looked a bit disapproving but I didn't care because I'd had two gin and tonics, three glasses of wine and a brandy. And, well, I got a bit uninhibited.'

'You went dancing? So? Dancing isn't a sackable offence.' I think of Kim and me, plus two businessmen, strutting our stuff in that deserted hotel bar in Scarborough. Dancing makes you feel alive. How can that be bad for someone as buttoned-up as Kate?

She slugs back another gulp of beer. She's working up to something.

'I slept with Charlie.'

'Ah.'

'I've always been scrupulous about keeping work and relationships separate. So that if it goes tits up, I don't have to face them every day. Plus you lose status, authority, if someone's seen you in, well, you know, in . . .'

'In the nuddy?'

'In an intimate context, I was going to say.'

Kate really does look shaken. Okay, it's not great but it's hardly the end of the world. I slept with my boss when I had the City job. More than once, as I recall. If anything, it shifted me one rung higher up the corporate ladder.

'Is Charlie discreet?' I ask. 'Can it stay your little secret?'

'I don't know. Yes. Probably.'

'Well, stop worrying then. If it doesn't affect your work relationship, you'll be fine, Kate. It takes two to tango. He's probably shitting bricks that he got rat-arsed and slept with the PR manager.'

'Charlie isn't a "he".'

I don't take it in when she says it the first time. She looks pained.

'I said, Charlie isn't a "he". He's a she. I don't know what I was thinking. I don't know who I am, Annie. I don't know any more.'

We park the conversation for an hour or two. I'm keen to dig deeper as Kate rarely, if ever, lets her defences down and does something so spontaneous . . . and so primal. But she's said enough for now and I don't want to push: even telling me this much is a personal best for her. I know about previous relationships but she's never been in full confessional mode before. She'd just throw out selected scraps of information for me to tack together. She was always in total control of how much I knew and what I was supposed to think.

This Charlie thing is totally new territory so it's best if I leave her to navigate, rather than steer her somewhere she doesn't want to go. I'm actually rather impressed with how sensitively I'm dealing with this. I'm being a proper big sister and I like it.

After our waistband-expanding curry, we go for a wander and find ourselves at the Southend Kursaal. We get a fiver's worth of two-pence pieces and feed them into a Penny Falls machine, always a favourite when we were kids. We won bugger all then too.

And now, here we are, lying alongside each other in our Airbnb bed. It's pitch dark, save for a stripe of moonlight under the blind. We're both wide awake, regretting that final scraping of sag aloo. With no eye contact possible, maybe we can pick up where we left off. I don't start with Charlie, though. I'm not daft.

'You said you'd tell me about Rory some time. How about now?'

Kate inhales deeply. In her current emotional turmoil, she'd forgotten about him. 'Ah, Rory. What a shit!'

I turn on the bedside light. 'Would this work better with a cup of cocoa? Look, they've given us two sachets.'

'On top of all that spicy food? Seriously, Annie?' Two seconds later: 'Oh, go on then.'

This must be our very first pyjama party, although I'm in my Boyzone T-shirt and a pair of Rob's boxers and Kate's in something silky, chemise-y and classy. We sit cross-legged on the bed, over-stirring our cocoa, and Kate begins.

'Well, you know my CV on the relationship front. I always pick unsuitable men or men who are already spoken for: Asif . . . Julian . . . that shitty little French toad who will remain nameless. So, when Rory said he was unhappily married, I believed him.'

'That he was unhappy?'

'That he was married. It was starting to get serious. You know, more than just a shag, talking about the future. And he kept saying if only he could leave his wife and his daughter but Sarah was so emotionally unstable and poor little Holly or Polly or Molly or whatever had special needs and relied hugely on him.

'He made me want him because he was unavailable and then it turned out he was lying through his teeth. No Sarah, no kid, no cute cat called Scampi with a bent tail. Just a photo of his cousin's wife and kid in his wallet, in case he needed to make a fast getaway. And then, can you believe it, when I found out, *he* dumped *me*!'

'Perhaps Charlie was a reaction to that,' I suggest. 'You know, to show Rory – and men in general – that you didn't need him?'

'Wouldn't that be convenient? Don't be daft. Course not, An-An. Charlie was a spur-of-the-moment thing. She knew exactly what she was doing. I didn't. But I was pissed and I wanted to see it through, to see how it made me feel.'

'And?'

'You're not getting every sleazy detail.'

'I don't *want* every sleazy detail, whether it's Charlie, Rory or that chinless boy scout you dated when you were 12. Eeeuw!'

'Sorry.'

She does look genuinely sorry. Sometimes Kate has no

idea who I am, just a version of me that suits her narrative.

'All I meant was . . . was this thing with Charlie just . . . a thing? Or a thing with a future.'

'Hardly. Not least because I work with her. She's out and proud to Ros and Ross and everyone. What if she tells someone about us? What if they find out? What will they think of me?'

I'm lost. What is Kate concerned about? Her privacy? Her sexuality? Her non-adherence to work protocol?

'Do you want to know what I think?' I ask.

'No. Yes. Only if you're on my side.'

'Now you're being ridiculous. I'm hardly rooting for Charlie, am I? What I think is: this is only an issue at work if you make it one. Pretend it's no biggie but don't do it again . . . unless you want to. *Do* you want to?'

Her instant reply takes a second or two longer than it should. 'It will never happen again. Not with another co-worker and certainly not with Charlie. That was a one-off, a mistake. I've drawn a line and moved on. Now I'm really tired and I think we should both get some sleep. God, I feel stuffed. Why did you make me have that cocoa?'

Next morning, I put away two of Jonny's sourdough rolls with fat pats of butter and Adrian's amazing raspberry conserve. Kate has a black coffee. We sit in the garden room, looking out on to a stunning garden: manicured, but not precious, cottagey but not chocolate-boxy.

It's easier to talk to Adrian about his Japanese acer and artfully random raised beds than it is to talk to my sister, whose face says: Don't go there. I mean it, Annie.

So I don't.

Chapter Fourteen

Dover

I've yet to make plans for the next leg of my journey with Dad. But Kate's ready to go home and assess how much shit has hit the fan, possibly thrown by Charlie. I could return the hire car and catch a train to London with her, then another one back down to the next sea area . . . Dover. But she's reverted to closed-up Kate again and I'd be unfeasibly dense not to pick up that she wants to be alone.

En route to Benfleet station, where I collected her only yesterday, I spot a little wool shop; I have yet to buy a ball in Thames. I tell Kate to keep an eye out for any parking wardens, dash into the shop, hastily select some salmon-pink yarn and slam a handful of coins on the counter.

'Why?' asks Kate, when I try to explain my project to her, starting with my encounter with the knitting club in Cromarty. She gazes out of the window as I tell her about it and the beautiful wool I bought in Edinburgh and the corner-to-corner knitting lesson from the woman on the train. She's not remotely interested.

I wait with her on the platform at Benfleet station for the imminent Fenchurch Street train. I've bought her a bag of humbugs, 'sucky sweets' for the journey. As kids, we never set off on any long drive without them; Dad indulged us, Mum worried that too many sweets would rot our teeth. I want my nostalgic gesture to make her smile and it does, but it's a sad smile and it makes me sad too.

'It'll be fine, Kate,' I say, giving her arm a squeeze.

'And you know that for certain because . . .?'

'Because you always bob up smelling of roses. I'm the fuck-up around here, the Stanley sister who digs herself a dirty great hole and jumps right in. You'll be fine.'

She nods to herself, as if she's been weighing up options all night. 'If Charlie's said anything to Ros and Ross, it's too late. If she hasn't, there's still time to tell her not to.'

'Why would she?'

'I don't know.'

'Even if she does, who cares? Listen, Katkin. You love your job and they love you. You know they do. It's 2019, not 1919. Who cares who people sleep with any more? Nobody, that's who. You can be whoever you want to be. It's totally up to you.'

The train approaches. The few post-commute passengers on the platform gather their bags, look up from their phones and position themselves by opening doors.

'Meaning?' Kate glares at me.

I'm not sure what I mean. I'm just trying to find some reassuring words to send her on her way. I've enjoyed being the Wise One and it's gone to my head.

'There's nothing wrong with being a lesbian,' I say. Because there isn't.

Kate throws her big pouchy leather bag over her shoulder and gets on the train. She doesn't even hug me goodbye, not that she was ever one of life's huggers.

As the doors close, she shouts: 'I am not a lesbian.'

It's a grand exit but perhaps not the one she had in mind. As the train pulls away, I see her trying to decide which fellow passengers heard her and who not to sit near.

I really was trying to help, to be the big sister who finds just the right words to reassure, comfort, to take away the worry. But I failed. I took something bad – in Kate's eyes anyway – and made it even worse.

Big mouth strikes again.

Sea area Dover stretches from the tip of Kent, just north of Broadstairs, to Beachy Head in East Sussex. That means I need to drive from Essex to Kent, then on to Sussex for my next sea area stopover. Dungeness? Duncan and I spent a weekend there when we first got together at university. Or Pevensey Bay Nature Reserve where I took a bunch of kids on a field trip? Eastbourne, maybe, or Hastings? I'm fairly sure an old colleague of mine, who walked out of her City job, moved to Hastings. Last I heard, she'd retrained as a psychotherapist. I bet I could find her on Facebook. Hastings is as good as anywhere – a bit faded, a bit funky. I think Dad would like it.

But right now, I'm feeling raw and stupid after screwing up my time with Kate. I don't need a psychotherapist to analyse my exposed nerve endings and give me a brutal diagnosis. I got that with knobs on from Duncan. I dismissed it at the time but now I can't shake it out of my head. Making bad things even worse must be my default setting, from Kim onwards. It's what I do. And yep, I've only gone and done it again.

I head for the Dartford Crossing, with *Woman's Hour* for company on the car radio. I learn about child mortality in

Mozambique and how to make kale pesto. Honestly, why would anyone do that? I attempt to follow episode six of a serial featuring a feisty woman cop who has missed out on promotion to her abusive ex. And he's rubbing her nose in it. I have no idea what's going on. I stop for a loo break, leg-stretch and coffee fix at Thurrock services.

Kate's phone goes straight to voicemail when I attempt to check in with her. Mum used to tell Dad off for 'bambling', which was a cross between rambling and burbling. I leave her a bambling message, hoping she's okay, hoping work will be okay, hoping that she really is okay. I end with 'love you, Katkin' and hang up before I can hope she's okay again.

There's a text from Rob: 'Call me asap.' And another: 'Annie, where are you?' And a third: 'I rang Kate. She told me what you're doing. Please call me.'

I call him. He picks up on the second ring. 'Annie? For fuck's sake, what's with the disappearing act?'

'I haven't disappeared. I'm right here. I'm just not in St Albans, that's all.'

'Where's here?'

'Thurrock services. Where are you?'

'Berkhamsted. Installing a bespoke kitchen for a pair of sarky, stingy whingers. I nearly walked off the job yesterday.'

'But you didn't. Well done you.'

'Yeah, well. It is what it is.' He sucks air through his teeth, a habit that used to drive me mad. But right now, I warm to the familiarity of it.

'Are you okay, Annie? Kate says you are, but she was in a rush, couldn't talk for long.'

'I'm fine, Rob. I really am.'

I hear him put his hand over the receiver and shout. 'Ooh,

lovely. Two sugars, please, Gill, and a splash of milk.' Then, softly, to me: 'Wouldn't put it past her to spit in it. We had words this morning about repositioning the island unit.'

'Spit or maybe washing-up liquid. So that she can pretend she hasn't rinsed your cup properly. That's what *I'd* do.'

Rob laughs. 'You bloody would and all. So. You stole your dad's urn from Bev and made off to— where did you make off to?'

'Cromarty, north of Inverness. And now you're going to tell me I've behaved appallingly and I should be ashamed of myself and I must return Dad's ashes to Bev asap before I make a bad thing worse.'

He laughs. 'Oh, you're way past "worse", Annie Lummox. You can't even see "worse" from where you are. At Thurrop services.'

'Thurrock. Well, go on then. Give me a bollocking. I'm all ready for it.'

'I won't. Want to know why?'

'Go on then.'

I hear clickety-clackety footsteps. Rob puts his hand over the receiver again. 'Cheers, Gill. Ooh, *and* a KitKat. Spoilt or what.' He waits till she click-clacks away.

'I won't give you a bollocking because I think it's bloody brilliant.'

'You do?'

'A hundred per cent. Bev's a nice woman and everything. She made your dad happy and she's lost without him. Well, we all are, obviously. But this feels right. When Kate told me, I saw my face in my rear-view mirror and I was grinning from here to here.'

'Ear to ear, you prat. You grinned, Rob? Really?' I feel my chin quivering.

'He was your dad and you want to do right by him. Which you did at the funeral when they played 'Sailing By'. God, that was emotional. And now this. This is so—so perfect, Annie. I'm dead impressed. Honestly.'

I can't find the words to respond. Rob totally gets it, just like he totally 'got' Dad.

And then he spits in my teacup. 'Fi thinks it's brilliant too. Obviously she never met Peter but she wanted me to tell you well done and she can't wait to meet you.'

'Fi. Terrific. Tell her thank you.'

'I will.'

There's a long pause as my bubble slowly deflates. Fi says well done and can't wait to meet me. Don't hold your breath, love.

'I'd better get back to work,' Rob sighs, breaking the silence. 'I'll probably be invoiced for the biscuit as it is. You take care, Annie. Ring me any time. Let me know how things are in Fisher and Faeroes or wherever you're heading.'

I don't bother telling him that Dad and I aren't visiting those sea areas. 'Bye then, Rob. Thanks for worrying about me.'

'Laters, Lummox.' He hangs up.

I sip the now cold Americano and take a bite out of my impulse-buy flapjack. I see myself sitting here, all alone in Thurrock services, and I want to cry.

My phone rings. It's Rob again. 'Annie, I've got a huge favour to ask. You can say no and I'll totally understand.'

'What? Tell me what it is first.'

'You know my godmother? Hilary. She moved into supported housing in Bexhill in March. Wanted to spend her final years by the sea. So she gave away her precious piano and most of her furniture, upped sticks and left Leighton Buzzard. We were gobsmacked.'

I remember Hilary. Retired headmistress. Wire-framed specs. Severe grey bob. In fact, that was my nickname for her, for Rob's ears only. Scary as fuck.

'I promised I'd visit her next week but this job's running me ragged and they'll sack me if I take time off. If you're passing, would you pop in on her for me? Just so's I know she's settled in all right. It would really take a weight off my mind.'

So now I have a destination. I never warmed to Hilary because she never warmed to me. She probably preferred Rob's ex-wife, Maggie. I will swing by Bexhill, though, and make the house call because I said I would. I can't *not* do it just because he suddenly started going on about Fi. Why shouldn't he? She's his girlfriend. Me not visiting Hilary just to get at Fi would be childish, daft and pointless. I need to be better than that. Then again, I could always give Bexhill a detour and tell Rob that Hilary was out when I rang her doorbell.

Once in Kent, and then Sussex, the signposts on the A21 keep tempting me to head for Hastings. But I ignore them. I *will* do this. I *will* go to Bexhill. I will take a bad thing – Rob and Fi – and make it better by checking in on Hilary.

While I drive the last leg, passing the vineyards at Lamberhurst and the abbey at Battle, I try to work through my resentment towards Fi, who I expect is a perfectly pleasant woman. I ended it with Rob because I knew I was sinking and I didn't want to drag him down with me. And not just that . . .

When we first met, I still hadn't given up on motherhood. But he had Josh and he didn't feel the same urge. We never really talked about it because I sensed from the start how he felt about having more kids. We should have talked. Why didn't we? After we parted, I knew it was unlikely that I'd meet someone who was keen to start a family but I needed that time apart from Rob to think it through, so stupidly certain that he'd be there, waiting for me, when I was ready to go back to him.

I desperately missed him but I didn't want him to love me out of obligation or pity. My only plan was to let him know when I was back in the real world and did he fancy meeting for a drink some time?

But while I was hibernating on my sofa, watching daytime telly or taking myself off to senior screenings at the cinema, while I was living in stained T-shirt and leggings, mainlining Tunnock's teacakes, he met someone he could see a proper future with.

It's hardly Fi's fault. But, for the time being, I'll settle on resenting her.

Hilary's supported housing development is called Beach View Point, which feels like one word too many . . . It looks purpose-built and very new; a gardener is still laying turf in one of the manicured lawns beside the car park. It smells new too . . . fresh paint and pristine lino in the communal corridors and a huge flower arrangement by the lifts which looks fake but isn't.

The father of one of my teacher pals moved into sheltered housing and it wasn't cheap. Lots of hidden extras that he didn't realize he'd signed up to, poor guy. I don't see anyone fleecing Hilary. They wouldn't dare.

All the front doors are the same colour – an uncontroversial magnolia – but residents have made an effort to personalize their own. A pair of china wellies packed with geraniums outside Flat 4 . . . a distressed wooden 'Life's a Beach' sign on twine, hanging from the door knob of Flat 6.

Hilary lives in Flat 8, at the end of the corridor. No cutesy knick-knacks or massed ranks of plant pots for her. Just a sisal doormat printed with the words: Paz, Paix, Shalom, Pace, Siochain, Vrede, Pau, Peace. Yes, this'll be her place. She's a great one for faded CND tote bags, feminist mugs and political posters.

As a clumsy teen, Josh broke the handle off her favourite Cambridge folk festival mug. He thought she'd be furious but she told him it was silly to become attached to things because they're just . . . things. 'Don't be a mug about a mug!' she chortled. Josh and Rob always quoted her every time something got broken after that.

I ring the doorbell long and hard. The last time I saw Hilary, she was refusing to wear her new hearing aid. I give it twenty seconds, then knock on the door with my knuckles. Still no reply. Even though I ought to be relieved that she's not here and now I don't have to lie to Rob, a small part of me is slightly disappointed. I'm curious now. How did she end up here? It couldn't be more un-Hilary-ish. What on earth was she thinking?

There's no point in slipping a note under her door. Better she doesn't know I was here than finds out she missed me. I head back down the corridor, wondering where I'll go now. Back to Plan A. Hastings then. I might even look up my old work friend, see if she's got a sofa bed. I really can't face another hotel or B&B, even though Dad and I are barely halfway through our grand tour. I'm trying to stick to a budget, but every day on the road costs money, not least a bed for the night.

As I pass Flat 6 – 'Life's a Beach' – the front door opens and a woman peers out. Her hair is peroxide blonde and beehived into a rock-hard pompom. Her face has the colour and texture of a gingernut. She's dressed in a jungle-print kaftan and glittery platform flip-flops.

'Can I help?' she asks.

'I was looking for Hilary in Flat 8. She's my – her godson used to be my – I'm an old friend from Leighton Buzzard.'

'Oh, she does *have* friends then? I was beginning to wonder.'

'I was just passing through Bexhill, hoped to say hello. Maybe next time, eh? Anyway, sorry to disturb you.' I head for the exit.

'It would be a shame if you missed her. You see, she's taking a while to settle in.'

I reach the end of the corridor but I can feel her awaiting a response. Rob would expect me to respond. I turn and return.

'I'm Toni, by the way,' she tells me and holds out a hand to be shaken.

'Annie. Pleased to meet you.'

'I'd invite you in only I'm making nibbles for our bridge club. I say "making". M&S did the donkey work.'

'Best not then. Especially if you've got those mini Yorkshire puds with horseradish. I'd scoff the lot.'

Toni titters, not sure if I'm joking. 'I expect you'll find Hilary at the De La Warr. I often seen her there when I'm passing.'

My face says 'huh?'

'On the seafront. Big building. You can't miss it. Now I'd better get on. They're due in half an hour.'

She beams lipsticked teeth and closes her front door.

I must have driven past the De La Warr on my way into Bexhill and, despite what Toni said, I really did miss it. It's a glorious Art Deco pavilion, all curved and sleek, with wide expanses of glass. I park and enter. I'm very hungry and a sign announces a cafe upstairs. But my first priority is to find Hilary.

On the sea side of the building, there are lawns, a watery play area for over-excited kids and dogs, and a strange modern structure that could possibly be a bandstand. It's a warm day so it's already busy with Bexhill folk taking the air or going for a run. If I lived by the sea, I'd do that too and get properly fit for the first time in my life.

If I lived by the sea, I might also finally commit to dog ownership, as compensation for not having kids, and take it for a run with me every morning, rain or shine. Unless it was pissing down, obviously. Running seems do-able if you live by the sea. It would never occur to me to put on my fit kit and do a quick circuit of St Albans or run that pretty route to Tyttenhanger, where Rob and I often went for a Saturday amble and sandwich at the pub on the green.

My stomach is now roaring for sustenance, ideally something that comes with a stack of fat chips and no salad garnish. I honestly think I've made enough effort to find Hilary. My conscience is clear. And then I spot a hidden deck, below the main outside area, which is less Art Deco and more Greco-Roman. More eating and shopping opportunities. More toddlers, more dogs.

And there, wrapped in a purple fleece and Palestinian scarf, ensconced on a mobility scooter and staring stoically out to sea, is Hilary's distinctive Prince Valiant hairstyle to hide her hearing aid: I have found Severe Grey Bob.

She hasn't seen me and isn't expecting me. For one final moment I think about getting back in my car and heading for Hastings. But she looks so forlorn and vulnerable sitting there, fringe flapping in the wind, chin out, that I can't walk on by. I approach at a diagonal, beaming a friendly smile. I don't want to give her a heart attack.

'Oh, you came, then,' she says, as I reach her. 'Robin WhatsApped to say you might, but I thought you'd steer well clear.'

'Absolutely not. I told Rob I would and here I am. I wanted to pop by and say hi, Hilary. So, yes, well, um . . . hi.' I flush with guilt. Has she read my mind?

'How did you know where to find me? Even I didn't know I'd be here an hour ago.'

'Your neighbour suggested it.'

Hilary pats a seat beside her. 'Sit, would you. I'd rather not talk to your chest. Which neighbour? The scratch-card queen in Flat 4, the bigot in Flat 2 or the orange nitwit in Flat 6?'

'Flat 6. Toni. She seemed nice.'

Hilary harrumphs so loudly it scares a passing spaniel. 'Nice? Nice? The woman's a fool. Did you see her hair? How can you have any regard for someone who takes styling tips from Donald Trump?'

I sit alongside her and angle my seat so that we can both face the sea. 'I thought she was really friendly actually.'

'It's all fake, all superficial. Like her "blonde" hair and her fake tan and those ridiculous false eyelashes. I bet her boobs came out of a packet.'

'While you, Hilary, are the one hundred per cent genuine article. What you see is what you get.'

She risks a half-smile. 'I do sometimes wonder how my life might have turned out with bigger tits.'

This catches me unawares and I let out a raucous guffaw. Hilary looks pleased.

'I'm 78 in September. Do you think there's an upper age

limit for 38DD implants? I could be Bexhill's answer to Dolly
Parton. That would put the orange nitwit in her place.'
My stomach growls. 'I need food. Can I treat you to lunch?'
'What? *Here?* Don't be ridiculous.' Hilary looks horrified.
'Besides, I've brought a hummus and Marmite Ryvita sand-
wich. And a hard-boiled egg.'
'In which case I'm doing you a favour. So . . . are you
coming or what?'

Hilary parks her mobility scooter in a corner of the cafe and
commandeers a table while I order us lunch at the counter.
I can't recall whether or not she likes a tipple but if she
doesn't want her mini bottle of Chardonnay, I'll keep it to
soften the edges of the next nasty hotel room in sea area
Wight or Portland. I order us two burgers and chips because
that's what *I* want.
'How do you know I'm not a card-carrying vegan?' she
demands when I tell her what's coming.
'Because you made that amazing lamb moussaka when
Rob and I came to lunch once. And you never demanded
the chestnut Wellington option for Christmas dinner.'
'Fair enough. Good call. People expect me to be some
kind of Quorn botherer so I like to order steak tartare, just
to outflank them. Could you tell the waitress I want my
burger practically mooing?'
The De La Warr cafe is full of yummy mummies and
well-heeled retirees, the sort you see in the Sunday supple-
ments, advertising stair lifts and equity release schemes.
Hardly kindred spirits of Hilary. I can't help wondering why
she moved here, from her delightful detached house in
Leighton Buzzard, but fear I might be opening a can of
worms if I dare to ask. Fortunately, I don't have to.

'And this is why I don't eat here,' she exclaims, glaring at the other diners. 'Look at them all. They should change Bexhill-on-Sea to Smughill-on-Sea. Welcome to our boring little town, where we take care of our own and bugger the rest of you.'

'They seem fine to me. I like that woman's jumper. It looks hand-knitted.'

'*You* live here then. You have the orange nitwit and the bigot as your neighbours. And I'll move back to Bedfordshire. I could even tolerate your poky little hovel, if I gave it a good spring clean and burnt a few joss sticks.'

If she's provoking me to ask the question, it's worked. 'So why move here in the first place? You must have known what you were letting yourself in for.'

She puts down her burger and starts to reply but thinks better of it and takes a few deep breaths. Then a little tear escapes from the corner of her right eye and trickles slowly down her cheek. We both wait while she composes herself. I pour the last of my wine into her glass.

'Why indeed?' she finally mutters, pushing her plate away. 'That's the million-dollar question, if ever there was one. And yet, here I am. It's Hotel California with ruddy great knobs on. But the only "checking out" people do at Beach View Point is toe-up in a wooden overcoat. That's if they don't ruddy well die before they move here and leave other people high and dry with no escape tunnel.'

I'm trying to follow. I really am. Who died? When? What escape tunnel? Hilary sees the confusion in my eyes and laughs. 'The mad ramblings of a daft old bat. Admit it, Annie. Isn't that what you're thinking?'

'You're old and you're probably a bat but you're not daft. Okay, I don't understand what you're saying.'

She slugs back the wine and explains. 'Do you remember

my pal, Val? She was at my seventy-fifth birthday party. In that Italian restaurant with the garden. Poured with rain all day. You and Rob made me a chocolate cake.'

I do. Hilary and Valerie. They'd been best friends since university. Valerie was widowed and lived in Reading. Hilary never married although I think she had her moments, more than once. After Val's husband died, they holidayed together every year: Rhine cruises, Turkish resort hotels, they even toured Cuba in a mini bus. Val often spent Christmas with Hilary in Leighton Buzzard because they were good company for each other and she couldn't stand more than an afternoon with her grandchildren.

'It was Val's idea. Selling her house in Reading and moving here. Her husband had never wanted to live by the sea but once he was gone, she could do as she pleased. Good for you, I thought. You go for it, Val. But then she said I should move here too and the more she pestered, the more I came around to the idea. What was there to keep me in Leighton Buzzard? Sweet eff all.'

'With ruddy great knobs on.'

'Exactly. Val found Beach Point View. And, honestly, Annie, isn't that the most ridiculous name? She suggested we come for the weekend so that she could give it the once-over. I just fancied a few days away. I had no idea she was going to rope me into her harebrained idea. She'd told the developers I was buying too, you see.

'So we came here and I saw the De La Warr Pavilion and I thought: Yes, I could live here, and I bought a flat too. I sold my lovely house and, because of space restrictions, I gave most of my furniture to a refuge for battered wives. I even parted with my beloved piano. But I thought it was worth it. It felt so cleansing, such a fresh start.

159

'Then, two weeks before the move, Val dropped dead. She'd had a dicky heart for years but it got her across Cuba, up mountains, down tin mines. And suddenly I was financially committed to Beach Point View and my appalling neighbours and Smughill-on-Sea.

'So here I am. Hell on earth minus the fire and the pitch-forks. But hey-ho, I've made my bed and now I must ruddy well lie in it until I pop my proverbials.'

After lunch, Hilary and I take a turn along the prom. She builds up quite a head of steam on her mobility scooter and I have to walk fast to keep up. A couple of people, also on mobility scooters or in wheelchairs, nod hello or say 'Hi' as we pass. Hilary acknowledges them with a swift grunt but she could be so much friendlier.

'He looks fun,' I comment about a man who has just whizzed past. He wears camouflage trousers, a deerstalker hat and has a Pokémon stuffed toy sitting in his basket.

'He looks deranged,' Hilary scoffs. 'He keeps suggesting I enter the Bexhill Wheel and Walk mini marathon next month, from the Angling Club to the De La Warr. It's in aid of the RNLI or I can get sponsored for a charity of my choice.'

'Worth doing then. Got one in mind?'

'How about Dignity in Dying? I could live with that.' She hoots at her accidental joke. 'Anyway, I've only got this scooter on a month's trial. Thought I might fancy one but I can still get about on Shanks's pony so it's going back next week.'

We walk for a bit longer, then Hilary demands that I accompany her back to Beach Point View. As we pass Flat 6, Toni is taking out a bin bag of empty bottles. She looks pleased to see us.

'How was bridge club?' I ask.

'Loud.' She giggles. 'Just as well Hilary wasn't here to bang her fist on the bathroom wall. Ooh, I've got something for you.'

As she nips into her flat, Hilary rolls her eyes. 'You see! Not just an orange nitwit but noisy with it.' I ssshh her; voices boom down this echoey corridor.

Toni returns with a paper plate covered in cling film. 'I kept you back some Yorkshire puds. Plus a few mini samosas and prawn toasts. *I'll* only eat them otherwise.'

Cranky as ever, Hilary says nothing so I take them. 'Ooh, lovely. That's tea sorted, then. Thank you, Toni.'

Hilary is already unlocking her front door so I volunteer to take Toni's empties down to the recycling skip. When I return, Hilary's already grudgingly polished off two samosas.

'Go on,' she says, mouth full. 'Tell me I'm rude and ungrateful and Toni was only being "nice".' She says it with a curl of her lip, as if it's the worst thing in the world to be.

'Someone has to be nice around here and it certainly isn't you.'

'I'm a cow. Always was, always will be. Valerie would have indulged her, invited her over for supper or a sherry. But Val's not here, is she, because she's dead. But I ruddy well am. And I'm a cow.'

'You really are. Silly me, I thought you might have mellowed.'

'Fermented, more like. If it makes you uncomfortable, you'd best be off. You can tell Robin you did your duty and checked I've still got a pulse.' She scrabbles in her handbag for her purse. 'How much do I owe you for lunch?'

'My treat.'

'You can bugger off then. Off you pop. Not that I even know where you're going or why.'

161

I walk to the door, relieved to be making my getaway. 'Shame. I might have told you, if you'd bothered to ask. Always a pleasure, Hilary.'

I'm done here. Finished. My conscience is clear. I can cross sea area Dover off my list. Next stop, sea area Wight. I stop briefly to hunt for my car keys before leaving. As I pass Flat 6, the door opens.

'She's crying in there,' Toni tells me in a stage whisper. 'I can hear her through my wall. I often hear her crying but she won't open up to me. You're her friend. You must know what she's like.'

I don't know what to do. I've been instructed quite clearly to bugger off. But Toni's beckoning me back to Hilary's front door. 'Well, go on, love. You wouldn't just leave her like that, would you?'

Beach Point View has guest accommodation but it's too late to reserve it for tonight. So I'll be dossing down on a row of Hilary's sofa cushions, wrapped in a sheet. She insists, even though I'm happy to seek out a last-minute hotel room nearby.

She also insists that I take advantage of the communal launderette, so I put all my clothes in the wash and borrow a pair of her pyjamas. Before tipping out the contents of my Star Wars wheelie suitcase, I carefully unpack Dad, happily intact in his travel urn, and place him by the window. Whatever Hilary says about Bexhill, she does have a breathtaking view, especially as dusk falls and a murmuration of starlings swoop past the Indian-influenced terraced houses beside the Pavilion.

Hilary pretended she hadn't been crying when I came back to see if she was okay. She even told me to 'bugger off' again. But her heart wasn't in it. I made some tea in her tiny kitchen;

CND mug for her, Greenham mug for me. She ordered me to sit while she went into the bathroom to tidy herself up. When she emerged, she looked stoic and Severe-Grey-Bob-like again. She asked if I'd care to stay the night and I said yes please.

Her flat is actually really cosy; like mine but with clever touches . . . a walk-in wet room and lots of well-placed sockets. It could be bland and beige but Hilary has filled it with posters, Indian throws and a faded kilim rug. If something goes wrong, she has 24/7 support, whereas I can take a fortnight to find a plumber or electrician. (Note to self: stop calling Rob to come to my aid. He's Fi's handyman now.)

'I'm sorry I lost my rag,' Hilary says as we polish off the last of Toni's leftovers, along with tomatoes and some slightly fizzy coleslaw from the fridge. 'I don't make a habit of it.'

I decide not to tell her what Toni told me, that she often hears her in tears. Hilary wants to keep up a capable front so I let her. After my attempt to counsel Kate about the 'Charlie thing', I figure less is more from me on the counselling front. Besides, she's dead keen to hear about Dad and my mad journey around the Shipping Forecast.

So I tell her . . . starting with my spontaneous flight to Cromarty with Keith's ashes. She loves it. Her face is suddenly free from the silent fury she carries around with her and she laughs uproariously.

She met Dad once, when Rob insisted we have both branches of the family over for a summer barbecue. We were still in our early, couply stage and we wanted everyone to see how happy we were. Rob wore an ironic apron and burnt a succession of sausages, I flitted around with a jug of Pimm's and Josh stayed upstairs with his mates, in Xbox heaven. Rob's at that loved-up stage with Fi now. I give it a year.

Hilary remembers Dad fondly. They disagreed on an awful lot but enjoyed the banter. 'What did we argue about at that barbecue?' she ponders. 'Politics, I expect. Lovely man and everything but I can't tolerate soft left Labour folk. What's the ruddy point if you only want to change things "a bit"?'

'You scared him. He said so afterwards.'

'Good. I don't think he'd hooked up with his ladyfriend yet. Or did I meet her but she made no impression?'

'Bev? No. He was still getting over Mum.'

'Ah,' says Hilary knowingly.

'Ah, what?'

'And then he met Bev and I bet you thought he'd got over your mother's death far too quickly and that's when the resentment set in. Culminating in this mad road trip to establish that you were more important in your father's life than her. Am I right or am I right?'

It's a fairly brutal precis of the last few years but I can't argue with it.

'And are you?' she asks, leaning forward like a barrister in a crime drama. 'More important than Bev? Will this trip prove it? How will you know?'

'Okay, okay, taking Dad's ashes was a ridiculous gesture but now I have to see it through. And Bev's fine with it. She told me so herself.'

Hilary gets up from the sofa with a painful 'oof' and totters to the kitchen. She returns a moment later with a bottle of Scotch and two tumblers. 'Val's favourite tipple. I bought it for our move. After she died, it seemed wrong to open it, but why the heck not?'

She pours generously, chinks glasses and waits for me to take a sip. Even after my tipple in Edinburgh with Duncan and Yasmin, I still don't like whisky, but when in Bexhill etc.

'This ashes business isn't just about your dad, though, is it.' Hilary says this as a statement, rather than a question. So I don't have to respond.

'Robin told me you gave up teaching. That's a shame. Not to mention a substantial loss to your profession.'

'I was ill. Chest pains, a heart thing. I had lots of tests but it was just an extreme form of burnout, combined with missing Mum. I got signed off for a few months and then, well, I just resigned. I haven't totally given up on teaching. Maybe it's given up on me.'

'And wouldn't that suit you? So you can convince yourself it's not your fault. Blame the job. Everything is someone else's fault. You're just a passive victim in all this.'

I gulp down more whisky. I still don't like it. I've committed to staying the night with Hilary but do I need to hear her cod psychologist routine?

'And, if you don't mind me being nosy, how did it end between you and Robin? I asked him, more than once, but he wouldn't say. Ever the gent, that boy. I'm guessing it wasn't his decision.'

'Spot on, Hilary. So that's hardly the action of a "passive victim", is it?'

Hilary gives an inscrutable smile. 'If you say so. More whisky?'

She tops up our glasses. Her silence is unnerving and it has the desired effect.

'I was such a poor excuse for a girlfriend. I knew he could do better. You think I was wrong to end it with him?' I'm forced to ask. Well, isn't that what she's implying with her raised eyebrow and tight-lipped smile?

'Passive victims know how to play the game. My chap, Frank, was like that. We were together for eleven years and he ran the relationship, even when he made it look as if I did.'

'I don't think I've heard about Frank before.'

'And you're not going to now. Water under the bridge. *Que sera sera.* You want to know what I think, regarding you and Robin?'

'No, but go on.'

'Lovely lad. Such a sunny little chap from the day he was born. Have you seen that photo of him on the donkey at Yarmouth, when he was about 6? Wearing a cowboy hat. Makes me smile every time I look at it. And he's grown into a decent, sensible man. A real catch, my old mum would have said.'

'Decent and sensible. That's Rob all right.'

'But when he introduced me to you, Annie, I thought: Hmmm. Not sure about this. Don't get me wrong, I took to you straight away. But that's one ruddy great stick of chalk getting together with one big fat lump of cheese. I know opposites attract but I had my doubts. I hate to say it but it looks like I was right.'

'Chalk and cheese can go together really well. Except in a quiche.'

'Is that regret talking? You let Robin go and now he's with this new woman.'

'Fi.'

'Robin's moved on and so should you. With someone new in your life, you might let go of all this sadness and self-doubt. It's not good for you, Annie. I can see that with my own eyes.'

Hilary has never held back, all the years I've known her. Calls a spade a spade, speaks as she finds, pulls no punches and tolerates no flim-flam. I totally hear what she's saying.

'So you don't think Rob and I should try again? I thought maybe you would. You know, as his godmother.'

'God, no! Draw a line and move on. Just as he has. Regret gets you nowhere. Look to the future, don't dwell on the past.'

Maybe it's the whisky, maybe it's the cosiness of Hilary's flat and the reassuringly soft cotton of her funny, stripy old jim-jams, but I feel fairly zen about her pronouncements. She hasn't pissed me off. Another perspective, from someone who knows both parties, is actually quite useful. But it cuts both ways and now it's time for her to be zen about *my* pronouncements.

I take a softly-softly approach. 'Draw a line, you say, Hilary. Move on. Look to the future, don't dwell on the past.'

'Absolutely.'

'Be open to new relationships. And friendships. Let new people into your life without prejudice.'

Hilary actually cheers when I say this. She looks thrilled that her lecture has paid off.

I'm not finished yet though. 'I've lost Rob. You've lost Val. So we both need to move on and look to the future. Perhaps you could start by getting to know your neighbours. Okay, Toni wasn't at Greenham Common or marching against the Iraq War. Or maybe she was. We don't know. But she's had a full life too and you might learn stuff from her. And from your other neighbours. And from the people who you see every day on the seafront. Like the man in the funny hat who wants you to take part in that marathon thing.'

Hilary has listened, expressionless, occasionally sipping her whisky. 'I don't think so,' she says, finally.

'You don't agree with anything I've said?'

'Some bits, yes. Some bits, no.'

'The point is: if I should move on, so should you. Otherwise you're a hypocrite.'

She looks shocked, and is actually silent – seemingly lost for words, for probably the first time ever – before conceding, 'I hate hypocrisy.'

I wait, eyebrows raised.

She sighs. 'Fair enough, I will try to be nicer to Toni and more open to my life here.' There's another pause. 'But I ruddy well draw the line at mobility scooter marathons so you can pull the plug on that suggestion right now, thank you very much.'

I sleep amazingly well on Hilary's row of sofa cushions and wake early. I make a mug of her fennel tea, which is surprisingly delicious, wrap myself in an ethnic throw and find a bench on the communal terrace. Toni is there, in a silk kimono, watering geraniums.

'Hello, love. You stayed over, did you? That's nice.' She drains the last drop of water from the watering can and sits beside me, declining a cuppa.

'I'll do myself a double decaff once I'm finished, thanks. Irene in Flat 4 is staying with her nephew in Horsham so I promised to take care of her pots. We look after each other here.'

'That's good to know,' I reply. 'You were right about Hilary not feeling at home yet.'

'It takes a while for all of us, love. I hated it for the first year. Wondered what the hell I'd let myself in for. Bexhill was so dull after twenty years in Ankara. But after my Ahmet died, I had this urge to come home, see if I could find my roots.'

'And have you?'

'I play bridge, I love Cornish pasties and I never miss *The Archers*. That'll do for now. You leave Hilary to me. I'll win her round, whether she likes it or not.'

When I get back to Hilary's flat, she looks relieved. 'At last! I saw you on the terrace with Toni. I didn't want to put the grill on until you got back.'

She makes us bacon rolls which were apparently Frank's favourite. 'You still want to know about Frank, don't you?' She grins mischievously. 'Well, hard cheese. All I will say is that he never saw the need for brown sauce and I couldn't contemplate a bacon roll without. A bit like life really.'

'Brown sauce is like life? Ketchup too?'

She sneers. 'Ketchup? Pah! Horrible stuff. Too cloying, too banal. Brown sauce adds spice, it adds oomph. You should never opt for the banal, Annie. You must know what you want and never settle for less. In bacon rolls and in life.'

I can't lie, this is a great bacon roll and Hilary's right. It needs the spice of brown sauce, rather than the syrupy sweetness of ketchup. I won't settle for banal. I will never eat a bacon roll without brown sauce again.

She's also folded all my clean laundry and carefully placed it, along with Dad's ashes, on the lid of my suitcase. 'It isn't ironed though. I don't iron. So, where to next?'

That's easy. According to my tea towel, sea area Wight begins at Beachy Head and finishes in Christchurch. I haven't been back to Brighton, where I went to university, for at least five years, apart from a friend's thirty-fifth birthday. And all I saw then were a series of cocktails bars, an Eighties club night and a twin-bedded hotel room. This is my chance to revisit properly.

'Ah, Brighton,' Hilary says, with a faraway look. 'Frank lived there for a while. Now where was it? Silkwood Street, no, Sillwood Street. I'd been such a dull little mouse in my twenties and thirties but I made up for it after that.'

'So you're saying there's hope for me yet?'

Hilary taps her nose and leans forward, as if she's about to be overheard. 'If you want to meet someone or just have some fun, surf the net. All human life there: gay, straight, bi, muscly, skinny . . . even a toe sucker or two. It's my little hobby but you mustn't tell Robin. He'll only worry.'

'You date men off the internet?' The sentence sounds alien to me, even as the words leave my mouth.

'Don't be daft. I don't date them. They'd be sorely disappointed if a flat-chested 77-year-old with legs like Stilton tottered up. No, I have alter egos: there's Dani C and Dreamgal. Ooh, and I've just invented Bella B. She's very open-minded, very wild. I may have to bump off the other two.'

'So what *do* you do then?'

'Online assignations. Occasionally quite steamy. But that's all. If they want to meet in the flesh – pardon the pun – I dump them. They're probably pensioners in Crawley anyway. Honestly, it's the best fun ever.'

I have no words. There are none. I try not to look *shocked*.

'I'm not suggesting you do what I'm doing, Annie. But there are plenty more fish in the sea, oodles of eligible chaps out there. I can say that because I ruddy well know. If you don't believe me, ask Bella.'

Chapter Fifteen

September 2004

Glynis and Jeremy were at it again. In the room above Annie's. Could they not stop shagging for an hour or so, just to give the futon frame a rest? And when they weren't shagging, they took over the kitchen, giggling while they shoved dripping spoonfuls of milk-sodden Cheerios into each other's mouths as if they were auditioning for a student production of *Last Tango in Paris*.

Or they were having a bath together and slopping water over the edge so that it created a damp patch on the downstairs hall ceiling. Annie had mentioned it to them more than once but they were too loved-up to care. Student houses were for now, not for keeps, so a little wear and tear went with the territory. Otherwise what were deposits for?

Had Annie and Duncan been so sex-crazed when they first moved into the Moulsecoomb student house together? Had they not given a fuck about when – or how noisily – they fucked? Possibly. Probably. But, like humming, snoring and farting, it isn't annoying when *you* do it.

Annie was pleased for Glynis. She really was. No, honestly, good for her. In the three years they'd been housemates, Annie had never expected her to get herself a boyfriend.

171

Some plain girls just look, well, not the shagging kind. Too busy studying late in the library or banging out essays at 4 a.m., under the glare of an unforgiving anglepoise. So, yes, it was great to be proved wrong. Yay Glynis. Yay Jeremy. If they could just stop grunting and shrieking 24/7.

Annie's mistake was staying on in the shared house after she graduated. Duncan hadn't been keen to move out plus it was ridiculously cheap and it suited them. He had regular work in a cafe in the Lanes and she combined part-time childcare for a family in Kemptown with her sales assistant job at the Body Shop. They were ticking over nicely. Whatever they planned to do with their lives post-uni could go on the back burner while they hung out with their mates in pubs, clubs, cafes and at music festivals. Why be boring at 23 when you can be boring at 33 and 43 and frigging forever after that?

After they split up, the room felt wrong. Duncan cleared out all his stuff in a matter of hours – the Chagall print above the fireplace, the Ikea duck-feather duvet and primary-coloured bed linen, the cheese plant, the ghetto blaster. She was left with her candle collection, her secret stash of Boyzone memorabilia and a single polyester duvet for a double mattress.

At night, she would cram in her ear plugs to drown out the shagfest above and write job application letters . . . an internship in Manchester, a planning job in Watford, voluntary work in Benin. She knew she was in a transitional period of her life and, years from now, she'd barely remember it. But right now it felt interminable. You can only march on the spot for so long without becoming worn down and exhausted.

It was a warm, sunny Indian summer Saturday and she wasn't working, made even better by the fact that when she tweaked her curtains, she saw Glynis and Jeremy going out. Great. She could have a nice quiet lie-in. She made herself poached eggs on toast and a jumbo mug of Gold Blend and took it to her room. She nearly turned on Radio 1 but silence was preferable. Silence was fucking golden. For the first time since she and Duncan had broken up, she felt hopeful, cheery. Hey, maybe she *was* in the driving seat of her life after all . . .

She was awoken by Glynis and Jeremy at it *on the floor* upstairs. They must have just popped out to the shops for yet more Cheerios and were now working up an appetite. The wafer-thin foam pillow over her head didn't work. Duncan's mum had bought him two good goosedown pillows, which had also left with him. She couldn't complain or ask the fuckers to tone it down; she'd just look bitter.

Ten minutes later, she was on a bus into Brighton. She needed to get her mother a birthday present anyway. She could mooch around for a few hours, try on frocks in her favourite vintage shops in Kensington Gardens, maybe even see what was on at the cinema. The North Laine neighbourhood buzzed every day of the week, but Saturdays were super-busy, with day-trippers and tourists keen to spend money and soak up the atmosphere.

In a print and frame shop, she found the perfect present for Mum: a poster for *The Man who Fell to Earth*, one of her favourite films. Plus it wouldn't be costly to stick in a cardboard tube and pop in the post. Better that than visit for the weekend and get the full-on, worried-parent interrogation on what her plans were and why she'd broken up with Duncan. ('Such a nice boy.')

As Annie walked past the open door of the Feathers, her and Duncan's favourite pub, she saw Simon serving behind the bar. Good old Simon. Nice guy, great sense of humour, but more Duncan's buddy than hers. She gave him a friendly wave that he returned, beckoning her to come in.

He leant over the bar and gave her a quick kiss as she hauled herself onto a stool. 'Howdy, Stannie Anley,' he said, pulling a pint and plonking it in front of her. 'Packet of dry roasteds to accompany it, madam?'

'Go on then. What's the damage?'

'Put your pennies away. *Mi casa su casa.*'

Simon had been in the same cohort as Duncan: both studying economics; hanging out together at the SU; even hitching to Spain with two mates during their first summer vac. Simon just scraped through his exams with a 2.2 and had forsworn a career in finance. In his second year, he'd appeared in a student fringe cabaret at the Brighton Festival and had gone down a storm, the overnight star of the show. He was now obsessed with learning the acting business at the coalface, rather than at RADA.

'So,' Annie asked, knowing she'd get a detailed response. 'How are you?'

'Pretty good, as it happens. Yep, things are on the up and up, I'd say.'

'Go on then. Spill.'

'You know I auditioned for a place with that agit-prop theatre group, the All-New Tree Huggers Roadshow? Well, they rang yesterday and I'm in. Three months taking a show around the UK. Art centres and church halls mostly. The Royal Court can wait, mate. I'm double-chuffed. It proves I'm not the only one who thinks I can do this.'

Annie raised her glass. 'That's brilliant, Si. I had every faith. That's another pal abandoning me in Brighton while I ponder my future.'

'You'll be okay, Stan. I know you will.' A customer caught

Simon's eye from the far end of the bar. 'Don't you move an inch. As the Schwarzenmeister would say, "Ah'll be bahck."'

He did return and she polished off another pint but this time she paid for it; she could see Simon's manager was on the war path. 'You can't just serve the sexy ones,' he'd snarked as he passed.

'Bloody jobsworth,' Simon moaned, once he was out of earshot. 'I can't wait to tell him to shove his job up his big fat rear end. This acting gig couldn't have come at a better time.'

Annie checked her watch. She'd been out of the house for nearly four hours. Surely she could go home now? If nothing else, Glynis and her newfound sex life was just the incentive she needed to do what so many of her friends had already done and find some kind of direction forward. Simon had done it, so could she.

She waved goodbye to him and gathered her shopping. On the street, in the few seconds she took to think about which bus stop to walk to, he ran out after her.

'Want to come to a party tonight? Emma and Tim's. Somewhere in darkest Hove. Promised I'd swing by, show my face. You're welcome to join me.'

Annie didn't have to think about it. 'Meet you back here at nine.'

You never know who might be at even the dullest of parties; maybe the man you'll spend the rest of your life with. So Annie made an effort; she pulled on her best black bootleg jeans, red ballet pumps, a red scoop-neck T-shirt and a ton of junk jewellery.

Simon whistled when he saw her and it suddenly dawned on her: 'Oh shit, he thinks I've done this for him.' He had changed his grey Gap T-shirt for a blue one. And he'd washed his hair. Bless. They had a swift pint, then caught a bus to beyond the far-flung fringes of Hove, to bloody Portslade. This end of town was alien to Annie. Here be dragons. But the bus ride gave them time to talk. Mostly about Duncan.

'He seems okay . . . now,' Simon said. 'But he was in bits when you two broke up. Really messed up. You must have been too, right?'

Annie nodded sagely, even though the voice inside her head replied, No, not really. She'd told Duncan that they'd come to the end of the road. She was calm and sensitive, every inch the thoughtful girlfriend. For some reason, he hadn't seen it like that.

Annie knew not to say this to Simon but she honestly thought Duncan had been a bit flouncy and histrionic when she broke the news. Didn't he know that university relation-ships rarely – if ever – last? Eras end and theirs had. If he couldn't see that, he was deluded.

'It was tough on both of us, Simon,' she said, looking out of the window for dramatic effect. 'But it's a well-known fact that university relationships rarely – if ever – last. We'd come to the end of the road and that was that. Have you spoken to him recently?'

'I rang him last week, as it happens. About my theatre gig. I thought he'd be pleased. Obviously he was. But he sounded quite, I don't know – distant. He was like, I'm back in Edinburgh. New job, new friends, new adventures. No time for nostalgia or regret. The only way is up. To quote Yazz. Not that he did. Quote Yazz, I mean. That was my little embellishment kind of thing.'

'There you are then. He's fine. We both are. New adven-tures all round, I say.'

Simon nodded eagerly and put his arm round her. 'Absolutely, Stannie Anley.'

When the bus terminated in Portslade, they didn't have to look far to find the party; it announced itself at full volume from the top of a side street: 'Hey Ya' by OutKast, so loud it made Annie's lungs judder. As they approached, they could see that the garden was rammed with people trying to get in, trying to get out, sitting on the garden wall, making out by the bins. She'd been to a gazillion parties like this since she started uni. In her first year, it had felt exciting, dangerous even. Now the density and intensity of it made her heart sink. People. Loud music. Crisps, if you were lucky. What was the fucking point?

'Let's push our way in,' Simon suggested. 'Or, look, we can go around the back and squeeze in through the kitchen.'

'The kitchen will be twice as heaving. You know it will. Is it even worth it?'

He sighed forlornly. But to give up, cut one's losses – that was the beginning of the end. A sign of getting old.

Annie hooked her arm in his. 'Come on, let's leave them to it. We don't need them.'

Simon assessed the situation and agreed. Crikey, was she coming on to him? He'd fancied her from afar ever since Dunk first introduced them.

His assessment was totally wrong, but that didn't stop Annie reciprocating when he kissed her, long and hard, in the bus shelter. It didn't stop her going back to his place, a pokey little bedsit in Seven Dials. It didn't stop them sleeping together that night and several more – plus a few mornings – after that. Simon was a thoughtful lover, with magic fingers and a strong sense of 'what women want'.

They even made a stab at being a 'couple' for a week or

two but both were distracted by more important things. Annie was offered a job in London and Simon was dumped by the agit-prop theatre group when their first choice became available after all, following a knock-back from *EastEnders*. They were both quietly relieved to pull the plug on their short-lived fling, now flung. Did it really only last a fortnight?

One thing united them. This hadn't been a proper 'thing'. Not really. So Duncan need never know. Agreed? Agreed.

Chapter Sixteen

Wight

I process Hilary's little secret on the train from Bexhill to Brighton and I'm still slightly shocked. Rob's godmother does sexy talk with strangers. Am I being a prude or just jealous of her chutzpah? I honestly think, if Toni can thaw the ice, those two could be best friends in no time.

I'd needed a break from driving so I returned the Kia to the Bexhill branch of the car-hire firm and was relieved when it was signed in as scratch-and-dent free. I swear the guy I handed the keys to was the same Wesley I hired it from four days ago in Scarborough. Only the accent was different. Maybe their diversity employment policy is a hundred per cent Wesley-centred.

I sit back in my window seat and enjoy the scenery, without having to negotiate jams, roundabouts and diversions. We trundle through the little towns of the south coast: Pevensey, Polegate, Berwick, plus the buzzing metropolis that is Eastbourne.

When I was packing, Hilary saw my expanding collection of yarns and knitted squares. She eagerly donated a ball of lumpy, muesli-like wool that she'd woven on a crafts retreat. She was happy to get shot of it and now I have my wool sample to represent sea area Dover.

In the hour or so it takes to get to Brighton, I crank out a quick square with the wool I bought in Benfleet. This little side project has turned into a bit of a chore but I tell myself it will be worth it when I've completed my journey around the British mainland and have the blanket to prove it. Mum would be gobsmacked – I wish I could show her.

That makes me sad for one brief moment but, actually, I'm feeling unfeasibly upbeat and that's down to Hilary. After I upset Kate with my misplaced words of wisdom, it felt good to give advice . . . and to receive it. I must call Kate, see if she's ready to talk to me again. She'll have bounced back. Kate always bounces back.

I'm not quite ready for that conversation just yet, however, so instead I dial a different number.

Rob picks up on the second ring.

'Hey Annie. I was just thinking about you. How's it going?'

'Fine. Good. I'm heading for Brighton.'

'And you visited Hilary? I didn't want to phone her before speaking to you.'

'I did. She even put me up for the night. She's fine, Rob.'

'Really? I know she can be a bit of a cranky old bird when she's unsettled.'

'She's not totally at home yet but she knows she needs to make more of an effort. We exchanged a few home truths.'

He chuckles. 'I can hear her giving it out. I can't hear her receiving it.'

'She did. She will. I'm sure of it.'

'And what home truths did *she* tell *you*? "Look sharp, wear a vest, fight the patriarchy."'

Wouldn't he like to know? 'Something like that, yes.'

'I'll try to get down to Bexhill once this job's finished but, honestly, it's like painting the Forth Bridge. Now they want a bigger larder and an extended wine rack in the utility room. Life would be so much easier if there weren't any customers. Just the work and the satisfaction of a job well done. Anyway, thanks, Annie. Seriously. I'm relieved to know she's okay. Is she making friends?'

'Slowly, but I have high hopes for her neighbour. Hilary's very sociable online, though. She's in loads of interesting chat rooms and forums. She's very popular there, by all accounts.'

'Wow! That's amazing. Good for her. Look, I'd better go or they'll send out a search party to the wood merchant's. Love you for doing that, Annie. Keep in touch, yeah? Bye.'

Rob loves me. For visiting Hilary. But he loves Fi for everything else. Hilary's ruddy well right. I need to spread my wings, open up to new relationships. Preferably not with a fake name and fake boobs in a closed group for toe-suckers.

I check in to a quirky little budget hotel on the Hove/Brighton borders, with views of what's left of the West Pier. My bank account is still healthy – I check the balance at every ATM – but there's no need to stay anywhere overly grand if it's just a bed for the night.

When I lived here in the mid-noughties, the structure of the pier was still identifiable, not long after the fire that had decimated it. Now it looks like a series of interlinked coat hangers. It has a kind of beauty, though. Worn away by wind and tide, standing proud and not going quietly. A bit like Hilary . . .

Brighton is exactly the same as I remember it and totally different, in equal measure. It still feels buzzy. It still has an energy that's almost tangible; I sensed it as soon as I moved here from St Albans as a fresh-faced student all those years ago. But it feels more corporate and grown-up now. There's

181

the i360, a doughnut-shaped viewing capsule on a pole, that dominates the skyline.

And stretched out across the horizon is a massive wind farm. Britain's offshore gales might toss around fishing boats and ferries but they also power factories and high streets and homes. 'Cyclonic later. Good.' Dad admired innovation, clever new ways of doing things. I'm not sure he'd have been a fan of the i360 though.

Wandering the slightly down-at-heel streets and squares that connect the seafront to the town centre, I regret that I never lived in the heart of Brighton. I had friends who did: Sally Wotsit, Dougie the dope dealer . . . didn't Hilary say she had a secret lover squirrelled away around here? Ah, Hilary. I know I dragged my heels when Rob asked me to visit her but it's definitely the highlight of my grand tour so far.

My favourite part of Brighton, the North Laine, is heaving with dawdling pedestrians, as it always was and, yes, some of my go-to shops appear to have survived, despite all the new eateries and vape outlets. I come across a wool shop and buy a ball of buttery-coloured cashmere that feels like Cromarty when you stroke it. I miss that cat.

As I walk up West Street, I pass a hen party teetering on unfeasibly high heels down from the station, each with a wheelie suitcase. They wear tiaras and fuchsia pink, person-ally sloganed, T-shirts: 'Slapper Sienna' . . . 'Treeza the Tart' . . . 'Big Boobs Bex'. Bex's T-shirt takes a moment to read because she does, indeed, have a splendid pair. Two older women are let off with 'Bride's Mum' and 'Groom's Mum'. The bride herself is easy to spot in her tiara, train and a T-shirt which reads: 'Shag Me While I'm Single'. A couple of cocky lads attempt to take her on but she bats them away. Plenty of time for that . . .

It's a hot summer's day so the benches outside the Feathers are packed with drinkers, mostly laidback locals by the look of them. The Feathers was always a bit of a dive and I'm relieved to see that it still is. It hasn't been transformed into one of those self-conscious gastro-pubs, with artfully mismatched furniture, artisanal ciders that smell of wee and shelves stuffed with books-by-the-yard.

Duncan and I often rocked up here, before or after doing something else. The call of the jukebox, the price of the lager, the general sleaziness, not to mention the occasional lock-in, were big draws. It was also a regular haunt for Brighton's duckers-and-divers and we loved shooting the breeze with them, doing a line or two of coke, as long as it was on them. In retrospect, they probably had a huge laugh at our expense: those two wet-behind-the-ears middle-class kids, desperate to impress, hanging with the big boys.

I can't resist. I take a peek inside the open door as I stroll by. Even the cracked, sticky lino hasn't changed and, omigod, there's a familiar face behind the bar. It's only bloody Simon . . . Duncan's friend Simon, who I had a mad fuckathon with before I left for London. He was always tall and wiry with long, dark-brown hair, often tied back haphazardly with a found scrunchie. Now he's shaven headed, muscly and fit. Simon has morphed into a total hunk and no one flipping told me.

He catches my eye just as I catch his. He comes out from behind the bar and strides over. Did he always stride like that? How come I missed it? Then he picks me up and swings me around. He seems pleased to see me. I could get used to reactions like this, even if my T-shirt is riding up, exposing flabby tummy, and I kick a stool over with my trainer.

'Shit-a-brick, Stannie Anley, it *is* you, isn't it? I haven't grabbed a total stranger?' He puts me down and stands back to check.

'It is me. Older but not wiser. Bloody hell, Simon. I didn't expect to see you here.'

'I know. Groundhog Day or what?'

He takes my hand and pulls me over to the bar so that he can finish serving the customer he just abandoned. Then he pours me a complimentary pint and brings it over.

'You are, ahem, conversing with the manager,' he boasts, with faux pride. 'How the not very mighty are fallen.'

How this can be? Has he been working at the Feathers since I left Brighton? What about his acting plans? He had such big plans.

Simon explains that he shouldn't even be here; it's his day off but he's holding the fort for a couple of hours while one of his staff has a doctor's appointment. When she arrives, he's free for the rest of the day if I am.

'How about half two at the falafel-and-wrap place across the road? And that's not a question, that's an order, Stannie Anley. That's if you're still a "Stanley". Are you? No, no, tell me at half two.'

He is jaw-droppingly hot. How can I refuse?

When I lived here, the falafel-and-wrap place was a grubby kebab shop. Now it's all Farrow & Ball walls and Middle Eastern tiles. Downstairs is busy but we have the first floor practically to ourselves. Simon eats with gusto and finishes my wrap when I give up. Eating with enthusiasm is surprisingly sexy, even when he gets tahini dressing down his chin and wipes it off with the back of a square, hairy hand. It suddenly feels hot in here. I gulp down some water.

'So,' he says, pushing away his empty plate. 'Who wants to start? My life story since we last saw each other. Or yours?'

'Yours. Obviously. Because you're taller than me.

'Obviously.' He laughs. He's got a great laugh. 'Okay then, here goes.'

He really didn't plan to return to the Feathers. It just sort of happened: part-time bar work when he was skint that then progressed to becoming manager when the previous one was caught with his hand in the till. And it suits him. That shithole is like a second home, right?

Then he rewinds to the beginning. Yes, he had high hopes of becoming the next Martin Freeman. He figured there was room for more than one and casting directors often compared them. But, well, it didn't happen.

'I gave it my best shot, Stannie. I really did. So many castings. So many nearly jobs. So many door-slams and knock-backs. I know it goes with the territory. I'm not daft. But after a while, you start to think maybe it's God's way of telling you that, sorry mate, you're a bit shit at this whole pretending-to-be-someone-else lark.'

'But you're good, Simon. I saw you in that show at the fringe. You blew everyone else off the stage.'

'My finest hour. Quite literally. All downhill from there.' He gives a brave smile. He knows he's good but now he has to believe he isn't, which is sad.

'I did have one ridiculously well-paid job for three years. Meant I could buy a motorbike, get a mortgage.' He pulls a discomfited face and points to it. 'Do you recognize Antacid Andy, the busy van driver who was a martyr to his heartburn? I was in three commercials over two years. Who knew chronic indigestion could be so lucrative? Did you see me? I often popped up in the *Corrie* breaks.'

'Um . . .'

'Yeah well, you'd probably nipped to the kitchen to make some tea. Or you zapped through the ads. My mum was dead proud. Even now, she won't take any other indigestion remedy, even though they sacked me. KJ loved the ads too. He could act them out off by heart.'

Simon sees my confused face. KJ? He whips a phone out of his pocket and shows me his screensaver: it's Simon and a mini-Simon, perched proudly on the pillion of his parked motorbike.

'That's from a couple of years ago. He's 11 now. Lives with his mum in Lewes.' Simon beams at the photo for a second or two. 'I know everyone says their kid's the best. But KJ actually is. Fact. He is, isn't he?'

'He's very cute. He's got your hair.'

'Which probably means he'll inherit my male pattern baldness too, poor little sod. Remember my ponytail? I actually had a ponytail. Now look at me. Baldy McBaldface.'

'You look a hundred per cent better without it, Si. Ponytails are for . . . ponies.'

He beams. Have I overdone it? Probably. But he really does look bloody good.

'Well, go on then,' he says. 'I've shown you mine. You show me yours. What's the story, Stannie?'

I wonder where to start, where to finish, what to leave out. 'I *am* still Annie Stanley. I've been in a couple of long-term relationships – not right now – but no wedding bells. I got that job in the City, didn't I, around the time we were – um, we were close.'

'"Close." Yes. Nicely put.'

'So I did that for a bit, got sick of it and retrained as a teacher. I'm taking a sabbatical at the moment because I got

186

poorly. I'm fine now, as you can see. I'm trying to decide whether to go back to it or—or –'

'Or what?'

'Exactly. Or what. I have no idea.'

'I can see you being a good teacher. You're assertive, confident, dare I say engaging.'

'Be my guest. It gets you down, though. It can be very stressful and draining. I miss it, of course I do, but I'm not ready to go there again. Not yet. Maybe never.'

'What do you teach?'

'Geography. It's what I studied at uni, after all.'

'Geography, eh? Okay then, how are you on wind farms?'

'Like the one off the coast here? I approve. Both as a geography teacher and an energy user. Wind farms are definitely a "good thing". Why?'

He stands and pulls me out of my chair, suddenly eager to leave. 'That, Stannie Anley, is the correct answer. Now, come with me.'

An hour and a bit later, we're at Brighton Marina, clambering onto a catamaran that will take us on a tour of Rampion, the offshore wind farm that dominates the horizon. There are six others in our group: two Danish students and two couples from Worthing who watched from the shore as the 116 turbines were constructed and are now keen to see it up close, as a birthday present for one of them. I'm not sure why *we're* here, though.

Once we pull away from the marina, our captain – Steve – provides a running commentary. Why the wind farm was built, how much power it generates, what renewable energy can do to fight climate change. My schoolkids would love this, especially Mason McIsaac . . . seeing innovative, energy-saving solutions at the coal face, so to speak. When – if – I return to teaching, I'll bring them here. Definitely.

Back at the cafe, Simon was laid back, funny and confident in a self-deprecating way. Now he hunkers down in his seat and stares straight ahead, as if he's on a long, dull coach trip. He barely speaks, even when I tell him what a treat this is. We hit choppy waters and he grips my hand so tightly that I have to unpeel his white knuckles to free my fingers.

'You're not enjoying this, are you, Si?'

'Not really, no.'

'But it was your idea.'

'I know, I know. I decided you were the person to do it with.'

'I don't get it.'

He sighs, defeated. 'I don't like the sea. I'm fucking petrified. I also hate swimming pools, lidos, lakes, the lot. Because I can't swim, okay. I hate this, Annie. You've no idea how much I hate this.'

'Then why put yourself through it?'

'I'm doing a one-man show. Two nights in a room above a pub. Not my pub. Another pub. A one-man show starring me. "Not Drowning but Drowning." That's the title and the programme's been printed so I'm stuck with it. Too late to change it now. I suppose I could call it something else on the night, but that isn't good marketing, is it? All about me and my hate-hate relationship with water. Fucking great deep, black, deep, fucking water like this.'

Now I take *his* hand and he slowly bambles to a halt. His palm is clammy and his forehead is beaded with sweat.

'Hey-ho, matey. Worse things happen at sea.'

Simon laughs, despite himself. 'I should have called it that. My show. Great title.'

I've made him laugh. This is an improvement. I even manage to convince him that we won't capsize if he gets up and goes to the loo. The trip there and back gives him confidence and when he returns, he looks a little less green.

'I need to get back on stage, Stannie,' he says, forcing himself to stare out of the sea-sprayed window. 'I know I can do it. I need KJ to see me as more than just a van driver with heartburn. See, I realized, I've lived by the sea nearly half my life so why's it got the better of me? Then I thought, Hey, I can do a show about this. About my sea phobia. From when I first encountered the seaside as a kid, swimming lessons at school, getting pushed in by the big boys. You know, confessional and uplifting. Funny and bittersweet. With a happy ending.'

'Which is?'

'That I conquer my fear of water on this catamaran and, at the ripe old age of 38, I learn to swim. And I finally swim in the sea, here in Brighton, with my lad. And then I swim the Channel and win an Olympic gold for butterfly and become Sports Personality of the Year. Okay, maybe not that last bit but a man can dream.'

'I still don't know why you asked me to come with you.'

'Because I feel relaxed with you. Not vulnerable and embarrassed. You're just passing through so you won't judge me. My everyday friends think I'm Macho Man because I run marathons and play five-a-side and I've got a six-pack.'

Simon's got a six-pack. I instantly visualize it. It's a very fine six-pack, with little tufts of dark baby hair around the belly button. *My* turn to get clammy hands.

'Thank you, Si,' I say and I mean it. 'I'm genuinely touched that you thought of me like that. How are you feeling now?'

'Still shit-scared, but at least I have the ending to my show.

I did it. I did this and it's marginally better than I expected, especially now I've had that piss.'

Duncan's words pop into my head, about me always taking a bad thing and making it worse. But he's wrong. I've helped Simon. I've made it better.

'We could maybe go for a little dip afterwards,' I suggest gently, not wanting to browbeat him. 'I'm a strong swimmer. I'd take care of you, cross my heart. What do you say, Si?'

'I say, Fuck off, Stannie Anley.'

We walk back from the marina, stopping for an ice cream along the boardwalk, and then for a coffee in Kemptown. It feels like we've been together for weeks. Something about Simon's confession has bonded us and we know it.

This isn't a 'date' but we're finding lame excuses to brush arms accidentally. We're comfortable in each other's company and it feels good. I have a soft spot for men who show their feelings. My relationship with Toby was all about him maintaining machismo 24/7, whereas Rob sobbed loudly in a packed cinema at the end of *Paddington 2* and made no apology for it. I loved him for that.

As we approach Brighton Pier, I spot the hen party. They've found a seafront bar and, although it's still only half five, they already look pretty wrecked. The Bride, Big Boobs Bex and Groom's Mum are dancing to Ibiza tracks from a neighbouring bar with a couple of bare-chested gay guys in tight denim cut-offs and cowboy hats.

I nearly tell Simon about Scarborough, when Kim and I danced to Boyzone and MC Hammer with those two guys in the deserted hotel bar and how fantastic it felt. But that would mean telling him why I was there and why I'm here and I'm not convinced it will come out right.

Explaining my tour of the Shipping Forecast with Dad's ashes is becoming increasingly hard to rationalize, even to myself. If I think about it too hard, I might give up and go home and I can't do that. I promised Dad.

The sun is giving out a late afternoon blast of warmth so we find a bench on the pier, share a portion of mouth-scalding doughnuts, and watch the world amble by.

'Piers aren't a problem,' Simon says, scattering sugar down his T-shirt. 'I can handle piers because I'm on solid ground . . . even though you can see the sea through those gaps in the decking. If I don't look down, I can pretend I'm on dry land.'

'You did it, though. You got on that catamaran and you stayed on it for the full two hours.'

'I was hardly going to dive off and swim for shore. Hey, that's quite funny. I can use that.' He pulls a little notepad and pencil from his back pocket and scribbles himself a reminder.

'Happy to be your comedy feed. Ernie to your Eric.'

'Seriously, though. Thanks for coming with me. You didn't need to but you did. You took it – me – seriously and you didn't take the piss.'

'Oh, I did a bit.' I grin. 'I was happy to, Si. It's been fun. Lunch, the boat trip, the pier, all of it.'

Simon looks around, taking in the day-trippers snapping selfies, the kids scoffing chips, the neon signage and kitsch gift shops. 'I love Brighton Pier. Me and KJ come here a lot. We know it's naff and cheesy but we don't care.'

'Back in the day, when we were students, we definitely thought it was naff and cheesy,' I recall. 'Because we were so damn cool. Hang on, I *did* come here when I was a student. With Dad. How could I have forgotten that?'

I know exactly why. I filed the memory in a rarely accessed compartment of my brain, where all the sad stuff goes. Now it's instantly front and centre and I get a cold shiver of repressed emotion. It's a sharp, stabbing hurt I wasn't expecting. I sit quietly, breathing deeply, waiting for it to fade. And then I'm crying.

Simon doesn't notice straight away – he's gazing out towards the marina – so I have time to pull myself together. But my grief escapes in a hiccuppy gulp and he finally sees my tears. He puts his arm round me, frowning with confusion and concern.

'It was during my first term,' I eventually explain. 'They were both supposed to visit, Mum and Dad. But Dad came alone because Mum was feeling so rough. And he said, Let's do the pier, because he loved piers. Plus I think he thought I'd get less upset if I was somewhere loud and bright and buzzy when we talked about Mum.'

'What about her?'

'He said that although her bowel cancer was quite aggressive, the doctors had high hopes that she'd come through. And that if *she* was cool about losing her hair from the chemo, I should be too. She was still my mum. So I was to crack on with my studies and not worry. And she did. She got through it. That first time. She said she wasn't going to let a frigging tumour get the better of her. She was bloody amazing.'

'I'm guessing it came back.'

'Six years ago. That was one of the reasons I chucked my job and moved back to St Albans. To be with her. She was so pleased that I'd decided to become a teacher. She had more faith in me than I did. I qualified two months before she died, so she never really got to see how much I loved it.'

I can't talk any more. I take deep breaths and Simon strokes my back. A toddler in a tutu runs past, heading for the funfair. A mother runs after her, attempting to plonk a sun hat on her head. A passing seagull generously offloads a big dollop of shit inches from our feet and, suddenly, we laugh.

'I'm sorry if I said anything, did anything, to upset you. Did I?' Simon asks.

'Talking helps. It really does. So there's nothing to apologize for.'

'Phew! I don't always engage brain. That's Melanie's theory. KJ's mum. When we were together, I'd come out with something, in all innocence, at a party, say, or to her mum. And hours later, she'd throw it back at me, accuse me of being insensitive and overbearing. Like I could even remember what I'd said. Fucking minefield.'

'So you're separated for good, you and Melanie?'

'Oh yes. Thank Christ. We get on much better now. KJ's happier too.' He glances at his watch. 'Flipping heck, it's nearly seven. It was beer o'clock two hours ago. Do you fancy one? I know I do.'

We get up to leave and I take one final look at the view from the pier. 'I wish I'd brought Dad with me today. Why didn't I?'

'Your dad's in Brighton?'

'Back at the hotel. Oh, Si, if I'd known I was coming here, I would have.'

'No time like the present,' Simon says striding off purposefully. 'Let's fetch him now. Sheesh, Annie, why didn't you say?'

Simon takes it surprisingly well when we get to my hotel room and I introduce him to Dad, who is perched on top of the wardrobe beside a high, round window. When I placed him there, a few hours earlier, I heard myself say: 'There you go, mister. Pretend it's a porthole.'

I am nuts. Mad. Queen of the Fruit Loops. I have truly lost it. Whenever I stop, take a deep breath and observe my actions through someone else's eyes, there's no other conclusion.

'Grief makes you do weird things,' Simon reassures me when I explain Dad's presence. 'My mum couldn't part with my grandad's dentures. I came across them in her sideboard when I was looking for an envelope. I never told her. She'd have been mortified.'

We're back at the pier, on the same bench as before, but now with a Sainsbury's carrier bag containing a bottle of New Zealand red, two teacups from my hotel room and . . . Dad. We sandwich the Pringles tube between us a) so that it doesn't tip over and scatter him prematurely through the slats and into the sea and b) so that it doesn't look super-creepy to any poor passer-by who realizes what it is.

I pour the wine and we clink cups. Simon clinks his with Dad, which nearly starts me off again. Simon is lovely.

I take the Shipping Forecast tea towel from my bag and spread it out on my lap so that I can show Simon where I've been. I point to the Black Isle, north of Inverness, where my journey began.

'Okay, we've been to Cromarty, me and Dad, in sea area Cromarty. Obviously. Then Edinburgh in sea area Forth. I caught up with Duncan in Edinburgh.'

'Wow, how was that?'

'Yeah, good. Fair. Moderate, occasionally rough.' I giggle slightly manically at my Shipping Forecast in-joke. 'I met Yasmin too. And one of their kids. Yasmin gave me this T-shirt.'

Simon peers at the map and shudders. 'All that sea, though, Annie. Miles and miles of it. What was Viking like? And Fisher and Forties and Dogger?'

'I didn't visit them. When I decided that I wanted to see it through, I knew I had to make it achievable, manageable, viable. I don't have a great track record for sticking at things: jobs, relationships, Zumba. So I eliminated all the sea areas that required a plane or a ferry; that way, I've got no excuse to give up. Anyway, after Forth I went to Scarborough in Tyne, Happisburgh in Humber, Canvey Island in Thames, Bexhill in Dover and now I'm here: Brighton in sea area Wight.'

He traces the journey still to come. 'So that just leaves Portland, Plymouth, Lundy . . .'

I whizz us through the final few. I know them off by heart. 'Irish Sea, Malin, Hebrides, Fair Isle. That's it. End of. Back to life, back to reality.'

'Why, though? What's it for? Sorry to be dense, but I still don't get it.'

I splosh more wine into our teacups. 'What's to get? I didn't want Dad scattered in Austria so I took his ashes. Well, I took Keith first of all, don't ask. I was going to scatter him – Dad, not Keith – in Cromarty but I just couldn't. So, um . . . I'm doing this. Don't look at me like that. Okay, it's slightly unhinged but then, hello, so am I.'

'No more than the rest of us. And I speak as someone who can't even look down between the slats of this pier in case I have a conniption.'

'Conniption. Top word.'

'Innit though. I'm using it in my show.'

'So *you* don't think I've lost the plot?'

'Nope. Well, yes. Kind of. But, like I say, let he – or indeed she – who has never behaved like a total twat cast the first stone.'

I'll have that. In my head, my actions made total sense. Mostly. But I can see that somewhere along the way I forgot about Bev's feelings or Kate's. Hilary pulled me up short, as I did her, but I just carried on regardless.

By ploughing on now, am I making a bad thing even worse? Or better? And if so, how exactly?

'Duncan had a theory, when we met up in Edinburgh,' I tell Si, trying to sound breezy.

'That sounds like Dunk.'

'He said I made our break-up worse by sleeping with you straight afterwards. Honestly, what was it to him? He'd moved back to Scotland, for fuck's sake. Anyway, it was over before it began. You and me. Wasn't it? I can't even remember how Duncan found out.'

'Your housemate grassed us up. The one with cold sores and the glasses. Who only ate soup.'

'Phil? Joey?'

'She was a she, the grass. Doing physics. Weird laugh.'

'Omigod, Glynis. Glynis told Duncan? But we never did it at my house. Did we?'

'I did stay at yours once. We were too wasted to shag but I got cramp in my foot and I made a bit of a racket trying to shake it out. It probably sounded like wild, unbridled sex to someone who wasn't getting any.'

'She so was, Simon. Trust me.'

I think back to the way I behaved. Perhaps I could have been nicer. 'I didn't mean to hurt Duncan. Or you. Oh God, did I hurt you without realizing?'

'Me? Course you didn't, you plank. We were both distracted,

unsettled, suddenly thrown into the real world after uni. We were both missing Dunk. Thus we sought solace in each other's arms.'

'Solace, eh? I thought we were just horny.'

'You didn't hurt me, Annie. But we both hurt Duncan by being sneaky behind his back. We behaved like a pair of kids. That's why I didn't try to contact you when you moved to London. Even though I moved to London too for a couple of years.'

'I wish you had.'

'Yeah, well, the moment passed and you met whoever and I met Melanie and then KJ came along and it wouldn't have made sense. Then.'

'Not then, no.'

'Maybe it would now. We wouldn't be hurting Dunk. And we're practically middle-aged.'

'Oi, speak for yourself!'

'We are, Annie. Okay, we're still fuck-ups but at least now we know we are.'

'You don't act like a fuck-up. Bringing up KJ, writing your one-man show, managing a pub.'

'I just hide it better than I did in my twenties. Perhaps we'd last longer than a fortnight this time around.'

He leans in, over Dad who is still nestled between us, and kisses me. It's a gentle, slow, sweet kiss and yes, it does seem possible, Si and me.

Maybe it could work. Now . . .

We pull away, suddenly feeling awkward. He tucks a strand of hair behind my ear. 'We could go back to my place, Annie. I promise I wouldn't get cramp. But there again, you wouldn't want to waste that hotel room of yours.'

'I've paid in advance. Whether I use it or not.'

I think about it. I really do. Pros and cons. I would so love to be loved right now.

He kisses my forehead. 'You're not going to, though, are you?'

'No, I'm not.'

'Because?'

'Because my head's heaving with stuff at the moment. Because I'm a mess. I am, Simon. Doesn't this road trip prove it?'

'Not to me. Okay then, call me as soon as you're done. We can pick up where we left off. See where the land lies, no pun intended.'

'Do you think we should?'

'Absolutely. Definitely. One hundred per cent.'

'Hey, let's meet right here on the pier. By then, you'll be up for a swim to the wind farm and back. Maybe some paddle-boarding or wind-surfing. What do you say, Si?'

'I say, Fuck off, Stannie Anley.'

As I walk back to my hotel, clutching the carrier bag that contains Dad, I see the hen party bride, her veil at a jaunty angle, outside a seafront club, looking as if she's just been sick.

'You okay?' I ask in sisterly solidarity as I pass.

'I'm still in Brighton, right?'

'You are.'

'And I'm still single?'

'You're on your hen weekend.'

'No worries then.' She teeters back into the club, adjusting her veil. 'Ta babe. Love ya, babe.'

Chapter Seventeen

Portland

My hotel room is airless and the stupid porthole window above the wardrobe is sealed shut with gloss paint, but I do eventually drop off and sleep fitfully, tangling my ankles in that strip of fabric that so many hotels like to put at the foot of beds these days. What is it for? Does it even have a name? I Google it and learn that it's a 'bed scarf'. Seriously? Beds need scarves? Please may I go back to sleep now?

By half four, I'm wide awake. By 5.15, I've thrown on some clothes, grabbed Dad and crossed Kingsway to watch morning break behind the West Pier. There are a few other early birds, on their way to work or heading home after a wild night out. I hope the hen party bride's okay. Should I have found her mum? Oh well, too late now.

I have a sudden urge to listen to the 5.20 Shipping Forecast. I find it on my phone and play it softly, but loud enough for Dad to hear it too.

The familiar intonations wash over me, read by a female voice I don't recognize. She must be new. Forth, Tyne, Dogger, Fisher . . . slight or moderate, occasionally rough . . . St David's Head to Great Orme's Head, including St George's Channel . . . Ardnamurchan Point to Cape Wrath.

It's as soothing as ever, comforting and encompassing, like an old blanket. I remind myself that I've travelled to this point – literally this one here on the Brighton seafront – because of . . . *this*.

I can explain it to other people: Don and Hazel in Cromarty, Hilary in Bexhill, Simon yesterday. It even makes a kind of sense if I put the right spin on it. I just need to be sure it still makes sense to me. And here, in this moment, it does.

Simon.

I could text him now. I could say I slept really badly because of him. I could even stay in Brighton for a few more days, to see if what we feel is real. It feels real. It feels even more real when I reread the text he sent last night, after we parted.

'Ooh-err, what a day. Not just our meet-up & catch-up. But I went to sea & didn't throw a wobbly. Thanks for holding my hand & not laughing at me. Much. Have gone straight to my PC to finish the frigging play. All down to you, lovely Ms Anley. Just listened to the Shipping Forecast. Is Fair Isle your final stop? Tell me when you're back on dry land. We've waited this long . . . xxx Si.'

We've waited this long. He may have, but have I? Can I honestly say I've thought of Simon constantly over the years? I can't because I haven't. Maybe that's a good thing. He's a new possibility, one that I hadn't factored-in. I think of Rob constantly but Rob is spoken for, Rob is history, Rob is Fi's. Maybe Simon will provide all my future fuzzy feelings whenever I need to remind myself that someone is thinking of me.

Simon is thinking of me. I'll work on that.

I've been putting off checking in on Kate. I meant to call her when I was in Bexhill. I definitely meant to call her when

I got to Brighton. And then Simon happened and she went on the back burner. Some sister I am.

It's too early to ring now but I can at least fire off a loving, caring hey-how-you-doing text. I even say I've been thinking of her lots which I have. Kind of. I apologize for being insensitive about the whole Charlie thing and hope it's blown over. Storm in a teacup. 'Big love, little sis.' I press send before I can edit or delete.

I'm back at the hotel and am about to get in the shower when my phone rings. Kate, of course. Her smartphone is practically welded to her arm and no message ever goes unanswered, even when a simple smiley face will suffice.

'Where are you?' she asks as a greeting.

'Sea area Wight. About to head to Portland.'

'Nope, not a clue where that is. This is your project, not mine. Are you okay?' She doesn't say it with warmth or concern, but that's Kate for you.

'I'm fine. I met an old friend. Simon. Friend of Duncan's. Do you remember Simon?'

'Not really, no. I handed in my notice. At work. I've got holiday owing so I just walked out.'

'Fuck, Kate! Seriously?'

'No, April Fool. Of course, seriously. You're not the only Stanley who can stomp off like a dipstick.'

'But why? I thought you loved that job. Are things awkward with Charlie?'

She sighs her weary 'Kate' sigh. 'It's got nothing to do with Charlie. Well, that's one factor, I suppose, but not *the* factor. I can't go into it all now. I'll explain it face to face, whenever that might be. When might that be, An-An?'

'Crikey, I don't know. I'm just taking it one sea area at a time.'

'What's to see in Portland?'

Kate has a point. I don't actually know. According to my trusty tea towel, it stretches from Christchurch to Salcombe. I only have one, half-baked stopover in mind.

'I might head for Poole.'

'Poole?' she laughs. 'Why Poole?'

It sounds ridiculous when I say it out loud. 'Because of Mum. Those Poole Pottery milk jugs she collected. You know, that went on the top shelf of the Welsh dresser and gathered greasy dust and we couldn't use them. When we had visitors, she served milk from the carton.'

No reply. I wait. Have we been cut off?

'Katkin? Are you still there?'

'Sorry, sorry.' She sounds tearful. 'I just miss her so much. Every day. Dad too, obviously. I miss them both. I miss you. Even when you're close by, I feel a distance. How did we let that happen?'

'My fault. Wallowing, shutting out the world. My fault, Katkin. We'll make it up, though. We've only got each other, haven't we?'

'Yeah. Let's try that.'

'Starting now?' I suggest. 'Tell me what happened at work, why you left.'

'I will, I promise. Soon. Sorry, got to catch a train. Bye-bye, An-An.'

That's Kate's other phone thing. She will always be the one to end the conversation, never me. Oh well . . .

'Rav' at Brighton station ticket office sorts out my route to Poole, with a change at Southampton. It will take me two hours and forty-one minutes. No worries, I have my buttery-coloured cashmere yarn and knitting needles at the top of my backpack, plus a well-thumbed psychological thriller I found in my hotel room. And I like being bored. Two hours and forty-one minutes? Pah! They will fly by.

Around West Worthing, I have finally crafted the right response to Simon's text. How to sound keen but not too keen, cool but not too cool. After much fiddling and finessing, it reads: 'Hi Si. So great to see you & hang out. I want to do it again too. Thanks for bearing with me. Really. Thanks. Will bring you back a Fair Isle bobble hat. Off to Dorset now. Lots of love, Stannie.'

Fair Isle bobble hat? Too twee? Too cool? Too late. It's sent. With any luck, he'll find it endearing. I sense that he's pretty smitten. Or am I fooling myself into thinking there's (love) life after Rob?

At Arundel, my phone beeps a notification. I put down my knitting and allow myself a little smile. Simon is *so* smitten and couldn't wait to reply. Good.

But no, it's from Kate. 'Giving you a heads-up to expect a call from your favourite father's ladyfriend's daughter. Pippa asked how/where you are, said she'll be in touch. Ha ha!!! xxx'

I'm instantly on edge. Pippa hasn't stuck her oar in yet, but it stands to reason that she'll be furious with me, on her mother's behalf. Especially if Bev's told her that, when I had my moment of madness and stole the ashes, I hurtled off with the remains of *her* dad and not mine.

Pippa is a pleasant enough woman. If I met her at a party, we'd manage a decent conversation for ten minutes, as long as we didn't stray into anything controversial or uncomfortable. I don't know her politics but I've got a fairly good idea what they are and they're from a very different hymn sheet to mine. Her husband, Mark, is a senior partner in a law firm and earns squillions. Elliott and Evie go to an independent school with fancy uniforms and a well-stocked stationery cupboard. When Elliott had his tonsils out, the NHS wasn't troubled.

I inherited my politics from Mum and Dad. Nothing too firebrandy or banner-wavy. Just a sense of what's right and fair and equal. I loved them for that and was happy to follow where they led. I suspect Dad had to rein in some of his more egalitarian views when he got together with Bev: she's resolutely apolitical and far happier talking about geraniums or *Strictly* than Prime Minister's Questions.

At Southampton Central I have five minutes to buy a coffee and a KitKat before boarding the Poole train. Pippa rings just as I'm settling into my seat and snapping off a chocolate finger.

'Annie, it's Pippa. Pippa Spencer. Bev's daughter, Pippa . . . Spencer.'

I stop myself from saying that I flipping know who she flipping is. Pippa has never done me any harm so my antagonism towards her is hardly her fault.

'Hi Pippa, how are you?'

'Fine thanks. Just getting over a cold. We've all had it.'

'That's good. That you're getting over it, I mean.'

A pause while she weighs up whether to continue the small talk or to cut to the chase, the reason she's ringing.

'Kate said you're in Dorset.'

'Not yet. I'm just pulling out of Southampton station right now, on my way to Poole. Sea area Portland.'

'Oh yes, the Shipping Forecast. Mark sometimes listens to it because of his sailing. The thing is, we're in Lulworth for the week, at the cottage we time-share with his brother and sister. There's always a tussle over who gets the summer hols. Your dad and my mum came to stay a few times.'

'That rings a bell. He said it was really chocolate-boxy. In a good way.'

'It is. Roses round the door and all that. Mark's forever banging his head on the low beams. Anyway, Mum's down for the week too and she – we – wondered if you'd like come for lunch, supper, whatever. If that fits into your schedule.'

'I don't have a schedule. Or a car. I'm not sure how I'd get to – where was it – Lulwood?'

'Lulworth. No probs. I can pick you up from Poole station. It's not far. What time does your train get in?'

'13.13, hold-ups permitting.'

'Great. I'll be in the car park. Metallic gold Renault Scenic.'

'I don't know what that is.'

'People carrier. Mark's pride and joy. It's got seagull business all over the bonnet. You can't miss it. Great. We have a plan. That's great. Call me if you're held up. See you in a bit. Byee.'

I could call her straight back, point out that I didn't say yes and, actually, I have other plans. But, apart from finding a B&B, I don't. I'm still not sure if Poole Pottery is even made in Poole.

An hour later, I'm sitting alongside Pippa in her guano-covered people carrier, driving through the Poole 'burbs, direction deepest Dorset. My Star Wars wheelie suitcase, with Dad ensconced within, is squeezed into a boot packed with wetsuits, surf boards, fishing rods, beach shoes, wellies, waterproofs, walking boots, two crates of beer and several six-packs of Pepsi. The Spencer clan clearly has a busy week planned.

Pippa has swapped her usual smart-casual wardrobe for a pale-yellow polo shirt, salmon-pink shorts and two-tone deck shoes. Her face is free of make-up, apart from a slick of lip gloss, and her bobbed hair is as neat and trained as ever. She looks good. I really should try to like her more.

'You travel light,' she says, as we leave Poole and she can finally shift into fifth gear.

'I only need a couple of changes of clothes and access to a washing machine.'

'Use ours while we have lunch. Mum's making seafood risotto. You do eat seafood?'

'I love seafood. My mum hated shellfish so I had to leave home to try my first lobster.'

Not much more to say about seafood. From either of us. Pippa knows the roads well and whips us swiftly past Wareham and Wool, past signs for Monkey World and the Tank Museum.

'Mark's out sailing with the kids,' Pippa tells me, over-taking a tractor. 'We've got a boat. Well, a third of one. He could practically sail before he could walk. He's so in his element. Elliott loves it too, Evie not so much. She's more land than sea, that one.'

'I've just caught up with an old friend in Brighton who has a fear of the sea. We did a tour of the wind farm.'

'Evie would love that. Anything with an engine, anything mechanical. She's always asking me how things work: the Nespresso, the retractable flex on the vacuum cleaner. Like I'd know. I always say: Ask your father.'

Pippa seems nervous around me, nattering nineteen to the dozen to fill any awkward pauses. I learn, in detail, that Mark grew up in Dorset and really misses living by the sea. Landlocked Potters Bar just doesn't cut it. Maybe my Shipping Forecast quest will resonate with him. His brother and sister never strayed as far away as he did: Julia is a dentist in Bridport, Tim is an accountant in Sherborne.

They've all done really well for themselves. Pippa so envies Mark his siblings, even though they often squabble, especially Mark and Julia, usually at Christmas.

Pippa envies Kate and me too. 'Such a tight unit. You two against the world. That's what it seems like to me, anyway. If you're an only child, it can be very lonely. When Dad died, I wish I'd had a big sister to hold my hand, tell me it would be all right. But there we are. If wishes were fishes. Do you know that song?'

'I thought wishes were horses.'

'Whatever.' She takes a deep breath, as if she's about to deliver a well-rehearsed speech. 'I do have one wish, Annie. That we make an effort. For Mum's sake. She's been through this twice now. Losing my dad, then yours. She's been so brave, so dignified, but she really doesn't deserve any of this.'

'Of course she doesn't. Who does?'

'Obviously you and Kate know all about the grieving process. Two steps forward, one step back. One good day, one bad day. You've been there twice, so you know the drill. Even so, Mum's been worried about you. That's why she invited you. She feels responsible for you, in lieu of your dad. She needs to know you're okay.'

'I'm fine. Under the circumstances. I'm fine, Pippa.'

'In that case, you'll want to know that *she's* fine too. Especially after the business with the ashes. Please will you check that she's still okay with what you did, Annie? Yes, she said she is but I'm really not sure.'

'Absolutely.'

And I will. I need to stop thinking this journey revolves around me.

* * *

The cottage is beautiful, hiding behind a bank of oak trees at the top of a quiet lane. There really are roses round the door, pink blowsy ones nodding in the breeze, and a neatly manicured cloud of white jasmine. As Pippa parks the people carrier, Mark and the kids rock up on bikes, looking wind-blown and hungry.

'Granny will find you a snack,' Pippa says, shooing them indoors. 'Do not touch the muffins. They're for later. And yes, I'm looking at you, Elliott Spencer.'

Mark retrieves their abandoned bikes, props them against the wall and ambles over. Like Pippa, he also favours salmon-pink shorts, but with a Jack Wills logo-ed T-shirt. I'd forgotten how unfeasibly tall he is, towering a good foot over Pippa and me. He's one of those men who exudes laidback, cocky confidence and, even though we barely know each other, he leans down and gives me a two-cheek kiss. I'm impressed. Men are usually crap at that. I nearly broke my nose once, trying to mwah-mwah Rob's nervous cousin.

I immediately decide that Mark's having a steamy affair with a colleague. Not his PA or secretary. That would be too easy, too cheesy. More likely a fellow lawyer who isn't remotely expecting wedding bells. Otherwise, his life with Pippa and the boys would be too cosy and comfortable. Obviously, Mark doesn't know that I know . . . even though my suspicions are based purely on an overactive imagination.

He goes to unload my Star Wars wheelie suitcase from the car boot, but I stop him.

'Might as well leave it in the car,' I point out, a bit too eagerly. 'I'm only here for lunch, then I'll head back to Poole.'

'I'll give that B&B a ring for you, Annie,' Pippa chips in. 'Our friends Roger and Sally stayed there. They said it was really cosy and friendly.'

Mark ignores her and takes my case to the house. 'Don't be silly. Stay with us.'

Pippa glares at his departing back. Did they discuss this at breakfast? Did Pippa say I wasn't welcome and Mark said nonsense? Or maybe Bev told them she didn't want me to stay. Because she's decided she needn't be nice to me any more . . . Because I've really, really upset her by taking Dad's ashes and he's turning in his urn?

But when I find her in the kitchen, in a Cath Kidston pinny, stirring a vast vat of risotto on the Aga, she couldn't be more pleased to see me. She wipes her hands on a towel and rushes over, open armed.

'Annie! How lovely that you could come. I want to hear all about your adventures.' She spots my suitcase, dumped in the hall by Mark. 'And you can stay too? It's a bit cramped but we'll squeeze you in somewhere.'

I marvel at my ability to lie on the spot. 'I wish I could stay, Bev, but I need to be back in Poole later. I'm meeting an old friend of Mum's tonight. Who lives in Poole. Her name's . . . Glynis. From university. They shared a student house at university. Yes. Glynis.'

'So you're looking up people on your travels, are you? That's good. I was worried you might get lonely.'

'Not at all. I've caught up with friends in, let's see, Forth, Tyne, Dover and Wight. And Kate joined me in sea area Thames.'

Bev remembers the risotto and loosens the grains with a splash of stock. 'Will you stir? I need to make the garlic bread.'

It's all very domestic and, on the surface, totally relaxed. Bev crams dollops of pungent butter into baguette crevices while I stir the rice. It smells bloody lovely.

'How *is* Kate?' Bev asks. 'I never seem to ring at a good time.'

'Oh, she's fine. Really well, as it happens.' Bev needn't be told that she's had a lesbian fling, walked out on her job and sounds desperately unhappy right now. I know exactly how that feels, apart from the lesbian thing. Been there, done that, got the T-shirt.

Pippa bustles in with the beer. 'Do you want to use our washing machine, Annie? It's in the futility room, as Mark likes to call it.'

He would. I'll bet he's never done anything as 'futile' as wash a load of bed linen or a muddy football kit in his life. You can tell.

I find the washing machine and tip my carrier bag of grubby clothes straight in. I can't believe I've travelled so far on so few clothes. It's a life lesson, actually. Don't pack what you don't need. Anyway, half the case is taken up by Dad's urn, wrapped in the jeans Yasmin gave me. I rest him on a nearby shelf as I add the detergent and set the dial to 'quick wash'. I don't intend to stay here any longer than I have to.

Bev shouts, 'Lunchtime, everyone!' from the kitchen and, after a bit of nagging to get the kids indoors with clean hands, we're all sitting around an ancient refectory table helping ourselves to risotto, salad, garlic bread, griddled courgettes and broad beans from the garden. We could be the cast of a TV commercial for home insurance or wholemeal bread or casual clothing. The Spencer crew are a great-looking family: Mark with his lanky Peter Crouch vibe, Pippa all petite and stylish, and the kids, already tanned from sailing, now squabbling over who will get the coveted crust-end of the baguette.

Bev beams at her brood. She must miss cooking for Dad,

fussing over him, finding recipes that would keep down his cholesterol and keep up his roughage. Not that it helped. He still died.

Pippa asks about Glynis and I find myself elaborating wildly on my lie; how she and Mum lost touch in their twenties but we found her phone number in an address book after Mum died, hoping she could come to the funeral. But she was in Australia and then we lost touch again and blah-blah-blah. I can't believe I'm churning this stuff out and that these people are listening, commenting, believing. I'm slightly ashamed that it comes so easily.

And then I am punished for my deceit. The god of duplicity and dentistry takes revenge. I bite on a chunk of baguette and find something hard, like a pebble, rattling around in my mouth. I remove it, wipe off the half-chewed breadcrumbs and study it.

Evie is fascinated too. 'Eeeuw! What's that?'

'A crown. My crown. It's come out.'

As I speak, wind whistles past the hole and catches on an exposed nerve. I wince.

Elliott peers at it. 'Is it like a denture or something?'

'It's a little fake tooth,' Bev explains. 'The dentist puts them in when your tooth isn't suitable for repair any more. Or if you ate too many toffee apples and sticks of Swanage rock when you were little.'

'Don't, Mum,' Pippa says firmly. 'Elliott and Evie take really good care of their teeth. Don't you, kids?'

Evie nods earnestly. 'Can I have it, Annie?'

Mark has been half engaged in a text on his phone. He says it's work related but he's probably arranging a liaison with his secret lover. 'Course not, Pickle. Annie needs to get it stuck back in.'

'There's some superglue in the kitchen drawer,' Evie points out helpfully. 'Mum used it yesterday to repair my Crocs. I have really steady hands when I make models.'

I feel almost invisible as they discuss me. I'm not in pain but I am in discomfort and suddenly feel far from home and the safe hands of my usual dentist, Dr Shah.

'Not to worry. I'll find an emergency dentist in Poole,' I suggest, feeling the wind on my nerve again.

Mark won't hear of it. 'Julia's closer. My sister. She's just down the road in Weymouth. I'll ring her now. See if she can squeeze you in by end-of-play today.'

I go to the bathroom to swill out my mouth. I scrutinize the gap in the mirror. It's my first and only crown. I have taken excellent care of my teeth my whole life so this feels distinctly unfair.

When I get back, there's news. Julia is on her way home from a conference in Birmingham. But she can see me tomorrow at 5 p.m. That means staying with the Spencers, whether I like it or not. Bloody great.

Bev asks if Glynis will mind not meeting up with me till tomorrow. 'Maybe she can join us for supper? She'd be most welcome.'

'We've not managed to connect this long,' I reply philosophically. 'One more day won't hurt. I'll suggest supper, though; thanks, Bev.'

After lunch, Pippa and Bev clear away and won't hear of me helping. Mark and the kids cycle to the farm shop to pick up strawberries for pudding. And I check out my accommodation. I've been offered either the lumpy fold-out sofa in the middle of the open-plan living room or an air bed in the summer house. There's no loo but if I don't mind using a potty, it will at least afford me a bit of privacy. Apparently the kids like to get up early, make themselves cereal and commandeer the sofa while they play on their tablets. No contest.

I've stayed in a variety of places since I set off: the fish-themed B&B in Cromarty, the posh hotel in Scarborough, the super-stylish loft conversion in Leigh-on-Sea, Hilary's agit-prop retirement flat in Bexhill. But this has to be the most magical sleepover so far. Yes, it's a glorified garden shed and, okay, I'm not a fan of spiders or weeing in a battered enamel chamber pot that's seen the business end of a fair few arses over the years. But if I can get past that – and I can – it's positively enchanting. There's an air bed, a paint-flaked Lloyd Loom chair, an old bentwood coat stand decorated with wire hangers and a little school desk. I may never leave . . . except if I need to do more than a midnight wee.

Despite the delights of the summer house, I feel trapped. I want to be able to leave when it suits me. Must I wait until Mark's sister can reattach my crown? I try Googling dentists in Poole but I have no signal. I can't even text Glynis to tell her what's happened. I honestly do process that thought for a split second, before reminding myself that she is fake news. Whenever I lie, I do it so convincingly that even *I* believe it. Get a grip, girl.

After supper (which sadly Glynis couldn't make because she's feeling unwell) the children watch a Japanese amination on Netflix, kiss everyone goodnight – even me – and head for bed. Bev is happy to babysit so that Mark and Pippa can nip to the pub. Would I care to join them? I decline. I can't see us having a huge amount to talk about once Elliott and Evie aren't buzzing around to distract us. Besides, I think

Bev's expecting some quality time with me and I daren't make up another bullshit story about craving an early night just in case God exacts further punishment and a wisdom tooth plinks out.

We take our teas onto the back porch and settle in two distressed Adirondack chairs. We agree that bats are amazing, resourceful little creatures but hope they don't fly too close. This is good. This is nice.

'Peter loved this house,' Bev tells me, balancing her mug on her armrest. 'He wondered if we should move to Dorset permanently. We even looked at a place in Swanage, near the pier. It ticked all the right boxes.'

'He never told me.'

'Because it didn't happen. We thought about it for a week or two but he didn't feel he could leave you and Kate, move so far away. I had the same qualms about Pippa and Mark and the kids. They rely on me for childcare and, besides, they're only ever down here a few weeks a year. He time-shares this cottage with Tim and Julia. Apparently they inherited some money from an uncle.'

'Lucky old Mark.'

'Isn't he? All this plus the partnership. You know he's a partner in his law firm now?'

'Lucky old Pippa.'

I mull over what Bev said just now about Dad not feeling able to leave us. I should let it pass. I know I should. Must I accept Bev's distorted spin on something I can't hear in Dad's own words? What if I don't like what she says? I should behave with maturity and let it pass . . .

'Why did Dad feel he couldn't leave us? Me and Kate? We're both grown-ups.'

Bev gives a little nod, as if she's weighing up what to say.

Just as I decide maybe I don't want to hear her reply after all, she launches in. 'Of course you're both grown-ups. And, oh, he was so proud of you: your teaching, Kate's, um, whatever it is she does with software. But your mother's death had hit you hard. He could see how much you needed him, especially when you had your, um, breakdo—when you broke up with Rob and gave up teaching.'

'Did he worry that I'd become a spicehead or a bag lady?'

As always, Bev laughs. She thinks I'm making a joke. As always, I let her.

'He adored you both. You know that, Annie. The simple reason is he couldn't bear to be so far away from you.' She waves an expansive hand around at the garden. 'All this – the garden, the countryside, the sea. It's lovely but it's for holidays, isn't it? Not for life.'

'He thought about it, though.'

'You do when you get to our age. Where you'll be happiest, cosiest. You think about your mortality too. We both did. But we reckoned we'd have plenty of years put aside to get old together. Sadly, it was not to be.'

I know it's irrational but I suddenly feel a huge wave of resentment towards Dad. He thought about abandoning Kate and me and moving to Dorset, to create ties with his 'new' family, plus the grandchildren we selfishly hadn't provided. And then he decided against it *because* of us.

'So let me get this right, Bev. We held him back from his dreams because we were too inadequate to look after ourselves. Not Kate maybe. Just me.'

However she glosses over it, I feel guilty. I pissed on his twilight years by being so useless.

'I knew this would be awkward. That isn't what I meant at all, Annie.'

215

I don't want to hear any more. I retire to the summer house, feigning tiredness. Once zipped into my sleeping bag, I compose a long text to Simon, saying way more than I mean to. Yes, maybe we could make a go of it. And yes, this time we wouldn't blunder into a relationship like a pair of self-obsessed, dopey kids. He makes me feel wanted again and I'm hugely grateful.

Then I delete the message which I can't send anyway because of the non-existent signal. Probably just as well . . .

I sleep so soundly that I have no need for the chamber pot, thank God. I occasionally half-hear the snuffle of a passing cat – or it could be a hedgehog – but I don't let it rouse me from dreams about teeth and Dad and madly stirring something over a scary open fire that isn't risotto and boils away anyway. In my dream, Dad wears a Fair Isle tank top. Dad never wore tank tops. I blame Bev.

At 5.45, Evie pops by, in PJs and Crocs. She isn't noisy but she doesn't tiptoe either.

'Have you seen my Star Wars escape pod? I think I left it in here.'

'Um, no. What does it look like?'

'Duh-err, like an escape pod. Wow, is that your suitcase? It's awesome.'

Nobody has commented on my suitcase since Yasmin gave it to me in Edinburgh, although I've had one or two strange looks in hotel receptions and at stations. Someone even told me his son had the same one. Who was that now? The car-hire guy in Scarborough, maybe? To have it admired so enthusiastically by Evie is pretty flattering.

'A boy called Fin gave it to me in Edinburgh because he already had one,' I tell her. 'It *is* awesome, isn't it?'

'How's your mouth? Can I see your crown again? Can I see where it came out of?'

I fish the fake tooth out of my purse. It's tooth-coloured and looks real. Evie picks it up and studies it closely. 'I want one of these when I grow up. It's so cool.'

'I'll show you the hole after I've brushed my teeth,' I tell her.

First the suitcase, now the tooth. I can do no wrong with Evie. She must think *I'm* pretty damned awesome too. We search for the Star Wars escape pod, which I find behind the Lloyd Loom chair. It's . . . awesome.

'Do you want some orange juice with bits in it?' Evie asks. 'I do.'

'My favourite kind. Yes please.'

She pads off to raid the fridge and returns a few minutes later with two half-full tumblers and a snack pack of popcorn, tucked into the waistband of her pyjamas.

'Won't that spoil your breakfast?' I ask, attempting to be the responsible adult.

'Not if we share it.'

She tips the popcorn onto my sleeping bag and divides it into two equal piles. I remember the science of sharing with Kate. Each square of chocolate or chunk of cheese had to be precisely the same size, weight and volume. It drove Mum mad.

There's no need for conversation as we sip our juice and eat our popcorn. Evie is comfortable in my company and that pleases me no end.

'We're going to Swanage Railway today to go on an old train. Are you coming too?'

'I haven't been asked.'

'I just did.'

217

'Thank you, Evie. I'd love to.'

'What's a fuck-up?'

Her innocent question catches me unawares. 'Pardon?'

'A fuck-up. Daddy said you're one. And Mummy said that's not fair.'

'Why don't we ask him?' I suggest.

Mark is super-nice to me at breakfast. Did I sleep well? Was I warm enough? More toast? More tea?

I tell Mark I'm just fine . . . for a fuck-up. Okay, I don't say that second bit. After last night's chat with Bev, I decide not to make a scene. It would probably only rubber-stamp my fucked-up-ness, not just to Mark but to the whole family.

Elliott has a litany of whinges to air over his Corn Flakes. Why did Evie wake him up at 5.30? Why isn't it sunny yet? Why didn't his favourite shorts go in the wash so he could wear them today?

'And why do we have to go on that stupid old train again?' he concludes, kicking his chair leg for emphasis. 'We do it every time we come here and it's boring.'

'It isn't,' Evie responds. 'And we don't do it every time. We didn't go at Easter because it was raining, even though the train was still running. Did we, Mum?'

'It really wasn't a day for going out, Pickle,' Pippa confirms. 'We'd have got soaked through.'

'So you said "next time, definitely" and this is next time. And Annie really wants to come, don't you, Annie.'

'Definitely.'

Elliott pushes his plate away and stomps into the garden. 'You always side with Evie. So not fair.'

Bev offers to go after him but Pippa shakes her head. 'He needs to know that losing your temper doesn't win arguments.'

Mark uses his lawyerly nous to broker an acceptable compromise. How about he takes Elliott sailing and everyone else does the Swanage thing? Deal? Deal. Evie gives a victorious grin and a little hop of happiness. Awesome.

So the people carrier, now spattered with a few more Jackson Pollock swirls of seagull shit, is a spacious, women-only affair: Pippa and Bev in the front, me and Evie in the back. We drive cross-country, along thin, lumpy roads, occasionally outstaring drivers coming the other way so that they have to reverse into a passing place. Pippa takes no prisoners.

We park at Norden station, in the middle of nowhere, so that we can enjoy the full experience of taking the train to Swanage, then back again.

'We've done it the other way too,' Evie explains. 'But this way's way better because then we have something to do when we get there.'

'What's that?'

'Swanage!' she shouts, hurtling ahead to the station entrance.

The platform isn't busy: just a few families like us, plus the inevitable train-spotting couple: the man wearing one of those khaki cricketer's sun hats and tucked-in shirt, the woman wearing a weary smile, wishing she was in a foldaway camping chair on the beach, with the latest Martina Cole.

Once on the train, Evie nabs us our very own compartment, with a corridor outside. And we're off, chuffing through Corfe Castle station, with its picture-perfect ruins on the hill.

Bev remembers travelling on trains like this when she was Evie's age. 'They even smell the same,' she says. 'Musty and dusty. And the seats had antimacassars, to soak up the Brylcreem.'

Evie looks to Pippa and me for a translation. We shrug. Not. A. Clue.

The train ride is pleasant but underwhelming. Once you're sitting inside a vintage train carriage, pulled by a vintage steam engine, it begins to feel normal. But on a normal train journey, you don't get waved at by families in campsites as you steam past or see over-excited men taking photos with fuck-off cameras at every station.

Evie is in heaven. I may be underwhelmed but I'm loving her excitement.

'How often have you done this, then?' I ask her.

'Four, no, five times,' she says, totting it up in her head. 'Well, ten times if you count the there and the back.'

'And the novelty hasn't worn off? You still love it?'

She stares at me as if I'm mad. 'Duh-err! Ye-es!'

A volunteer guard, in full uniform plus peaked cap, slides our door open and Bev hands him our tickets. He clicks a hole in them, under Evie's watchful gaze.

'Can I hold them, Nana?'

'Until we get to Swanage. Then I'll keep them safe for the journey home.'

The guard, a cross between David Attenborough and the Werther's grandad, shows Evie how his ticket clicker works. He must have to do this for every child on the train but, give him his due, he makes it look as if he just thought of it.

'And what's your name, miss?'

'Evie.'

'Are you enjoying yourself, Evie?'

'Yes.' She's suddenly all shy and goofy, staring hard at her Crocs.

'That's good. Because if I see anyone who isn't enjoying themselves, I tell them they'll be tossed off.'

Evie and Bev nod earnestly at his warning. Pippa catches my eye and we swallow down our laughter. It has to escape as soon as he's gone.

'What?' says Evie, perplexed.

'What?' says Bev, puzzled.

By now, we're too hysterical to explain. Evie shrugs and moves to the corridor to watch Swanage appear. Grown-ups are so silly. They laugh at stuff that isn't even funny.

'What?' Bev asks again. 'What did I miss?'

Pippa whispers an explanation into Bev's ear while I watch the penny drop. She is at first horrified, then embarrassed. Just as I'm thinking this is going to turn eggy and awkward, she emits a loud, fruity hoot of laughter. She turns pink, flaps her hand at her face and mops her eyes with a hanky.

'It's just – I wouldn't have – I honestly didn't know it was called that.'

I've never seen her so uninhibited. Dad must have seen her like this, loved her for this. It suits her.

Another day, another Great British seaside resort. In travelling around the coastline, I am bound to experience one or two. Perhaps I should write a guide, comparing Scarborough with Southend with Swanage. The tourist tat in the shops is the same: sun hats that resemble watermelon slices . . . rubber rings that resemble doughnuts. The fish and chips smell of fish and chips and the streets heave with day-trippers, whether you're in Tyne, Thames, Portland or Plymouth.

That said, I'm starting to take a shine to Swanage, probably because I'm seeing it through Evie's eyes. She's such a sunny, upbeat little girl. She's curious about everything: the train; the ship-in-a-bottle in a junk shop window; my stupid crown, twenty-four hours on.

221

Evie helps me choose a £1 ball of red wool from a bin outside a charity shop. It reminds me of the wool I bought to knit the hat for Stephen Gately. Then we stop for a cup of tea and Evie shares my jam tart. It's definitely home-made, rather than cash-and-carry, with very buttery pastry and the darkest raspberry jam. Evie declares it's the best she's ever eaten, and she's right. It is really, really good. I hadn't noticed. Too busy chewing on the side without the missing crown. I should notice stuff more.

Then we walk onto the pier, with Evie running ahead to observe an angler landing a fish. 'Don't go far,' Pippa shouts.

Evie waves and I wave back, rather over-eagerly. Am I enjoying her company just because she's enjoying mine? Or is this the ongoing broodiness I've become brilliant at locking away? I honestly don't think I felt the same connection with Duncan and Yasmin's boy. I just envied them their family unit, as I envied Kim in Scarborough, even though her two are practically grown up. So perhaps this isn't broodiness; perhaps it's regret. It looks as if I've missed the boat and it makes me particularly sad when I meet amazing children like Evie.

'You've got a new best friend,' Bev tells me as we find a bench, leaving Pippa and Evie to explore the end of the pier.

'Evie, you mean? She's a sweetie.'

'She adored Peter too. Maybe she sees him in you. I certainly do.'

'Do you?'

'Well, obviously I never met Jackie so I don't know what you inherited from her. I've only seen photos. Kate looks more like her, I think. Her hair, her lovely long legs.'

'While I got Dad's rugby player legs.'

'You and me both. Peter was always trying to get me into shorts on our hiking holidays but I dug my heels in.'

I try again. 'Why am I like Dad?'

'Apart from the legs?' She chuckles. 'You have his temperament, his eyes. You both do that shoulder-heaving thing when you laugh and your eyes go all crinkly. You must know what I mean.'

I do. Of course I do. 'Dad and I used to make each other laugh all the time. Mum called it "acting the giddy goat". Silly voices, silly walks. Kate hated it. She'd hang back, pretend we weren't her family.'

'I have to ask, Annie. Is Kate okay?' Bev looks genuinely concerned. 'I can't help it, I worry about you both. I don't expect you to ring me every day, like Pip does. But Peter would want me to keep an eye on the two of you.'

Well, according to Bev's oh-so-perfect son-in-law, I'm officially a fuck-up. And Kate's going through all sorts of emotional shit right now, most of which she won't talk about even to me. I'm fairly sure the lesbian thing isn't the half of it.

'Oh, we're muddling through, Bev. We came out the other side after Mum died. Mind you, we had Dad then. We know the drill. The good days, the bad days, the bad nights. Well, you know all that too, from losing Keith.'

'I lost Keith a second time when you ran off with him.' She's smiling. She doesn't hate me.

'I'm so sorry about that, Bev. I don't know what came over me.'

'When he was alive, he never got north of Edinburgh. We went there before Pippa was born, to see the Tattoo. So you gave him a bit of an adventure. And now your father's having one too, thanks to you.'

Bev's understanding is making my eyes fill. She's not meant to be nice. I'd kind of hoped this would be the last time we'd need to be together. This niceness really isn't helping.

'See those flats over there,' she says, out of the blue, pointing to a modern development, beside a rather ornate Victorian clock tower. 'That's where we thought about moving to. Second floor, the one with the porthole window. Peter was very taken with that window. Such splendid views of the pier and the bay.'

And now I do start crying because I'm staring at Dad's dream home in sea area Portland. Who wouldn't want to spend their final years here? But he stayed in St Albans because he couldn't trust me to look after myself.

'Hey, hey,' Bev says gently, putting an arm round me. 'You'll start *me* off in a minute.'

'I've behaved like a child. Before he died and afterwards. So selfish. I stopped you and Dad moving here. I've gone on this mad trip and now I have to see it through because everyone thinks I should.'

'Only if *you* want to, love. Do you?'

'Maybe. Yes. Or what about here?'

Bev doesn't understand. I'm not sure I do. Yet. I let the words tumble out to see where they take me. 'If Dad loved Swanage so much, maybe we could scatter him off the pier. Right here. I bet people do it all the time. If this is where he wanted to spend his final years, we could make that happen.'

'Ah, I'm with you now.'

'Kate can join us. If I rang her, she could be here tomorrow. Tonight, even.'

'She's got a very responsible job, Annie. She can't just swan off to Swanage.' Bev beams briefly at her accidental pun.

Kate definitely wouldn't want me to tell Bev that there is no job and it looks like both Stanley girls are quitters. So I wing it. 'I bet she could swan off. And Pippa and Mark and the kids would be here too. What do you think?'

Bev stares down at the pier planks beneath our feet. I've stopped crying but I fear I've set her off and she's too distraught to talk. She's quiet for a really long time, just looking down, and I don't know what to say. I've upset her. The flats on the shoreline have reminded her of the happy ending that was stolen from her. All I can do is pat her hand. Then she pats mine and I pat that one. We create a little tower of hands and laugh.

'To Rosemary & Bob. Our much-missed holiday pals,' she says at last, still looking down.

'Sorry?'

'For Paddy the poodle who loved this pier.'

'Who's Paddy the poodle? Are you okay, Bev?'

She points to the planks at our feet. Each one bears a little metal plaque with a short message: Rosemary & Bob; Paddy the poodle; Nana Jean 1949–2009; Ronnie Wright, loved to bits by Suzi. Swanage pier is covered in them and I hadn't even noticed.

'Peter didn't like things unfinished,' she says, now looking at me. 'Jars of jam, the Sunday papers, Scandi dramas on BBC4. It used to drive me potty.'

'You're right, he didn't. Even now, I hardly ever have leftovers. Drummed in by Dad.'

Bev laughs. 'He used to get so furious with Cromarty when he didn't eat all his Go Cat. I want you to finish this, Annie. You'll be disappointed in yourself if you don't. We can remember him right here with one of these little brass plaques. He'd get such a kick out of that, don't you think?'

Evie makes friends with the guard on our return journey to Norden and he lets her click all the tickets in our carriage. The train-spotting couple are also on this train and the man looks dead jealous. Why wasn't he asked to do that? He's always wanted to do that.

Pippa gets a text from Mark. There's been a change of plan. Julia's appointments are running late and she can't re-install my crown at 5 p.m. after all. Will first thing tomorrow do? That means another night with Bev and the Spencers. And, actually, that's fine with me.

Mark and Elliott are back before us and have slathered a couple of giant pizzas with whatever they could find: olives, sweetcorn, pineapple, half a tin of tuna and a shedload of red onion. I'm nervous about biting into the crust, because of my missing crown, so Pippa makes me a special dish of overcooked pasta and pesto. Sweet of her. She didn't need to. Even so, we'll never be besties and we know it. Which is fine.

After supper, we take over the refectory table for a very noisy game of cards that I never quite get the name or the hang of. It's like musical chairs; if you don't grab a card when everyone else does, you lose a life. Dad adored this game, apparently, and was a ruthless, devious, win-at-all-costs player. That doesn't surprise me. Bev is the opposite and is the first to lose all five lives.

When I'm knocked out too, I head for the kitchen to make tea for the grown-ups. I can hear low-volume talking from the futility room; it's Mark in muttered tones on his mobile. I can't make out what he's saying until the kettle's finished boiling, then I pick up everything, whether I want to or not.

'No, just listen okay, I can't talk now. I'll ring later. Stop making such a thing of it. You know, don't you, how difficult it is when I'm in Dorset. So please don't make it worse. Yes. Soon. Promise. Love you. Love you.'

I knew it. I bloody knew it. Sometimes my imagination isn't overactive or biased. Sometimes I'm just plain right.

I try to busy myself with the tea as he hangs up: peppermint for Bev to settle her imminent heartburn from the pizza, soya milk for Pippa, weak for me, strong for Mark. He manages to hide his surprise at finding me within earshot and offers to carry the mugs through. We exchange a look. He knows I know. I know he knows I know. Nothing is said. Nothing needs to be said.

For now . . .

Later, zipped into my sleeping bag, I think this through. Mark doesn't deserve my silence but I really don't want to get involved. Should I tell Bev? Pippa? Or keep schtum and save Mark's skin? Will my collusion make a bad thing worse or better?

I'll sleep on it. And I do . . .

Julia has texted to confirm that she'll fix my crown if I can get to her Bridport surgery by 8.45 latest. Mark offers to take me, probably so that he can spin me some line that the conversation I overheard last night was with his sick granny.

'That's really nice of you,' I reply, the soul of friendliness. 'But I don't want to ruin your plans. You take the family to Monkey World. I can easily order a taxi.'

Mark won't hear of it and neither will Pippa. He can take me to Bridport, then they'll go to Monkey World after that. 'No worries, Annie.' I'm cornered.

I retreat to the summer house to pack my few things. Dad has spent his time in sea area Portland, his well-travelled urn relaxing against a faded cushion on the Lloyd Loom chair.

'You nearly got scattered in Swanage,' I tell him as I wrap him in the Shipping Forecast tea towel. 'But Bev talked me out of it. She's okay, your Bev. I should have told you that before but I didn't know. I'm sorry, Dad.'

Last night, she and I knitted blanket squares in front of *Love Actually*, her favourite film ever, bar none. I'm not a fan but was happy to go along with it if I could catch up on my ridiculous project. Thanks to Bev, I now have eight completed squares to represent sea areas Cromarty, Forth, Tyne, Humber, Thames, Dover, Wight and Portland. Some are less lumpy and sweated over than others, but the end result was never going to be a thing of beauty.

I even taught Evie how to knit, like I'm suddenly the expert, and left her the remains of all the yarns so that she can make herself a stripy scarf. She's promised to send me a photo when it's finished.

'Where next?' Pippa asks as Mark loads my case into the people carrier.

'Sea area Plymouth. That's anywhere between Salcombe and Land's End.'

'What about Glynis?' Bev wants to know.

I have no idea who she's talking about. Glynis? Glynis? Then I remember Mum's fictional friend. 'She's going down with a cold. She texted to say maybe next time.'

'Oh, that's a shame. Still, her loss our gain.'

Pippa frowns. 'I don't know how you do it, Annie. Heading off into the unknown. No plan, no destination.'

'Got any suggestions?' I ask. Has to be better than sticking a pin in a tea towel.

'You could stop in Exeter. Lots of options from there.'

'Rightio, Exeter it is.'

She gives me a hug, an egg sandwich and a banana. 'Don't bite into anything crusty until the glue's dried.'

I still need to say goodbye to Bev, Evie and Elliott, not that I've made much of an impression on him. They come out of the house together to wave me off. More hugs – except from Elliott, who's way too cool – and more jokey warnings from everyone about taking care of my teeth.

I'm trying to find the words to thank Bev for being so understanding and Evie for being such a delight, when Bev suddenly suggests she comes on the drive to Bridport too.

'I'm just not ready to say goodbye yet. Is that okay?'

'I'd love that, Bev.'

'Then I'll come too,' Evie announces, slipping her hand in mine.

Chapter Eighteen

Plymouth

Bev has given me another reason to feel gratitude towards her. And she didn't even do it on purpose. By inviting herself along on the drive to Bridport, she's saved me from an excruciating conversation with Mark about what I did or didn't overhear last night in the kitchen.

That has to be the only reason he offered me a lift. He's barely exchanged twenty words with me since I arrived. Why converse with a fuck-up? What's in it for him? Well, nothing until last night. Now he needs to win me round, keep me sweet, make sure I don't spill any beans that might splat on him.

And Evie's come too because she didn't want to miss out. I flatter myself that she wanted to enjoy every last bit of my company. Why shouldn't I think that . . . as long as I don't let it go to my head.

'When will you get home?' she asks from the back seat of the Scenic. Bev insisted on putting me up front, alongside Mark, which makes his silent proximity all the more loaded.

'Hard to say. Couple of weeks maybe. A month max. There again, I might take a shine to Lundy or Liverpool and never return.'

'You *are* joking, Annie?' I can see Bev's frown in the rear-view mirror.

'Course I am. I might prefer Swansea or Stornoway.'

Evie invites me for tea when I've finished my trip. She will make double-choc cupcakes, her signature bake.

'I love cupcakes,' I tell her. 'If you show me how to get them double-chocolatey, I'll give you my Mum's secret carrot cake recipe. It's Delia Smith but with extra added – nope. Can't say. And if I write it down, you have to eat the piece of paper.'

Evie giggles. Job done.

I know I'm talking gibberish, partly because she's lapping it up and partly to block any openings from Mark. If I engage one word with him, it will feel as if I'm colluding. I still don't know what to do. What if I misheard the conversation and it's all perfectly innocent? I can't accuse him of having an affair; I can only accuse him of sounding furtive.

If pressed, I would testify that he's guilty as fuck, your honour. Written all over his wind-tanned, attractive, smug face.

He does speak eventually, but just to piss on my chips. 'You do know there are no trains from Bridport to Exeter?'

I didn't. 'Of course I do.'

'So how are you going to get there?' Evie wants to know. 'Can *we* take her, Dad?'

'And be the reason you miss Monkey World? I'd never forgive myself.'

'What about a bus?' Bev suggests. 'Or maybe we could drop you in Crewkerne. That's the nearest station, I think.'

I haven't thought any of this through but they don't need to know that. 'I'll hire a car in Bridport. That way I can drive on to Lundy, once I've knocked off sea area Plymouth.'

Pippa was right to be impressed. I am bloody intrepid. I'll drive to Exeter and beyond. I am so on it.

Julia is brisk and businesslike, probably because she has a packed day of fillings and extractions after me. My cavity is cleaned out and my crown stuck back in. It takes all of ten minutes and she doesn't charge me. Bev wanted to wait, to see if there were any problems, but I made them drive back to Lulworth. Those monkeys won't visit themselves.

I stand in the street, enjoying the feeling of a full set of teeth. No more wind whistling past exposed nerves, no more avoiding ice cream. I am complete again, ready to continue my journey. And, thanks to Bev, I can walk past a bin of random balls of wool outside a craft shop without having to buy one. Like my mouth, my yarn-based project is up to date and I don't need to knit another square until I'm past Salcombe.

Onward and upward. Or rather, westward. Yay me!

After a quick phone search, I find that I'm just around the corner from the car-hire firm I used in Scarborough. They'll do just fine.

This time I'm driving a silver-grey Hyundai i10. 'Stacy' tells me it's a popular choice and I'll love how it drives. I nod. It's a car. As long as there's a wheel in each corner and the radio isn't stuck on easy listening, I'm ready to hit the road. Stacy is satisfied that I'm satisfied.

Just as I'm signing the paperwork, my phone rings. I suddenly panic. Oh God, did I leave Dad in the summer house? Course not. He's safe, sound and snug in my Star Wars suit-case.

It's Josh, my nearly stepson. He's Fi's nearly stepson now. I can't help it. I resent her. Josh was the closest I got to parenthood and I blew it.

'Hey there, Miss Stanley,' he says, shouting to drown out a muffled PA.

'Hey there, yourself, Master Dwyer.'

'I'm on a train and my signal keeps fading. D'you mind if I cut to the chase?'

'Go on then.'

He launches straight in. 'So what it is is . . . Bev rang Dad and Dad rang me to say you'd just left Dorset and are heading for Exeter.'

'I am. Or I will be as soon as I've uploaded my route.'

'Fancy some company? I've got a thing to do in Exeter, then I'm meeting a mate in Cornwall.'

'And your dad's okay with this?'

'Annie, he suggested it. Go on, I'm an awesome navigator.'

'I'd love it.'

'Result! So I'm just pulling out of Reading, due into Exeter St David's at 13.03. The thing is, Anni—'

He's gone. I never know the etiquette for who phones who back in such situations. My phone vibrates and we pick up where we left off.

'That sounds good, Josh. See you in the car park. I'm driving a silver-grey Hyundai iPad or something. Do you know what they look like?'

'Not a clue. I have a small favour. Dad said you're too busy with your trip and not to ask. But I'm like, Annie won't mind.'

'Try me.'

'So what it is is—' And he's gone again. There's no point trying to find out now. It'll have to wait until 13.03.

My drive to Exeter is smooth – thanks to the Hyundai Wotsit – and jam-free, apart from some roadworks outside Honiton. I opt for the fast A35 and A30, rather than the scenic route closer to the coast, because I now have a place to go, a person to meet and a time to be there. I have to say, having Josh along for the ride to wherever is really appealing.

Initially it was awkward when he found out that his dad was dating Miss Stanley, albeit fairly innocently in those early days. I was really careful not to get involved with Rob until it was perfectly clear that he and Maggie were history. Until that point, our contact with each other was purely a business arrangement. He made me a kitchen cabinet. I paid him the going rate and hoped he'd never finish it.

We bumped into each other once, in WHSmith, and chatted in that polite, how-are-you style, although it was now pretty apparent that we majorly fancied each other. We even went for a coffee afterwards in Starbucks and he was super-keen to explain that his separation from Maggie was, by mutual consent, about to become permanent.

'Oh, that's a shame,' I said, not meaning it. Rob nodded. By now, we knew we were a matter of weeks from getting together and it was unbearably agonizing and erotic.

Josh gradually accepted that his dad and a teacher at his school were now a 'thing'. Even so, Rob and I were careful to keep our relationship under wraps for the first few months, in case any of my colleagues thought I was out of line, not that I was teaching him geography any more. When we finally went public, at a school fundraiser, nobody looked shocked or horrified.

Josh was going through a rough patch with Maggie, so all I had to do was be laidback, low-key and endlessly supportive. We had – we still have – the same sense of humour so we liked hanging out together, making each other laugh. Rob got a kick out of that too and it took the pressure off what could have been a difficult time.

I'm ensconced in the car park at Exeter St David's with ten minutes to spare. I nip to a mini-supermarket for some bottled water, humbugs and biscuits and then can't find my car. It's an excellent vehicle and has served me well so far but, to a non-petrolhead, it has no distinguishing features. Eventually I recognize it by my jean jacket on the back seat.

I'm just thinking about taking a photo of the car and registration plate so that I don't lose it again when Josh appears, in cut-off jeans, T-shirt and work boots, wearing a backpack the size of Cornwall. He looked pretty bloody grown-up at Dad's funeral but he's even more adult now. He towers above me and practically pulls me off my feet when we hug.

The thump in the pit of my stomach is back, the one that I also felt from my connection with Evie. It's the physical manifestation of missed chances at motherhood. But I'm not going to let it bring me down. I've connected with Josh and Evie in my own way and that's more than good enough. All the pleasure, none of the pain, and no stretch marks or stitches in my fanny either.

We set off, windows wide open for a welcome through-draught, and Josh gets me up to speed on why he's here and what this favour is.

'So what it is is—'

I can't help it, I laugh.

'What?' He looks aggrieved.

'"So what it is is." Oh, I've just missed you, Josher, that's all. Well, go on, what "is" is it?'

'You know I've got a place at Exeter Uni. English and film studies?'

'I did know that. I've just been way too self-obsessed lately. Course you have, clever old you.'

'I knuckled down at the last minute, just scraped through. Well, anyway, what it – the thing is, Dad wants me to stay in halls for my first year because that's what you do, right? That's what all my mates are doing. I get that. But Barney O'Hara from school, remember him?'

I do. Instantly. Shoulder-length hair, yappy and over-excited like an annoying spaniel.

'So his brother's in his third year at Exeter and he's moving in with his girlfriend and he's like: Do *I* want to take over his room in a rented student house?'

'But your dad doesn't want you to?'

'Stupid, isn't it? When I didn't even have to look for it. *It* found me.'

'What does your mum say?'

'Oh, she's too distracted with her shop. She's opening an online gift shop. It's all she thinks about, 24/7. She says whatever I decide is cool with her.'

'So you want *me* to approve? I don't think so, Josh.'

He looks worried, as if I'm not going to provide the solution he requires. 'I persuaded Dad that if you come with me, look at the room, look at the house, check out the neighbourhood, that might convince him it's all good.'

'Ah.'

'He trusts your judgement, Annie. If you say it's okay, he'll believe you. So you just need to give it the once-over and say it's okay. Okay?'

'And if it's a crack house or a squat, I can say that too?'

Another flaw in Josh's foolproof plan. 'Yeah, I suppose. But it won't be.'

It isn't a crack house or a squat. It's a terraced house in a pleasant part of Exeter, called Pennsylvania, not far from

the campus, not far from the football grounds, not far from
the town centre. Judging by the crates of empties in front
gardens, there are several other student houses along this
street.

Number 56 has two bikes padlocked to the railings and
a neglected lawn. The front window has the obligatory
pinned-up Indian throw, pretending to be a curtain, and
there's music blasting from the back. It's like my student
house in Moulsecoomb. It's as if time stood still.

We're shown around by Dinah whose parents, she tells us
within ten seconds, own the house. She's keen to point out
that she's just one of the gang but it's obvious she's taken
on Head Girl responsibilities, which is fair enough if The
Bank of Mum and Dad has to pick up the tab when bills
aren't paid or furnishings are trashed.

'Kitchen,' she says, stating the obvious, as we follow her
in. Like Josh, she's also in cut-off jeans but, whereas his
flap round his knees and expose the first four inches of
his tighty whities, hers are pretty much denim knickers:
snug, torn and showcasing a pert little bum. Josh can't
take his eyes off it, even when I give him a hefty nudge.
Dinah also has long white-blonde hair and, beneath a
cropped T-shirt, the kind of bra-less boobs I never had,
even when I was her age. Josh is quite taken with *them*
too.

'Depending on who's around, someone will make a shedload of chilli or mac 'n' cheese. Otherwise, people prefer to
do their own thing, foodwise.' Dinah opens the fridge and
each shelf encapsulates a differing nutritional approach: tofu
burgers and muddy carrots; half-consumed tinned beans and
budget trifle; beer, just beer.

'How many live here?' I ask, knowing Josh is unable to

conduct any major interrogation while his tongue is hanging out of his mouth.

'Me, Lula plus new person upstairs,' Dinah recites. 'Mo and Edwin downstairs.'

That sounds like a lot of housemates for one modest house. 'So there's no communal living room, no dining room?'

Dinah imperceptibly rolls her eyes. Josh follows suit. I'm not fussed. I'm here to be Nasty Cop and if she takes offence, that's not my problem.

'Hey, who needs a dining room?' Josh jokes, willing me to shut up.

Dinah nods, her hair bouncing animatedly. 'Absolutely, Josh. People stay in their rooms when they're not on campus. Sleeping, eating, studying . . . entertaining. We did have a communal living room when Mum and Dad first let the house but it was hardly used.'

More to the point, turn it in to a bedroom and that's another rent coming in.

I remember a joke someone told me when I was a student. I can't recall which university it referenced but, for the sake of argument, let's say it was Exeter.

Question: How many Exeter students does it take to change a lightbulb?

Answer: No need. Daddy just buys them a new house.

We tramp upstairs to see the vacant room. The door of the master bedroom is ajar and it doesn't take a detective to deduce that Dinah's got the best room in the house: neat as a pin, slatted wooden blinds, a smart Ikea desk-and-bed combo. Head Girl's perks.

The bathroom looks well used and there's a rota on the door: it's Edwin's turn to clean it . . . the day before yesterday. But there's no cross in the 'done' column. There's an Edwin in every shared house: slobby, lazy and dozy. Leave it long enough and someone else will relent and buy the new loo roll, empty the bin, wipe up the cider.

I can tell, from the layout of the house, which is identical to several I've lived in over the years, that the vacant room will be the box room. And it is. Not even big enough to swing a small rodent: single bed, clothes rail fitted wonkily in an alcove and two small chests of drawers topped by a plank of wood to make a desk.

'Wow,' says Josh. 'Dinky.'

'That's one way of describing it.' I nod. 'Where will you put everything?'

'I don't have much "everything". And I'm not going to get any "everything" when I'm here. Just books and stuff. Yeah, no, it looks great, Dinah.'

I give him a warning glare. Her arse has clouded his judgement and I've a duty to Rob – and Maggie – not to let his dick decide.

'Is the rent lower for this room because it's so much smaller?' I ask. 'And can Josh – or whoever moves in here – can they upgrade if a bigger room becomes vacant?'

'A bit less. And yes, they can upgrade. This used to be Lula's room,' she replies, starting to tire of her managerial duties. 'We've got two more people coming this afternoon to check it out. I need to know before then. Your friend vouched for you so it's yours if you want it, Josh.'

'Don't the other tenants have to meet him first? And him them? That's what we did when I was a student.'

'Back in the Ice Age,' Josh mutters.

'I'm in charge. I decide.' Dinah heads back downstairs. 'I'll give you five minutes to think about it.'

We wait until she's out of earshot, then both speak at once.

'You *did* want my opinion,' I say.

'I really like it,' Josh says.

'Oh, I know what you "really like" and trust me, Josher, she's way out of your league.'

'Don't call me that here,' he hisses.

Josh swears he'll be happy in this claustrophobic little room. But I'm the responsible adult and I think it would be a big mistake. And Rob would never forgive me if I don't say what I truly think.

'Are you sure you mightn't be better in halls?' I try. 'Just for the first year. To get the hang of student life.'

But he's made up his mind and my misgivings are surplus to requirements. All I can suggest is that he says 'yes' to Dinah and I'll work on him on the drive to Cornwall.

'I won't change my mind, though,' he says, jutting out a determined jaw. He looks so like his dad. Rob used to pull the same face when he ordered an over-hot curry, then ploughed through it, rather than admit his eyeballs were on fire.

Dinah looks underwhelmed by Josh's thumbs-up. As long as the rent's paid, she doesn't care who's squeezed into the box room. My guess is that Josh won't make any kind of impression on her. But right now, he reckons he's on a promise and I have to admire his optimism.

We hit the road for Cornwall, taking the fastest route via the A30, rather than driving across Dartmoor. Before we've even left the Exeter, Josh starts his pitch on why the student house will suit him. He doesn't mention Dinah. Not once. He claims he wants to strike out, to be independent, not bound by university rules and restrictions.

'Dad says if I choose catered halls, I don't have to cook for a whole year.'

'That's a good thing, isn't it?' I suggest tentatively. 'More time for settling in and studying.'

'But I like cooking. Nana taught me. I make a blinding crumble. What if I *want* to cook?'

'You can't live on crumble. Anyway, aren't there self-catered halls of residence?'

'Yeah? So? I just don't want to stay in halls.'

'If Rob asks me what I think, I won't lie, Josh.'

'Tell him you respect my decision. Because you do, don't you? End of.'

End of. I can keep up the pressure and piss him off or I can let him figure it out for himself. Dinah will be his landlady, nothing more. If she's after some Netflix and chill, she'll draw from a different pool of eager guys. And if Josh has to learn that lesson the hard way, so be it. Especially if the walls are thin and he hears every last grunt and groan, as I did with Glynis and Jeremy.

'Remind me where we're going?' I say breezily, opting to change the subject . . . for now.

'Fowey but it's pronounced Foy. Do you know it?'

'Like Happy's Berg and Haisbro.'

'Huh?'

'I talked about it at Dad's funeral. Or did I dream that? Never mind. Why-ee Foy-ee?'

Josh laughs. It isn't that funny, I know, but we allow each other bad jokes.

'Got a promise of some summer work down there. Rhys's Auntie Julie does B&B in her pub and she said she'd try us out, helping with the breakfasts and cleaning and stuff. Rhys has a tent so we won't have to fork out on accommodation. I'm going to get a six-pack and learn to surf.'

'That's quite an art, cooking a full English breakfast. Hey, you can always serve them crumble.'

'Crumble, egg and bacon, poached crumble on toast, the full crumble. She probably won't let us near the cooking, just serving and clearing away. I've brought proper trousers and a school shirt.'

I'm impressed. Before I went to uni, I took a summer job in a factory but I only lasted three days. It was too hard. After that, I mostly slept. Mum was tired and weak from the radiotherapy, so when I wasn't sleeping, I was keeping her company, doing laundry or burning sausages. It drove her mad, watching me do housework badly.

'So,' I say as we head for Okehampton with Josh's Spotify playlist blasting from the speakers. 'Student houses. Did you know I lived in one in Brighton?'

'Is this one of those stories where you say how rank it was, to try and put me off?'

'It was great. I loved it. I stayed there after I graduated. Big mistake. Leave before you're ready to go. Rule for life, that one.'

'Why did you stay?'

'The usual reason. Boyfriend. Plus I was loving the student life even though I wasn't a student any more. Then we broke up and he went back to Scotland – Duncan, my boyfriend – and, well, I realized I was ready to be a grown-up. I couldn't put it off any longer.'

'And how's that working out for you? The grown-up thing?'

'I'll tell you when I start.'

* * *

I need a 'comfort stop' and Josh announces loudly that he's 'gagging for a slash'. Same difference. Rather than hunt the streets for a public loo, we head for Okehampton Waitrose. The car park is heaving but I eventually find a space.

'If I give you a tenner, will you buy Rhys's aunt some flowers?' I ask Josh, after we've both done what we stopped for.

'Why?'

'Because she's giving you a summer job and it's a nice gesture. Because she'll remember you as "that thoughtful lad" when you break a plate or swear in front of the guests.'

'I meant: why should you have to pay for them?'

I'm impressed. Josh is a sweet, sensitive boy. He can do way better than Dinah. I give him a little hug.

'What it is is there's no need for you to pay. Dad gave me some dosh to get her chocolates but flowers are nicer. Even now, you two are *so* in each other's heads. Scary or what?'

It is. We are. Maybe we always will be, even when he and Fi are collecting their pensions. But he's not mine so it means nothing.

Back at the car, we carefully lay a mixed bouquet of summer blooms on the back seat. I've also treated Josh and Rhys to three six-packs of beer and a five-litre bottle of mineral water. I create a space for them in the boot while Josh gets cash from the ATM. My phone rings.

'Annie, it's Bev. I just wanted to know how you are. And where you are, come to that.'

'I'm fine. I'm in Okehampton.'

'How's the tooth? All shipshape?'

I chuckle at the nautical reference. 'Firmly anchored. Mark's sister did me proud. So, yes, I'm fine. I've got Josh with me. We're heading for Cornwall.'

'Oh, that's nice. I always liked Josh. I'm pleased you have a travel companion.'

Bev carries on talking but her words are drowned out by a deafening volley of car horn over my left shoulder. An impatient woman in a grubby Land Rover wants me to terminate my phone call and depart so that she can have my parking space. I beckon Josh back and tell Bev I'll call from Cornwall. As we drive off, Josh pulls a face at Grubby Land Rover Woman because she won't stop hooting. So rude.

Bev's right; I am lucky to have Josh alongside me. I wish I'd had a passenger on that interminable drive from Scarborough to Happisburgh. It makes such a difference, even when you're not chatting or sharing the driving. Occasionally, without prompting, Josh will unwrap a humbug and post it into my mouth, then he has one too and we see whose lasts the longest. Even though I'm super-careful not to chew into the sticky centre after losing my crown, Josh wins every time.

'How are you, Annie?' he suddenly asks.

'Well, I'll be hungry in about half an hour. Hey, we can have a Cornish Cornish pasty.'

'Not "how are you right now?" I mean, how are you from . . . all this? This trip with the ashes. Is it helping? Dad worries about you. He doesn't say so, but he does.'

What can I tell him? That I'm okay. But am I? That I'm so glad I took on this ridiculous project. But am I? That I look forward to getting back to St Albans when I'm finished? But will I? Dad will still be gone, Rob will still be with Fi, Kate will still be grieving and messed up and I'm still not sure I'm ready to go back to teaching.

The only difference between now and when I set off is

that I've found a way forward with Bev. She isn't the Enemy any more. That has to be worth all the miles I've covered since I set off for Luton Airport.

'How do *you* think I am, Josh?' Answering a question with a question was one of my favourite tricks with demanding pupils.

'I think you're better than you were because now you're, like, doing something, instead of just vegging out on the sofa.'

'Anything else?'

'I think you miss Dad.'

His words come out of left field and I nearly bite clear through the latest humbug, which he only popped into my mouth seconds ago.

'*Do* you miss him, Annie?'

'Well, yes. Course I do. I loved Rob. I still do . . . as a friend. But, well, I was a mess and I needed to sort myself out. It's just taken longer than I expected.'

'I still don't get why you had to break up with Dad to sort yourself out.'

When Josh says it like that, I find it hard to answer. What was I thinking when I pulled the plug on us? I know why I broke up with Toby and I think I know why I broke up with Duncan. But Rob? Couldn't we have ridden the storm together? At the time, I thought I was better off battling through it alone. I didn't want to drag him under the waves with me. But he wouldn't have let that happen. He'd have held my hand, pulled me through the undertow, saved me.

I stare at the A30 ahead and the road signs for Thrushelton, Stowford, Broadwoodwidger, Dingles Fairground Heritage Centre. I try to explain. 'Here's what I've learned from this trip, Josh. In the past, I've had a tendency to take a bad thing and make it even worse. Mum died. We knew she would. It didn't come as a surprise, like it did with Dad. Afterwards, I tried to bounce back, get on with my life, and that's when I met your dad. But it didn't happen. I couldn't "bounce". Ridiculous idea, if I'd only been rational enough to see that. So then I thought a bit of space and self-reliance would sort me out. Just me. By myself. No Rob to hurt or worry. It made sense at the time. I made a bad thing worse for both of us.

'But I'm trying to change the habit of a lifetime and make things better from now on. That's the plan anyway. So . . . how am I doing?'

'You're getting there. Bugger, I just crunched my humbug.'

When our stomachs won't stop rumbling, we make a pit stop in Launceston. So many market towns these past few weeks. So many loo- and lunch-breaks. So many pay-and-display tickets cluttering glove compartments. Launceston has the usual quota of narrow streets, clogged with parked cars, the usual range of cafes, charity shops and chain stores. It will do.

We pass a wool shop and my 'yarn alert' activates. Josh is checking his phone to see if Rhys has reached Fowey yet. I yank him into the shop to select my sea area Plymouth wool. Until now, I've been choosing colours that complement each other: maroon, red and dark pink; khaki, camel and honey tones. Josh selects a lurid lime green because it matches the logo on his T-shirt. As good a reason as any.

'What's it for?' he asks, not really that interested.

'I started squares knitting in Cromarty. For a blanket to represent all the sea – oh, never mind. How about this cafe?'

It's practically empty. The woman behind the counter is sealing tubs of egg mayonnaise and coronation chicken before packing up for the day. Why is Britain so unprepared for the late luncher? But she's still serving coffee and offers to warm us up a couple of half-price home-made pasties, because 'they won't keep'. She serves them with a little leafy garnish which Josh instantly sidelines. We barely exchange a word until our plates are empty.

I think we've re-bonded sufficiently to ask him the question that's been in my head ever since Exeter. 'So. Fi. What's she like then?'

Josh is unwrapping an Eccles cake and doesn't look up. 'Yeah. She's okay. Nice smile. Want some of this?'

I shake my head. No, I don't want a bite of his cake and no, that really won't do as an answer.

'Smiles are meant to be nice, Josh. That's what they're for. I need more than that.'

'Why?'

'Because I want to know Rob's happy. That he's made a good choice.'

'You want to know if she's as great as you?'

'Well, obviously.'

He looks uncomfortable, puts his cake down and over-stirs the last dregs of coffee. 'This isn't fair, Annie. I don't like being piggy in the middle.'

'I'm curious, that's all.'

'Mum did this. She wanted to know all about you when you first started seeing Dad.'

Of course she did. I would have done, if I'd been her. 'I'm sorry. Must be weird for you.'

'I'm not a kid, Annie. I wasn't a kid when Dad met you, was I? He can do what he likes, date who he likes. It's none of my business.'

'So, what did you say? When your mum asked about me?'

Josh glares at me. If I haven't already crossed the line, I'm just millimetres from it. 'That was different.'

'How? How was it different?' And there I go. Line crossed. Too late now.

He takes a big bite of his Eccles cake and doesn't reply until he's ready. 'Well, for one thing Mum and Dad were *so* over when you came along. She was horrible to him. Bullying, doing him down all the time. I was like: Stop it, leave him alone. But she wouldn't. Which is why I was pleased when you two got together, even though you'd been my teacher and all my mates took the piss.'

'Sorry about that.'

'So, yeah. They're much happier apart. Mum met Karl and Dad met you and they remembered how to be nice to each other again.'

'Thank you for accepting me. I didn't appreciate it at the time.'

'No problem,' he says shyly from under his ridiculously long lashes. 'You and Dad went well together. Anyone could see that. We laughed a lot, didn't we? All three of us.'

'Oh yes.'

'That meal for his birthday. Remember? When the restaurant was so shit.'

'God, yes. Big rows in the kitchen because the chef was splitting up with his wife.'

'And the waiter spilled wine everywhere and blamed you.'

'It was my fault actually but I wasn't going to tell *him* that. They didn't charge us in the end. And then I ruined everything by breaking up with him.'

'You really did, Annie. For no good reason, as far as I can see. But now he's getting over – he's got over it. You. With Fi. Maybe you need to leave them be.'

'I am.'

'You're a good-looking woman, for your age. There must be loads of guys out there who'd be like: She's hot.'

'For my age.'

'So what's stopping you?'

'Nothing.'

I think about Simon, who's been sending me regular texts from Brighton to see how I am. Simon is a lovely man. Simon will take me on unconditionally, just as soon as I give him the nod. Rob has moved on. Now it's my turn. With Simon.

Josh finishes his coffee and wipes pastry flakes off his T-shirt. From the serious expression on his face I can tell that this will be his final word on the subject. 'So. Fi. You want to know about Fi. Right . . . choppy blonde hair, sort of long and short at the same time. Nice smile. Skinny but not too skinny. Tiny feet. I mean, seriously tiny. She's a good cook. Vegetarian, but her van's vegan. She's got a snack van, takes it to festivals. She said I could work for her this summer but I'd rather hang out with my mates.'

Shit. She sounds perfect. 'How old?'

'I dunno, early thirties? Doesn't ever want kids. When she told me that, I was like: Whoa, too much information, lady.'

That would suit Rob. He's done the dad thing. So that's every box ticked. Fi sounds perfect.

'There's just one thing,' Josh says, lowering his voice as if the cafe owner might grass him up. 'Maybe it's not important. Maybe, after you, Dad reckoned it wasn't a deal-breaker.'

'What? What one thing, Josh?'

'So what it is is, she's got a sense of humour. But it's just a bit, I don't know . . . vanilla. She doesn't do sarcasm or irony like you do or make me laugh till my lungs literally burst. She can watch a whole episode of *The Big Bang Theory* without even cracking a smile. I feel bad saying it out loud. I mean, she can't help it, can she?'

'Your dad doesn't seem to mind.'

Josh looks thoughtful, weighing up whether or not to say more. But I know how to stare him out and he relents. 'To be honest, I think Dad does mind sometimes. He's always quoting you, things you've said, little in-jokes, stuff that makes him smile to himself when he doesn't know I'm looking. Fi's great and everything but she doesn't fit the space you left.'

As we walk back to the car, Josh rings Rhys, who has arrived at his aunt's pub in Fowey, to see if she has a spare room for me tonight. She does. So we can head straight there, without worrying about where I'll sleep. Even with a passenger to keep me awake, it's been a long drive and I'm knackered.

Launceston to Fowey takes less than an hour. We cross Bodmin Moor, passing Jamaica Inn. I tell Josh it was one of my favourite books when I was his age but he's never heard of it.

'Are you sure it's not a Bob Marley album?' he asks, a bit too pleased with himself.

We listen to Dr Feelgood, via Josh's Bluetooth, for the last leg from Lostwithiel. He really likes it, which I find amazing, so I tell him about Dad's love of them and meeting a fellow fan, with a dog called Olga, on Canvey Island.

'He was a dude, your dad,' Josh says with a sigh. 'Well, apart from whenever he wore those walking trousers with the zip-off legs. I won't lie, Annie, they were bad.'

We get to Fowey in good time and find the pub. We're feeling pretty chilled after the drive, ready for a pint or three of local cider and a hot meal. And then everything changes.

The suitcase. The wheelie Star Wars suitcase, which has been with me since sea area Forth, which contains Dad's ashes . . . it isn't in the boot. At first I freeze. Then I frantically pull everything out and dump it on the ground – Josh's backpack, the beer, the mineral water – as if the suitcase will suddenly, magically, reappear.

Josh has been in the pub, letting Rhys know we've arrived. He finds me rooted to the spot, staring at an empty space where the suitcase should be.

I point. 'Suitcase. Not there. Gone.'

'Are you sure?' Josh asks, trying to sound calm and grown-up.

'Look, it's so not there. Oh God, someone's nicked it. With Dad's ashes in it. Oh God, oh God.'

And then I remember the flap I was in, trying to load the already over-stuffed car boot at Waitrose while talking to Bev on the phone and getting hassled by Grubby Land Rover Woman. I must have put the suitcase on the ground and, in the ensuing chaos, accelerated off without it. No wonder she wouldn't stop hooting.

I launch into loud wails that scare me and horrify poor Josh. He tries to hug me but I won't be hugged. No one should be nice to me after I let this happen. How can I break it to Bev? What will Kate call me when she hears what I've done? I've taken a bad thing – this ridiculous trip – and made it a hundred and fifty per cent worse by my sheer incompetence and thoughtlessness.

'You're not though, Annie,' Josh tells me. 'Incompetent or thoughtless. This is just a case of shit happening and today it happened in – where was it?'

'Okehampton. Should I tell her yet?

'Tell who?'

'Bev. Should I tell her I've lost Dad?'

'You haven't lost him. He's been mislaid. I'll ring Waitrose now. Your suitcase will be put away safely in the manager's office, all ready to collect tomorrow.'

'I don't care about my clothes, my shoes, that daft fucking suitcase. I just want Dad back. God, I'm such a twat.'

'You need to stop saying that because it's not true, okay.'

'Okay.' (I am.)

Julie, who is calm and reassuring, makes me a cup of tea and shows me to my room, while I await news from Josh. It's up in the eaves, with an amazing view of the estuary. But I can't relax until Josh returns to tell me *panic over, what are you like?*

He knocks tentatively on my door and the lightness of his knuckles says it all. No 'panic over, what are you like?' No suitcase. No Dad. No end to my self-flagellation.

'I spoke to the deputy manager, the manager and the guy who collects trolleys. No one handed in a suitcase. Doesn't mean they won't, though. Whoever found it might have been in a hurry to get somewhere and they'll rock up with it tomorrow.'

Bless him, he knows that's bollocks but he can't bear to see me in such a state.

'Julie's putting together toothpaste, toothbrush, a little bottle of detergent. And you're to tell her if you need any, you know, women-type things. I can lend you spare clothes until you get your case back. And your dad. Tomorrow. You will, Annie. Get him back. People always hand stuff in. People are good, mostly.'

I can't eat a thing. I can't relax. Kate rings and I let her go to voicemail. How can I tell her what's happened? But I can't lie either. I feel the start of a headache.

I remember when my purse was stolen in a bar in St Albans a couple of years ago. I didn't care about the cash or the credit cards, which were easily stopped anyway. I didn't care about the sodding store cards or the card that would gain me a free coffee if I got every square rubber-stamped. There was a photo in the little plastic window of me, Mum and Kate, when she treated us to a mini break at a health spa. The purse was found and handed in, minus cash and cards, obviously. The photo was intact.

In it, we're all wearing thick-pile, white towelling dressing gowns, wet hair scraped back, faces free of make-up, bunched together on a lounger for one. We look happy but I remember it as a difficult day. Those cheesy smiles were just for the camera.

My stupid purse didn't matter but the photo did. My stupid suitcase doesn't matter. I just want my dad back.

Soon after eight, and when I've refused food three times, Julie gives me a couple of naproxen and a cup of cocoa. 'You need to sleep off that headache. I get them too so I know how you're feeling. It'll all be sorted by morning, love. Promise you it will.'

I sleep fitfully. Whenever I'm awake, I'm loading the car boot again and again, ensuring each time that the suitcase is safely stowed away. When I sleep, I dream about Simon. He's taking Dad and me out on his boat. He's a brilliant sailor: knowledgeable, confident, keen. He has long hair and is the Simon of our student days. I'm fifteen years older. Dad is just Dad.

When all this is over, I need to see Simon. I need to know how I feel about him. The dream has created a kind of intimacy, but it's just a dream. When all this is over. . .

* * *

Even up here in the eaves, I can smell frying bacon, toasting bread, strong coffee. My headache is gone, my appetite returned, my pants clean and dry on the shower rail.

Breakfast is served by Josh, looking semi-smart in black trousers and a polo shirt. He gets a bit fumbly taking down my order of poached eggs and has to come back to check if I'd asked for tea or coffee. Rhys is helping out in the kitchen; he worked here last summer and apparently does a mean scramble.

I polish off my eggs, two slices of toast and jam, plus a yoghurt. My stomach is full, my head is clear and I've stopped beating myself up. Now I'm ready to turn my anger on whoever took my suitcase. I shall return to the scene of the crime, stand outside the supermarket and interrogate every shopper. I'll report the theft – because that's what it bloody well is – to Okehampton police. I'm ready to kick ass and get my dad back.

I'm just relaying my plans to Josh when Julie runs in from the kitchen, talking on her mobile. 'She's here now. You're a star, Melanie. Just let me tell her, okay.'

Julie holds the phone out to me. 'Melanie. Daughter of a neighbour. She works for SWitch Community Radio. She reckons she can get you on air right now to put out an appeal for your suitcase. They're always doing shout-outs for missing cats and lost wedding rings. Well, go on.'

I take the phone. 'Hello?'

'Annie? Hi. Julie's told you, right. Look, I can't promise anything.' Melanie lowers her voice. 'Himself's just finishing the breakfast show and he's in a stinking mood. I'll put you on hold for a mo while I see if we can squeeze you in before nine.'

I wait. Julie waits. Josh serves a couple kippers, then waits too.

Julie uses the hiatus to explain. 'I told Melanie about your father's ashes and she really felt for you. SWitch covers all the South-West so you never know. Fingers crossed, eh?'

Melanie is back. I hear her sad little sigh before she speaks. 'He's got his jacket on. He'll be out the door and off for breakfast in ten seconds. I told him your story but he said it's not local because you're not. I'm so sorry. He's such a bastard. Got to go. Sorry.'

I pass the phone back to Julie and shake my head. 'Not happening. Never mind.'

Josh wants to comfort me but the kipper couple require more coffee. Julie bundles me into the kitchen, wipes her hands on her apron and grips mine.

'Oh, that's a shame. I should have checked with Melanie before bringing you into it. I shouldn't have raised your hopes.'

'I'm not local.'

'Your story is, though. And it's a bloody sight more news-worthy than a school fete or a guinea pig that looks like James Corden. Actually that one was quite good, as it happens.'

'I'll call Waitrose again, then go back to Okehampton, see if anyone saw anything.'

'Want me to come with you? I'm more than happy to.'

'I'm fine, Julie. Honestly.'

She's about to insist when 'La Bamba' erupts from her jeans pocket. She answers her mobile, listens earnestly, then gives me an exuberant thumbs-up. 'Oh, that's brilliant, Melanie. She will. I'm sure she will. Leave it with me. You're a star. No, you are. Thanks, love.'

What it is is . . . Melanie told my story to Shell, who does the afternoon phone-in show. Can I come in and talk about my journey and Dad's ashes? 'Shell's a lovely presenter. Not like that morning chap. I've told her yes but you just say if you don't want to do it.'

I drive to a trading estate on the outer fringes of Plymouth. SWitch Community Radio shares an industrial unit with an upholsterer's and an importer of Chinese noodles. Who said showbiz isn't glamorous? The radio station is a tiny operation: a scruffy open-plan office, a goldfish-bowl studio and a 'green room' which doubles as a dumping ground for dead rubber plants, redundant ring binders and four white plastic garden chairs.

I should have listened to SWitch in the car, to learn what I'm letting myself in for. I hear it now, piped around the green room. Shell introduces 'Top of the World' by the Carpenters and flags up the phone-in to follow. She's playing the Carpenters under faux duress and takes the mickey, with gentle affection, of the listener who requested it. She has a rich, fruity West Country accent and a throaty giggle. I like her already.

Shell's producer, barely older than Josh, finds me and thrusts a mug of tea at me. 'Annie? I'm Milo. Thanks for coming in. I could jot down some bullet points for Shell but you're on in five so I'll let her get the full story, okay?' He bustles me into the studio.

Shell is about 50, with long, purple, crinkly hair, crammed under headphones. I bet she keeps chickens, has a pierced navel and never misses Glastonbury. She waves me to sit opposite her and put on headphones. 'Top of the World' fades to a close.

'There you go, Iris. Because I promised. But I'm warning you, no more Carpenters requests for a fortnight or you're banned.' Another throaty chuckle. 'Take care, my lover. Catch you later. More music dreckly but, before that, let's get to know our guest.'

She means me. I smile, which does not make great radio.

'Annie Stanley, welcome to SWitch, Community Radio for the South West. So tell us why you're here and how we can help.'

'My suitcase. It's gone missing. With my dad in it. Someone took it. I don't know why. I was in a flap and I put it down and someone took it. It's all my fault.'

'Deep breath, and start again.'

I rewind to the beginning: Dad's death; the Shipping Forecast; our journey from sea areas Cromarty to Plymouth. Because Shell is such a good listener, I even tell her about my eight knitted squares. If I sound unhinged, I can't do anything about that now.

'And you're sure nobody handed your suitcase in to the supermarket?' Shell asks when I finally putter to a halt.

'Positive. Someone took it. It's not as if they picked up the wrong Bag for Life by mistake; it's a Star Wars wheelie suitcase. Containing a bunch of creased clothes and my dad's ashes in a cardboard travel urn. The case is worth more than the contents, but even that can be bought for £15 on any high street.'

'So it's a double tragedy, isn't it, Annie?' Shell sounds like a therapist. Maybe she is. 'You lost your father once when he died. And now you've lost him again.'

'Because I'm an idiot.'

'Course you're not. And we're here to help, aren't we, SWitchers? Anyone listening who's from Okehampton, or passing through Okehampton, who might have stopped at Waitrose yesterday? What time was this, Annie?'

'About three. Yes, just after 3 p.m.'

'So that would include afternoon shoppers, late lunchers, parents chauffeuring their kids. Did you see a Star Wars suitcase in Waitrose car park? Did you see someone take it? Annie's putting on a brave face but we can all tell, can't we, what a trauma this must be. Come on SWitchers. Let's reunite her with her dad. While you get dialling, here's Fleetwood Mac.'

Shell fades up 'Rhiannon', then down again so that we can talk over it, off mic. 'We had a rambler on last year who dropped his great-uncle's compass from his back pocket when he took a dump on Bodmin Moor. We only got it back! A dog found it. Wingnut, that was his name. An Airedale called Wingnut. Our listeners voted him Pooch of the Year.'

The phone lines start going. Milo weeds out the 'wingnuts' and puts through any potential leads. These include a Star Wars fanatic who can do impressions of Darth Vader and a woman with a supermarket phobia. Shell dispatches them with tact and charm.

Then there's Phil from Saltash, whose wife gave his late nan's best trifle bowl to a jumble sale; Rosie from Kingsbridge, whose family photo albums were washed away in a flood and June from Highhampton, who can't find her bus pass. Mostly they want to talk to Shell, whom they view as a virtual friend, a bit of company when they haven't spoken to anyone for days.

'Let's not get distracted here,' Shell reminds her listeners. 'Our primary mission is to reunite Annie with her father so that they can finish their journey. Lundy next, isn't it?'

'Lundy, Irish Sea, Malin, Hebrides, Fair Isle. But I'll give up and go home if I don't get Dad back.' I try to cover the quaver in my voice. Returning urn-less to St Albans is too painful to contemplate.

'We've got Pauline from Liskeard on the line. All right, my lover? Do you have any good news for Annie?'

'I wish I did, Shell.' She sounds old and frail. 'I've been thinking about what you said about two kinds of loss: losing a person and losing something that's, you know, them. Like Phil's nan's trifle bowl. With Annie, it's the same thing, isn't it? Can I speak to her?'

'She's right here, my lover.'

'Hello, Annie.'

'Hello, Pauline.'

She pauses for a moment, to find the words. 'As I see it, even if you get the ashes back, you can't get your father back. He's gone. I hope I'm not upsetting you.'

Surprisingly, she isn't.

'Is your mother still alive?' she asks.

'She died a few years ago.'

'So you're an orphan, Annie.' We all laugh at her inadvertent pun. 'My folks died a year apart. 1959 and 1960. I have photos but I can't remember how they walked or smiled or how many sugars they took. All I know is that they loved me and they wanted me to have a happy life. And I have. I really have. Whatever goodness they passed on, well, it taught me how to find it in Bill, my husband. So I lost something – them – but I gained something too. Oh, listen to me rambling on. I knew I'd make a hash of it.'

'You haven't, my lover. Has she, Annie?'

'Not at all. My parents wanted *me* to have a happy life too but I haven't always managed it.'

'Have you found someone who'll make you happy, like I did with Bill?' Pauline asks. 'Not that it's any of my business.'

'Maybe.' Simon? Not Rob. It has to be Simon.

'Well, you'd best make it more than maybe. This isn't a dress rehearsal.'

Shell waves to Milo; let's bring this call to a close. 'Sound advice as ever, Pauline. Thanks for your call.'

'I felt I had to. I hope you find your ashes, Annie. Bye now.'

I'm fazed by Pauline's words. Shell bungs on 'Both Sides Now' to give me space to get my thoughts ordered.

'Pauline always comes up trumps. We love Pauline. You okay, my lover?'

'Maybe.'

'We can do six more minutes on your suitcase, then I'll have to cut to the news.'

So we take a few more calls, some sympathetic, one querying cremation over burial and Gerald from Polperro who lost a fiver and found a tenner.

I drive back to Fowey, still a little dazed. Simon? Really? Am I over Rob? Really? Has the phone-in clarified my feelings for him? It wasn't the outcome I expected. To be fair, I had no expectations. I certainly didn't expect to find meaning in a conversation with a woman called Pauline. So much to process. Losing Dad. Twice. Losing Simon when we were young and selfish and then finding him again. (Maybe.) Treasuring the goodness my parents gave me. Not squandering it in self-pity and self-doubt.

I may have to adjust to the fact that Dad is gone forever: both the dad who hugged me and loved me *and* his ashes. But even if I accept that I've lost this second version of him, will Kate accept it? Will Bev?

On the drive back to Fowey, I try to put the suitcase out of my mind because nothing's changed on that front. Instead I think about my conversation with Josh in the Launceston cafe, what seems like weeks ago. I was grilling him about Fi and what he'd told Maggie, when she grilled him about me.

He was thirteen when Rob and I got together. Not an easy age and harder, I reckon, on boys. Girls have that network to talk periods and eyebrows and anxiety with. And yet he was prepared to take me on and to tell Maggie I was okay. He could see from the very start that I made his dad happy.

When my dad told me he'd met a nice woman called Beverley and she made *him* happy and he hoped I'd accept her into the family, I behaved like a brat. Maybe I had an excuse: Josh still *had* his mum whereas I'd watched mine fade away. Two entirely different situations. Yet Josh saw his dad's happiness as the most important thing while I stomped and snarked and sneered at Bev; her cloying niceness, her politics (which I never actually discussed with her); her seat at *my* family table, the seat previously occupied by my beloved mother.

Somewhere along the way, I'd blamed Bev for Mum being gone. I don't think Kate did. Just me. It made sense at the time. Now I feel huge waves of remorse and shame. Bev gave Dad a future, after our collective grief at losing Mum, and that felt so wrong to me.

Josh is sitting on a bench outside the pub as I park. He looks distracted, excited. He rushes over as I get out of the car.

'Annie, for fuck's sake, I've been ringing you this past hour. Why didn't you pick up?'

'I was driving. Thinking. I stopped off at Tesco to buy a change of clothing. But see, I'm here now.'

He takes my hand and leads – no, drags – me into Julie's little office, behind the kitchen. I know he's young and impetuous – it's part of his charm – but this is annoying. What's so urgent that I can't have a wee first?

There, on her desk, is Dad in his urn, looking none the worse for his absence. And parked beside the desk is my suitcase. I have never loved Star Wars so much.

I don't cry because I'm too surprised to find any tears. All I can manage is a squeaky: 'How?'

'Everything's there, Annie.' Josh beams. 'Your clothes, your washbag and stuff. And your dad. You can stop beating yourself up now.'

He parks me in a quiet corner of the pub garden and fetches me a brandy. He can't wait to explain what happened.

'We listened to you on the radio in the kitchen, all of us. You were really good, even with some of those nutjobs. Then, about twenty minutes after you finished, Julie got a call from her friend at the radio station. Melissa.'

'Melanie.'

'Melanie. Right. What it is is, a woman rang in after the show but you'd already left. Her son and his mate saw your suitcase in the car park yesterday afternoon. And because they're stupid, thoughtless kids, they just took it. But they didn't know what to do with it after that. Obviously, there's nothing of value, apart from your dad and even then, he's no use to them. So one of the boys hid the case under his bed. His mum found it this morning when she was hoovering, then she heard you on SWitch. Melanie told her where to find you and she drove straight here. She didn't want to stay and meet you. Too embarrassed. She was like, "I'm so sorry, I'm so sorry. He is so for it." Her son. Grounded for a month at least. So. Happy fucking ending or what!'

I take my case up to my room. I put Dad on the window sill to enjoy the view of the estuary. I tell him I'm sorry, but he's cool about it. I sleep soundly for three hours until I'm awoken by my rumbling tummy. I stumble downstairs, ready to order anything comforting from the pub menu.

Josh and Rhys are propping up the bar. Judging by their pink cheeks and loud guffaws, they've been sampling the local ciders.

'Hey, Miss Stanley.' Rhys beams. 'Pull up a stool. What are you drinking?'

'A half of whatever that is please.'

While he's getting the drinks, Josh leans over and whispers in my ear, 'Rhys has fancied you since Year 9. Go on, Miss Stanley, fill yer boots. What happens in Fowey stays in Fowey.'

Rhys gives a cheery wave. Would I like peanuts?

Maybe it's the cider, maybe it's the sheer bloody relief, but I manage another ten hours straight through, despite the flimsy pillow and squidgy mattress. When I wake, the bed looks totally undisturbed, as if someone has made it around me.

I didn't stay with the lads too long last night and I'm sure, if I'd have tried to take Rhys up on his fantasy of one night of passion with Miss Stanley, he'd have run a mile. A couple of lads at Rangewood had the hots for me. Fancying your teacher is all part of growing up. I had crushes on Mr Goldberg and Miss Long when I was at school. Girl crushes are also part of growing up.

I think about Kate. I'll give her a ring, whether she wants me to or not.

After the stress of yesterday, I feel alive and refreshed. Maybe I'll stay in Fowey for an extra day, if Julie has space, to recharge my batteries. That way, I can also tell Rob that I made sure Josh was properly settled in before I left.

Simon has texted. 'How you doing, Stannie? Hoping all well and your dad's enjoying his adventure. I've changed the ending of my play. Now you have a part in it because I'm a sucker for happy ever after. Take care, lovely girl xxx.'

I wander up Fore Street, buy a little bag of salted caramel fudge and a painted starfish tile for Kate. Yes, Fowey is a bit twee and touristy but then, so am I. It's also heaving with young people; Josh will have a great summer here.

I find a bench, looking out onto the estuary, scoff a square of fudge even though I'm not hungry, and dial Kate's number. It goes straight to voicemail. We haven't spoken since Brighton . . . after agreeing that we should be closer. But I'm the older sister and I shouldn't leave it to her to keep us connected.

'Hey, Katkin. I need to debrief about Dorset and Bev and stuff. It was fine actually, apart from me catching Mark phoning his fancy piece. I think he was. Couldn't be sure. Wouldn't put it past him. I know you'll say no, but if you're kicking your heels, come and join me. I'll be heading for sea area Lundy in the next day or two. Love you and miss you, little sis. Byee.'

When I see her, I'll tell her about losing Dad in Okehampton. Now that I have him back, it can be an anecdote, rather than a crisis. I really want to see Kate and I desperately want to be a better sister.

I must try harder.

In the afternoon, I catch up with Josh in the pub garden. He's back in his usual T-shirt, low-slung cut-offs and a pair of flip-flops so worn and thin, they look like crispbread. His beach-bum get-up is practically a uniform with all the under-twenties in Fowey.

'Where are you camped?' I ask, belatedly aware of my 'responsible adult' duties.

'Just out of town. The tent's a bit cramped and Rhys snores. But I bloody love this place, so no worries.'

'You're going to have an amazing summer, Josher.'

'Yeah, no, definitely.'

I sense that he's distracted by something behind me. I turn to see a stunning girl with an orange buzz cut and Maori tattoos clearing glasses from a distant table.

'Who's that?'

'Josie. Her folks have a place here. Second home, lucky sods. We got chatting after you went to bed.'

Josh and Josie. Josie and Josh. Back when I was a kid, people would stick their names on the windscreen strips of their cars to denote coupledom. 'Josh and Josie' is just asking to be immortalized in big white letters on a green background.

'And?'

'And what?' Josh sounds prickly, defensive. As if this is none of my business. Well, of course it isn't – but even so . . .

She sees us, gives a broad smile and a friendly wave, then enters the pub with her tray of empties.

'What else did you find out about her?'

'Not much. She plays bass guitar, her sister was on *Love Island*, she liked my T-shirt, she's got a tongue stud, she reckons she's a hundred per cent compatible with Capricorns. And she's in halls at Exeter.'

'Bummer that you're not. You did tell her you're settling for a shoebox off campus, with an Ice Queen landlady?'

'No, yeah. I haven't decided for definite yet.'

'You should ring Dinah today. To confirm that you still want the room.'

He grins at me, one of those grins that makes me want

to hug him. 'I don't think I'll bother. Anyway, someone's probably got there ahead of me.'

He hauls himself to his feet and kisses the top of my head. I've always loved that this boy is so giving of affection. Just like his dad. 'Anyway, I'm running late. What it is is, Josie's teaching me to surf this afternoon.'

'Take it slowly,' I tell his retreating back. 'Don't show off, protect your knees . . . and wear a condom.'

Chapter Nineteen

June 2013

Eggs Benedict with a side of hash browns and a full-fat latte or . . . an egg-white omelette, raw spinach and a glass of hot water? Annie thought about it for all of five seconds. Yes, obviously, it would be great to shift a few pounds while she was here. But she'd made herself a rule years ago, when Toby first introduced her to eggs Benedict: if they're on a breakfast menu, you must, repeat *must*, order them. She couldn't waver now.

Mum opted for a boiled egg and Marmite soldiers and Kate said she'd be fine with a black coffee. She didn't do breakfast at home so why change her habits, just because she was here?

'Oh go on. Push the boat out,' Mum wheedled. 'How about smoked salmon and scrambled eggs? You love smoked salmon, Katkin. Or, let's see, "a freshly-baked muffin"?'

Kate glared. 'I'm fine thanks, Mum. I'm here, aren't I? Even though I'm a premium member of my gym and can do all this at home.'

Annie's turn to glare. 'We know, Kate. Of course, you can do your kettle bell workouts and have your massages and pedicures and sludge smoothies back in St Albans. But not with Mum and me, you can't.'

'I've invited you lots of times, as my guest. Both of you.'

'Hey, hey, we're meant to be enjoying this,' Mum said with a sigh. 'I'm here to de-stress, relax and stop eating biscuits. But I can't if you're bickering like a pair of kids.'

They ordered their breakfasts from Magda, the shy Polish waitress. Kate relented and requested fruit salad and yoghurt. Progress. And Annie decided against the hash browns. So that was progress too. Mum smiled. Maybe this was going to be okay.

It had been her idea: three days, two nights, at a health spa near Aylesbury. A flyer had come through her door, offering a special deal if you booked by a certain date which turned out to be the following day. So she made a booking instantly for the three of them and paid up front. No cancellations, no refunds.

If Kate and Annie couldn't come, she'd have to ask her best friends, Judy and Moira. And they'd each demand their own room and Judy would keep sneaking off for a crafty ciggie and Moira has a laugh that grates after four hours. So Annie and Kate *had to* come. Anyway, it was her treat so it would be churlish to turn it down.

Mum had even managed to book them two rooms linked by a shared bathroom. Hers was small, dominated by a big double bed; Annie and Kate had twin beds with a six-inch strip of floor between them, an unnerving flashback to their childhoods.

After breakfast, Kate dashed off to her circuit class. Within an hour of arriving, she had booked a busy schedule of classes, power walks and treatments. Annie intended to sleep, eat, sleep and maybe fit in a few lengths of the pool.

Mum also wanted to keep it simple. If she finished her Ann Cleeves thriller, she could swap it for another from the library of abandoned books. Her only aim was to spend quality time with her busy daughters and if she had to confine them in a luxury country-house spa to do it, so be it.

After breakfast, Annie put the 'Do not disturb' sign on her door knob and went back to bed. It was such a luxury to lie in. Teaching was a different kind of tough to her frenetic job at Canary Wharf. She'd always found she could disassociate herself from stress in the City, despite all the pressures. With teaching, the 'product' would be people, small people who expected her to know what she was doing. Just learning how to do that with confidence was exhausting. Maybe it would get easier once she was qualified, employed, actually doing it for real. She bloody hoped so.

She awoke to retching. It took a second to find her bearings, then to remember the shared bathroom.

'Mum? Are you okay?'

She heard a faint, faux upbeat 'Yes, thanks' from behind the door. She knocked and entered to find Mum perched on the closed seat of the loo, vomiting bile into the sink. Mum's face was a mix of embarrassment and relief. She hadn't wanted to be found like this but at least now she could stop the pretence.

Annie dampened a flannel and gently washed Mum's face. She found a fresh T-shirt, neatly unpacked in the chest of drawers, and helped her change. Mum allowed herself to be cleaned and tidied, teary gratitude in her eyes.

'Remember when you drank all that orange juice at your nana's and you puked it up in the car?' she said weakly. 'And I had to wipe you down with a tartan blanket until I got you home.'

'Oh God, the orange juice. Why didn't you stop me drinking it?'

'Because you'd have thrown one of your hissy-fit wobblers if I had. You never did it again, though, did you?'

Annie filled a tumbler with tap water and got Mum to swill out her mouth. Then they stared at each other. It didn't need to be said, but even so . . .

'It's back, isn't it?'

Mum nodded. 'And I'm so bloody furious. I knew it was a possibility. Dr Golding said as much. And I'm not stupid. But I told myself I'd be one of the lucky ones.'

'You still could be. And you'd be more prepared for the chemo this time.'

Mum shook her head. 'I've accepted it, love. Your dad too. At least he says he has. This isn't going to get better. D'you know what, I think I'd like a little nap now. Wake me up in an hour, will you?'

Annie was angry, teary, helpless. Kate had gone straight from her circuit class to an Indian head massage so she had no one to debrief with. Maybe Kate didn't know yet, in which case was it her news to tell, or Mum's?

She went to the indoor pool and angrily thrashed back and forth . . . five lengths, six . . . ten. In the tepid water, with only one other swimmer to get in her way, she could cry, hit out, push against the tiles with a force she didn't know she had. In rhythm with her strokes, her head pounded: not fair, not fair, what about us . . . what about Dad . . . not fair, not fair . . . It was a release but it was only temporary.

She put on her white towelling bathrobe, lay on a lounger and closed her eyes to gather her thoughts. There was absolutely nothing she could do to make this less awful, less . . . terminal. When would Mum die? How should they spend the time they had left? How would they cope without her?

Too many thoughts, too many questions . . .

She must have disengaged her brain long enough to doze because when she opened them again, Kate and Mum were sitting beside her in director's chairs, also wearing their fluffy white bathrobes. Kate, as ever, had her phone in her pocket and, when Magda brought them a carafe of iced water, asked her to take a photo of them, all scrunched together on Annie's lounger with Mum in the middle, like a Stanley sandwich.

It was so obvious: Kate didn't know yet. Her phone suddenly rang and she sprinted out onto the lawn to take the call.

'Do you want me to tell her?' Annie asked, half fearing the answer.

'No, no, I'll do it. But thanks, love. That's sweet of you.'

'Okay, but I will if you change your mind.'

Mum encased her in a tight towelling hug. 'I'm so proud of you, you know. I don't say it enough, my darling girl, but I am.'

'Me too.' Annie ran a fluffy cuff across her cheek, to mop up a stray tear.

'Promise you'll look after each other. Kate pretends to be hard as nails but we know different, don't we?'

Annie nodded as Kate rushed, excitedly, back from the garden.

'Hey, hey, good news. In fact, the best news ever.'

Annie and Mum exchanged looks. 'Well, tell us.'

Kate sat beside Mum and clapped her hands, like a happy child. 'I didn't want to say before in case it was a no. Who needs bad news on a spa break! But it's official. I've got a new job with a software start-up run by this amazing couple, Ros and Ross Lomax. Apparently I was the best candidate by a country mile. They bloody love me. Ros just said so.'

'Oh, that's splendid,' said Mum. 'Let's have champagne with our lunch.'

'Congratulations, Katkin. Well done, sis.'

'I'm sorry I've been a bit tense and snarky since we got here. Now you know why. I have such a good feeling about this job, this year, every flipping thing. Seriously, I really do. Bring it the hell on!'

Chapter Twenty

Lundy

Fowey fully recharges my batteries. I swim, I sleep, I eat fish and chips with mushy peas, I knit. I hang out with Josh, Rhys and Josie and sample more of the amazing local cider. Not to be outdone by 'Josh+Josie', Rhys makes a move on a super-tanned Dutch girl called Tineke. She's clearly stringing him along but he doesn't seem to mind.

I even feel relaxed enough to ring Rob and confirm that Josh is really pleased to be staying in halls for his first year at Exeter. Josh doesn't let on to his dad that he was tempted to take Dinah's room. Our little secret.

I tell Rob about fabulous Fowey and Josh's B&B job and how much he's going to enjoy his summer here. I keep my tone upbeat and breezy. But Rob sounds distracted.

'Have I called at a bad time?' I ask.

'What? No, sorry, Annie. I'm driving and you're on speaker.'

'Anywhere nice?'

Suddenly a female voice chips in. 'Hi Annie, this is Fi. We're just coming into – where are we, Rob?'

'Battle. We're on our way to Bexhill to visit Hilary.'

I bristle.

Reason #1: I now have a voice for Fi. She's no longer just a name. It's an attractive voice too, not a squeaky or silly one. Shit.

Reason #2: Even though Hilary is Rob's godmother, I experience a twinge of annoyance. Didn't I go out of my way to visit her when he was too busy? Didn't I check that she was okay? Over a couple of days, I learned stuff about her that I'm guessing Rob – or humourless Fi – will never know, not least her big love, Frank, and her secret life on Tinder.

The other big thing Hilary told me was to put Rob behind me and move on. And she was bloody right. I think I already have.

'Hi to you too, Fi,' I gush. 'Give Hilary a great big hug from me, won't you? Tell her I'm definitely following her advice. And do say hi to her neighbour, Toni.'

'Will do,' Rob replies. 'Sorry, got to go. We need to stop for petrol.'

I text Kate again. Does she fancy joining me in sea area Lundy or what? Her reply is typically terse. 'Yeah, what the hell, why not. Send deets of where + when.'

Before setting off from Fowey the next morning, I take advantage of the available Wi-Fi to establish the full 'deets'. Over breakfast, I text Kate and instruct her to catch a train to Barnstaple; I'll meet her in the station car park. There's a ferry to Lundy island from Bideford or Ilfracombe. It looks a bit barren, with just puffins for company, but there is accommodation. I wonder if Kate fancies that. I tell her to pack walking boots, just in case.

Josh brings me a mug of coffee and a generous serving of eggs, expertly scrambled by Rhys. When I pop into the kitchen half an hour later to tell him I'm off, he abandons his pot scrubbing to give me a massive, soap-suddy hug.

'All good?' I ask.

'All good,' he replies.

'Good. Don't break her heart and don't let her break yours.'

'Blah-blah-blah.' He grins. 'And you take care too, Miss Stanley. You are seriously bloody amazing.'

'Blah-blah-blah,' I say, as I exit, before he makes me cry.

The cross-country drive is trouble-free although I do a detour around Okehampton, not wishing to tempt fate. At a service station near Torrington, I give Kate a ring. No reply so she gets one of my bambling voicemails.

'Are you on the train? Do you have an ETA? I'll be in the car park. Silver-grey Hyundai with a Z and a 3 and maybe a G in the number plate, I think. Or an 8. Keep me posted, Katkin, or are you just going to rock up without warning, like you did in Canvey Island? Laters.'

I get to Bideford at noon and visit the tourist office for information about the Lundy ferry and accommodation on the island. I'm told it gets booked up months, years, in advance, so I settle on a printed list of Bideford hotels. Maybe this is the night we treat ourselves to something five-star because I haven't run out of money yet and because we're worth it.

Still no word from Kate.

I buy my Lundy wool and succumb to a Devon cream tea in a doily-ridden cafe but I'm starting to get annoyed. Kate said she was coming, so where the fuck is she? How long should I leave it before I give up on her? What is she playing at?

I'm just about to pay for a twin-bedded room in a

mid-range hotel near the pannier market when my phone rings.

Kate.

My aim is to stay calm. 'Are you at Barnstaple? Why didn't you say? Get a coffee, find a bench and I'll pick you up in half an hour. Forty minutes tops.'

'I'm not there. I'm at home.' She sounds snotty and teary.

'Oh Kate, you could have said. I've been expecting you all afternoon.'

'I don't know what to do, An-An. I've ruined everything: my work, my life. What am I meant to do now?'

'What's happened? Hey, I can't help if I don't know what's happened.' There's an ominous silence. 'Katkin, are you still there?'

'I'm just grateful that Mum and Dad aren't around to see how useless I am.'

'No, no,' I tell her. '*I'm* useless. You're the sensible one. Are you coming to Devon? Please come to Devon. We can talk, make it better.'

'I don't want to come to fucking Devon. I'll still be fucking useless, won't I?'

I have to ask. How can I not? 'Okay then. Do you want me to come to you?'

Kate's faint reply is drowned out by a passing car.

'Do you want me to come to you?'

'Yes,' she replies, sounding like a little girl. 'Could you, An-An?'

PART III

Chapter Twenty-One

Irish Sea

I'm just grateful that I caught up on all that sleep in Fowey because the next ten hours are mental. The first five involve getting from Bideford to St Albans by car, train, Tube, train and, finally, a taxi. I doze for all of ten minutes on the Exeter to Paddington leg and dream quite vividly that I leave my suitcase on the luggage rack. For the rest of the journey, I keep it on my lap, which isn't easy . . . especially in the taxi. There would be a certain irony in losing Dad again, just as I reach home.

Josh texts to ask how I'm doing in Lundy. Explaining why I'm heading back to St Albans is too complicated. Plus it's Kate's emergency, not mine. I give him the bare bones and it seems to be enough, probably because he's keener to keep name-checking Josie than hear where I am. Josie is so amazing. Josie is so clever. Josie calls him 'Josh the Nosh' because he's always hungry. He can't believe his luck. I tell him she'll be pinching herself too.

Kate's living-room blinds are closed and there are no lights on upstairs. Perhaps she's gone to bed. She knows I'm coming. I texted her every half-hour, more for my own reassurance than hers. A couple of half-arsed thumbs-up emoji replies make me wonder if she's changed her mind and the last thing she wants is her chaotic sister rocking up at . . . crikey, nearly 11 p.m. Too bad. I urgently need the loo, two mugs of tea and some Ambrosia creamed rice straight from the tin, if she has such a thing.

She gives me a huge hug when she finds me on her doorstep. As a rule, Kate doesn't hug. Or if she does, they're brittle, unsatisfying affairs. She's wearing the towelling bathrobe from our spa weekend with Mum. It looks as fresh and fluffy as the day she bought it. Her hair is pulled back in a headband and her face is cleansed and creamed. She is incapable of looking shit, even when she feels like seven shades of it. How does she *do* that?

I follow her into the kitchen. She has been scrubbing cupboards, scouring fridge shelves, running a bleach cycle through the washing machine, polishing the pedal bin . . . possibly even descaling the U-bend. The smell of chemicals and cleaning agents practically takes my eyebrows off.

She slumps on a kitchen stool, exhausted, so I put the kettle on and, in the absence of tinned rice, bung a couple of restorative slices of wholemeal into the gleaming toaster.

'So,' I say, once tea and toast are ready. 'Tell me what's happened.'

Kate is no longer teary or furious with herself. Those hours scrubbing every available kitchen surface must have calmed her down. It's as if she's composed her crisis into a concise business report, free from emotional masochism or irrational thought.

'I'm fine, An-An. Anyway, aren't you meant to be in Lundy?'

'I am. I was. But you wanted me to come home.'

'I didn't think you would.'

'Of course I came. You sounded so upset. How could I not come?'

'Well, as you can see, I'm fine now. I'm happy to pay for the return trip, if you need to get back to Bidecombe tomorrow.'

'Bideford!' I bellow, surprising us both.

I abandon my toast and tea and leave the room before I lose my temper further. Can't she see how hurtful her fake indifference is? She's always had a problem with looking vulnerable. God knows, it's never been an issue for me. I can't get angry, though, or I'll never find out what's happened.

But I *am* angry. In fact, I'm quietly furious. Dad and I still have Irish Sea, Malin, Hebrides and Fair Isle on our schedule. I want to finish this ridiculous trip. I need to finish it. Then I can see Simon and take a punt on my future. And now I'm hundreds of miles off course. I was hoping to make a bad thing better by coming home but this time it's Kate who's made it worse.

She gives me a minute to regain my composure, then finds me in the living room. She's put my toast and a fresh cup of tea on a tray, as well as two Tunnock's teacakes. I can't believe she has a supply of these. So very me but so *not* Kate. It makes me smile and love her even more.

'We're both tired,' she says, sounding like that sad little girl again. 'Why don't we talk in the morning? I'll make up the spare bed while you drink your tea.'

She gives my arm a stroke. 'Thank you, An-An. I'm really glad you came.'

Before falling asleep, I listen to the Shipping Forecast. I realize that the slog of getting from one sea area to the next, hiring cars, returning cars, catching trains, watching the pennies, finding a bed, a cash machine, a petrol station . . .

all the details have taken my eye off the ball. Or urn, in this case. *This*. This is why I'm doing it. For Dad.

I scoot around the coast in my head: Cromarty, Edinburgh, Scarborough, Happisburgh, Canvey Island, Bexhill, Brighton, Lulworth, Fowey, Bideford. I think about Duncan, Kim, Hilary and Simon, not to mention Kate, Bev, Pippa, Evie and Josh.

I am amazed by how far Dad and I have travelled.

In every sense.

Kate's nineties semi is on the other side of St Albans to my flat, in a quiet cul-de-sac. She was on a good salary at LoMax and spent much of it on making the house her own. It's very monochrome and restrained. She doesn't do knick-knacks or ornaments and she prefers moody black-and-white photos of Manhattan to anything colourful, ethnic or challenging. I gave her a framed Bridget Riley primary-coloured Op Art print as a housewarming gift; she hung it in the downstairs loo.

We're both up early the next morning and decide on a walk before breakfast. Kate is ready to talk and I'm certainly up for listening, in a sisterly, supportive way. It's another of those conversations where we won't have to maintain eye contact, just walk, hands in pockets, looking straight ahead. That's how Kate will want to play it, this heart-to-heart of ours: focused, factual and unemotional. I can do that.

We walk the path behind her house, towards Tyttenhanger. I could murder some toast but I sense that Kate's ready to unburden, so I will my tummy to stop gurgling.

'Right,' she says, as if she's starting a conference call. 'I'm just thinking of a good place to begin.'

'Jump right in and work backwards. Would that help?'

'O-kay.' She doesn't sound convinced. Too disorderly for Kate.

We walk on for a bit while she collects her thoughts. A dad runs by, chasing after a child who has just learned to ride a bike and now can't stop. A spaniel runs after the dad. Kate and I laugh.

'O-kay,' she says again. 'The Charlie thing.'

'Hang on, you told me it wasn't a thing. Or rather, it wasn't the reason you chucked in your job.'

'No, see, this will only work if you don't interrupt.'

'Sorry.'

'The thing with Charlie . . . you know, when we were all in Coventry on business and I was drunk and everything . . . and I was mortified because it was so unprofessional and I'd never done anything like that before . . . you know, slept with a colleague and slept with um, well, you know . . . a woman.'

'Can I say something?'

'No. Yes. What?'

'Sleeping with a colleague can definitely be a mistake. Been there, done that, got the P45. But I won't have you beating yourself up about something that just kind of happened and isn't "wrong" in any sense of the word.'

'I know that. I'm not stupid. I know that, okay. It just freaked me out because it wasn't who I thought I was. Am. And, afterwards, seeing Charlie every day at work, well, it totally messed with my head. I couldn't concentrate. I made stupid mistakes. I booked a venue for a big presentation on the wrong day and only just cancelled it in time. I lost the firm's credit card and found it in my gym bag a week later. I ate a whole box of Belgian chocolates that I'd bought for Bev. You know me, An-An. I don't *do* stuff like that. You do but I don't.'

We laugh because it's true. Kate has always been perfect. My sister has never flooded a neighbour's bathroom or bought a vintage rug heaving with moths or lost her pants on the London Eye.

'And Ros and Ross were very sweet and very tolerant but I could see they were getting really pissed off with me. You can't fuck up when you're a small business like LoMax because it affects everyone. So I quit. I jumped before I was pushed. I had no choice.'

I'm less interested in lost credit cards and scoffed chocolates. 'What about you and Charlie?'

'Oh, An-An, I got it really wrong.'

'Crikey, she isn't gay?'

'For fuck's sake, just listen, will you? I thought I was just a drunken shag in another town, a notch on her bedpost. And that she was as keen to forget about what happened as I was. But she wasn't. She can't forget. She's desperate to see me again. She says she's never felt like this before.'

I stop in my tracks. Not at all what I was expecting.

'And now I'm even more confused. You know me, An-An. I'm even more shit than you at relationships. Why would this work any better, just because we're both women? And if I've never felt like this before either, how do I know it's real?'

'You mean, you have feelings for Charlie?'

'Yes.' Said so quietly I nearly miss it.

'What if you've never felt like this before because you hadn't met Charlie before? Anyway, how do you know it wouldn't work? Based on what? Proved by what? You don't know, Katkin. None of us do. That's why relationships are scary.'

'So what should I do?'

'Talk to her, listen to what she has to say. Tell her you're scared. There's nothing wrong with showing your vulnerability.'

Kate nods. The kid on the bike whizzes past going the other way, with dad and dog still in pursuit. We watch them retreat down the path.

'You're right. You really are, An-An,' Kate says eventually. 'Hey, that must be a personal best for you.'

'Ha bloody ha!'

'Sorry. Uncalled for. I know you're right. I do.'

'Good. Because I am. Remember that spa break with Mum? When she told us the cancer was back?'

'She tried to play it down but we knew it was bad.'

I make us stop walking so that Kate can take this in. 'Mum said I was to look after you, be a proper big sister. This is me doing it. Here. Now. Talk to Charlie. You have to, Kate. You can't keep your feelings to yourself. Not if your happiness is at stake.'

She kisses my forehead. She agrees. I squeeze her hand. We go home for breakfast.

My flat smells musty, claggy, as if I left a damp sock in the washing machine. In fact, it's a tea towel. Inspired by Kate, I resolve to give the whole place a belated spring clean. I got into some bad habits before I scarpered to Cromarty. I can't let myself sink back into them again. I should check the cupboard under the sink for cleaning products. Tomorrow. I'll do that tomorrow.

Dad must be expecting a seascape of Lundy island at the very least. But for now, he'll have to make do with the view from my bedroom windowsill. Parked cars. Communal flower beds and bins. A laminated sign for a lost cat stuck to a lamppost. The occasional fox. I hope those last two aren't connected . . .

I also resolve to contact Cameron about going back to Rangewood for the autumn term. He's always been a big fan, even after I rebuffed an over-eager kiss from him at the last staff Christmas party. If I'm teaching again, my days will have a structure. I need structure. That way, I won't have time to get into my old ways, like living in slob-around gear and vegging out on the sofa, which is still dented with my pre-Cromarty bum shape.

I fling the seat and back cushions onto the floor, give them a dust-releasing thump, turn them over, swap them round and put them back. Instantly, the sofa looks tidy. See how easy it is to start afresh, Annie . . .

Tiring, though. I find my favourite leggings and Boyzone T-shirt, heat up a long-forgotten M&S moussaka from the freezer, carve a new bum dent in the sofa and watch *Escape to the Country*. For today at least, I've earned it.

Rob texts: 'Are you back?'

I reply: 'Yes.'

'Are you home now?'

'Yes.'

Sixty seconds later, the doorbell rings and there he is with a bag of supermarket shopping. 'Eggs, milk, loo roll, orange juice, muesli, apples,' he says, unpacking it onto my worktop.

'Apples?' I query. 'Apples?'

'I thought you'll probably have been eating rubbish from garages and station buffets these past few weeks. Chocolate and chips and pasties. Apples are good for you.'

Rob knows me so well, the bastard. Even so . . . apples!

'Josh told me you were coming home but he didn't know why. Are you okay, Annie?'

'I'm fine. Really. Couldn't be better. It's Kate. She's not very – she hasn't been well and I was worried about her.'

'Not like her to ask for help.'

'She didn't. I offered. We're all we've got now. Can I get you a cup of tea? Or coffee? An apple?'

It's a flying visit. He can't stop. He's meant to be popping by that nightmare job in Tring. They don't like the finish on the drawer handles. They don't want them replaced but can he make them more 'antiquey'?

'I've had shitty clients before but these two take the gold medal.' He sighs. 'I said to Fi, I'm almost tempted to give them their money back and just walk away. She said I should charge them double for all their nit-picky time-wasting. Fi's way tougher than me. Ooh, that reminds me.'

I know what he's going to say before he can get the words out.

'She'd love to meet you, Annie. You two will really get on.'

'Because we've got *you* in common?'

'We're going for a pizza tonight. That restaurant in Market Place. Fancy joining us?'

'When I've got all these apples?'

'I'll take that as a yes. See you at 7.30. You and Fi will definitely get on.'

'Yeah, you said.'

'She wants us to meet,' Kate gabbles down the phone before I can even say 'Hello'.

'Fi does?'

'Fi? Why Fi? That's Rob's girlfriend, isn't it?'

'Ah, you mean Charlie. And by "us" you mean you, not me. She wants you and her to meet.'

'Well, duh-err,' Kate groans. 'Why would she want to meet *you*?'

'To check she's smitten by the right sister?'

It's a joke, and a lame one at that, but Kate doesn't respond. When she's as jittery and vulnerable as this, I can't even risk a stupid throwaway line.

'No, you're right,' she says, after a thoughtful pause. 'You really should meet Charlie, see what you think, see if I'm way off base here.'

'Seriously, Kate? You've never asked me to vet any other relationships before. God knows, you didn't want anyone to meet that architect, all the time you were with him.'

'Because I knew you'd judge him and you'd judge me for being with him.'

'Then don't ask me to judge Charlie.'

'Please, An-An,' she says, in her little voice. 'I'm a mess. I can't think straight about anything.' She laughs at her accidental joke.

'I'm not keen, Katkin.'

'Ten minutes. That's all I ask. I'm meeting her for a drink tonight. Half seven in the Peahen. You swing by, say hi, then pretend you've got to be somewhere.'

'I *do* have to be somewhere, as it happens.'

She laughs as she hangs up. The very idea.

That afternoon, I actually do some cleaning and tidying. Plus I polish off all the apples. Rob was right. I have been eating too many big breakfasts, too much fast food. I must fill the fridge with veg and try that Zumba class again.

After living out of a suitcase for weeks, I now have a whole wardrobe of clothes to choose from again: trousers and tops, skirts and shirts, a couple of Sixties frocks from my favourite vintage shop. I even unearth the luminous dress I bought for Dad's funeral. I was going to give it to Oxfam but I can't. Not yet. I remember wearing it and this makes me cry.

But weirdly, when I get ready for my night out, I feel most at home in the freshly laundered boyfriend jeans and sailor-striped T-shirt Yasmin gave me in Edinburgh. I check myself out in the full-length mirror. I look leaner and stronger, and not just because I've been hauling that Star Wars suitcase around the British Isles.

Something's changed. I can't put my finger on it but I like what I see. I couldn't have said that six months ago. I pull a silly face to puncture the moment. Even the silly face feels real. This is the authentic Annie Stanley. Maybe she was there all along, hidden beneath the sweatpants and a permanent cloud of gloom. I must remember this moment, in case I need to draw on it in an emergency.

Kate told me to 'swing by' the pub where she's meeting Charlie. What does that even mean? What's my story? Am I 'swinging' spontaneously or on purpose? Do I know Kate'll be there or should I just stumble across her and Charlie by accident? I mustn't mess up.

I spot Kate through the pub window so no subterfuge is required. She's just downed a glass of white wine and is topping it up as I approach. No Charlie. No wonder she's in need of Dutch courage. She looks so relieved to see me, like the cavalry's arrived. She's already pulled a paper napkin to shreds and is starting to worry a beer mat. I grab the debris and shove it in my pocket. That's what sisters are for.

She pours me a generous glass of Chablis. I'm in need of Dutch courage too. I'm not worried about meeting Charlie but meeting Fi is another story. That strong woman I saw in my bedroom mirror seems to have done a runner.

'Too much lippy?' Kate asks, kissing a paper hankie. 'Or not enough? Have I missed my mouth? I don't want to look like Auntie Jan.'

'You look flipping gorgeous, Katkin.' She does. Always. Khaki linen sweater, tailored navy shorts, bronzed dimpled knees. Only one thing spoils the look: an expression of sheer bloody terror.

'Just chill, okay,' I tell her. 'Remind yourself what you want from this. Don't put up barriers. Be open, honest and receptive. You bloody deserve this.'

She nods, then her face freezes into a grinning rictus. She kicks me hard under the table to signal that Charlie is approaching. I catch the bottle of wine that Kate sends flying as she jumps up to greet the person approaching behind me.

Charlie sits and I get a proper look: long straight grey hair, that stainless-steel shade that's almost lilac; heavy horn rims; shortish, curvy, mid-forties; rocking the smart-casual look, just like Kate. Not sure what I was expecting but, if first impressions are anything to go by . . . I'm impressed.

'Don't mind me,' I say. 'I'm Annie, the big sister.'

She shakes my hand. Hers is clammy. She's nervous. 'Charlie. Hi.'

'Kate and I needed a quick catch-up. I've been away.'

'The Shipping Forecast. Kate told me all about it.' Charlie grins. 'Even the cock-up with Keith.'

Oh, God. Keith. My face reddens.

She looks awkward. 'I'm so sorry. I didn't mean to make light of it. It must have been a nightmare for you.'

'Just a bit.'

'It's a brilliant thing you're doing, Annie. What a fine tribute to your dad.'

I wasn't expecting that. Her response makes my voice quaver. 'Or an utterly bonkers one. The jury's still out.'

Charlie goes to the bar for another bottle of wine and Kate can't decide whether to give me a warning glare or a hopeful smile.

'Well?' she stage-whispers.

'She seems nice, based on all of twenty seconds.'

'She *is* nice. Why wouldn't she be? Listen, you don't have to stay. Seriously, An-An. I thought I needed you but maybe I don't any more.'

'I've barely exchanged pleasantries. Are you sure?'

'Just bugger off, will you? I'm fine.'

So I slug back my wine, make my excuses and go. Charlie wishes me luck for the next leg of my journey. I think she means Lundy to Irish Sea, not the pizza place two minutes up the high street.

Rob was right: Fi and I do get on. She's warm and friendly and it's written all over her face that she's potty about Rob. I sit facing them, as if at a job interview. But then what's the seating etiquette in a situation like this? Why wouldn't Rob sit next to Fi and opposite me? That way, they can hold hands under the table.

We're all anxious. We all seek approval. Although me not so much because I'm history. But Rob needs reassurance that I like Fi and I need to reassure him that I do. Fi just has to make it clear that she has a firm grip of the baton now. In true Annie Lummox style, I dropped it and she picked it up. I get that. I do.

The first time I met Maggie at a barbecue, she gave me the once-over, desperate to know who Rob had replaced her with. She asked me a few questions: where was my dress from, how long had I lived here, what was my preferred sexual position? Okay, maybe not that last one, but I bet she was dying to know. Whatever answers I gave were sufficient for her to abandon me for griddled sweetcorn and a chicken wing within four minutes. No point hanging around: she'd established that Rob hadn't found someone quite as fabulous as her.

When I met Bev for the first time, how could I not compare her to Mum? But whereas Maggie got huge satisfaction from Rob dropping his standards, I was hurt that Dad thought Bev was good enough to fill Mum's shoes. This friendly woman, in her turquoise blouse and peach lipstick, didn't even come close. Now that I know Bev better, I see that it isn't fair to compare them.

Mum was Mum and Bev is Bev. Two women with Dad in common.

Just like Rob, Fi and me.

Fi is as Josh described her: choppy blonde hair, slim build, toned arms. I bet she's got a six-pack. She puts down her bruschetta, cocks her head to one side and gives me a look.

'What?' I ask. 'Have I got pesto down my front?'

'I know you, Annie. I know I know you.'

'Fi's amazing,' Rob says. 'She never forgets a face. I keep telling her she could be one of those super-recognizers the cops use.'

Her face looks familiar too. Josh said she doesn't have kids so she can't be a school parent. Maybe she was in the same year as Kate.

'Got it!' Fi says, clapping her hands. 'Scoff's. You were one of our regulars.'

Nope. Not. A. Clue.

'Scoff's. The little cafe near the cathedral. Purple-painted brick walls. Breeze-block counter. All us staff wore red aprons. Okay, here's a clue: "Would you like your frittata warmed?"'

Scoff's. Of course. I often nipped in on a Saturday for a chai latte or smashed avo on sourdough. When I stopped teaching, but before I qualified as a full-time couch potato, I'd spend an hour or two over a couple of coffees at a window table. They always had a good selection of newspapers and gossip rags, plus some choice glossies.

'Aha, I remember you now. And the other guy who always wore a baseball cap.'

'Danny. My shit of an ex.'

'That frittata was to die for. I asked you for the recipe once and you pretended not to hear me. Small world, though. I caught up with an ex-boyfriend when I was in Edinburgh. Duncan. Josh told me you do food markets. He does too. Home-smoked fish in a floury bap. Bloody gorgeous.'

Rob watches us bonding and beams with joy. No fisticuffs, no sarkiness or snarkiness. I bet he's thinking: If only Maggie and Annie could have hit it off like this.

Fi isn't finished. 'You came to Zumba once and never returned, right?'

'I did. That class was my worst nightmare. I just wanted a bit of cardio, you know, work up a sweat so I could have cake afterwards. But it was like I was auditioning for Beyoncé's dance crew. Plus, I kept forgetting left and right. Horrifying.'

'Marco. He was brutal. It's Fleur now. She's amazing. Come with me next week. I can nudge you if you get lost.'

Our pizzas arrive. Mine groans under the weight of three kinds of meat. Rob and Fi have chosen veggie options and spend several minutes trying to swap slippery halves; his courgette and sun-dried tomato for her spinach and goat's cheese.

293

Rob loves pepperoni but he's going meat-free for Fi. If they were *The Lady and the Tramp*, they'd be sucking up the same strand of spaghetti. I want to hate them but they're not making it easy.

Fi fills me in on the Scoff's saga. She and Danny had an acrimonious break-up but fortunately, it came at the same time as an offer to buy them out by one of the big coffee chains. So he went to Spain and she bought an old ice-cream van off a mate.

'I was the grafter, not him,' she explains. 'My tabbouleh recipe, *my* fig flapjacks, *my* spinach frittata. Not Danny's. So that's what I sell now, at farmers' markets and summer fayres and festivals. I couldn't be happier, especially since I met this one.'

She takes Rob's hand and they smile at each other. My prosciutto sticks in my throat.

I feel obliged to break the gooey silence. 'I remember that flapjack. God, it was good.'

Rob pats his waistline. 'Don't I know it.'

We chat, with no awkward pauses, for the rest of the meal. Fi is nice, Rob is happy, I am cool. Maybe it's a good thing. I can draw a line and move on. And now I have someone to move on with/for/to. Simon is imperceptibly becoming part of my future by the day, not that he knows it yet. And it means that, instead of thinking the world revolves around me (which of course it does), I can be pleased for Rob. For Rob and Fi. They've found each other and the world is blessed with one more blissed-out couple.

A tiny, pointy shard of me is still slightly narked by their happiness. I over-compensate by following my pizza with a sticky stack of profiteroles and, four hours later, a Gaviscon.

* * *

Kate rings my doorbell at quarter to nine the next morning. I've been sleeping in since I got back from Bideford. It's easier than deciding what to do next and I've always thought my bed was the best in the world; the pillow/mattress/duvet relationship is perfect.

She bears croissants from the French patisserie, classy raspberry jam and freshly ground beans; she heads straight for the kitchen to make coffee. How did she know my Nescafe has solidified into one grey lump that I have to chip at with a knife to extract granules?

I know she's dying to tell me what happened last night with Charlie, but I also know my control-freak sister well enough not to pester her until the coffee is brewed, the croissants are warmed and plated, the jam has a clean spoon in it.

'Well, bloody go on then,' I say as we sit cross-legged on the floor around the coffee table.

Kate smiles. It's a smile I haven't seen in years: a relaxed, laidback, stress-free smile that tells me all I need to know. Well, not quite but she's my sister and I don't need every last detail.

'Charlie was petrified,' Kate says. 'Did you see how nervous she was when she arrived? That's when I knew it would be okay.'

'You weren't exactly a picture of confidence yourself. Pour the coffee, will you? I'm gagging for it.'

Kate has found my two matching mugs. Another sign that only the best will do for this important family moment.

'She knew how she felt about me right from when I came for the interview. She told Ros and Ross I was the best candidate and they had to give me the job. But really it was because she thought she might not see me again, if they chose someone else.'

'Oh great. You only got the gig because of her.' I am outraged on Kate's behalf.

'Course not. I *was* the best candidate. Flattering, though, that she had feelings for me so quickly. I liked her from the off too. But I wasn't expecting . . . *this*.'

'And what is "this" exactly?'

Kate coyly tears off a chunk of croissant and dunks it in her coffee. 'What do you think it is?'

'I've got a pretty good idea, judging by that look on your face. Just flipping tell me, will you?'

'It's good, An-An. It's bloody brilliant. Charlie's brilliant. I don't want to assume anything because that's the kiss of death. But today, right now, me and Charlie are, I don't know what to call it. We're together. We're a "thing".'

'No shit, Sherlock.'

'And not just that. She told Ros and Ross that she was meeting me. Just about work, not the other stuff. And they said they want me to come back. They put my silly mistakes down to grief. I'd come back to work too soon after Dad died and I was going through delayed bereavement. I suppose I was.'

'Will you tell them you're a "thing"? You and Charlie?'

'Probably. Best to be upfront. After all, they're a couple and *they* work together so they can hardly forbid it.'

I hug her and she hugs back. I'm so pleased that my little sis is happy. Finally.

She pulls away, tempering the moment. This is Kate, after all. 'I need to be cautious, An-An. I won't jump into this with both feet. Not yet. I know it sounds silly, but I'm not ready to believe what's staring me in the face, just in case I've got it wrong.'

'What's staring you in the face?'

'That your blinds need a bloody good clean. They really are rank.'

'Katkin! What!'

She smiles her wonderful smile again. 'That I've met "The One".'

I look at maps and train timetables, to pick up where I left off on my circuit of the British mainland. Maybe I can cheat, skirt round the Bristol Channel and head straight for sea area Irish Sea in Fishguard or Aberystwyth. I think back to the drive down the east coast from Tyne, through Humber, and on to Thames. Even though I'm a geography teacher, I hadn't realized how flipping far that would be. And now I need to make the equivalent journey back up the west coast. My heart sinks . . .

Another long drive in a hire car, probably alone. Another hunt for a half-decent B&B, an available washing machine, a functioning ATM and a fish supper. There's money left in my bank account. I can afford to do this. Just. But the urgency is gone. I'm back in the familiar bum dent on my sofa and I'm not sure I have it in me.

Before I fall asleep, I listen to the Shipping Forecast. Perhaps it will recharge my flat battery and spur me on. But it doesn't. I'm not defeated by the miles to cover or the effort it will take. My pessimistic mood comes out of sheer bloody loneliness. If I take Dad to Irish Sea, Malin, Hebrides and Fair Isle, what will I come home to?

This.

Who will I come home to?

No one.

Rob has Fi. They're an adorable couple. Even our waiter in the pizza restaurant commented on it. I was merely 'interim girlfriend', to tide him over after he broke up with Maggie. Now he has Fi. She is The One.

I can't bank on Simon being my 'One'. Yes, I feel hopeful but I couldn't bear it if we hooked up and fizzled out after a fortnight, like last time. And no matter how much I tell myself that it'll be different – that we're different, older, more fearful of being alone, that we'll make it work – I can't be sure.

Before Dad died – and more so in the weeks after – I still had Kate. We were a unit. We looked out for each other. Mum asked me to take care of her, when the cancer returned, but it took Dad dying for me to finally get my arse in gear. After that, I tried to make up for my years of selfishness and laziness. To be a proper big sister, the one Kate deserved. Shit, I even rushed home from Bideford without a second thought, because she was in such obvious distress.

Her words in the pub have rung in my head, ever since she said them. 'I thought I needed you but maybe I don't any more.' Okay, I know she meant I could leave her and Charlie to their hot date. But right now, I'm in the mood to pick masochistically at what she said, to pull it apart and find the truth beneath.

Kate has Charlie. Rob has Fi. Who do I have?

Kate's in that honeymoon period of the New Relationship. She's consciously *not* dropping Charlie's name into every sentence but her lover is present in every happy sigh, every enigmatic smile about nothing at all, every *zhuzh* of her hair or glance at her phone. I've become the thing she has to tolerate before returning to Charlie.

The good news is that she's got her old job back. Apparently Kate had singlehandedly kept the business running these past few years and they were grinding to a halt without her. Ros was particularly understanding; she lost *her* father eighteen months ago so she put Kate's out-of-character cock-ups down to grief at our dad's passing.

Kate and Charlie have decided not to go public for a week or two, while they get used to each other. Serious relationships need to be built around more than steamy sex on the kitchen table. It's all good, though, Kate says, with one of her more enigmatic smiles. I don't like to think about my sister's sex life but I'd say she's not complaining. Lucky old Kate.

I get back into my old routine. It suits me. It doesn't challenge me. It's like I never left the sofa. I compose an email to Cameron about getting my old job back but I don't send it. I will send it. When I'm ready. Soon.

One evening, I'm all set for Netflix and chilli, washed down with half a bottle of Lidl Chardonnay, when I get a text from Fi. Do I fancy going to Zumba with her? I politely decline, even when she offers to pick me up from my door. I know she means well and I can't dislike her, but why would I, saddo ex-girlfriend, reveal myself to the gorgeous proper girlfriend as a funk-free wobble-bottom? I don't need pity. I have no wish to be humiliated, patronized or, worse, totally ignored just as soon as she sees how crap I am.

So I lie. I say sorry, I'm visiting Bev that night. I know Fi won't give up so I'll need to come up with another excuse for next week. I'll say I've started a cupcake course and it clashes or I've lost a foot. Or I could just say: Thanks all the same, but I don't bloody want to, okay.

Anyway, who passed a law saying that Fi and I should be besties? If she wasn't with Rob, I'd be happy to meet her for lunch/brunch/cocktails. She is lovely. But no. Sorry. Not going to happen. Hell is scheduled to freeze over first.

Chilli dispatched, I'm just polishing off an ancient almond

Magnum when my doorbell rings. It can't be Fi. The class started ten minutes ago. What part of 'no' didn't she understand?

It's Rob, still in faded work shirt and paint-spattered jeans. 'I know you don't need checking on, Annie, but I wanted to see if you're okay.'

'I'm tip-top. A hundred per cent. Couldn't be better, thank you for asking.'

He hovers, as if there's more to say. There isn't. But I don't want to appear rude or a-woman-spurned so I invite him in and pour him a tiny wine, because he's got the van outside. I can be civilized. I can be grown up. I just wish my shorts and T-shirt weren't so creased, but who irons slob-around gear? (Fi, probably.)

Rob sips his wine, takes in the detritus of my TV dinner and a pile of dirty plates on the kitchen worktop. 'How's the new dishwasher?'

'It's a dishwasher. It washes dishes. I can't ask more of it than that.'

'So it's all working for you again.' He waves a hand around the room. 'This.'

'This what?'

'Telly, microwave, sofa . . . perhaps not the iron.'

'And your point is?'

'Look at yourself, Annie. This is how you were before your dad died. *And* afterwards. It was only the threat of his ashes going to Austria that got you off your arse. It's like you never left your sofa.'

'I did leave. I visited ten sea areas and I've got the knitted squares to prove it.'

'What's changed, though? What's *really* changed? Looking at you, here, now, as far as I can see, bugger all.'

I'm not having that. He can't swan in and make value judgements on my sad little life, just because Fi's at Zumba and he's got a couple of hours to kill.

'What's changed?' I say, putting down my wine so that I can rant properly. 'Okay, how about I've made my peace with Bev and her family, apart from Mark who's still a shit bag. How about that Kate's way more open and honest with me than she ever used to be? That's a huge step forward, Rob. I learned stuff about me too. Big stuff. Important stuff. Slow-burning stuff like who I once was, who I am now. Let's see, what else . . .? Oh, I know. I got to hang out with Hilary who is bloody amazing *and* with Josh who I honestly didn't think I could love any more. Will that do for now?'

'It's mutual,' Rob replies. 'Hilary and Josh have separately given me grief for breaking up with you. I kept reminding them it was your call. You pulled the plug, not me. But that's history. We're history. And we're cool with it, right? We've moved on.'

'Absolutely.'

'I'm with Fi now. What did you think of her, by the way?'

'She's great. You've fallen on your feet there, Rob.'

'So why didn't you want to go to Zumba with her?'

Bloody Zumba! I hadn't realized my attendance was crucial.

'Let's see: a) I hate Zumba and b) just because Fi's your girlfriend doesn't mean *we* have to be best friends. Seriously, Rob, it's not the law.'

'Fair enough. But you *are* okay that I'm with her? I'd hate to hurt you.'

'For fuck's sake, you're not hurting me. I'm totally okay about Fi. And you can be okay that I'm with Simon.'

Ha! His face! He hadn't reckoned on *me* moving on. Yes,

301

okay, I'm jumping the gun a little. But it's more a case of 'when', not 'if' I'm with Simon. I see that now, clear as day. Like Rob says, he's history.

'Who's Simon?'

So I tell him: ex-boyfriend from years ago, who I met up with in Brighton. Hugely successful actor, about to tour with a one-man play. I even embroider the truth about those indigestion commercials, implying that he's still spearheading a major TV ad campaign and it's earned him a fortune. Rob doesn't watch much telly; he won't know I'm lying.

'It's so brilliant that Si and I reconnected,' I conclude. 'The years just fell away. You two must meet. You'd really get on.'

Rob takes my words at face value. I'm not lying as such, just previewing the inevitable. Simon won't mind. On the contrary, he'd be thrilled to hear me bigging him up like this.

'So,' I conclude, 'we've both met someone, we've both moved on. We're both in a happy place and we can be friends, just like we are now, without any awkwardness or emotional baggage. Okay with you?'

'Absolutely.' Rob nods enthusiastically, to show just how okay it is.

I honestly think we've turned a corner.

I wake up to the loo flushing. My alarm clock says 2.20 a.m.

Fuck, fuck, fuck! This isn't a dream. This is really bad. Annie Lummox strikes again.

Rob tiptoes into the bedroom but doesn't get back under the duvet. I pretend to be asleep. I hear him pull on his jeans, stumble into the dressing table, fumble for his watch. I stay motionless. There is no alternative.

'Annie?' he says softly. 'Are you awake?'

I'm tempted to launch into loud snoring but I decide against it. I snuffle and turn over. See, Rob, I'm out for the count so there's no need to wake me and make clunky conversation. And at least he won't have to explain himself to Fi when he gets home because they don't live together yet. Small mercies.

He must be dressed by now. What's he waiting for? He stands still for a moment. He'll be thinking: Will I look like a total creep if I scarper without even saying goodbye? I hear the rustle of paper. He scribbles me a note which he leaves on the dressing table. Then, like a total creep, he scarpers without even saying goodbye.

The note reads: 'Didn't want to wake you. Talk soon xxx R.'

I give him a full minute after my front door closes, then twitch the blinds to see him get into his van and drive off. I make myself a cup of tea, sit on the sofa in the dark and scroll back to last night.

We finished the wine and opened another bottle. Platonic friends can get pissed together, no problem. But I must have said something, touched his arm, given him a look, Christ knows. He made the first move but I prompted it. I must have. What was I thinking? We snogged on the sofa like a pair of hormonal teens and it was so good; the same but different, wrong but right.

Wrong really. So wrong.

It felt too frantic to be called making love. It felt too familiar to be called fucking. There were no surprises, no awkward moments about what he likes, what I like. How gentle, how urgent, how intense. Because we knew. It was like riding a bike, you never forget. Shit, I think I even said that out loud, before we moved to the bedroom, and we both giggled.

I should have stopped it after the first kiss. I shouldn't have smiled or made eye contact or whatever I did that caused . . . this.

He has Fi. I have Simon . . . pretty much.

This can never happen again.

As the days go by, and despite his note, we can't talk about it. So, by silent, mutual consent, we don't. We don't talk at all because this is too unwieldy to deny or ignore.

I've made a bad thing much worse; sleeping with Rob, then losing him, even as a friend.

A week after my return to St Albans, I have to accept that Dad and I aren't going to complete our tour of the Shipping Forecast. So perhaps he should be quietly returned to Bev and scattered in the South Tyrol or off Swanage Pier. It's her call, after all. I've had my hissy-fit. It made sense at the time. Now it seems childish and selfish.

I nearly ring her to invite myself round for the symbolic Return of the Urn but I get distracted by a Chinese takeaway and eight back-to-back episodes of *Friends* and then it's half eleven and too late and yadda-yadda-yadda and I'll do it tomorrow.

Probably . . .

Before I can, I get a call from Hilary in Bexhill and everything changes. I've just popped out for Sunday papers, eggs and milk. My only plans for the day are eggy bread and another afternoon on the sofa with the gang at Central Perk.

'So,' she says in her familiar bossy voice. 'By my reckoning, you must be in Wales by now. Sea area Irish Sea. I got arrested in Rhyl once, but that's another story.'

'Not quite. I'm in sea area St Albans. Moderate to good, occasionally poor. And how are you, Hilary?'

'I'm very well, thank you. Apart from a bit of heartburn from last night's imam bayildi. Stuffed aubergine to you. Toni was somewhat heavy handed with the smoked paprika.'

'You and Toni are friends? Oh, that's made my day. I knew you'd have to stop being so anti-social sooner or later.'

'Nonsense. I've been very gracious and responsive to all my neighbours, apart from that pound-shop Tory on the next landing. Anyone who wears a cravat is using up someone else's oxygen.'

I leave the newsagent's and perch on a bench outside. Hilary has never rung before, so she must have something to say.

She cuts to the chase. 'I spoke to Robin the other day.'

Oh God, he hasn't told her, has he? He wouldn't.

'Oh yes?' I bleat weakly.

'He said that you've found this Shipping Forecast business rather exhausting. Is that correct?'

'It has been hard to keep going.'

'But you'll see it through?'

This is my first opportunity to say out loud what I've lately been thinking. I may as well try it out on Hilary. 'Nope. I'm done. Thus far and no further. Yay me for even attempting it.'

I detect tutting. I'm about to be dressed down. But all I get is a loaded silence.

'Well, say something, Hilary. It's not like you to be speechless.'

'I'm sad, that's all. I thought your little adventure was such a splendid idea. For you *and* for your late father. I can see that it was tiring and emotionally draining, but all the best adventures are.'

'It really was. And who honestly gives a stuff if I don't finish?'

'I ruddy well do, Miss. And, a year from now, won't you kick yourself if you don't complete the task?'

Well, yes, the thought had occurred to me. What's that saying: only regret the things you haven't done. But I won't be bullied into seeing it through if I don't feel up to it.

'Sorry. Got to go. I'm late for my Zumba class.'

I hang up on her. I really do. It was only a teensy white lie. I do have stuff to do. That eggy bread won't fry itself.

Two weeks later, Dad and I are on a train to Liverpool. We're all set to finish what we started a gazillion weeks ago in sea area Cromarty. I told myself I wouldn't to be bullied or arm-twisted into anything, but my resistance was low and there are only so many episodes of *Friends* a girl can watch in one sitting. And eggy bread can't sustain anyone for more than two days, even if you drown it in golden syrup.

Bloody Hilary. She wouldn't let it lie. She refused to respect my feelings and, ultimately, her solution was so well-conceived and brilliant that I had no choice but to go along with it. Will I regret it? Quite possibly . . .

Apparently she and Toni took it upon themselves to get me and Dad back on track and complete my circuit of the British mainland. They Googled train timetables and coach tours, figuring that if they could come up with an all-inclusive itinerary, I might be more inclined to follow it. And then Toni found (cue drum roll) the cruise: a five-night voyage, taking in the final four sea areas: Irish Sea, Malin, Hebrides and Fair Isle.

Hilary, in a rare moment of self-knowledge, realized that her haranguing me into doing it was always going to be a non-starter. So she sent her emissary Rob to run through the details over coffee in a favourite cafe. He didn't bring up our drunken shag, so I took my lead from him. If we gave it oxygen, it would exist. Better to suffocate it with over-enthusiastic talk of Hilary's solution. That way, we could pretend there *was* no shag.

'The ship departs from Liverpool and visits Greenock, Tobermory and Kirkwall,' he explained, via a map on his phone. 'Six days out of your busy schedule and it's job done. Plus she's paying. Hilary is picking up the tab. She's not short of dosh and she has no one to spend it on. So you'd be a special kind of prat not to accept, Annie. Well, what do you say?'

What could I say?

It was only after I agreed and Hilary had bought the tickets that I was made aware of some unexpected Terms & Conditions. Hilary didn't want me travelling alone – I'd done more than enough of that – and wondered if Kate might join me. But Kate was otherwise engaged with Charlie and I didn't want to drag her away.

Rob was the obvious companion. Hilary would pay not only for his ticket but Fi's too. Yep, Fi was joining us on the cruise. Her great-grandfather came from Mull and she'd never been there. So I could either throw a hissy-fit and say 'No way' or accept their couply company for six days. Less than a week. No time at all in the scheme of things. Even if it was only a fortnight ago that I was shagging her boyfriend.

Suck it up, Annie Stanley, I told myself. You can do this. Suck it the fuck up!

Fi suggests we three travel to Liverpool together but I can't face that, on top of the cruise. So I pretend I'm setting off early, to see an old friend for lunch, and we'll meet at Lime

Street Station. I'm getting super-good at lying but, just in case, I plant a picture of Kim in my head so that I can bullshit better, if interrogated on who I met.

The train journey is uneventful. I sleep, I listen to one of Josh's Spotify playlists on Bluetooth, I knit my square of Lundy wool and study my phone to check sea area borders. Irish Sea is St David's Head to Portpatrick, Malin is Portpatrick to the Sleat Peninsula, Hebrides is Sleat to Kearvaig and Fair Isle is Kearvaig to John O'Groats. And then I'm done.

Liverpool is my only chance to buy some Irish Sea yarn before we set sail and I snap up what I'm after at a charity shop in St John's Shopping Centre. At 1 p.m., I am fed, watered and ready to meet Rob and Fi by the Ken Dodd statue on the station forecourt.

Rob appears first, steering two suitcases, one streamlined and modern, the other looking like a car boot sale cast-off; battered tan leatherette and covered in faded stickers. Rob is frazzled and knackered, even before we begin our 'adventure'.

'Slight change of plan,' he mutters, mopping his sweaty brow. 'Well, a pretty major change of plan, actually. I should have told you but it was all a bit . . . fluid.'

I look around for Fi. Is she buying sensible snacks from the shop? Has she nipped to the rather fancy Lime Street loos? That's when Hilary appears, wiping wet hands on her patchwork Indian trousers.

'I hate those ruddy hand dryers. All they do is warm the water and you're still damp as a dog at the end of it.'

My dropped jaw prompts a full explanation from Rob. 'Sorry, Annie. It all went tits up two days ago. Fi got a last-minute slot at a fancy new food festival in Shropshire. She'd applied months ago and they'd said they were full.

But then, well, they had a cancellation and she couldn't turn it down.'

Hilary can keep quiet no longer. 'Therefore I shall be Fi for the next five days. Robin was keen to tell you but I said it'll be much more jolly if we keep it a secret until, well, now. Surprise!'

Rob gives an apologetic shrug. Hilary is Hilary; you stand in her way at your peril, particularly if you're her godson.

I try to get my head round it. 'What about the cabins?'

'Easy-peasy,' says Hilary, still beside herself with excitement. 'Toni got on to the ship people and made them sort it out. You and I shall occupy the twin cabin and Robin's got your single. Howzat?'

In the cab to the quayside, I queasily think this through. On the plus side, I don't have to be pally with Fi for the next five days, even though I'm still avoiding eye contact with Rob. On the minus side, I'm sharing a cabin with an elderly, eccentric, short-fused woman.

Hilary, on the other hand, couldn't be happier. 'I took all of twenty seconds to take Fi's place. Didn't I, Robin? I've always felt drawn to the Scottish isles: Lewis, Shetland, Orkney. I never thought I'd see them before I popped my proverbials, but here I am. And I have a little adventure of my own in Glasgow.'

Rob looks surprised. First he's heard of it. 'Well, spill the beans.'

'I will. Tonight.'

I hope it's nothing to do with Dani C, Dreamgal or Bella B.

We're told that our ship, the *Black Watch*, is a wee thing compared to some of the twenty-storey floating cities that rule the waves, but it looks pretty bloody huge from the quayside. We are swiftly processed and go on board to find our cabins, with luggage already deposited outside our doors.

I'm sad not to be using my dinky Star Wars wheelie suitcase for this final leg of the grand tour. It served me well through ten sea areas – apart from that little adventure in Okehampton – but it's just not big enough. As soon as I started to pack, I realized I'd need more than a couple of changes of clothing and some spare knickers. Plus a safe corner of the case for Dad, obviously.

When I get back home, I'll ask Bev to pass the suitcase on to Evie because she thought it was 'awesome'.

'Dressing for dinner' isn't in my DNA, but I can hardly rock up five meals running in manky leggings and a sweatshirt. Fortunately I found a couple of silky tops and a pair of black trousers at the back of my wardrobe, and Kate's donated a dress from Toast – midnight blue, slinky and sleeveless – which I'll wear with bronze Birkies and a turquoise pebble necklace given to me by Bev.

I must see her on my return. I must, must, must.

Hilary is impressed with our cabin. Yes, it's small and, okay, we may need a bit of forward planning if we want to pass each other by the dressing table. But at least the beds are far apart, which we're both silently relieved about. And there's heaps of wardrobe space for our meagre selection of 'outfits'. The chambermaid has thoughtfully folded the first sheaf of loo roll into a little paper boat shape and, on each bed, our flannels have been fashioned into a rather scary *Donnie Darko*-style rabbit.

I wish there was a window sill – or should that be porthole sill? – where I could put Dad's urn for the duration of the cruise. But there isn't so he must settle on a side table and feel the sea beneath him.

310

Hilary bags the bed by the porthole, which is only fair since she's picked up the tab, and I offer her all the high shelves and drawers so that she doesn't have to bend. Once unpacked, we lie on our beds and sigh. It's been an exhausting day and we haven't even set sail yet.

'What do you make of our fellow travellers?' Hilary asks, all set to slag them off.

I won't rise to it. 'They look okay. More your age group than mine. Yeah, they look fine to me.'

'You do know we're expected to dine with the same people every night? I can't promise to bite my tongue if we have fundamental differences on austerity or the death penalty or vegans.'

'Since when have you been a vegan? You wolfed down that burger at the De La Warr.'

'Me? Heavens, no. I can't abide them. Smugness personified. I'm afraid I get more intolerant with advancing years.'

'You were certainly pretty harsh about Toni and now you're best pals. What happened?'

Hilary emits a faint fart. 'Ah, now, I should have warned you about that. I'm rather a windbag, in every sense. Toni is a decent person and a good neighbour under all that orange hair. I locked myself out of my ruddy flat one day and she came to my aid. She's got a spare key now and I have hers. She's actually lived a fascinating life, which I hadn't expected.'

'I'm really pleased,' I tell her. Because I really am. 'Does she know about your secret life on Tinder?'

'She's joined me. She calls herself Super Cougar. And don't you tut, Miss Holier-Than-Thou. We're having the time of our lives and we're not hurting anyone. You should try it some time.'

* * *

We've been assigned a table for six in the rather swanky restaurant and wonder who the other three will be. Looking around, this 'dressing for dinner' thing seems to cover a wide range: a fair few sequinned cocktail dresses and evening bags from the women while the men mostly make minimal effort with a clean shirt and chinos, plus the occasional blazer and fancy waistcoat.

Hilary has thrown on a rather spectacular purple kaftan, loaned by Toni, which she accessorizes with some well-worn hiking sandals. Rob looks freshly washed, neatly pressed and slightly anxious in a flower-print shirt and his best jeans. This is so not his natural habitat. Him and me both. I opt for innocuous black trousers and paisley silk top. We blend in quite successfully with our fellow diners.

Rob barely has time to tell us about the cosiness of his single, windowless cabin when our three dining companions arrive: a tanned older couple holding hands, in lairy Hawaiian prints; and a woman of about my age, wearing a little black dress, a zebra-striped shawl and a resentful frown.

'Nice to see you, to see you nice,' the man says, pulling a chair out for his partner. 'The gang's all here so uncork the Chateau Nerf du Plonk and let's get ready to rumble.'

Hilary kicks me under the table which I ignore. I have been known to make instant value judgements on people, but this is way too soon, even for me.

'Dad!' the younger woman hisses. 'Remember what we said in the taxi.'

'I heard you, love. Loud and clear. But I'm that pleased to be here.'

They introduce themselves: Mim and Barry from Bury, and their daughter, Dawn. We nod hello Britishly.

'Hilary . . . Robin . . . Annie,' Hilary replies, waving a

mein Host hand across our side of the table. 'I'm his godmother, she's his ex. If you come across another set-up like us over the next five days, you win a prize.'

'You're on, Hilary,' says Barry, rubbing his hands. 'I like a challenge, me. Don't I, Mim?'

Before our starters have arrived, we're regaled with all the cruises Barry and Mim have been on these past ten years. Every ship, including the *Queen Mary* and the infamous one with the novo virus outbreak; every destination from Cambodia to Tasmania, Alaska to Madagascar. This is their third trip on the *Black Watch* so they're on bantering terms with several waiters, bar staff and crew. They are more than ready to rumble.

'Are you a seasoned cruiser too?' I ask Dawn, who, so far, has let her folks do all the talking.

'I'm a newbie like you. I always fancied it, but Liam didn't. My husband.'

'Your *ex*-husband,' Mim chips in. 'And good riddance, I say.'

Barry gives Mim a warning look and we three pretend not to notice the tension.

'The kids are off doing their own thing,' Dawn continues. 'So I thought, it's now or never.'

Barry takes this as a cue for a song. 'It's now or never. Come hold me tight. Kiss me, my darling. Be mine tonight.'

I sneak a look at Hilary, expecting her to be appalled. But she isn't. She even applauds. 'Oh, I adored Elvis. Such a sexy man before he discovered deep-fried peanut-butter sandwiches.'

Barry beams. 'I thank yew, I thank yew. I'm here all week.'

Mim's eyes shine with love. 'Shut up and eat your crab cakes, you great daft lump.'

The three courses are delicious, the service is friendly and all six of us make a dent in several bottles of wine. I could get used to this, although I fear Hilary's choice of artichokes, cassoulet and plum compote will come back to haunt me later in our airless cabin.

We adjourn to the Neptune Bar – Hilary fancies a cognac. The sea has been calm since we left ('moderate or good') and the night is clear and starry, with the occasional twinkle of light from the coast.

I suddenly realize that, apart from bobbing around the Rampion Wind Farm with Simon, this is my first proper experience at sea since I began my journey. I run through a mental image of the Shipping Forecast map: have we passed the Isle of Man yet, or the Mull of Galloway? Where are Arnamurchan Point and Macrihanish Automatic, and will I know them when I see them? What do they even look like?

I've been subconsciously aware of these magical place names all my life, shushed by Dad over Saturday bangers and beans when he wanted to catch every gale warning and wind speed. And now here I am, quite literally 'sailing by'.

There were times, when I was hurtling towards Humber or Portland, that I forgot the point of this lunatic venture. I got so caught up in the where-to and the how-to that I couldn't see beyond the next sea area. This is good. This is right and I'm so grateful to Hilary for making it happen. Dad would be dead impressed. I really think he would.

Rob and Hilary are discussing tomorrow's first stop in Greenock. I interrupt them to make a toast. 'To Peter Stanley, who'd be absolutely loving this. And to Jackie Stanley, who'd be taking the piss something rotten.'

We clink. We drink. Hilary raises her glass again. 'To

family, friends and lovers, past, present and future. To us. And to hell with what people think.'

We drink again, moved by her words. Then Rob picks up where he left off and breaks the moment.

'I've told you what I think, Hilary. Inside your head you're Wonder Woman. But outside, you're a 77-year-old pensioner who's none too steady on her pins in a strange city taking on, as far as I can tell, a complicated outing. You think so too, don't you, Annie?'

'Sorry. Miles away. What outing?'

Rob's about to speak but Hilary silences him with a stern finger to her lips. 'It's my outing so it's my explanation, if you please, Robin. I'm going to Glasgow tomorrow.'

'We all are,' I tell her. 'It's way more interesting than Greenock.'

Now it's my turn to get the finger-to-lip treatment.

'Could you both just ruddy well listen?' she snaps. 'I've done my research. Well, Toni did, but that's by the by. I know precisely where I'm going and I know how I'm getting there. I will be perfectly fine and I don't need you inviting your-selves along as my carers.'

'Where *are* you going?' Rob and I say the words in unison.

'A bookshop on Glasgow University campus. I shall get a taxi to Greenock Central, a train to Glasgow Central and a Tube train – or whatever they call it – to Kelvinbridge. From there, it's a short walk. I walk all the time in Bexhill. That mobility scooter was just a whim. So sod right off with ruddy great nobs on, the pair of you.'

Rob gives me a quick nod to indicate a change of tactic. Pestering Hilary will only make her all the more stubborn.

'What's so special about this bookshop?' he asks calmly.

Hilary sips her cognac, refusing to answer. We let the

silence sit until she can keep quiet no longer. 'Frank is at the bookshop. He's giving a reading at lunchtime. If that's not fortuitous, I don't know what is. And now I think I shall retire. Don't crash about when you come to bed, Annie. I'm an exceptionally light sleeper. And may I suggest we both adhere to the "if it's yellow, let it mellow" rule with regard to nocturnal flushing.'

After she's tottered off, Rob and I debrief.

'Frank, Frank . . .' I recall. 'She mentioned him a couple of times when I visited her.'

'Frank who?' He's peeved that I've heard of him and he hasn't.

'Ex-lover. I get the impression she's had quite a lively past. She kept teasing me. Dropping his name into the conversation, then saying no more.'

'Why didn't she tell *me* about him?'

I have no idea. And Hilary will only elaborate when she feels like it. *If* she feels like it.

'We need to go with her,' I say. 'That's quite a trek for someone her age in a strange city. That way, we'll find out who Frank is.'

While I have this moment alone with Rob, I decide to bite the bullet and use it to shoot the elephant in the room. We can both relax, enjoy this cruise, if we stop skirting around what happened.

'That night,' I say and Rob knows instantly which night I mean. 'It was a thing but it wasn't a "Thing". Not for me anyway. So if you've been feeling awkward about it, please don't.'

'We got pissed, we got silly, we got over it,' he replies. 'It wasn't a "Thing" for me either.'

'Phew, what a relief. I was worried you'd read more into

it than what it was. Just sex, nothing more. No strings, no agenda. It only happened because we're still a bit too comfortable with each other, that's all.'

'True.'

'I like Fi. I really do, Rob. And I wouldn't want to hurt her. I still can't believe we did that. I hate women who do that. So bloody selfish and stupid.'

Rob fiddles with a hang nail. 'I wouldn't want to hurt Simon and I've never even met the guy. It won't happen again. Thanks, Annie.'

'What for?'

'For being so sensible and up front about it. I knew you would be.'

'Why didn't *you* bring it up then?'

'Because I'm a shit-for-brains Neanderthal man and we're rubbish at stuff like that.'

'You really are. So, line drawn? Clean slate? End of?'

'Definitely.' He looks ridiculously relieved. We've dispatched that pesky elephant with no blood spilled.

Chapter Twenty-Two

Malin

We're on the train from Greenock Central into Glasgow Central, all three of us. Rob and I had a secret strategy chat over breakfast and agreed on how best to play this. We're coming to the bookshop with Hilary, whether she likes it or not. She may be more worldly and well-travelled than me but she's also forty years older.

Initially she assumes we three just happen to be on the same train because we shared a taxi from the quayside. At the first stop, Port Glasgow, Rob gazes out of the window and innocently asks Hilary if he's ever met this Frank. 'I must have done, right?'

It gets just the response he was after. 'Of course you ruddy well haven't, Robin. Why would I introduce my lover to my godson? I may be many things but I've always been a strict respecter of boundaries.'

'Fair enough,' Rob replies, pretending this is all the information he requires.

My turn. 'Is Frank Glaswegian? Maybe he can suggest a nice place for lunch.'

Hilary feigns weariness at having to explain all this. But it's obvious she wants to unload. 'Originally. He moved to

London in his twenties. He lives in Toronto now. Has done for years. He's a visiting professor at Glasgow University. As I understand it, this reading at the bookshop is his last gig before he returns to Canada. Anything else you want to know, Nosy Nora?'

'I remember you mentioning him when I visited. Wasn't he your fiancé?' I know this will jolt another snappy reply and I'm ready for it.

'Fiancé . . . what a ridiculous concept. He was my lover, on and off, through most of the eighties. Ten years my junior. Arrogant, controlling, needy. But, by God, I gave as good as I got.'

'What happened?' Rob asks, knowing she's finally ready to talk now.

'I got tired of him banging on about his precious poetry all the time, without ever picking up a pen to write any. He was always meaning to do things and never getting around to it. When he finally left Vivienne so that we could be together, I was living with my darling Hans and he never forgave me. So he took a teaching job in Toronto and we lost touch. Hard to be lovers when there's an ocean in between.'

'Wow, Hilary, you really were quite the, quite the –' I can't think of the right word.

She grins. 'I had my moments. I'm not saying Frank was the love of my life but he was most definitely one of them. It's just that I can't abide unfinished business. He was always a little troubled, emotionally. I need to know he's okay.'

At Glasgow Central, we suggest Hilary dispenses with the subway ride and hails a cab. And, here's an idea: why don't we hitch a ride to the bookshop as we're thinking of going to the Mackintosh House, which happens to be nearby?

'You won't let me do this alone, will you?' she observes as our taxi takes us, rather symbolically, along Hope Street.

Rob and I smile. Busted. Hilary smiles back. She looks relieved to have us here, despite her bluster.

Glasgow University is gothic and grand, just as a university should be. The bookshop is a modern, sandstone building across the road from the campus, up a sloping hill.

We're ten minutes early and are rather smug at how clever we've been to find our way here in good time. Hilary approaches an assistant stacking books on a table.

'The Professor Stern event. Where do we go?'

She doesn't know. She finds a colleague who does. 'Ah,' he tells us, his face full of professional regret. 'Cancelled, I'm afraid. Professor Stern has a bad head cold. We only found out an hour ago. You can still buy one of his books, though.'

He finds us a copy, a slim volume of poems called *Russet Apples: Late Thoughts, Lost Stanzas*. While Hilary flicks through it, Rob pulls a tenner from his wallet. Now what? We regroup over coffee.

'Back to the ship?' I suggest. 'We gave it our best shot. Or we really could go to the Mackintosh House. I've heard it's amazing.'

Hilary says nothing but continues to turn the pages of Frank's book. She stops at the title poem, 'Russet Apples'. 'He was always tinkering with this one, never finishing it. I told him: leave it be. It's done, it's good. Leave it ruddy well be.'

Rob catches my eye. What to do for the best. Is Hilary ready to leave Frank ruddy well be?

'I need a wee,' she announces and heads for the Ladies'.

'At least we tried, Annie,' Rob says when she's out of earshot.

I agree. 'Sometimes unfinished business has to stay . . . unfinished. You can't write "The End" on every chapter of your life.'

I think about the relief on Rob's face when I told him I was cool about That Night. He truly is happy-ever-after with Fi and now it's my turn. I honestly feel I have a future with Simon. Or should I leave it ruddy well be? As soon as I get back, I need to find out.

Hilary returns from the loo, purposeful and triumphant. 'I found that chap who sold us the book and, after much prevarication, he told me where Frank's staying. So. Next stop, the Hilton Glasgow Grosvenor. It's not far so if you could just look sharp, we'll be on our way.'

I'm not sure why we thought Hilary would get lost in Glasgow without us. While Rob and I faff and fiddle with GPS and Google Maps on our phones, Hilary assertively leads the way to the Hilton. She got directions from the guy in the bookshop.

At Reception, she wastes no time with politeness. 'Professor Stern. Please ascertain if he's in his room.'

'Of course, madam,' a smartly suited young woman name-badged 'Lila' replies. 'And who shall I say you are?'

'His lover? The inspiration for a rather thin book of poems? No, on second thoughts, just say it's Hilary.'

Lila rings his room. We wait. She smiles at us to show that she's endlessly happy to help. We wait. Eventually she hangs up. 'No reply, I'm afraid.' She offers us a Hilton notepad and pen (which Hilary later pockets). 'Would you like to leave him a message?'

'I hardly think so. What on earth would I say?'

We regroup . . . again. We tried. We were unsuccessful.

You can't force an ending when there isn't one. But, as we turn to the door, ready to leave, Hilary suddenly exclaims: 'There he is. I'd know that hair anywhere.'

Sitting in an armchair, with his back to us, is an unruly mop of grey curly – verging on frizzy – hair. Professor Frank Stern. We've only ruddy well found him.

Rob and I are all set to approach but Hilary holds up a 'halt' hand to stop us. This is *her* unfinished business, not ours, so back off. We watch her walk to the armchair. She stops. She looks uncertain, then she forces herself on. We still can't see Frank but we can see Hilary's face as she reaches him. Ten seconds pass, maybe twenty, and she doesn't say a word. Then she returns.

'Well?' Rob asks. 'Why didn't you speak to him?'

She shakes her head. 'He was fast asleep. Snoring a little. Frank was always the most terrible snorer. I looked at him and I realized we were finished business decades ago. What on earth would be the point in raking it over now?'

'Are you sure?' I ask. 'We've come all this way.'

'Of course I'm ruddy well sure. Now, if we can just get back to the ship before 2 p.m., we'll still be in time for lunch.'

Rob has learned that five laps around the deck of the *Black Watch* equals one mile so he's aiming to get some serious running in while we're at sea. Apparently Fi is addicted to Park Runs and has been trying, unsuccessfully so far, to enthuse Rob. He reckons, if he can improve his endurance and stamina while he's away, he'll be all set to take her on.

'Starting now,' he says, jogging on the spot in baggy shorts and an Arsenal T-shirt. 'I think I'll do a few circuits before dinner. Want to join me?'

'Nice of you to ask, Robin,' Hilary replies with a twinkle,

'but I forgot to pack my high-impact sports bra. Annie might be interested, though.'

I pat my tummy. 'After that lunch?'

'I'll take that as a no, then.'

'Ask me tomorrow.'

So Hilary and I secure ourselves a couple of deckchairs for a spot of people- and scenery-watching. Next stop, Tobermory, on the Isle of Mull.

When I was packing, I decided to leave my precious Shipping Forecast map tea towel back at home (although, coincidentally, the very same one is framed and hung on a wood-panelled wall near the ship shop), so I trace the next stage of our route via my phone.

I show Hilary, who is failing to turn beyond page two of the Harlan Coben thriller she borrowed from the ship's library. 'Looks like we'll be looping down past Arran and the Mull of Kintyre, then round Islay and Jura and north to Mull.'

'Whatever.'

Not the response I was expecting. She's bound to be pining for Frank, wishing she'd spoken to him at the hotel, wondering what might have been. She was very subdued – for Hilary – on the journey back to the ship.

'Penny for them.' It's an icky phrase I've always avoided but I'm hoping it might kick-start a conversation.

Hilary ponders. 'That strudel was too dense for my liking,' she says finally. 'I should have had the fresh raspberries.'

'And Frank? Are you cool about not talking to him at the hotel?'

'Am I cool? Am I cool? What do you think I am? A ruddy Frigidaire?'

Rob jogs past and we give him a wave. He looks a little

pink in the face. Perhaps he should walk before he runs, but I know he won't be told.

'Yes, I'm "cool",' Hilary declares, doing those annoying quote marks. 'As you might put it, I'm "totally cool".'

'Maybe you are . . . right now. But it's only been a few hours since you saw him. The regret's bound to hit you, sooner or later.'

'My only regret is that strudel. What would have been the point in talking to him, Annie? Where would it have got either of us? Nowhere. That's where.'

'You just don't know.'

'I just *do* know, Miss Agony Aunt. Frank's part of my past. He has no place in my present and certainly not in my future, if I have much of one at 77.'

'You were dead set on seeing him, though. You were, Hilary, so there's no point denying it.'

'Brown sauce,' she says suddenly, apropos of nothing.

'Huh?'

'Bacon rolls need brown sauce. Frank didn't add spice . . . oomph. I need spice. Too many couples on this ship are the bland leading the bland. They've settled, not striven for what they really want. That's not for me.'

I'd forgotten her brown sauce lecture in Bexhill. So daft, so Hilary.

She's not done. 'I was curious, that's all. Haven't *you* ever wanted to meet up with an old lover, Annie, to see how they've fared over the years? Merely out of curiosity, nothing more? I very much doubt it. You're not exactly proactive, are you? You prefer to stay in your cosy little comfort zone. Unchallenged. Passive. Safe.'

Here we go again. Hilary, the disher-outer of home truths. Is she provoking me? Is that her game? I don't understand why, but it's working. 'Okay,' I say, aiming to remain calm. 'Firstly, I think this journey with Dad's ashes is pretty bloody proactive. And secondly, I *did* meet up with an old lover in Brighton, as it happens. Not on purpose, I grant you, but it was a big deal for both of us. We talked about the past and the future. Our future. Like you and Frank, it's unfinished business.'

'Do you have a future with this chap?'

'He thinks we do. His name's Simon.'

'Aha, but you don't. Any reason for that?'

'Guess what? I do. We're meeting up when I've finished my trip.'

Hilary harrumphs and turns a page although she's obviously not reading.

'Go on then,' I snap. 'You're going to tell me what you think, so let's get it over with.'

'I'm pleased for you and Simon. Just as I'm pleased for Robin and Fi. He's my godson, after all. He may be – how old is he now?'

'41.'

'He may be 41 but I will always give him my perspective on his life choices.'

'I don't doubt it, Hilary.'

'What do you make of Fi? I'd genuinely love to know.'

'I like her. They seem very happy together. I was an interim girlfriend, after Maggie. Now he's with Fi and they're for keeps. Anyone can see that. So, good for him. Good for them.'

'Hmm.' That's all Hilary says. 'Hmm.'

'What's that meant to mean?'

'They visited me a few weeks ago, Robin and Fi. And, yes, I like her too. Charming girl. Lovely eyes.'

'She *is* charming. Rob's moved on and he's found The One, so it can't have been me. You said yourself that we were chalk and cheese. You told me I should move on too. Start afresh. Find a new man. You did, Hilary.'

'And you took my advice. With this Simon chap. Excellent.'

'We've all moved on. Even you. You've drawn a line under Frank.'

She rubs her temples. 'Fi is very engaging. She made two lentil lasagnes and a cauliflower cheese for my freezer, which I thought was most thoughtful. So did Toni and she loathes lentils. Fi is very engaging.'

'Yeah. You said. There's a "but", though, isn't there?'

She nods. 'And there's the ruddy rub and I hate myself for even thinking it because of chalk and cheese and you moving on and meeting Simon.'

'But what?'

'But . . . Fi isn't you.'

Rob runs by. We wave.

At dinner, Hilary, Rob and I have no need to speak, from the chicken liver parfait through to the tarte Tatin, as Barry and Mim take it upon themselves to regale us with every last detail of their four-hour coach excursion to Loch Lomond: the beautiful scenery; Barry's purchase of a tartan waistcoat; the stop at Helensburgh for a chance to snap our ship at anchor across the Clyde. We see several of these photos on Mim's tablet, with one or both of them in the foreground, plus another with Kirsty, their excellent guide. There's also a photo of Dawn squinting into the sun, alongside a lanky, smiley man in a *Game of Thrones* baseball cap.

'That's Steven. We got chatting on the coach,' Mim explains. 'Dawn's dining with him in the Brigadoon buffet tonight. He's a paramedic and he lives in Cardiff. He's such a pleasant man. Isn't he, Barry?'

'Give it a rest, Mim love,' Barry says with a twinkly smile to show he's not telling her off. 'Don't buy the wedding hat just yet.'

'Her ex was a good-for-nothing, wasn't he, Barry? A lazy layabout who expected to be waited on, hand and foot. Well, he was. Tell them about her thirtieth birthday. Go on, Barry. Tell them what Liam did to ruin it.'

'Let's keep our dirty linen private, eh, Mim love?'

Hilary raises a glass. 'To Steven from Cardiff. And to finding The One. You'll drink to that, won't you, Annie.'

After dinner, Hilary shoos Rob and me away. 'Small talk is so ruddy tiring. I should like to be silent for an hour or two with my Harlan Coben and a whisky Mac.'

We spot Dawn and Steven in the bar on Deck 9. They wave us over to make up a foursome for the 10 p.m. general-knowledge quiz. If it wasn't for their slightly hesitant body language, they could easily be a couple. Maybe they will be by the time we sail back up the Mersey.

I wonder if Rob and I look like a couple to anyone glancing our way.

Steven is in three different pub quiz teams in Cardiff and appeared on *Pointless* with his brother two years ago. He really does know his stuff, so why waste time conferring with his team before scribbling down the answer, especially as he holds the pencil?

'Wasn't Henry VIII's first wife Lady Jane Grey?' I try, at one point.

Steven overrules me with a weary sigh. 'Catherine of Aragon.'

So I choose not to tell him he's wrong about the capital

of Paraguay (it's Asunción, not Montevideo) and he's gutted when our team comes second by just one point.

'What a tool!' Rob says afterwards as we sip brandies, studiously ignoring Hilary hunkered down with her book in the far side of the bar.

'Quizzes do that to some people. It's just as well I'm not remotely competitive.'

Rob practically spits his brandy at me. 'You're one of the most competitive people I've ever met.'

'Bollocks.'

He recovers himself. 'I will say just three words. Crazy golf, Great Yarmouth.'

'Aha! That's four words, clever clogs.'

'I had to take you to one side, tell you to calm down. Josh thought it was hilarious. It was the very first time he'd seen you as a human being, not just his geography teacher.'

'Back when I still *was* a geography teacher.'

'You still are. You're just not one right now. And I never thanked you properly for taking Josh under your wing in Exeter. And getting him to Fowey.'

'Did he tell you about Okehampton? When my suitcase got nicked.'

'With Peter's ashes in it. Yep. Nightmare.'

'Josh was brilliant. Calm, sensible, not awkward about holding my hand or giving me a hug.'

'He loves you to bits. You must know that.'

'And me him.'

'I'm not sure Fi's got the hang of him yet though.'

'Really?' I ask, hoping he'll dish. 'Why d'you think that is?'

'To be honest, Josh hasn't made much of an effort. His head's been too full of other stuff: exams, girls, life. Plus it's still early days between her and me. Not even six months.'

'Yeah. You can't rush these things. I'll be sure to take it slowly when I meet KJ.'

'Who's KJ?'

'Simon's son. He's 13, lives with his mum, stays with Simon at weekends. You'll know what *that's* like.'

'I'm pleased for you, Annie. I really am. That you've found someone. I didn't like to think of you cocooned in that flat, not caring about yourself.'

'I was fine. I am fine.'

'Will you move to Brighton?'

'God, I don't know. Me and Simon are even earlier days than you and Fi. But yes, it's a possibility.'

It wasn't until two seconds ago. Will I move to Brighton? I wonder . . .

We're still in sea area Malin when we dock off Tobermory early the next morning. Back when she booked the cruise, Hilary also reserved two seats on the seven-hour Scenic Mull coach excursion, thinking Fi might like to see the island of her great-grandfather. But Fi isn't here: she's parked in a Shropshire field flogging frittata.

Over breakfast, Hilary runs through today's schedule. 'I rather regretted not booking a place for myself on the Mull tour, especially when I learned that it includes a visit to Iona. So now I can go in Fi's place. You don't mind accompanying me, do you, Robin?'

'It'll be good to have some you-and-me time. But what about Annie?'

I look up from my eggs Benedict. 'Don't worry about me. I'm happy to mooch.'

'Are you sure?'

His concern is slightly annoying. 'Rob, I've just travelled

around nine-tenths of the British coastline. I reckon I can kick my heels in Tobermory for a couple of hours.'

So they head off to the lounge to be checked in to their coach party and I have a second cup of coffee and a Danish pastry. After yesterday's frantic dash around Glasgow, I'm quite happy to rely on my own company and keep it simple today.

Tenders ferry us from the *Black Watch* to the quayside. As soon as we step onto dry land, we're extras in what must be one of the quaintest high streets in the British Isles. There's a photo of it in every Scottish guidebook, a poster of it on the wall of every Scottish tourist office. If you've watched *Balamory*, you'll recognize it in an instant.

I've seen some pretty places since I started this trip but Tobermory wins hands down on sheer unadulterated cuteness. I amble along the main drag, dodging all the other tourists checking out the shops: Highland crafts, chocolate, candles, pottery, Tobermory whisky. In a community hall, I come across a charity shop and buy a pretty ball of muddy yellow yarn for all of 50p.

I find a bench, with a fine view of the *Black Watch* anchored in the hazy distance, and wonder if I should phone Kate. When I first started seeing Rob, our regular phone chats got postponed or forgotten. Obviously, I didn't stop thinking about her or wondering how she was.

Actually, that's not true. I *did* stop thinking about her. Rob was front and centre of every sentient thought and I dreamt about him too. I was totally caught up in my new relationship, so desperate not to fuck it up. I can only assume Kate's too busy, enjoying every minute with Charlie, to want to waste time talking to me.

When I told her about the cruise, she was pleased. Ever

the completist, she knew I had to see my journey with Dad's ashes through to the finish line. She met Hilary once, at a family gathering, and liked her spirit.

'I'll be a Hilary when I'm her age,' she'd said at the time. 'Cranky and independent, speaks as she finds. Doesn't care what she looks like.'

I'd laughed at that last bit. Kate will always look immaculate. I'll be the one in mismatched socks and yolk-stained cardies. I already am.

So. To phone or not to phone. In the end, I message her, with a photo attached of Tobermory harbour. 'Hey Katkin. This is my view RIGHT NOW. Adorable innit. Hope you + Charlie having fun. Miss you. Don't want to disturb your weekend. Big love, An-An.'

I resend the photo to Simon because he's also inhabiting a big chunk of my thoughts right now. 'Just two sea areas from finishing. Let's catch up after that? xxx Stannie.'

My nostrils suddenly twitch at a familiar seaside smell. A fifty-something woman has sat with an 'oof' at the far end of the bench, digging into a steaming parcel of fish and chips. She sees me inhale and proffers a chip. I decline, still full from that pastry.

'You'll be missing out,' she says, bobbing it in front of me again. 'Best in all the Hebrides. His deep-fried scallops are legendary.'

She waves at the takeaway van behind us, where there's quite a queue. I don't want to be labelled as That Snooty Tourist, so I take a chip. It's very good, not flabby, not greasy. I nod an approving 'yum'.

'Told you so.' She grins. 'Are you touring? You know, "If it's Tuesday, it must be Tobermory"?'

'I'm cruising. On that.' I point to the *Black Watch*.

'Oh, very nice. I prefer trains myself. I did the Orient Express for my fortieth. But you can't beat Scotland for the best rail journeys. Me and my other half, we've done them all. Some twice.'

She tells me she's come to Tobermory on the bus from Dervaig, which is west of here. She babysits twice a week for her son and daughter-in-law, and her grandson, Lewis, is a little monster.

'So cheeky, such a fibber. He'll go far. Do you have children?'

My heart catches. I hate it when people ask. It isn't going to happen.

'No, I don't.'

'My son works out there.' She nods seaward. 'Taking folk like you out on his boat to see the wildlife: porpoise, dolphins, minke, even the occasional killer whale. You'll not have time while you're here, will you?'

'Afraid not. Once everyone's back on board, we sail to Orkney.'

'Ah, "If it's Wednesday, it must be Kirkwall." That's no way to see Scotland, hen. You'll need to come back and do it properly.'

'I will. Definitely. I bet your son never misses the Shipping Forecast. Especially when there's a storm brewing and he's got a boatload of tourists booked for the next day.'

'The Shipping Forecast? Och, that's just for townies.'

'Seriously?'

'He uses an app on his phone. They all do. Stands to reason. What if you turn on the radio a minute late and the announcer's already done Malin or Hebrides or wherever? You'd need to wait six hours until the next forecast. Proper sea folk don't have time for that. But it's a nice wee relic and it works better than counting sheep.'

I need a moment to take this in. The Shipping Forecast is for people who have no need of it? What would Dad think? Should I be disappointed on his behalf? I have a brief moment of sadness, as if this news has devalued my trip around the British coast.

I decide it hasn't, and not just because I've nearly reached the finish line. Dad would laugh. A 'wee relic' for landlubbers. He'd be hugely tickled by that.

Chapter Twenty-Three

Hebrides

Our waiter asks where everyone is; our table for six has four empty chairs. I can answer for Hilary: today's tour of Mull has wiped her out and she's ordering dinner from room service. And Rob bumped into Barry and Mim on deck earlier, who told him they're 'pushing the boat out' and have a table booked in the fine dining restaurant with Dawn . . . *and Steven*.

'Mim's beside herself,' Rob relates as we study our menus. 'She hoped there'd be some eligible men on board. "Our Dawnie deserves a bit of happiness after all she's been through."'

I'm briefly distracted by the selection of starters. 'Ooh, good, goat's cheese fritters. Poor Dawn, though. Imagine getting to know someone new, especially if the last one was "a lazy layabout", and your parents have ringside seats and are watching your every move.'

'Plus you're at sea so there's no escape.' Rob pours the wine. 'At least Barry and Mim approve of Steven. Your dad wasn't too thrilled when *we* got together.'

'He was cross with me, not you. Dad thought I was a marriage wrecker.'

'He didn't want to see you hurt. Understandable dad behaviour.' Rob clinks my glass. 'To Peter, who I still miss like crazy. You look great, by the way.'

I'm finally wearing Kate's blue dress. When I checked myself out in the cabin mirror, I wondered if it was too tight. But Hilary told me to stop being so ruddy silly. 'You're curvy. You're sexy. Flaunt it, you noodle.'

'I do, don't I? Dress from Kate, necklace from Bev, pashmina from Hilary. I didn't want it but she wouldn't take no for an answer. She's quite the force of nature.'

'Always has been. She was full-on excited today. So thrilled by what we saw, especially Iona. I'm not surprised she's flaked out, though. How was your day?'

There's not much to tell; a bit of mooching, a bit of shopping, a chip and a chat on a harbour bench. 'Guess what I learned? You'll never guess.'

'I hate it when you do that.'

'Proper sea folk don't use the Shipping Forecast any more, not when you can check weather conditions there and then on your phone. So it's become aural cocoa for landlubbers like us. Cricket on the green, bobbies on the beat, "Sailing By" on the wireless and God save the Queen. Three cheers for nostalgia.'

'Wow, I wonder what Peter would have made of that.'

'He was no Little Englander and he couldn't bear anyone who was. The Shipping Forecast was his one concession to patriotism because he felt it on a gut level. It gave him a sense of belonging: Lundy, Fastnet, Irish Sea, Wight, Portland, Plymouth. *That* was Dad's national anthem. And don't look so worried, I'm not about to make myself cry. Right, I fancy the lamb tonight. What are you having?'

* * *

When I get back to the cabin, there's a done-with room service tray outside our door and gentle snoring from the other bed. I undress and wash as silently as I can and slip into bed.

I hadn't relished sharing a cabin with Hilary but we make a good team. We're sharing her toothpaste, rather than have two tubes on the go, I've taken to her fennel tea bags and I enjoyed wearing her pashmina tonight. It was strangely reassuring, despite the occasional straight grey hair threaded through the weave.

I think about Rob.

Dining together felt so normal. Our ease with each other can't just switch off, despite The Shag. He was always generous with compliments and I'd have been miffed if he hadn't paid me one tonight; I did look good in Kate's dress. When I got close to tears, he was genuinely concerned.

I think about Kate.

I can't find it in me to envy her happiness with Charlie, even though they're still in the honeymoon period. Charlie has months to go before learning that Kate turns into Scrooge at Christmas. She despises mince pies and figgy pudding but will happily put away a whole tub of brandy butter. (Mum was furious.)

Kate texted a reply to mine from the Tobermory bench but I only see it as I'm about to turn off my bedside light. 'You always told me to relax, unclench, chill. At last I'm learning how. V V V happy with C & starting to believe it's for keeps. Love you so much, my best big sis. Katkin.'

I lie in my narrow cabin bed, finding the swell of the waves strangely soothing. Hebrides is the only sea area where I won't have a stop-off point or to buy the yarn for a knitted square. Dad's ashes will simply be sailing by. At this penultimate leg of our journey, with only Fair Isle to go, I reckon it's okay to tick Hebrides off as 'visited'. I took the urn, I make the rules.

I'm ready to sleep . . .

'They had a big barney,' Hilary suddenly announces from her bed beside the porthole.

'You what?'

'I was taught to say "I beg your pardon," but civility is *de trop* these days.'

'I beg your pardon, Hilary. Who did?'

'Robin and Fi. I got the impression it was quite acrimonious but he was giving very little away. That's why she didn't come on the cruise and you've been blessed with me as your cabin mate.'

'What about?'

'I told you. Robin wouldn't be pressed.'

'But what was your impression? Just a lovers' tiff or have they broken up proper?'

'It did sound serious. However, I have no solid evidence to back that up. Ask him tomorrow, why don't you? Now could you please desist with this interrogation and let's get some shut-eye.'

Chapter Twenty-Four

July 2015

Rob gave Annie a shove, waking her from her stress dream about getting locked in the staff room overnight.

'It's burning! Annie, get up. Your quiche's burning!'

She threw herself out of bed and ran into the kitchen, just in pants and half asleep. They'd only popped back to bed for a twenty-minute cuddle but must have dropped off. Where did Rob keep his oven glove? Did he even have one? Or had Maggie taken it when they shared out the stuff of their marriage? A folded tea towel would have to do.

She rescued the flan tin and flung it on to the worktop, where it hit some spilled tea and emitted a hiss. The quiche itself wasn't totally burnt but the crust was charcoal.

'Fuck, fuck, fuck, Rob. Your fucking oven is a bastard.'

Rob padded into the kitchen and held out the faded plaid shirt Annie had adopted as her dressing gown. Clothed, she was calmer. But the quiche was still inedible. She could hardly cover it in squirty cream and grated chocolate, her usual solution to burnt baking.

'Hey, it's not the end of the world,' Rob said, buttoning up the shirt and enveloping her in a hug. 'We can pop into Sainsbury's on the way to the picnic. See? Sorted. Let's go back to bed, eh? We don't need to get ready for another hour.'

Annie shook her head angrily. Why didn't he get this? What was so difficult to get? She'd promised to bring home-made quiche, pasta salad, grapes and two kinds of Kettle Chip. She'd told Bev she was making the quiche from scratch, saying it was Mum's favourite recipe. Her mother never had a favourite quiche recipe but Annie desperately needed to include her in Dad's sixtieth birthday picnic or she'd be forgotten. Who was this bloody Bev anyway, and who had appointed her 'menu monitor'?

Back in bed, Annie couldn't relax, even though Rob's work-calloused hands knew where to go to de-stress her. 'At least I made the pasta salad,' she sighed, 'but any idiot can make pasta salad.'

'It looks delicious. They'll love it. Relax, Annie. You're all tensed up.'

'Kate's bringing summer pudding. She makes an amazing summer pudding. Pippa's a rubbish cook so she won't have made anything. But she'll be bringing Elliott and Evie so that more than compensates for any shop-bought dips.'

Rob gave up his attempt to distract her and pulled both hands out from under the covers. There'd be no sex now. Oh well, he'd try again later, when they got back from the picnic.

'Listen, lovely, you're over-thinking this. Your dad's having a birthday picnic for family and friends. A nice day out. Nothing to stress over. And if you do get stressed, I'll be there to hold your hand and eat your pasta salad. Even if it *is* a bit heavy on the spring onions.' Rob tensed for the inevitable thump in the ribs.

Annie leapt out of bed . . . again. 'There's enough pastry left to make another quiche. I'd better not burn this one.'

The smell of warm pastry now pervaded Rob's car as they drove at speed to Verulamium Park. Annie had sat on the kitchen floor watching the second quiche cook and, this time, it was perfect. That left her just ten minutes to throw on a favourite summer dress and her Sunday-best Skechers trainers. No time to tidy her hair but it would be fine pulled back in a random clamp. Rob was in his usual linen shorts and T-shirt.

They were five minutes away, just enough time for Rob to fit in a quick whinge about Josh. 'So is he trying to score points off *me* or off his mum, because I've actually lost track? I've told him, I'll buy the sodding Xbox if he can just stop acting like a 5-year-old.'

'I thought Maggie was buying it?' Annie asked, tentatively. The Xbox saga had been rumbling on for weeks. Every time she thought it was sorted, there would be a new twist, an unexpected subplot.

'It won't be Maggie who buys it, though, will it? It'll be that sweaty-handed prat she's shagging. To stick it to me that I should have bought it ages ago but I can't be relied on to do anything right because I'm such a useless dad.'

'You're starting to repeat yourself, Rob.'

'Sorry. I'm just pissed off that Josh is so good at winding me up. I know his game. I was just the same with my mum and dad. *And* he should be at the picnic today. That was purely to get at me, Annie. Peter will be so disappointed.'

'He won't even notice. Not when Bev's busy fussing over him or handing out her amazing Thai prawns and pouring her delicious Pimm's.'

Rob laughed. 'You're annoyed with your dad for taking up with Bev, and I'm annoyed with my son for being a manipulative little shit. The joys of parenting, eh?'

'There are joys, though, aren't there? Josh hasn't put you off kids for life?'

'I'm hardly going to disown him. I might need him to wipe my arse when I'm 90. As for me having any more, well, we're both on the same page there, aren't we?'

What page? When was that decided? Annie was keen to query his words, but they were turning into the Verulamium car park so she bit her tongue. They could discuss it some other time, when she wasn't so wound up about this sodding picnic. Their relationship was still so new; she'd hold back with talk of having kids until she was sure they had a future. She hoped they did. Rob was a keeper.

They unloaded their picnic things from the car: food; blanket to sit on; Cava; frisbee; plus Dad's birthday present – a book of black-and-white Magnum photos of all the Shipping Forecast sea areas. Annie took two of the heaviest bags but Rob made her put them down again, alerted by her anxious frown. He placed a reassuring hand on each shoulder and kissed her. It was important to sound loving but firm.

'This is your dad's day, Annie. This is all for him. Your quiche is perfect and the picnic will be perfect. Trust me, it will *all* be perfect.'

'Even with too many spring onions in the pasta salad?'

'Even then. You love your dad, I love your dad. All this is for him.'

'I know, I know.' Annie risked a tut. She didn't need a flipping lecture.

'I'm nearly done here. Bev loves your dad too. Okay, she

isn't your mum but she makes him happy. And that's fantastic, isn't it? You didn't think it possible but Peter's found happiness. Just like *we* have.'

Rob went to pick up the picnic things but now Annie wouldn't let him. He had to be hugged.

'I won't be a bitch. I promise.'

'And you'll thank Bev for organizing everything?'

'Brownies' Honour.' Annie even did the salute. 'I'll gush once when we get there and once when we leave.'

'Right then. To the picnic?'

'To the picnic.'

Chapter Twenty-Five

Fair Isle

Hilary insists and I accept. She'd booked two seats on the Highlights of Orkney excursion and it's my turn to have one of them. With Rob – because she's still tired from the previous trip. The three of us have already had a morning wander around Kirkwall; the museum, St Magnus Cathedral, another pedestrianized street of tastefully touristy shops, another craft centre where I buy a twisted skein of sheep-coloured hand-spun Orkney yarn for the final square of my blanket.

We sit behind Dawn and Steven on the coach. Steven's keen to show how much he knows about military history; he applied to *Mastermind*, with Scapa Flow as his specialist subject, but was sadly unsuccessful. Dawn looks underwhelmed. Our guide, Elizabeth, is a native Orcadian and she's led this tour over forty times. Fortunately she has sole custody of the microphone so Steven is forced to bow to her superior knowledge.

The scenery beyond 'bustling' Kirkwall is as stark and dramatic as you'd expect so far north, with only the Shetland Islands beyond. Trees are a rarity on Orkney – you soon get used to not seeing them – but their absence is more than made up for by scattered clusters of Neolithic stones.

Our first stop is the Ring of Brodgar. Another coach has

just pulled out of the car park so our little group has the site to ourselves. Elizabeth gives us half an hour to walk around the Stone Age monument, take our photos, take our time, take it in.

It's moody and broody, especially with a bank of grey clouds above: twenty-seven stones (originally sixty, says Steven) like worn teeth set in a circle. It's also quite nippy and I wish I'd brought my fleece. Rob offers me his jacket but why should he freeze so that I don't?

'Just flipping take it, you wazzock!' he insists. 'I'm wearing three layers and I'm boiling.' I flipping take it and it smells of him: barky, soapy, slightly spicy. He's worn the same aftershave for as long as I've known him. Creature of habit. Maybe Fi will wean him off it.

I remember Hilary's comment that Fi and Rob had a row. God, I hope she didn't find out about The Shag.

Rob stops and fiddles with his phone to find the camera setting. He's never been good with technology. Josh thinks it's hilarious. I watch him. He looks up and focuses his phone on me so I pull a silly face. I'm feeling nervous with him today. I must be over-compensating.

'Hilary would love this,' we agree as we walk a circuit of the stones, accidentally photo-bombing Steven's selfie with Dawn. As we pass, she mouths 'Help' and puts an imaginary gun to her temple.

'She did her godmother duty and dragged me to the British Museum when I was doing a school project on Ancient Egypt,' Rob recalls. 'She went all weepy at the Rosetta Stone. She doesn't do God but she connects on a spiritual level with ancient stones and bones, bits of old pottery. Then we had afternoon tea in this big grand hotel – can't remember which one – and she nicked the sugar tongs.'

'We'd better check her suitcase for cutlery before we dock at Liverpool.'

'She is enjoying it, though, isn't she?' Rob asks as we pause beside another huge shard of stone. 'It's not too much for her?'

'Honestly, she's loving it. Food, company, scenery, so many people to bitch about. She'd soon let us know if she was unhappy. Plus she's crossed Frank off her "to-do" list, and emotional housekeeping like that has to be a good thing when you're her age.'

'He had a lucky escape too, I reckon.' Rob walks on. 'Some relationships just aren't meant to be.'

Is he still talking about Hilary and Frank or speculating on his future with Fi? I will find out about their argument. But not yet.

After Brodgar, our coach skims past the Scapa Flow coastline and Elizabeth relates the extraordinary tale of the scuttling of the German Fleet in 1919. Steven nods sagely throughout, with the occasional pained wince when he disagrees with her commentary, the silent version of mansplaining. God forbid that she might know more than he does. Dawn moves to the seat in front, ostensibly so that they each have a clear view of the imposing bay, with Hoy, South Ronaldsay and Burra beyond. No wedding hat for Mim, then.

Stromness rivals Tobermory for cuteness, minus the brightly coloured cottages. We have free time to explore. Rob buys a tweedy flat cap in a shop that smells of mothballs. I treat us each to a cone of artisan ice cream, Orkney fudge flavour. We sit on a bench in the main square overlooking the harbour, eating them fast before they drip down our arms.

'How's Fi's foodie thing going?' I ask between slurps. 'Shropshire, isn't it?'

'Not a clue. We haven't spoken.'

'Yeah, the phone signal's been dodgy since we left Greenock.'

'Or texted or messaged.' He finishes his cone and bins the serviette. 'I nearly rang her from Mull but I thought better of it.'

'Oh? I bet she's wondering how you are.'

Rob's sigh comes from deep in his chest. 'We had a row. Our first. Who knows, maybe our last. Better not to talk than get angry all over again.'

I feel my cheeks redden and it's not from the Orkney wind. Has Fi found out about us? Did Rob tell her? Why the fuck would he do that?

'Has Fi found out about us? Did you tell her?'

'Why the fuck would I do that? Of course not,' he replies tetchily. 'You have nothing to do with this, Annie.'

'That's all right then.' My cheeks slowly unflush. 'Maybe I can help? I was agony aunt to Kate and now she's blissfully happy. All down to me. Nothing to do with her falling head over heels in love.'

He looks dubious.

'Only if you want to,' I say in my best therapist voice.

We gaze out at a ferry in Stromness harbour while he thinks about it. It's excruciating, hoping to hear what happened between them. Outwardly I remain the soul of calmness.

Finally, he speaks. 'It might help to run it by you, Annie, see what you think.'

'Try me.'

'Okay then, three things really pissed me off. First, she thought *I* should cancel the cruise too so that I could be an extra pair of hands at the food fair. After Hilary had treated us both. No way could I do that.

'Second, a mate of hers needs someone to refit a shop and

346

she's told him I'll do it, without even asking me. I could do it, course I could. But it's not the sort of work I enjoy and she should have bloody asked.'

'It doesn't sound very you.'

'Fi says I'm not ambitious enough. I am in my way. All I want to do is a good job, make something that people will appreciate. You have more control over that if you keep things small-scale. I like being my own boss. It suits me. You always got that, didn't you?'

'You'd hate giving orders to electricians, doing spread-sheets, keeping "the Man" on side. It isn't who you are. And the third thing?'

I'm sensing this one's the biggie.

'She thinks I should have a vasectomy.'

'Wow!' I didn't see that coming.

'She doesn't want kids, which is cool and I respect that. But she assumes I don't either, so why don't I have the snip? Logically, I'm with her, totally. But I won't lie, Annie, it's really hacked me off. I'm like: Who made her God of our relationship? Do I have a say in it?'

'That does sound major. I'm sure you can talk it through when you get back, though. If you want to.'

'I do. I really want to. I can't bear another failed relation-ship on my CV. Fi and I should be able to meet in the middle, don't you think?'

'Definitely. And this time apart can't hurt either.'

He likes my response. So he doesn't want to break up with Fi. And I want him to be happy. Of course I do. But as we're sitting there, it suddenly hits me, even though I've known it all along: I want him to be happy with me, not her.

What have I done?

* * *

Back on the ship, my head is bursting with questions, feelings, possibilities. I avoid the cabin; Hilary will be super-curious and I'm still processing what Rob told me. He's gone off to do another of his jogs round the deck. After unburdening, he must be wondering if he said too much. Maybe he's beating himself up for being disloyal to Fi. I know where *my* loyalties lie and, sorry to be unsisterly, but they're not with her.

I toy with treating myself to a massage before dinner. I need to zone out, turn my brain off, stop trying to make sense of all this. But there are no available slots and I'm too ticklish anyway. Eventually I find a big squishy armchair in a hidden corner of the library where I can curl my legs under me, sip a hot chocolate and think.

Something he said plays on a persistent loop in my head: 'Our first row. Who knows, *maybe our last.*'

Does Rob think Fi intends to dump him when he gets back? Maybe *she's* his interim girlfriend and The One is still out there: not long single, needs bookshelves for her new flat, gets his name from a friend. So Rob pops round with his tape measure, their eyes meet across an empty alcove and, wallop, happy ever after.

Fi doesn't want children but Rob does? Because he's had a change of heart now that Josh is about to fly the nest? Or because Fi's demand is too final and it's dawned on him that he isn't ready to have the kiddie option taken away?

I get that because it's how I feel. But is what I'm experiencing a genuine ache or a knee-jerk what-if regret because the world is so child-centred? I don't know.

When I still had a social life, I could get quite upset if my friends were invited to a party and I wasn't. Maybe I didn't want to go to the sodding party but it hurt that I hadn't even been asked. If I did receive an invitation, the choice was mine: 'I *can* go but, guess what? I don't want to.' I'm in control again.

Same with babies? Do I want kids? Really? Okay, I could go it alone but I don't think I'm grown-up enough. Kate could do single parenthood, no problem, but she has Charlie now. They'd make great parents. Do I only want the chance to have children with the right man? Is that Rob? Was it always Rob?

I need to let this sit. I might have got it all wrong; his row with Fi is already resolved and he's booking a vasectomy appointment first thing next week, to prove his commitment to her.

I must have my eyes closed because I'm suddenly aware of someone slumping into the armchair opposite me.

I thought I was hidden here but Dawn's found me. 'Hiya, how are you doing?'

'Me? Fine. Totally. You?'

'He's a wanker, isn't he? Steven. Nice-looking, good job, great arse. But up here –' she taps her head – 'one hundred per cent wanker. Mum won't be told but Dad gets it.'

'They just want you to be happy.'

'Why swap a bastard for a wanker? All that proves is that I'm too scared to be alone.'

'It's hard. But it's better than being with the wrong person.'

'Easy for you to say. You've got Rob. He's great.'

'He is great but he isn't mine.'

Dawn looks genuinely gobsmacked. 'Are you serious? You mean I could have chatted him up days ago, instead of lumbering myself with Mr Mastermind?'

'He's someone else's, although they had a big bust-up before the cruise.'

'And?'

'And what?'

'And is he in bits without her? Doesn't look like it from where I'm sitting. From where I'm sitting, he's got feelings for someone else. And I don't mean Hilary.'

I laugh. Dawn looks pleased that she's perked me up. 'Bloody go for it, Annie!' she urges. 'If you don't, I will, and you can have Steven.'

While we dress for dinner, Hilary respects my monosyllabic responses and doesn't press me for gossip. All she does say, as she eases her bunions into her sandals, is: 'Fi. Daft ruddy name, if you ask me. How would it be if I went around calling myself "Hi"?'

The six of us are reconvened at our designated table for dinner. We bat around small talk, avoiding politics and Steven, who has returned to his mixed singles group across the restaurant. Barry and Mim went on the wartime history excursion this morning, so that's conversation covered for most of the meal anyway.

Dawn gives me a nudge and nods her head Rob's way as our entrees are served. She still wants me to 'bloody go for it'. I shoot back a warning glare: bloody leave it.

We adjourn to the bar for brandies but Rob is restless and wonders if we can see the Scottish coastline on our port side. Barry and Mim nearly join us but Dawn persuades them to stay in the bar with Hilary; they can make up a foursome for the 10 p.m. quiz.

Rob and I huddle on deck and peer into the distance for twinkling lights. I think of Dad. Would this cruise have suited him? With Mum? With Bev? I doubt it. He hated being over-organized; told what to do, where to go, when to eat. He liked being spontaneous, a free spirit, ideally with a thumping Feelgood soundtrack.

But this, here, now . . . he'd have taken pleasure in the slap of the waves on the side of the ship, the salty, seaweedy smell of the North Minch, the knowledge that the *Black Watch* is just one wee link in a chain of ferries, ships, trawlers, tugs and yachts, looped around the British coastline, from Forties to Fitzroy, Bailey to Biscay. Imagining him here on deck, weathered face to the wind, makes me quite emotional.

I tell Rob I'm nipping back to the cabin for my fleece. I return with Dad's ashes.

He's taken aback. 'Really? You're ready to scatter him?'

That hadn't even occurred to me. 'I wanted him to smell sea area Fair Isle. Duncansby Head must be over there somewhere, on the north-east tip of the mainland. And I think Cape Wrath's on the north-west. Dad would know. Do you think I *should* scatter him here then?'

'It's your call, Annie.'

'I had a thought about that, actually.'

'Oh yes?'

It's getting blowy, so we find a bench, still on deck but protected from the wind. We tuck Dad's urn between us, just like I did with Simon on Brighton Pier.

'So what's this thought then?'

'Remember Dad's sixtieth birthday, when Bev organized that picnic for him?

'Yeah?'

'And we all brought food and it was such a lovely day and he looked really happy.'

'And you were in a strop because you burnt your quiche and you had it in for Bev big time.'

I'm shocked that Rob would misremember what happened. Yes, okay, I did burn the quiche but I'm sure I was perfectly friendly with Bev by then. I'm positive I was.

'Mum and Dad loved that park. When we were kids, they were always making us go for Sunday walks there. And then, at his birthday picnic, Dad looked so, so . . . revived, rebooted. He didn't have Mum but he had a reason to keep going. Bev.'

Rob can hear the tremor in my voice as I try to articulate my thoughts.

'We should scatter Dad in Verulamium Park. With everyone. Friends, family, everyone. Shouldn't we? We could have another picnic. We should scatter him there, Rob.'

'Bev would love that. Good for you, Annie.'

We sit quietly, feeling the ebb and bob of the current, enjoying the heft of Dad's urn safely wedged between us. Dawn is right: I should 'go for it'. I need to tell Rob that Simon isn't my future and he was barely a chapter of my past. I need to tell him that he mustn't get back with Fi or meet someone new because I can't contemplate anyone else having him.

I need to tell him that The Shag *was* a big deal and I've been lying to myself every day since it happened. I said it meant nothing; just a no-strings fuck for old times' sake. Who was I fooling? Not me. Did I fool Rob? Does he believe we're cool and we've moved on?

But if I say any of this out loud and he shakes his head, all hope is gone. He'll go back to Fi and I'll be alone on my stupid sofa with my stupid grief and my pointless longing for a life I sabotaged.

I need to tell Rob all this but I can't risk it. My self-created hurt is manageable because I'm used to it. I did something bad but trying to make it better will just make it even worse.

So we chat about the Ring of Brodgar and the Dawn and

Steven saga. We laugh at some of Hilary's more outrageous moments and how much we'll miss the massive breakfasts but not the tiny beds. Then I give Rob a kiss goodnight on the top of his head, take Dad's urn and go to my cabin where, thank God, Hilary is snoring for England and I won't have to talk to her.

As I lie there, stone-cold wide awake, I accept that I can't use Simon as a consolation prize. If we were meant to be, it would have happened that night on Brighton Pier. It didn't. We're not. And that makes me sad too.

'Any update on that row?' Hilary asks from her bed by the porthole. 'Will Rob and Fi kiss and make up?'

'I think so.'

'Bugger. Double bugger with ruddy great nobs on.'

We have one full day's sailing, from Kirkwall back to Liverpool. I treat myself to a massage, then a pedicure and a haircut, mostly to keep out of Rob's way. I couldn't bear him asking me for tips on how to win back Fi. And I don't need Hilary sticking her oar in either. If she was so good at relationships, she'd be with Frank, not having virtual sex with all the other fake profiles on Tinder.

When she brings up Fi over breakfast, I nearly throw that back at her but I bite my tongue. I mustn't be spiteful or ungrateful; she helped me to complete my journey with Dad and I've become so fond of her, despite the farting and wet towels everywhere.

So . . . Rob runs round the deck for much of the day, Hilary requisitions a favourite armchair in the library to finish her Harlan Coben and I acquire ruby toenails and honey highlights in the ship's salon. Rob and I have lunch together in the buffet but, apart from him thanking me for listening last night, we don't talk about Fi. I keep us off the subject by telling him my plans.

'I've decided: I'm going back to teaching but not at Rangewood. I need a fresh start, a clean slate. It's time to get off my arse and get on with my life.'

'That's great, Annie. You're a born teacher. It's what you're good at, it's who you are.'

I could have been more than that, I want to say. We could. But I blew it.

In the evening, we dine with Barry, Mim and Dawn and we're all quietly relieved that this will be the last time we have to fill the space with inane conversation.

'You must let us know if ever you're in Bury,' Mim suggests over tiramisu and Muscatel.

'Oh, I don't think so.' Hilary's jovial reply shuts down any discussion and Mim has no idea she's just been snubbed. I have so much to learn from Hilary.

Dawn nabs me in the Ladies'. Like Hilary, she's desperate for a happy ending. 'Well? What happened with Rob?'

'Nothing. That ship has sailed.'

She looks crestfallen. 'Really?'

'It's fine, Dawn. Honestly. Rob and I are mates, that's all. Ship mates.'

Back in sea area Irish Sea, the *Black Watch* docks in the shadow of the Liver Birds and we are efficiently disembarked. I now know what a cruise is like and am in no hurry to experience another, even when all around us are planning their next trip.

Hilary looks knackered and frail, so Rob and I waste no time getting a taxi to Lime Street Station, with half an hour to spare before our 12.33 train takes us back to the real world.

I use the station loos and study my reflection in the mirror. Did this woman staring back at me have any expectations when she washed her hands at this very sink six days ago?

Well, yes, six days ago I thought I was off on a Scottish cruise with Rob and Fi. Would I feel like a gooseberry? Would Fi and I become proper besties, not just for Orkney but for life? Instead Hilary was my cabin mate and shifted the whole dynamic. Little else has changed, apart from me finally realizing that I'm done with self-pity and regret.

I've been bobbing about at sea, rudderless and without a compass. Now it's time to head for the shore.

Rob and I are friends. We have too much shared history not to be. But that's all we are. Little orphan Annie has no more parents to lose so I won't need Rob for emotional or practical support. I can't shut myself off any more. I've done too much of that.

We find our train carriage and settle in our seats. God love Hilary, she's snoring by Runcorn. I really don't want to chat, and I sense Rob doesn't either. So he reads Hilary's newspaper and I noodle about on my phone or gaze out of the window.

Over the last few weeks, I've explored the edges of the British Isles, from Cromarty through Dover and Plymouth to Fair Isle. Now I'm seeing the inner workings . . . Crewe, Stoke, Stafford. Some small-town names flash by, too fast to read. Places you go through to get to somewhere else, in our case St Albans Abbey Station, via Watford Junction.

'I need tea,' I tell Rob. 'Can I get you one too?'

'Please. And biscuits. You choose. Should we wake Hilary, see what she wants?'

'No, don't. I'll get her a peppermint tea.'

I wave away his £20 note and make the six-car trek to the

buffet, negotiating numerous feet in aisles, a wandering toddler and a student type with a massive rucksack, snoozing on the floor in that dead space between carriages. Just the sort of thing Josh would do and right in front of the toilet too.

Service is speedy and I'm soon at the front of the queue. Rob shouldn't ask me to choose his biscuits. Of course I know he loves shortcake and can't abide custard creams. Will archived trivia like that fade with time?

I head back, carefully clutching my paper carrier bag so I don't tip scalding tea down my thighs. The student is still asleep on the floor, making access awkward for anyone needing the loo. As I weave past him, Rob appears.

'I got you shortcake so it's too late to change your mind.'

'I've been sent by Hilary. She is so bossy.'

'Does she want proper tea?'

We smile. No need to complete a favourite joke about proper tea being theft.

'She said to tell you she wants a bacon roll but she'll only have it if there's brown sauce. Or did she say ketchup?'

'Ketchup is banal. Brown sauce adds spice, oomph.'

Rob looks exasperated. 'She called me back twice to make sure I relayed her precise words. What was it: "If Annie doesn't say what she wants, she's an idiot." About brown bloody sauce? I hope she isn't losing her marbles.'

I get it. Hilary doesn't do subtle and I totally get what she's trying to tell me: I can live the rest of my life without Rob but it will be like a bacon roll without brown sauce.

If I don't say what I want, I'm an idiot.

I want Rob.

Rob holds out his hands to take the teas. 'Or *I* can get the bacon roll, if that's easier. But if I forget the brown sauce, that's me deleted from her will.'

'I love you!' I hear myself say more forcefully than I planned.

Rob looks shocked. A woman coming out of the loo looks shocked. The sleeping student on the floor turns over, grunts and hugs his rucksack.

I don't have time to order my thoughts or practise my words. 'I shouldn't have let you go, Rob. I was all over the place. And then I was literally all over the place, taking Dad round the Shipping Forecast. Cromarty, Canvey Island, Okehampton flipping Waitrose, everywhere. But I'm not all over the place now and I won't let you go again.'

The woman gives me a reassuring smile and leaves the three of us to it: me, Rob and the sleeping student.

'But if you want to be with Fi, I can't stop you. Do you, really?'

He looks exasperated. 'Bloody hell, Annie. What do you want me to say?'

'"Yes, Annie, I really, really want to be with you."'

He nods. 'I do. Ever since we broke up.'

'I'm so sorry, Rob. For being such an arse. It's just . . . I was so scared.'

'On your trip?'

'Before the trip. Before Dad died. After Dad died. I didn't think I deserved to be happy. So I let you go. That's what turned me into such a – such a failure, such a nothing. I'm so sorry I hurt you, Rob. I thought by letting you go, I was making it better for both of us. But I made it worse. That's been a bit of a habit with me.'

Rob takes the carrier bag of teas from me – I hadn't realized I was still holding it – puts it on the floor and wraps his arms around me. I feel safe. Anchored.

'Is that a sympathy hug or am I getting somewhere?' I ask into the muffled warmth of his armpit.

'I love you too, Annie. So bloody much. I thought with Fi, I could move on. But it's never felt right. This, though. This feels right.'

I cry. I cry so much these days. It's partly relief – Dad and I have finished our journey – plus I'm so exhausted. But it's not the kind of wasteful, pointless exhaustion I wallowed in six months ago, in that permanent bum dent on my sofa.

Something's still niggling me. 'The vasectomy. You don't want it because you *do* want kids?'

'I always thought Josh was enough. Now I'm not sure. Do *you* want kids, Annie?'

'I don't know either. I have to want them for the right reasons. Not just "because".'

The student wakes with a judder. His first sight is us two, hugging and crying. He shrugs and turns over.

'Will we be all right, do you think?' I ask Rob.

'For the rest of our lives, definitely. But I'll be bollocked all the way home if I don't get Hilary her bacon roll.' He kisses my forehead. 'We're good, though. Aren't we, Annie Lummox?'

'We're good. Previously cyclonic, occasionally moderate. Now we're good.'

Coda

July 2020

Annie woke with a jolt. She'd overslept, today of all days. But the digital clock said 05.15 so she could close her eyes for a couple more hours. Rob snored gently beside her, his hand curled under his cheek. She felt his familiar fuggy breath on her face and the body warmth he gave out so unconditionally, even in his sleep.

The Shipping Forecast would be starting soon on Radio 4 but she didn't need to hear the familiar sing-song of sea areas. She had her own version: Cromarty, Edinburgh, Scarborough, Happisburgh, Canvey Island, Bexhill, Brighton, Lulworth, Fowey, Bideford, St Albans, Liverpool, Glasgow, Tobermory, Kirkwall.

Good.

She turned onto her back, crossed her arms behind her head and planned her morning. She'd decided against buying a special outfit for the occasion. That wasn't her. She remembered the dress she'd bought for Dad's funeral. God, it was awful. Today she'd wear the freshly washed jeans and sailor-striped T-shirt Yasmin had given her in Edinburgh, her go-to outfit for every occasion. She might even run a quick iron over them, just to give Bev and Kate a shock.

359

When, on her return from the cruise last year, she'd suggested the picnic and scattering of Dad's ashes in Verulamium Park, to celebrate what would have been Dad's sixty-seventh birthday, Bev and Kate agreed instantly. Quiche was mentioned . . . summer pudding . . . Thai prawns . . . Pimm's.

In the past few weeks, Hilary and Toni had booked their train journey from Bexhill; Josh and Josie hoped to get away for a couple of days off from their holiday jobs in Fowey; and Pippa insisted she and the kids would be fine if Mark was there too but Bev said absolutely not. She'd never liked him and, now that he'd been kicked out, she had no desire to see him ever again, thank you very much.

The debate around Mark's presence, plus Kate's ongoing stress over her first IVF cycle, made the decision to simplify the proceedings all the easier. Bev suggested they pare everything down to the minimum: no picnic, no friends and family from far and wide (although they'd be joining them later – all except Mark), no speeches, no fuss.

Just Annie, Kate, Bev, Dad and a moment to be together before his ashes enriched the grass.

Annie slipped out of bed, padded into the kitchen and turned on Rob's bastard oven. She'd agreed with Bev and Kate to keep it simple. But who'd say no to a bit of home-made quiche and a paper cup of Cava?

Acknowledgements

I wrote Annie Stanley, All at Sea in 2019, hence the absence of face masks, furloughs and lockdowns. I'm sure these references won't be missed. If I'd written it in 2020, I wouldn't have been able to visit so many sea areas or go on the cruise to Mull and Orkney, as Annie, Rob and Hilary did.

Conversations with various friends gave me the nudge I needed to make the leap from script to prose. Thank you, Isabel Ashdown, Kate Harrison, Donna Hay and Karen Rose. I'm also very grateful to Lizzie Enfield, Katie Fforde and David Nicholls for providing just the right words of encouragement at just the right time.

I'm proud to be a member of the Beach Hut Writers, an informal network of Brighton and Hove published writers, and am sure I've learned much of my craft simply by listening to them in the pub, on the beach or over Christmas lunch. Special mention to Araminta Hall, who gave me an early kick-start via her excellent novel-writing workshop.

Thank you to all the friends around the UK who supplemented my research trips and Google searches. Those who answered my plaintive pleas on social media (and have probably forgotten that they did) include Jos Bell, Henrietta Hardy, Sharon Nixon, John Phelps, Pauline Smith and Lucy Sweet. The Women's Quilt Facebook group assisted with a

Sue Teddern

knitting query; how to create same-size squares with different ply yarns. My St Albans insiders were Helen Singer and Jon Meier, and it was great to hang out with Nick and Helen Fisher in Dorset. I couldn't visit every sea area so please forgive any omissions or inaccuracies.

I'm grateful to all my Brighton and Hove friends for gee-ing me up whenever I wondered how I'd transport Annie and her emotional baggage to the next sea area. Special mention to Fleur Peacock, for encouraging me to hoist that kettle bell and perfect that plank.

Then there are the Material Girls; we've laughed and cried together over hummus and Kettle Chips for half a lifetime at least. Plus ca change. Big love to Alison, Blake, Georgia, Gerry, Jo, RK and Rosy. We miss Annie and Gilda every day.

I fell on my feet when Sheil Land added me to their client list. Lucy Fawcett has held my hand through (mostly) happy scriptwriting experiences. Gaia Banks told me I should write a novel and kept reminding me to do so. Her feedback and encouragement have been invaluable.

I love being part of the Mantle family and have enjoyed the process, from one-paragraph idea to end result. Sam Humphreys, my editor, is such a reassuring presence and I'm grateful to Kate, Rebecca and Jess for getting my words onto the page, Mel Four for her cover design, and Philippa McEwan in publicity.

My unofficial editor has been my amazing, inspiring, resilient sister, Ruth. I'd like to pretend the 'bacon roll with brown sauce' idea was mine, but the spark came from her.

My travel companion has been my husband, Edward. We've so enjoyed exploring our coastline together, from Cromarty, through Canvey Island, to Mull and Orkney. His love, patience and support have made this, my first novel, possible.